WARMAGE: UNCONTROLLED

WARMAGE: UNCONTROLLED

THE NEVER ENDING WAR™ BOOK THREE

MARTHA CARR

MICHAEL ANDERLE

DISRUPTIVE IMAGINATION®

Copyright © 2020 Martha Carr & Michael Anderle
Cover by Mihaela Voicu http://www.mihaelavoicu.com/
Cover copyright © LMBPN Publishing
A Michael Anderle Production

LMBPN Publishing
PMB 196, 2540 South Maryland Pkwy
Las Vegas, NV 89109

First US edition, April 2020
ebook ISBN: 978-1-64202-862-1
Print ISBN: 978-1-64202-863-8

THE WARMAGE: UNCONTROLLED TEAM

Thanks to our JIT Readers

Larry Omans
Dorothy Lloyd
Veronica Stephan-Miller
Diane L. Smith
Jackey Hankard-Brodie
James Caplan
Deb Mader
Kelly O'Donnell
Dave Hicks
Paul Westman
Debi Sateren

Editor

SkyHunter Editing Team

CHAPTER ONE

"*Sequantur Flamma!*" Raven Alby raced across the field at Fowler Academy as her dragon's massive column of fire burst from his mouth. Her spell manipulated his attack and corrected it enough to streak into the wooden dummy with the burlap sack of pebbles at its base. The target ignited and she pumped her fist. "You were very close with that one."

"I merely wanted to give you something to do," Leander muttered, his wings spread a little as he ran beside her.

"Ha. Well, thanks."

Despite the fact that it cracked and split in the flames, the dummy unleashed another attack spell of green light directly toward the young mage in training.

Her dragon sensed her intention and lowered himself to the ground. She leapt onto the base of his tail and ran up the ridges of his red-scaled back as he launched himself skyward. The dummy's attack hurtled past them at the last second but of course, it missed.

"She didn't tell us they were rigged to keep attacking," she muttered.

Leander wheeled a few yards above the field's rippling green grass. Below them, Bella Chase and her firedrake Wesley darted continuously to dodge the magical attacks launched by the other five dummies stationed around the field.

"Let's go in and help."

The great dragon flapped his translucent red wings and swooped downward even before she finished the sentence.

She grinned from her seat on her familiar's back. *I don't even need to say it.*

The other girl evaded two more hurtling green balls of magic, then faced the closest dummy squarely and shouted, "*Adsulto protentia!*"

The rocking force of her spell careened into its wooden chest and head and the target splintered dramatically while the base, weighed down with pebbles, wobbled madly.

"Careful," Raven shouted seconds before her dragon landed behind the other dark-haired mage in training.

"I got it, thanks." Bella didn't acknowledge the young dragon rider any more than that as she searched the sky for her firedrake. "Wesley!"

The small flying lizard the size of a large bird uttered a high-pitched screech and followed his mage's wordless command. He swooped toward the dummies from behind and released an impressive column of flames for such a small creature. The fire crackled along each wooden head before he wheeled to return to her.

The girl folded her arms and darted a satisfied smirk at

Raven seated on her dragon. "Don't worry about it, Raven. I took care of the rest for you."

"Bella, they're not—"

"Where's Alessandra? I'm ready to move onto something else—"

"Watch out!" She vaulted from Leander's back and ducked as she barreled into Bella.

The dark-haired mage grunted as she was thrown across the grass onto her hands and knees in time to avoid one of the burning dummy's next attacks that rocketed over both their heads.

Bella whipped her head up and settled onto her knees, although she made no effort to stand. She pushed strands of hair away from her face.

"They're rigged to keep attacking, Bella."

"What?" The girl pushed to her feet and scanned the flaming, smoking remains of the wooden heads and torsos. "That's cheating."

"Yeah, I had the same—"

Her words were cut short when the dummies unleashed another round of hurtling green spheres toward the young mages at the same time. Leander took to the air to evade two of them, and Raven ducked to avoid the others before she attempted the spell she'd only heard Bella use. "*Adsulto protentia!*"

Two of their lifeless adversaries exploded at their bases and hurled scraps of burlap and pebbles in all directions.

With a surprised grin, she straightened and studied the damage. "That was awesome."

"How did you learn that spell?" the other girl demanded.

"What? I didn't. I heard you cast it and thought I'd give it a try."

"You—" Bella clicked her tongue and folded her arms. "You can't trust 'give it a try.' I spent weeks learning that spell."

Raven simply shrugged and offered her a wry smile. "And you're really good at it."

"You're so condescending, you know that?"

"Bella, I'm not trying to—"

"No, you're merely trying to make me look like an idiot. There's no way you haven't practiced that force spell."

"You're not an idiot—"

"I know that! We're already stuck in war mage training together, Raven. What are you trying to prove?"

She stared at her in surprise. "That's the point. We're training together—"

Above them, Wesley uttered a piercing shriek and darted toward his mage. Both girls looked up and scowled at two more churning green dummy attacks that careened toward them.

Bella raised her hand. *"Defle—"*

The assaults found target on both young mages in training and catapulted them across the grass.

Raven lay motionless for a few seconds, stunned, then slowly pushed to a seated position in the grass and rubbed her chest. "Damn. That was way more like getting kicked by a goat than I expected."

Bella growled in frustration and thumped her fist on the earth. With a groan, she scrambled to her feet as Wesley swooped to land on her shoulder. "Now look what you did. I got hit and now, we have to start all over at the beginning."

With a tiny frown, Raven glanced at the other young mage as Leander landed gracefully in the grass behind her. "We both got hit."

"And that wouldn't have happened if you weren't trying to be such a showoff." The girl's nostrils flared.

"Hey, I didn't have to tell you those dummies keep firing after we blow them up."

Bella scoffed and folded her arms. "Yeah, a lotta good that did us."

Wesley curled his long, slender tail around one side of his mage's neck and snorted twin plumes of steam.

The dummies flashed with a pale green light in unison, and Alessandra slid from her perch on the roof of the huge domed barn. She landed gracefully on her feet with a muted thump and placed both hands on her hips. "What happened this time?"

Raven chuckled. "We both got hit."

"Obviously." The older woman with the tight knot of a gray bun at the back of her head stepped forward toward her war mage trainees. "Why?"

"Because Raven thinks lying about how long it takes her to learn spells is gonna get her anywhere."

She stood as well and raised her arm to pat the top of Leander's ridged muzzle gently when he nudged it against her side with a loud sniff. "Wait a minute. That has nothing to do with it, and I didn't lie."

"Of course not." Bella wouldn't look at her. "You're perfect."

"Seriously, Bella? What's—"

"That's enough." Alessandra approached them, took a deep breath, and glanced from the one girl to the other with an expression of exasperation. "You've been at this for a week already, and you still haven't learned that this is about more than only you as individual mages. This is about how you can work together to get the results you need without blowing holes in each other." When Bella cut a scathing glance toward their trainer, the woman raised a warning finger. "Or your instructor."

Wesley launched himself from the girl's shoulder and darted toward Leander. The tiny firedrake wings batted fiercely barely inches from the red dragon's face. Raven didn't turn to look, although she was tempted. *He'll take care of it.*

As soon as she had the thought, his huge, powerful jaws snapped shut with a startling crack. He raised a front paw to swipe at the firedrake, missed deliberately, and put Wesley off-balance enough to make the flying lizard topple onto the grass. The firedrake uttered an angry screech, but Leander merely lowered himself onto the ground to rest his huge head on his forepaws with a snort.

Wesley hopped back and immediately left the little spat to find his perch on Bella's shoulder again.

Alessandra watched the whole thing with an expression of distaste. Finally, she tossed a dismissive hand in the air. "We'll pick this up again tomorrow. You two need to find some space. Maybe from each other too, huh?"

"It's like you can read my mind." Bella gave their trainer a quick smile, turned on her heel, and stormed across the field.

"Bella, wait." Raven hurried after her and had to jog a

little to catch up. "I wanted to talk to you about something."

"You heard her, Raven. Running after me isn't exactly finding space."

"I'm sorry I pissed you off so much by using your spell. It's a very good one."

"Go back to your dragon." The other young mage didn't slow or turn to look at her rival and new training partner, which didn't exactly come as a surprise.

Raven stopped short and dropped her hands against her thighs with a little slap. "See you tomorrow, then," she muttered.

When she turned, Alessandra and Leander hadn't moved from where she'd left them. The war mage—with the patch on her shoulder to prove her competence and authority—darted the red dragon a perfunctory glance but said nothing.

She approached them and shrugged at her trainer. "Apparently, that force spell belongs to Bella."

Alessandra raised an eyebrow. "Sarcasm won't get you where you need to be either, Miss Alby. I suggest you tuck that away while you're training as well."

Leander snorted and both mages glanced at him. The red dragon closed his eyes and said nothing.

"I don't know why she hates me so much."

"I don't think it's hate, Miss Alby. But if you want to know what it really is, you're the one who has to figure that out." Alessandra cleared her throat. "Now go do something else while I clean up the mess you two made by trying to outdo each other."

Without waiting for a response, the war mage turned

swiftly and headed toward the dummies, which were now all reduced to smoldering remains and a few tattered strips of burlap.

With a sigh, Raven approached her dragon and stopped in front of his face. She lowered into a squat and stared at him until he opened one huge, glowing yellow eye. "I won't apologize for being me. This is who I am."

"Would you apologize even if you were pretending?"

A tiny smile lifted the corners of her mouth. "I don't know, Leander. I haven't tried pretending yet."

"And if you want to keep this dragon around, you won't start."

She laughed. "I won't start anyway, and you know it."

A low rumble escaped him.

"So. We were cut loose early. What could we possibly do with all this extra time today?"

With another rumble, he spread his wings in a quick whoosh of air and opened his other eye too. "I can't think of a single thing."

"Oh, too bad. It looks like we're out of options." Raven straightened quickly and paced slowly along the agile length of the red dragon's body. She took one step onto his tail and hovered her other boot above the ground. "We have such a boring life, don't we?"

"Raven, if you don't hurry, I'll launch you across this field. A week in that human pen they call an infirmary would be very boring indeed."

The young mage uttered a mocking gasp. "You wouldn't."

"Try me."

The image of all the countless times Leander had batted

her across the dragon pen and into metal walls at Moss Ranch made her laugh. She ran up the great dragon's back and her boots found easy purchase on the ridges of his hardened scales. When she reached the base of his long neck, she stood and spread her arms. "I already spent a week in the infirmary, thanks. Let's—"

Leander pushed to his feet and she crouched to steady herself against his scales before she sat fully on his back and gave his neck a little pat.

"Ready when you—"

The beat of his powerful wings cut her off as Leander launched skyward. Raven squeezed with her thighs and wrapped her arms around his neck as far as she could as they rocketed almost vertically toward the thin wisps of clouds in the blue sky. *Yeah, he's always ready. So am I.*

CHAPTER TWO

The young mage uttered a whoop of joy as Fowler Academy disappeared below them. Leander finally leveled out and found a current of air to support them in a gliding sweep that whipped her hair around her face. Air ruffled across the thin edges of his translucent wings with a tiny flutter. The fresh spring air buffeted her face again as they banked, turned, and descended slightly to the right.

Raven straightened fully on her dragon's back and spread her arms. She couldn't help the tears that streamed from her eyes and were whisked away past the long red braid that fluttered behind her. *But at least I've learned how to be able to breathe up here.*

"Anywhere you wanna go today?"

He scanned the green valley racing below them and his massive dark shadow flickered across the tops of the forest. "You want to see William."

She laughed. "Well, we haven't yet since we knocked out the Swarm. I feel a little bad about it."

"You want to see him." The dragon released a rumbling

purr and turned to fly in a wide arc around the town of Brighton.

Dragons might not be so much of a terror after this one saved them two weeks ago. But it's good to be careful anyway.

Leander elevated a little and brought the range of the Mountains of Jordan into view as they headed south toward Moss Ranch. She closed her eyes and didn't care about the chill in the air or the wind that buffeted her clothes. *This is where we were meant to be.*

Ten minutes later, they swooped over the huge dragon paddock of Moss Ranch. He uttered a piercing screech and a great red dragon below raised her head to echo the cry.

That call sounds very different now. Almost happy.

Raven leaned forward to stroke the scales along his neck. "We could go see her again if you want."

"She knows I'm here. We're fine."

"Okay. But let me know if you want to."

They slowed beyond the stables and came to a graceful, hovering halt. William Moss leapt from where he worked on the stables' roof and grinned at them, waving his hat. Leander beat his wings a few more times before he landed in the trodden dirt that sustained only a few patches of grass here and there. A spray of earth and dust rose beneath his final wingbeat, and Raven leapt from his back.

"I thought we'd stop by for a surprise visit." She grinned at the man and shrugged a little apologetically. "Sorry it took us so long."

"I know you're busy, Raven. I can't hold it against you." William chuckled and jammed his wide-brimmed hat over his shoulder-length, dirty-blond hair. "Honestly, I like surprises. And you—" He frowned at the huge red dragon who had landed on his dad's ranch, then took a step sideways to get a better view.

A few sharp, quick hisses escaped Leander as he folded his wings and settled onto his belly in the dirt.

She darted the dragon a glance and folded her arms. "Now you're showing off."

"Raven." William took his hat off again to wipe the sweat from his brow and completely forgot about putting it on. "What are you doing?"

"Flying a dragon to visit a friend." She grinned. "What does it look like?"

He stared with wide eyes at Leander's bare back before he flicked his gaze toward the young mage. "It looks like you forgot to saddle that dragon."

"What? No. I didn't forget." She waved him off. "Leander and I realized how much better it is to ride without one and we've been practicing. It is so much better, let me tell ya."

William's head nodded vigorously as he bit on his bottom lip. "Yeah, I know you like to do things your way, Raven. And that's great. But this is suicidal."

"You're being dramatic."

"Dramatic? Dramatic!" He tossed his hands into the air. His hat slipped from his grasp and he fumbled to catch it before he shoved it onto his head with both hands. "Honestly, I think I'm underreacting."

"William, we're fine. This isn't the first time we've done this. Trust me. We worked our way up from quick, short flights barely off the ground first. And it saves so much time."

"Time? That's what you're worried about before you

simply climb onto a dragon that size and fly away wherever you want."

Oh, boy. Raven pressed her lips together and lowered her chin, trying to get him to look at her. He continued to stare with wide eyes at Leander's bare back. As if to drive the point home, the dragon snorted, rolled in the dirt, and wiggled for a good back-scratch.

"Of course he likes it more. He never wanted one in the first place."

Raven approached her friend and placed a hand on his shoulder. "I like it more too."

"That doesn't matter, Raven. You can like it all you want, but this is more reckless than anything I've seen—including your attempt to train Leander yourself."

She tried not to laugh at that. "And it worked out well, didn't it?"

William fixed her with a deadpan stare and cocked his head.

"Look, we have it under control, okay? I promise. And the whole time thing? Yeah, it's a big deal. What would've happened if I took five minutes to put a saddle on him while what was left of the Swarm raced across the kingdom toward Fowler Academy?"

"You know I can't answer that."

"Hey, I can't either so it's a good thing I don't have to. Five minutes is too much time to throw down the drain."

He cleared his throat and folded his arms. "Compared to all the time wasted if you fall off your dragon from above the clouds? I don't think so."

"Okay." Raven stepped back and raised her hands in mock surrender. "I obviously can't change your mind."

"Nope."

"And I'm okay with that. But if you can trust that we know what we're doing, you could save yourself considerable worry about it."

William took a deep breath but he chuckled when he exhaled again. "I shouldn't be surprised by this."

"Of course not."

"You, Raven Alby, are more terrifying than the Swarm."

The young mage kicked her boot heel out and offered a wide, sweeping bow. "Why, thank you."

"I'm not sure that's a compliment." He scratched the side of his face and squinted at the red dragon, who continued to take a dirt bath and snorted with pleasure.

"I choose to take it as one."

"Choose whatever you like, Raven," Leander muttered as the back of his long neck dragged from side to side in the dirt. "This one has a tiny brain."

William snorted. "And you talk a big game, Leander."

The dragon stopped his wiggling and rolled halfway over so he could fix the dragon trainer with one yellow eye. "Really?"

Swallowing, the young man nodded slowly and stepped back. "We'll let him do his thing over there, huh?"

Raven fought back another laugh and pointed at Leander. "Are you okay over there?"

"I'm busy."

"That's a yes." She turned toward William and shrugged as they headed down the long length of the stables.

He kicked up a few sprays of dust with the toes of his boots as they walked. "Despite my suspicion that you've lost all common sense, Raven, I'm glad you guys stopped by."

She chuckled. "Doing things my way and breaking tradition isn't necessarily a lack of common sense."

"Well, maybe with some things." He sent her a sidelong glance, smirked, and bumped his shoulder against hers. "Before you ask, yes. I did hear about everything that happened at the school that night. You and another mage in training eliminated the rest of the Swarm all on your own, huh?"

"Not completely alone. We couldn't have done it without Leander."

"I bet."

"It's simply another example of how much sense it makes to have no common sense, right?" Raven wrinkled her nose at him and laughed when the dragon trainer sighed at the sky.

"My own words thrown back to bite me."

"Just sayin'. And I heard you came for a visit while I was still super-unconscious."

"I thought I'd give you time to get back on your feet. And I know you can't stay away from Moss Ranch." He chuckled but it faded quickly. "I'm proud of you, Raven. Both of you. Really."

Raven frowned a little over a secret smile as she studied his profile. *That's either a sunburn under his hat or a little blush.* "Thanks."

"It's everyone else who should thank you, isn't it?"

"Go ahead. I'll wait."

William threw his head back and laughed. He turned to her, pressed his hands together, and shook them melodramatically as he lowered himself to one knee. "Oh, Raven Alby, war mage and dragon rider, thank you for delivering the kingdom from peril—woah."

He toppled when she shoved his shoulder jokingly.

"Oh. Sorry." She choked back a laugh and stuck her hand out to help him up. "It was my automatic reaction."

"To being thanked?" He chuckled and dusted his work pants.

"More like to seeing you down on one knee and blowing things wildly out of proportion."

At that, he froze and gave her a quick glance before he stared out over the field beyond the stables that stretched toward the tree line of the forest. "Huh."

What's that about?

Raven laughed it off. "I appreciate the thank you, though."

"Uh-huh." William clicked his tongue and laughed with her. "So, what's life like now for the dragon-riding mage in training who saved the day?"

"All right, you can cut that out. I'll be a great mage one day but I'll always still be me."

For a few seconds, he studied her face thoughtfully. "I'd say you're already a great mage."

She stared at him, a little uncertain. *I'm not sure I like the way he's looking at me. What is that?*

His scrutiny ended abruptly when he burst out laughing. "A great mage with a death wish and no saddle."

"Yeah, laugh it up. Are you sure you're not the one with the death wish?"

He shrugged and leaned against the small section of the

fence directly outside the stables. "I'm only testing the limits. You know all about that."

Raven leaned beside him and kicked her heel up onto the bottom rung of the fence. "That might be my style, sure. And life's moving on the same as it did before. Mostly."

"Ooh. There's an exception."

She snorted. "Headmaster Flynn took Bella and me straight out of the infirmary and down to the stables on the grounds for detention."

"Oh, the horror."

"Shut up. It turns out it wasn't detention. He called in a war mage to train us after what we did."

"Woah." William turned to face her and leaned sideways against the fence. "Actual war mage training, huh?"

"Yeah. Alessandra's a real…piece of work, I guess."

"It sounds like a perfect match."

"Ha, ha. Honestly, I enjoy it. We get to run around practicing our battle magic, Leander gets good exercise in, and I'm always learning. Bella has a way of making it…interesting."

"Who's Bella?"

Raven sighed—a little dramatically, but her irritation with the girl had resurfaced. "Another mage, obviously. She's very talented and competitive."

"Uh-oh." He chuckled when she rolled her eyes.

"We both found out at the same time that our moms were war mages too. They fought together."

"And now their daughters are following in their footsteps."

"Kind of." She settled her forearms on the top of the

fence behind her and gazed at the woods on the other side of the ranch property. "It's hard to follow in my mother's footsteps when I don't even know where they are. Or where they stopped."

"Hmm." William nodded. "But at least now you know where they started. That's something."

"Yeah. I think she'd be proud of me."

"Of course she would." They stood in companionable silence for a few minutes before he finally turned to lean against the fence again. "Any word from Connor?"

"Nope. No matter how hard I try, I can't seem to make sense of that at all."

"Well, wherever he is, I'm sure he's missing you badly by now."

Raven nodded. "I miss him too. But there's more than enough other stuff to keep me distracted, right? War mage training, a new friend-not-friend who thinks I stole her spells, all my classes still in full swing, and a dragon who wants to be out of his pen and flying as much as I do."

William pressed a hand against his cheek and released a mocking sigh. "How do you find the time?"

"Do you want me to push you into the dirt again?"

"Not really. Hey, what about your boyfriend? Is he not part of the war mage's busy schedule?"

Raven choked on a surprised laugh and turned quickly to stare at him. "My what?"

"So he's not your boyfriend?"

"Oh, come on. No. If you're talking about Daniel Smith, he asked me to be his date for the spring gala and I wasn't even thinking when I told him yes. But no boyfriends. That's ridiculous."

He smirked. "I can only assume that night didn't turn out as he expected."

"Ha! It didn't turn out as anyone expected. And honestly, I've been too busy to even think about why he's avoided me."

"Aw. Maybe you broke his heart?"

She shook her head. "It's better than letting the Swarm get to him, though."

They laughed again, and William glanced at the roof of the stables behind them. "Well, I'm glad you have enough going on to keep you busy and out of trouble."

"That was sarcasm, wasn't it?"

"Maybe." He shrugged. "We've been busy around here too, actually."

"Do you have a group of new dragons to train?"

"I wish. Come take a look at this. It'll bore your socks off."

CHAPTER THREE

With a smirk, Raven pushed herself away from the fence and followed William to the front of the stables. "Woah."

"Yeah. It's kind of ridiculous, isn't it?" He folded his arms and looked at the new stable doors with a frown. "We're reinforcing everything. With steel this time, if you can believe it."

"Those doors look like they belong on a dungeon somewhere."

He chuckled. "Well, thanks. They were a bitch to put up."

"And why exactly would you want to put dungeon doors on your dragon stables?"

"Orders from the top." He sent her a sidelong glance and shrugged. "My dad wanted them up and I'm only another employee to do the job as far as he's concerned."

"Okay, let me rephrase. Why is your dad putting dungeon doors on your dragon stables?"

"He's trying to beef security up here a little, I guess. A

few other dragon trainers stopped by on their way to... I can't remember. Some huge city way out east. They stayed for the night and put their dragons up for a while. Dad always asks about news from other places, although I don't think he's been much farther than Harpertown, honestly. And all the news was of nothing but trouble."

Raven frowned. "What kind of trouble?"

"Well, I assume you know about that giant hole in the wall, right?"

"Yeah. I heard it break and saw it myself when Leander and I went to check."

William nodded and lifted his hat again to scratch his hair. "Apparently, the capital and all the major cities in Lomberdoon are trying to get the word out there for people to double down on security for their properties. They're all talking about raiders and being prepared."

"Seriously?"

"I heard it directly from the dragon trainers flying between major cities." He shrugged.

"You don't seem all that worried about raiders."

"It's only talk, Raven. People like to do that, don't they? Okay, maybe there are raiders heading to that giant hole in the wall, but I don't read too much into it."

"Maybe your dad has it right, though, to increase security like this." Raven nodded toward the laughably huge door.

"He's merely overreacting, which isn't anything new. I don't care how bloodthirsty and greedy raiders are. If they're stupid enough to try to steal from a dragon ranch with a number of trained dragons around, they deserve everything that's coming to 'em."

"Okay, that's a fair point."

"And then a whole piece of the roof fell off once I finally got this stupid door up so now, I gotta take care of that too. We can't let spring rain get into the dragon feed and all that."

"Right. Is there anything I can help with?"

William chuckled. "I don't think either one of us wants me breathing down your neck if I gave you something to do. My dad made it perfectly clear that he wants all this done a specific way."

"You'd only have to tell me once. I can follow directions."

He turned toward her and raised an eyebrow. "Even I had to write it down."

"Ugh."

They laughed and he stepped away from the front of the stables to catch another glimpse of Leander. The huge red dragon was now a giant, copper-colored mound and his scales flashed in the sun here and there between the thick layer of dirt that coated his body. "I think your dragon fell asleep."

Raven smirked. "That's what he wants you to think."

"Uh-huh."

"Well, I don't wanna keep distracting you from your work."

William met her gaze and narrowed his eyes. "You're always a welcome distraction, Raven."

"Well, thanks." She laughed casually and shook her head. "But I'm not very good at having to double-check every tiny detail, so I probably won't be any help."

"Nah. You have your busy schedule to get back to at

mage school." He stepped toward her and wrapped his arms around her before she even realized what he was doing. "I'm really glad you stopped by. And that you didn't get yourself killed when you saved us all."

She hugged him in return before he released her. "Yeah, me too."

"Now, please don't get yourself killed flying around without a saddle. Hey, let me get you one from inside, huh? We have plenty."

"Nice try." She pointed at him and grinned as she stepped backward across the dirt and patches of grass toward Leander. "I don't think he'll ever put a saddle on again. And honestly, I'm not all that interested in trying."

"Of course not." William folded his arms and shook his head. "You stay safe, Raven."

"You too. Nothing's gettin' through that dungeon door." She spun and hurried toward Leander while the trainer's laughter followed her across the ranch. "You look like you're enjoying yourself."

"It was spontaneous." The dragon was curled in the dirt, his head resting on his forepaws again as his sides swelled and compressed with long, slow breaths. "But I still prefer the grass."

"That doesn't surprise me. Hey, we still have more than enough time to see Zora if you want to."

He snorted. "She's busy."

Raven looked across the huge open space where the Moss Ranch dragons were allowed to roam freely after they'd been satisfactorily trained. It was easy to tell the clans apart. Little pockets of dragons lounged in the sun together, batted their wings, and released a few streams of fire into the sky as they played.

Finally, she located the other massive red dragon not quite as large as Leander but still impressive. Zora lay in the scattered patches of grass out in the paddock too, curled like her son. The female dragon's wings stretched in enjoyment to catch the warm sunlight as two other dragons—a long, lithe beast like a dragon-sized firedrake and a shimmering blue one —danced around her in some kind of playful sparring match.

"She has a clan out there, doesn't she?"

"Of course she does. And she's happy. So am I."

"Good." *He wouldn't lie to me about it.* Raven nodded and stooped to run her hand along the ridges of her dragon familiar's snout and along the back of his long, curled neck as she walked around him. "Do you need more nap time?"

Leander snorted and raised his head. "I don't need a babysitter."

"Well, okay, then." She smirked and brushed that comment aside as she looked at the dragons in the field again. *He's happy knowing Zora's happy. I wish I could say the same about Grandpa.*

"You know you don't even have to ask, Raven." He pushed to his feet and shook like an oversized, scaly dog.

"Woah." The young mage turned away and covered her face with her forearm as dust and blades of grass flurried around them. Leander's tail flicked at the end, and when she turned again, his red scales shimmered in the sun again.

William's laughter rang across the ranch in the moment of surprised silence.

She turned to wave, then folded her arms at Leander and fixed him with an exasperated glance. "A little warning next time would be awesome."

"I didn't know that would happen until I did it." He swiveled his head toward her and grinned and his scaly lips pulled back from two rows of razor-sharp teeth. "It felt very good."

"Yeah, I bet." With a chuckle, she brushed the dirt off her clothes as best she could. "So, I had one more place in mind—"

"I said you don't have to ask." The dragon crouched enough for her to vault a little higher onto the base of his tale and climb up his back. "I expect you to listen."

"Ha. Well, I expected you to not share your dirt bath. We'll call it even."

Without a word from the young mage, Leander spread his wings, rose fully on all fours, and took to flight.

William watched them sail toward the clouds and shook his head. "That girl's gonna find herself in some serious trouble one day." He grunted, laughed, and returned to work. "But she'll fight her way out of it, of course." *She always does.*

He climbed quickly onto the roof and rummaged around in the bag he'd nestled up there for a few more nails. "No saddle. Psh."

CHAPTER FOUR

L eander landed gently at the top of the hill behind her
grandfather's house on the Alby Ranch. A few of the
dwarf goats bleated at him in greeting and hopped around
each other, but generally, they moved away from the huge
flying beast beyond their large grazing pen.

Raven slid off his back and gave his scaly shoulder a pat
as she studied the dozens of goats that bounced down the
side of the hill. "I hope that fence got fixed and this isn't
another great goat escape."

The dragon snorted. "There is nothing great about
them."

"Oh, come on. Have you ever had goat's milk?"

He swiveled his head to stare at her with his yellow
eyes.

"Okay, probably not. But that's their one redeeming
quality. That and they're always happy to see an old friend."

"They're not your friends, Raven. To them, you smell
like food."

"No, to you I smell like food. To them, I smell like the

person who used to bring them their food. There is a big difference."

"I would never eat you." The dragon hissed a laugh and nodded his head on his long neck.

"That's why we're so good together, Leander." With a chuckle, Raven patted his shoulder again and nodded. "I won't be too long. I only wanted to check in and make sure things are still running smoothly here."

Unperturbed, he lowered himself lazily to the ground and rested his huge head on his forepaws again. "Take your time. I'll be here."

She left her dragon familiar at the top of the hill but didn't approach her grandfather's house yet. *If that fence isn't fixed by now, we're gonna have some seriously frustrated ranch hands running around.*

When she finally reached the other side of the goat pen and the little shelter where they were put up at night, she found the entire stretch of fence along that side fully repaired. "Huh. So there's no great escape after all."

A loud bump inside the goat shelter was followed by a curse and a loud hiss. Deacon ducked to step out of the low wooden building and rubbed the back of his head. "Raven?"

"Hey, Deacon. Sorry. I didn't mean to sneak up on you."

"I would've jumped outta my skin if that beam wasn't there to stop me." The man chuckled, grimaced again, and put his hands on his hips as he studied her. "It's good to see ya, girl. Although I'm not quite sure why you came out here today. I hope it wasn't 'cause you don't think we can handle things while you and Connor are gone."

Raven grinned. "No, I know you can handle it. I came to

check on a few things inside the house but I saw the goats were out."

"Oh, yeah..." He smiled and rubbed his head again. The dwarf goats bounded energetically and bleated at the two of them. "They've been itching to get out into wider spaces, as I'm sure you know. We got the rest of the new fence posted up and nailed down about four days ago. I think they're trying to adjust all over—what? Get—Glennie. Go on. My sleeve ain't hay, girl."

She couldn't help a laugh while the man flapped his hand to shoo the curiously nibbling goat away from him. "That means she likes you," she said as she brushed loose hair out of her face.

"Oh, sure. She likes my shirt even more, huh?" Deacon laughed with affectionate mirth and shook his head. "These animals, I swear. Now I know you and Connor have your work cut out for you with the goats and the milk and all that and we're handlin' it fine. But I tell you what, girl. The best part of my day is still headin' out on that cart with Presley and gettin' away from these jumpy, weird-eyed little fluffballs on four legs."

"Well, Presley is a good horse."

"Yeah, and she knows the difference between a hand and her feed. She can't talk with words like your dragon but sometimes, I swear I can hear her thinkin' anyway." The man paused and tilted his head warily. "Did you, uh... fly here?"

"Yep." Raven stepped aside and pointed up the hill behind the Alby house. "I think he likes that position."

He dusted dirt and dry, brittle straw off his pants as he stepped toward her. Curiously, he leaned over the fence of the goat pen and the new wide goat paddock and nodded slowly. "Uh-huh. I don't think I'll ever get used to seeing a big red dragon on this ranch."

"Well, we'll keep coming until you do." She nodded at Leander, and he stretched his wings in response before he settled them against his back again. "Hey, Deacon?"

"Yeah." The man sighed as he stared at the dragon, then shook his head and looked at her.

"Have you heard anything from my grandpa?"

He pressed his lips together in a small, tense grimace. "No. But that'll change. He'll be back and it's simply business as usual around here until then, huh?"

She drew a deep breath and exhaled slowly as she settled her gaze on the house that was still her home. "Thanks to you and Patrick and the other hands."

"Well, the way you and Connor run this place makes it real easy for us to keep runnin' it for a time. Things are goin' well."

"Thank you again."

"Naw. There's no need to thank us. We might be gettin' the better end of the deal." Deacon winked and she responded with a laugh.

"I'm still gonna thank you. The goats look happy and I think that new fence might hold them in this time. Mostly."

"Don't jinx it, girl!" Deacon laughed when she made a face at him and he scanned the goat pen as she wandered up the gentle slope of the hill toward her grandfather's house.

The door to the screened-in porch looked a little crooked. *I thought we had that fixed before I started school.*

With a shrug, she opened the door—which screeched

loudly and stuck halfway open—and stepped across the porch and into the house. The front door didn't give her any problem, but she completely forgot to close it behind her when her gaze fell on the massive hole in the center of the main room.

The wooden floor had thrust up from below in jagged, shattered spears, and sawdust, dirt, and wood chips covered almost everything.

"What the hell?" she shouted and stepped back hastily. Her startled gaze located Connor's huge, heavy metal trunk they'd left against the far wall beside the hearth. It now rested at a crooked angle like someone had dragged it away from the wall.

Footsteps pounded up the steps to the porch and Deacon raced inside with his hat in his hand. "Raven? Are you okay in here—what the hell?"

"Well, at least I know I didn't overreact." Raven darted him a sideways glance and chuckled. "Did you know about this?"

The man shook his head. "If I'd known about this, girl, it would've been patched and it would be impossible to tell the difference by now. How in the world did somethin' like that happen?"

With a frown, she stepped closer to the massive hole and peered over the edge.

"Careful, girl."

"It's okay, Deac. I'm fairly sure I know what made this." She glanced at the metal trunk, which seemed unscathed aside from the fact that it had been moved.

"Oh, yeah? Do they teach you about crazy exploding floors at that magic school of yours too?"

"Not quite." The breach in the floor wasn't all that deep as there were only a few feet between the opening and the earth beneath the house. As she suspected, the soil looked like someone had stuck a giant spoon in it and stirred it into a swirling mess. "But the school did teach us enough about working with familiars to get rid of the Swarm. What was left of it, anyway."

Deacon drew a sharp breath and took two wary steps forward as he clutched his wide-brimmed hat to his chest. "Are you tellin' me one of those cursed things bust a hole in your grandfather's floor and then…what? It simply left?"

Raven wrinkled her nose and twisted over her shoulder to shrug at the ranch hand. "Basically, yeah."

"Now why in the hell would a brainless beast do somethin' like that?"

"They weren't that brainless. One of them came here looking for something."

The ranch hand cleared his throat in evident discomfort.

"Something that wasn't here, obviously. And now, that something doesn't exist and neither does the Swarm."

"Uh-huh. I heard about that too." He stared at his hat for a moment as if surprised to find it in his hands, then shoved it onto his head. "I heard you had something to do with it."

She chuckled. "A little."

"Phew. Girl, I know not to expect the same old thing from you as from everyone else, but what are you doin' gettin' yourself mixed up in that kinda mess?"

When she looked at him again, he grinned at her like he knew the answer already. "Only being myself."

Deacon roared with laughter and clapped both hands on his stomach. "You are somethin' else, Raven. I tell you what."

"Thank you." She stepped nimbly around the massive, jagged hole and approached the metal trunk. Once she'd opened it, she peered briefly inside but none of Connor's old things looked even slightly disturbed. *The Swarm really did come here for that skull. If I hadn't taken it to Bixby's class, things would be so much worse right now.*

Raven closed the trunk and shoved it into its previous position against the wall. "At least it was a quick break-in."

"Oh, ha. Yeah. Sure. Don't mind the giant hole or the fact that one of those monsters got their nasty...well, I don't know what they used. Claws?"

"Tentacles, probably."

Deacon exhaled a loud, quick sigh and shook his head. "Too much. It's all too much."

"Are you okay?"

"Sure. Sure. I'm standing in here looking at something I don't know how any of us missed, talking to my employer's granddaughter who happened to eliminate the rest of the Swarm everyone else thought was gone for good." He rubbed his forehead but his frown remained. "I need fresh air, I think."

"It is a little musty in here."

The man laughed and stepped out of the house, shook his head, and muttered inaudibly.

Raven smiled as she watched him leave. She allowed herself a final glance at the hole in the floor and sighed. *Things worked out exactly the way they were supposed to.*

The thought made her feel a little better and she skirted

the destruction and headed toward the back of her house. In the short, narrow hallway, she stopped to peer into her bedroom, which looked empty now that she'd moved into the dormitories at Fowler Academy. She turned in the opposite direction and peered into her grandfather's room. *It's still a mess.*

She stepped through the door anyway and moved toward his twin bed nestled against the far wall. The bedframe creaked when she sat—exactly like she'd heard it creak under Connor's weight for as long as she remembered—and it made her smile. She took a deep breath in through her nose, closed her eyes, and settled her hands in her lap. *It still smells like him. He could be here right now if I keep my eyes closed.*

"I miss you," she whispered. "You told me to do what's right while you're gone, and I'm sure that's what I've been doing. It's always nice to hear you tell me anyway, though."

A lump caught in her throat and she exhaled another long breath. "Be safe, wherever you are. Things aren't the same around here without you, even if I'm not here all the time either. And I heard one of the other students talking about how the goat milk doesn't taste the same this spring, so you might wanna hurry up and get back."

A short laugh escaped her, and when she opened her eyes to stare at the piles of scattered clothes on the floor, she realized her cheeks were wet with tears.

Leander uttered a shrill cry from his position at the top of the hill. Raven startled, wiped the tears away with the back of her hand, and nodded. *We'll be fine. We always are. So is Grandpa.*

The bed creaked again when she stood and with a final

glance around the room, she hurried to the door. The young mage's fingers trailed across the doorway and she strode quickly to the front of the house, across the porch, and out onto the grass.

By now, Patrick had also abandoned whatever he'd been working on to stand beside Deacon. Both ranch hands stared at the dragon on the hill with wide eyes.

"Everything's okay," she reassured them.

"It don't sound like it." Patrick nodded at the red dragon and scratched the side of his head. "I about fell over when I heard that scream."

"Leander doesn't scream." Raven chuckled. "He's being supportive, that's all."

"Of what?" Deacon's chuckle sounded nervous. "Are you tryin' to scare the water out of everyone on this ranch, girl?"

"Not on purpose." The young mage tossed her head and sniffed. "I'm sorry if we did."

"No, don't you apologize for a thing." Patrick took a few steps toward her and shook his head. "We all heard what you did with the army, Raven. If you ask me, you shouldn't have to apologize for anything for the rest of your life." The man placed a hand gently on her shoulder and shook her exuberantly.

"Okay, okay." She raised her hands and backed away as Deacon joined them, laughing. "I don't think I've seen you this enthusiastic before."

Patrick nodded with wide eyes. "Sure, I'm enthusiastic. We're not worried about whether or not those damn monsters are comin' anywhere around us when we least expect it, and that's thanks to you. I'm only glad those foul things never made it onto the ranch."

The other two exchanged a glance. "Speakin' of which," Deacon said, "we have some repairs to do in the main house, Pat."

The other man frowned at him and cocked his head. "We weren't speakin' of repairs."

"I know." Deacon nodded at her and smiled. "We'll get that whole thing sorted out first thing, girl. By the time your grandfather comes home, he won't notice a thing."

"I wouldn't be so sure about that." Raven chuckled. "Connor Alby notices more than people think."

"That's the real truth right there." Patrick nodded and pointed at the young mage. "I bet you get that from him, don't you?"

"Probably." *And my mom.* Her fingers went instinctually to the place she normally would have felt her mom's pin on her shoulder, but she hadn't retrieved her jacket between training with Alessandra and taking off with Leander. She lowered her head and gave both men a little wave. "Thanks for everything you're doing here. I couldn't think of better guys for the job while the Albys aren't actually on Alby Ranch."

"Ha. Flattery. Do you hear that, Deac?"

"Uh-huh. Now you and your flattered self can come with me to the house and take a look at these repairs."

"See ya later," she said cheerfully. They turned to wave to her before they headed toward Connor's house. Patrick mumbled questions about what kind of repairs in the empty house were so important that they need their attention then and there.

Raven climbed the hill until she reached Leander, who still lay on his belly in the grass with his head on his forepaws. "I guess you felt that too, huh?"

"I always feel you, Raven." The dragon sounded a little huffy.

"I can't help it." She shrugged. "I try not to but I miss him terribly. It's so weird not having him here when I come home, even if I don't live here either."

"I understand."

She grinned and studied his shimmering red scales that glinted in the afternoon sun. "I know you do."

"Let me guess. It's time to go back to your funny little school so I can pretend to not be on display?"

With a snort, she climbed onto his back, which was much easier when he was prone, and stepped to the base of his neck. "You're a dragon, Leander. Everywhere you go, you're kind of on display."

"Oh, yes. I'd forgotten how seamlessly you blend in with other humans."

"Hey, I wasn't talking about me. But yeah. I guess we're both on display."

The dragon snorted and pushed himself to his feet. His wings spread wide to either side and rustled the blades of long grass on the hilltop. "Let them watch, Raven Alby. People could learn a thing or two."

He soared skyward to return to Fowler Academy. Her laughter was carried away by the wind.

CHAPTER FIVE

"All right." Raven folded the empty burlap sack of dragon feed and stepped away from the trough. "*Bon Appetit.*"

Leander snorted and his tail snaked from side to side across the grass of his pen at Fowler Academy. "Should I expect a change in the menu tonight?"

"Not really. I'm fairly sure dragon feed only comes in one flavor. Meat and—"

"Blood."

She looked away from the full trough to fix her dragon with a mock frown. "Come on. You can't say stuff like that out loud."

"Why not? It's what I am."

With a low snort, she grimaced at the trough. "Does it really taste like blood?"

"Unfortunately, the best flavors are all removed. But the smell is almost as good."

"I have a hard time imagining you eating anything else to compare this to."

Leander's scaly lips drew back in a dragon's grin and his yellow eyes flashed in the evening light. "You didn't meet me as a hatchling, Raven."

"Huh. No, that's very true." *And now I'm glad I didn't.* "Okay, well, I'll leave you to it while you pretend you're eating…whatever else." She made a face and stepped toward her dragon familiar. "It's time for my dinner too. I'll come to say goodnight."

"You don't have to. I'm perfectly fine out here and I can see you in the window."

The young mage stepped aside to peer over the edge of the pen's high metal wall. "I can't."

"You are not a dragon." He nudged her with his muzzle and she chuckled as she wound her arms around his huge head and scaly neck.

"Definitely not. And I'm glad. I wouldn't have you as one of the perks, otherwise."

"Correct."

She released him and patted the side of his massive jaw. "I'll let you have the night to yourself, then. You did a great job during training this morning, by the way."

"Yes. My skills in hopping around an open field and dodging nonlethal magic are vastly improved."

Laughing, she shook her head and moved toward the open gate of his pen. "I'll be back in the morning."

"Like every morning." Without another word, Leander lowered his head and focused all his attention on the overflowing trough of dragon feed.

Raven knew she'd been dismissed, slipped out of the pen, and pushed the gate shut behind her with a little click. The sound of her dragon familiar crunching ravenously through his dinner made her wrinkle her nose. *I bet he's imagining crunching bones right now instead.*

She laughed, even when a little shiver of disgust ran through her. "You can take the dragon out of the wild..."

The mage in training headed quickly across the open field on the school grounds and toward the stone archway that led into the school's main group of buildings. The girls' dormitory was on the right as she stepped through the aperture. She practically jogged to the front door before she hauled it open and stepped into the common room.

The smell of the elaborate dinner Fowler Academy provided for its resident students overwhelmed her immediately. Her stomach growled and she patted it gently. *Perfect timing.*

The area bustled with all the live-in students at the girls' dormitory, who chatted at the tables that lined the long room on the first floor. She went immediately to the tables along the left wall and took a silver plate. As she moved along the length of the buffet, she piled it high with buttered rolls, slices of ham, an ear of roasted corn, a few slices of cheese, and a large bunch of purple grapes. She poured herself a cup of water from the pitchers at the end, then turned and scanned the faces of the other girls seated at the tables.

Although her roommate sat with her back toward her and her head bent over a book, she recognized Elizabeth Kinsley immediately. *Same thing, different night.* With a grin, Raven strolled toward the table before she realized that three other girls were on the other side. None of them spoke to Elizabeth, but that might have been because the girl didn't speak to any of them.

"Hey." She slid into the chair beside her roommate and picked up a warm roll.

"Hey." The girl tossed her head to the side but her curtain of black bangs fell into place again over one eye even before she'd completed the motion.

"What'd you get up to today?"

Elizabeth thumped the back of her fingers on her book but didn't look up. "You're lookin' at it."

"It sounds like a busy Sunday."

The other girl smirked and took a huge, crunching bite from the apple in her other hand. When she lowered the fruit into her lap, her bat familiar Iggy uttered a squeak and nibbled on it too. "How was your super not-so-secret war mage training?"

"Not-so-secret, huh?" Raven glanced at the other three girls seated opposite them. She didn't seem to be of interest to them and she shrugged her reticence aside. "It was fine. Leander did well. I merely wonder when Bella's gonna stop blaming me for things that aren't a problem."

"That's why she stormed off the grounds in such a huff, huh?"

She rolled a piece of ham and stuffed it into her mouth. Then, she laughed and tried to keep it between her lips when she realized she should've waited. Elizabeth looked slowly at her, raised an eyebrow, and returned her attention to her book.

After a huge gulp of water, she leaned back in her chair and picked a few grapes from the bunch. "She thinks I 'stole her spell.'"

"Of course she thought that. Did you?"

"Is that a serious question?" Her nose wrinkled, Raven couldn't help but laugh a little at her friend.

The girl shrugged.

"No, I didn't steal her stupid spell. It's a great spell, though. She used it that day in Fellows' class where he made us all fight each other in teams, remember?"

"The force spell? Yeah, I remember. I bet she practiced it for months."

"She said weeks, actually."

Elizabeth simply hummed in response and lowered her head.

"So she wasn't all that happy when I tried it today."

Her roommate stiffened and closed her book slowly before she stared at her with an expression that vacillated between amusement and disbelief. "You tried it?"

"Tried and succeeded." Raven wiggled her eyebrows.

"And how long did it take you to learn?"

"Um." She bit back a laugh. "About five seconds."

The girl snorted and shook her head. The other students at the table finally looked at the two roommates. Mostly, they smiled only at Raven. One of them—she thought her name might have been Ally—propped her chin in both hands and grinned. "Have you talked to Daniel recently, Raven?"

"Uh...what?" She laughed and tore a slice of cheese in half before she popped it in her mouth.

"You know, the guy most girls in this school would fight hard to have a date with like you did the night of the gala."

"Yeah, I know who Daniel is." She glanced at Elizabeth, who had conveniently returned to her book. "I'm not sure our date was anything special, though, given that I left him in the middle of the dance and ran off to…fight some stuff."

Her friend snorted.

"But you had a great time before that, didn't you?" A girl with tight ringlets of brown curls wiggled her eyebrows and grinned.

"I guess."

"Is it true he's, like, the best kisser ever?"

Raven folded her arms and leaned back in her chair to regard them warily. "I have no idea."

"Really?" Maybe-Ally turned and glanced at her friends with wide eyes. "That's not what he said."

She yanked a handful of grapes off the bunch and shoved them all into her mouth at once. *You've gotta be kidding me.*

The curly-haired girl frowned with an empathetic little smile. "He's told the whole school for the last two weeks that you guys made out behind the dorms before you even got to the dance."

"Wow." She chuckled. "That would explain why he's avoided me for two weeks, wouldn't it?"

The other girls' eyes widened and their mouths fell open in surprise. "You didn't?"

"No. We didn't. So go ahead and spread that one around if you feel like it. It's definitely not a rumor." With a little shrug, Raven smiled at the other girls before she pulled another hunk from her roll and slid it into her mouth.

The upperclassmen laughed a little and collected their empty plates. "Have a good night, Raven."

"Yeah, you too."

"There's no way she's lying," the third girl whispered as they took their plates to the cart beside the banquet tables. "Who wouldn't want everyone to think they kissed Daniel Smith?"

Raven shook her head and turned to Elizabeth. "Did you hear about this?"

Her roommate shrugged.

"And you—" She laughed. "You didn't think that was something I might wanna hear about?"

"It's none of my business."

"You know what? I can't even pretend to be upset after an answer like that."

The girl smiled and closed her book. "Thank you." She lifted Iggy to her chest so he could grab hold of her shirt with his tiny bat claws and stood. "I'm calling it a night in public places, I think."

"Yeah, I'm right behind you."

With her book tucked under her arm, Elizabeth turned and wandered down the stretch of the common room toward the huge hallway in the back. Her head remained lowered as she offered her familiar more of the apple they were sharing.

Raven shook her head and rolled another slice of ham. *Telling everyone we made out. Someone needs to cut that off at the source.* The thought made her smirk, and she finished her dinner at an empty table, completely happy to be done with everyone else's crazy rumors for the night.

CHAPTER SIX

When she reached her room, Raven closed the door behind her and leaned against it with a little sigh. The noise of all the other girls in the dormitory talking and laughing and settling before classes started for the week the next day cut off instantly. "This might be the only completely quiet room in the entire school."

"Thank you for that too." Elizabeth sat cross-legged on her bed, hunched over the book in her lap again. "One of the benefits of having Raven Alby for a roommate, right?"

"I guess." She swiped her hair out of her face and went to her bed on the left side of the room. Her expression a little disgruntled, she sat on the mattress with a thump and untied the laces of her boots. "No rumors about you yet simply from sharing a room with me, huh?"

"People were already talking about me before you moved in here." The other girl smirked but didn't look up from her reading. "I couldn't care less what anyone says about me."

"I'm right there with you. But I'm still gonna have a chat

with the guy." Her boots thudded on the floor and she undid the leather thong that held her braid together before she shook her long red hair out. "Otherwise, the next thing you know, I'll hear at breakfast that we got married."

Elizabeth snorted. "I bet it was super *cool*."

Raven laughed and followed it with a groan as she flopped back onto the bed. "Daniel's an okay guy. Telling everyone we made out, though? I'm not so sure that gets him extra points."

"Maybe not with you." Shaking her hair out of her eyes, her roommate straightened and closed her book again. She set it on the bed beside her and leaned back to prop herself with both hands. "But I bet everyone else thinks he's *so cool* for doing anything with you."

"That's so stupid."

"Yep."

Her hand thumped against the wall, and she drummed her fingers against it for a few seconds. "Whatever. If I've been too busy to hear anyone say anything about it, I'm still too busy to care that much."

"He knows you'll call him out on it. That's why he's been hiding from you."

"Avoiding me? Yeah, probably."

"Hiding, Raven."

They laughed, and she coughed a little before she rubbed her chest. "Ow."

"Please don't tell me the spring cold's going around already." The girl studied her warily and leaned away toward the wall beside her bed. "And if it is, stay away from me. I don't handle crowds of people very well if I'm sick."

Raven turned her head slowly to catch the other girl's

gaze across the room and raised an eyebrow. "You don't handle crowds very well anyway."

"And you don't wanna see what happens when I feel like crap." Elizabeth pursed her lips and tried not to laugh, but she couldn't help it.

"I'm not sick. I was struck in the chest by one of Alessandra's attacks today and might have a bruise in the morning."

"I'm not sure your trainer's supposed to actually hit you. Even a war-mage trainer. What did she use? A practice sword?"

She laughed a little acidly. "A horde of dummies that kept shooting spells off even after Leander and Wesley burned them."

"Ouch."

"Yeah."

"Whose idea was it to train you and Bella every single day, anyway? The weekends are supposed to be for sitting around all day doing fun stuff."

"Alessandra told us it was necessary if we wanted a chance to earn a war mage's patch." She raised her fingers automatically to where her mom's red pin would be but her jacket was still folded over the back of the chair at her desk. "Honestly, I like it. And I don't even mind technically not getting a 'day off.' It's good practice for Leander, at least, being around other people."

"You mean your dragon isn't a huge people person like you?"

"Very funny." Raven smirked at her roommate before she turned her head to look at the ceiling. "And we still get the rest of the afternoon after training to do whatever we want. Which is mostly flying."

"Yeah, I bet." Elizabeth returned her attention to her book. "I'm good sitting here and reading all day."

"I noticed." The dorm room fell incredibly silent, and she remained focused on the ceiling. *Reading. If I wasn't so ready to pass out, I might try that.*

She closed her eyes and tried to let everything from the day filter out of her mind. Unfortunately, the image of Connor Alby's old journals wouldn't leave her alone. *I bet there's something in there about raiders too. It's not the first time they've been a problem for the kingdom.*

The moment the thought crept in, she bolted to a seated position with a sigh.

"Are you okay?" Elizabeth didn't look at her.

"Definitely. I'm trying to turn my brain off." She spun to lower her feet onto the floor and hurried to the dresser on the other side of her desk. The bottom drawer opened smoothly and she rummaged in the mostly empty oilskin bag she'd borrowed from her grandfather. *One journal's enough to start with.*

Raven took out the first one she'd looked through with Bella a few weeks before and took it with her when she returned to her bed. A hasty glance told her that her roommate was completely engaged in her reading again. The young war mage in training opened the old journal slowly and caught the scent of dusty, yellowed pages and decades-old ink. She flipped through to the place she'd found immediately after the Magic Meld spell and forced herself to keep reading.

This was where I left off last time. It has more details about

Sarah Alby and Vanessa Chase. I'm ready.

It opened with a brief introduction and a list of all the war mages who'd been a part of forming that branch of Lomberdoon's military during that time. Each name came with a page or two of what they'd excelled at and how they'd initiated new safety protocols for the kingdom. She found Alessandra's name and skimmed the page briefly, which provided information about the woman's role in training other war mages. *It looks like she's been doing that for a while.*

She reached her mother's name again. Sarah Alby was listed next to Vanessa Chase and the first summary introduced them together as two of the most influential founders of the war mages as a whole.

War mages Alby and Chase were instrumental in convincing Lomberdoon's King Reginald and six of the kingdom's largest cities—Kemfiir, Azerad, Delton's Crossing, Morningstar City, Sethvarin, and Pelinor—of the importance of young witches and wizards trained in combat magic. War Mage Alby excelled in battle strategy and rallying soldiers from all sectors of the kingdom. She implemented many of the kingdom's current battle preparations in the outer towns closest to the wall, including Brighton, her hometown. War Mage Chase occupied a status all her own in diplomatic relations with the larger cities, bringing most of them together with her sharp wit and ability to find the common threads linking them together. The war mage sector would not have become a reality without Sarah Alby and Vanessa Chase, and it is with this in mind that the following pages have been dedicated to recounting their numerous acts of valor, bravery, and sacrifice in the name of Lomberdoon's safety, peace, and prosperity.

Cautiously, she turned the page and found her mom's name again in large bold letters at the top. She released a long sigh and butterflies raced in her stomach as she glanced at her dresser across the dorm room. *Sacrifice. Mom didn't sacrifice everything if she died with Dad in that overturned wagon.*

Tears swam in her vision and she wiped them away hastily. *I should read this when I'm not already exhausted.*

She flipped the pages twice more and didn't dare to stop and read about all her exploits and accomplishments as a war mage, although there seemed to be far more under Sarah Alby's name than any of the others. The next name, of course, was Vanessa Chase, and she stopped again. *This feels private. Maybe I should let Bella read this first.*

With another sigh, Raven slipped the strip of leather attached to the journal's spine between the pages to mark her place. She snapped it shut, returned it to the bottom drawer of the dresser, and changed into her flannel pajamas for the night. *I've already waited for sixteen years. Another day or two won't hurt.*

Weariness settled over her and she climbed into bed and rolled to face the wall.

"Are you callin' it a night?" Elizabeth asked softly.

"I think so. It's been a long day."

"Yeah. I'm right there with you." The girl set her book on the nightstand and climbed under her covers before she stretched her hand to the magical light that hovered in the center of the ceiling and muttered, "*Nullen lucidis.*"

The glow blinked out, and Raven closed her eyes. *I'll make a fresh start in the morning.*

CHAPTER SEVEN

Bright and early, Raven went through her usual routine of waking up hours before anyone else on Fowler Academy's grounds and hurried to Leander's pen. She filled his trough with dragon feed again, which he normally didn't touch until after she'd left him for the day. This morning, the huge red dragon familiar didn't even stand when she rolled up the empty burlap sack.

"Come here." Still curled on the grass he enjoyed so much, he raised his head a few inches from where he'd rested it on his forepaws. His yellow eyes blazed like lanterns in the gray-blue light before sunrise.

"What's wrong?" She dropped the empty sack near the closed gate and made her way toward him.

"I'm wondering the same thing." A puff of steam rose from the dragon's nostrils with his next heavy breath. "Something's bothering you."

She chuckled when he nudged his snout against her hip and she gave the ridges between his eyes a little rub. Slowly, she lowered herself to the grass beside his long flank and leaned against his side. He curled around her a little tighter, and their breath puffed steam into the early-morning air. "Not bothering so much as running around in my head."

Leander's chest rumbled as the young mage pulled her knees up to her chest and wrapped her arms around them. "I'm listening."

With a smile, she glanced at his huge head now only inches from her on the ground as he curved his long neck so he could face her. "My grandpa's journals."

"And the mention of your mother."

Raven's eyes widened. "Are you sure you can't read my mind?"

"I don't have to, Raven. Did you find what you were looking for?"

"Maybe. I don't know." She leaned her head against the dragon's warm, scaly side and stared at the last few stars visible before the sun came up. "I couldn't bring myself to keep reading last night."

He curled closer around her and his body heat chased away the last of the pre-dawn chill. "The idea of the truth can be more terrifying than what we already know."

She laughed. "A dragon's philosophy is priceless, you know that?"

"It doesn't only apply to dragons. I felt the same thing the day you persuaded me into that field with Zora. I did not trust the truth until it was there in front of me. Not only that, I wouldn't have trusted it if you weren't standing there too."

"That's..." The young mage nodded and stretched a hand to stroke the ridges of scales between the great dragon's glowing eyes. "I made you a promise, Leander, and I followed through on it."

"I will always be grateful for that." Another low rumble escaped him. "I cannot promise you will find what you're looking for in those journals, but I will always be here."

"Is that an invitation for me to hang out in this pen with you and read those journals all the way through?" Raven smirked when her dragon snorted.

"As long as you don't read out loud. I'm not interested in storytime."

With a laugh, she rested her head against his side again. "I'm sure the history of war mages would be incredibly boring to a dragon."

"Unless there's something about us in those pages, then yes."

"Well, when I do finally go through them, I'll let you know."

"I'll already know."

Raven shook her head and stared at her dragon in amazement. "Of course you will. Thank you."

"For what?"

"Simply for being here. With Grandpa gone, the list of people I can talk to first thing in the morning is very small."

"It's nonexistent." Leander snorted again. "I'm not a person."

"That might be the best part."

They sat in silence and watched the sun come up, both of them warm where they curled together in the grass of Leander's pen. When the sky lit with pink and orange and bright blue, her stomach rumbled on cue.

"I guess I'd better get to breakfast before everyone else in the dorms picks those tables clean." Raven pushed herself to her feet and ran her hand down his long neck. "We have a few classes together today. Business as usual, right?"

"If you say so." He butted his head against her thigh and she turned toward the pen's gate.

Laughing, she turned again and pointed at him. "Your little nudges are not so subtle."

"If I wanted to be subtle, Raven, you'd never know."

"I'll come get you before the next class. Enjoy your breakfast."

The dragon didn't answer and he didn't move from his curled position. She snatched the empty feed bag and took it with her as she left her familiar's roomy pen. The gate shut rapidly behind her with a click and her stomach rumbled again. *As far as subtlety goes, I'm fairly sure Leander takes the win.*

After a hurried breakfast of a few steaming rolls and a bowl of oatmeal with berries, Raven adjusted the straps of her satchel over both shoulders and left the dorms with the last few girls. They chatted noisily as they prepared to start another day at magic school. She hung back a little as she always did and followed them into the main square of Fowler Academy.

The center courtyard immediately inside the school's front gates already bustled with activity. She caught sight of her friends beyond a huge group of upperclassmen practicing their mischievous spells and waved.

"What's up, Alby?" Henry grinned and slid an arm

around her shoulders when she managed to navigate through the crowd to join them.

She stumbled under the weight of it and shrugged it off her shoulders with a laugh. "You mean besides you trying to knock me over with that arm, Derks?"

"Hey, it's a show of love and respect." He shrugged and glanced at his toad familiar Maxwell, who poked his head beneath the flap of his mage's messenger bag. "How was your weekend at Fowler?"

On the other side of him, Murphy chuckled. "Nice and relaxing I bet, huh?"

He nodded vigorously. "Yeah, with all the extra time spent lounging around the school doing nothing."

"Totally." Raven shook her head and waved airily. "I had the relaxation beaten out of me by indestructible training dummies before William Moss called me suicidal."

"Yep. Merely another day in the life of Raven Alby, war mage, huh?" Henry burst out laughing and flinched when she socked him playfully in the shoulder. "What did you guys get up to over the weekend?"

"Fritz and I did more training between helping my mom darn holes in socks." Murphy shrugged and smiled at her barn cat familiar, who sat at her feet and gazed intently at Maxwell where he continued to peek out of the bag.

Henry noticed the cat staring and nudged his toad gently into his bag. "I hope you two worked on not attacking other people's familiars."

The other girl smirked and caught Raven's eye. "Well, we didn't have anyone else's familiar around. You should come by sometime and test it."

Raven barked a laugh.

He fixed Murphy with a wide-eyed stare. "I hope that was only a joke. I've seen that cat pounce."

She blushed a deep red and shrugged. "Yeah, I'm only kidding."

"I wouldn't be so sure, Derks." Raven nodded at the other girl. "You guys could get practice in on all your walks to and from home and school."

"Yeah, sure. And then I'll train with my familiar stuck inside Murphy's." Henry ran a hand through his already disheveled blond hair and shook his head. "I can't exactly use a toad's healing properties when the toad needs healing, right?"

"The only way to find out is to try." She gestured expansively and grinned.

"Not funny, Alby." He gave Fritz another wary glance, then double-checked his bag to make sure Maxwell was still nestled safely inside.

Murphy gazed at the crowd of students and her blush faded slowly. "It looks like we're ready to get going. Our first class today is—"

"Bixby," Henry grumbled.

Raven grimaced. "She hasn't exactly warmed to me again after I brought that Skiffling skull to class."

"Well, she should. You—hey!" He almost stumbled over Fritz as the trio moved with the other first-year students toward Professor Bixby's History of Magic class.

Murphy scooped her cat up and couldn't bring herself to look at him. "Sorry."

"No worries." Henry stuck his tongue out at Fritz, then picked up where he'd left off. "Alby, I don't care how much you freaked Bixby out. If you hadn't brought that skull, we might not even have a school to go to anymore."

"Yeah, I'm aware, Derks." Raven fought back a smile as they made their way down the stone hallways of Fowler's main building.

"Now that I think about it, no classes for a while wouldn't be all that bad." He grinned. "It would give me more time to catch up on that report for Gilliam."

"Haven't you finished that yet?" Murphy leaned forward and stared at him.

He scratched his head and looked a little sheepish. "Uh...it's almost done. Come on. The school was almost destroyed by the last of the Swarm. They can't expect us to be completely caught up with work after that."

"That was over two weeks ago." The two girls shared a laugh. "And nothing happened to the school."

"Oh, sure. Well, near-death experiences affect everyone differently, Alby. You saved the day and spent a few more in the infirmary, and I'm still a little shell-shocked."

"Yeah, you look real traumatized."

Henry smirked and stepped into the classroom, threw his head back, and slapped the back of his hand against his forehead. "Is this more convincing?"

"Not even a little," Murphy responded with a laugh.

Raven raised an eyebrow. "The only way you'll convince anyone that you're too traumatized for mage school is the day you stop eating, Derks."

"Ha. Fat chance of that."

The trio chose three empty desks on the far side of the room. The classroom droned with conversation from all the other first-years settling in for a day of learning before Professor Bixby waddled quickly through the door. The short, stout woman with wild, frizzy copper hair could barely be seen as she made her way down the center aisle between the desks toward the front of the room. She climbed onto the platform behind her podium and clapped quickly three times.

"Bring it down, all of you. My goodness. If I had my way, you'd all take classes every day of the week simply to avoid this rowdy nonsense when you come into my class." The woman held the edge of her podium and leaned forward. "That applies to you too, Mr. Cotton."

With a lazy smile, Bennett turned away from Mike and Percy and promptly shut his mouth.

"That's much better. Thank you."

CHAPTER EIGHT

"Now today," the professor began, "I've laid out a slightly different lesson. Most of you already know Brighton quite well, as many of you have spent most of your lives in this very town. Also, many of you are visitors from other surrounding towns here in Lomberdoon's southern region. Normally, the wider exploration of our kingdom is delayed until your second year at Fowler."

Bixby tapped her wand once on the edge of her podium and muttered, "*Tabula regnum.*"

A yellow light erupted from the tip of her wand and in seconds, it materialized into a giant floating map beside the professor's podium. It clearly depicted the mostly circular wall that surrounded the entire kingdom of Lomberdoon. "Now, I'm certain someone can tell me where we are on this map."

A few students raised their hands, but Bella Chase beat them all to it. A flash of silver light darted from the second row of desks and struck the map with a flash to illuminate the small area of Fowler Academy beyond Brighton's town square.

Bixby shook her head furiously and settled her gaze on the girl. "Very good, Miss Chase. Although I would prefer it if you waited to be called on next time."

Bella merely smiled sweetly at their History of Magic professor, with Wesley perched on her shoulder.

Henry turned to shoot Raven an exasperated look. His eyebrows raised before he rolled his eyes.

She has her moments, though. Raven glanced at the back of Bella's head and the firedrake's tail curled around the other girl's neck.

"Yes. Miss Chase has it perfectly." Bixby returned to her attention to the floating map. "Brighton is quite far south, as you can see, and quite close to the wall—"

"Where's the giant hole?" Thomas asked. A few of the other students chuckled.

"That, Mr. Sinclaire, is an entirely useless question. The wall remains and it's currently being repaired as we speak. Rest assured, I will not waste all our time by noting a place on this map that will soon become obsolete anyway. Don't ask me again."

Murphy leaned toward Raven and muttered, "She's too scared to talk about it."

"I think she's scared of everything that hasn't already happened."

"Moving on." The woman clapped briskly again and pointed her wand at the map. "While life goes on in Brighton and the surrounding villages, Lomberdoon has a number of much larger cities protected within the circle of our great wall. Some of these will become much more relevant after this week. Yes, yes." She tittered and shook her head at her private joke.

Henry frowned and leaned toward Raven. "How would that be relevant? Next week is spring break."

She shrugged.

"As you can see here, the larger cities in our kingdom's southern region are more spread out and farther from the wall, although a few are within a day's ride from Brighton. Maybe two." Points on the map lit up with small round seals as Bixby's wand darted another bright yellow light toward each. "Azerad, Delton's Crossing, Sethvarin."

With wide eyes, Raven straightened quickly in her desk. *Exactly like in Grandpa's journal.*

"I believe you're from Delton's Crossing, Miss Hambridge, are you not?"

Tessa shrugged and propped her chin in both hands as her elbows thumped on the desk. "A few miles outside it, actually."

"Close enough. And of course, the northern and eastern regions have their major cities as well," Bixby continued. "Kemfiir and Morningstar City in the east. Pelinor in the west. And no map of our great kingdom is complete without the capital itself, Havendom."

The seal that lit up with the capital of Lomberdoon—a spear crossed over a sword with a tower and a flying dragon in the background—made Raven lean forward. *Those flyers were from the capital. And that letter Grandpa burned.*

"Now, of course, having our capital city and the seat of the king north of the kingdom's center has kept both our monarch safe and all of Lomberdoon's people within relatively easy reach. It can't be easy keeping so many cities and outlying towns under his watchful gaze, but as far as I'm concerned, King Vaughn has done a very good job of it all the same."

"And the dragons," Erin added.

"I'm sorry?"

"The soldier patrols on dragons." The girl gestured toward the map. "That's how Havendom keeps an eye on everything too, right? We see them flying all the time."

"Yes, yes. Dragons are an important part of it as well." Professor Bixby's gaze darted to Raven but she forced herself to turn toward her map. "But this is not a class on dragons, Miss Barnaby. This is history."

"And geography," Henry muttered with a smirk. She didn't hear him, fortunately.

"And all of this is only the beginning." The professor tapped her wand on her podium again and sent another flash of yellow light toward the map.

The mostly circular ring of Lomberdoon's great wall shrank and the seals of so many large cities contracted into tiny, bright points of light. The map populated itself with outlines of the entire continent, two others across two different oceans, and a curving spatter of island dots in the southeastern corner of the map.

"Before the Great War and before Lomberdoon raised the wall around its people to keep us all safe, King Reginald had a prosperous relationship with the other kingdoms across the Empty Plains. Currently, that area of unclaimed land is populated by a few satellite ranches, the owners of which still conduct business with both Lomberdoon and the two other kingdoms on the greater continent of

Threndor. Can anyone tell me what those other two kingdoms are?"

The students cast each other curious glances and most of them shrugged or shook their heads. A few turned to Bella, including Professor Bixby.

"Miss Chase, now would be the perfect time to cast another focus charm if you have the answer."

The girl folded her arms and shook her head.

Murphy nodded at Raven. "So there is something she doesn't know."

Bella either heard the comment or assumed someone would say something about her. She turned and scanned the students in the room. Her eyebrows twitched together when she caught Raven's gaze, who merely gave her a reassuring smile in return. For a second, the girl looked more confused than upset before she turned to face the front.

"Very well. I'm at least a little relieved to know that I can teach each and every one of you something you don't already think you know." The woman cleared her throat and whisked her wand a few more times at the map. "As I mentioned, there are two other kingdoms on Threndor. Sterlin Velt is ruled by King Hamish and Queen Thelise. Everwiel is governed not by a monarch but by a party of high-ranking officials who call themselves The Four-Handed Circle. Careful, Mr. Cotton. Frowning like that won't help you understand the way a kingdom can be run without a king. As far as I know, The Four-Handed Circle keep Everwiel running with expert efficiency. They're a trading kingdom. We deal far more with them than with Sterlin Velt, although not nearly as much as we used to before the Great War—for obvious reasons, I should think.

"Now, this second smaller continent to the northeast of Threndor is Malenspire. The last I heard of it, the people were divided between agriculture—much like in Lomberdoon—and fishing villages."

"Do they have dragons?"

Bixby looked unimpressed. "You're remarkably interested in that subject, aren't you, Miss Barnaby? Perhaps you and Miss Alby should get together for a discussion."

A few of the students laughed. Raven shook her head and sent Erin a sympathetic smile when the girl's cheeks flushed.

"The answer, Miss Barnaby, is no. To the best of my knowledge, I don't believe the people of Malenspire deal with dragons of any kind. That said, I hear they're much more adept at training and utilizing sea serpents."

"Are you kidding?" Henry shouted.

The classroom erupted in laughter, and the professor almost fell from her perch behind the podium.

She glowered furiously and caught herself barely in time. "Mr. Derks, I most certainly do not make a habit of kidding in this class. Sea serpents have been around almost as long as dragons, and I daresay they may even be related. You'd have to ask Professor Worley about that. Now, before anyone else decides it's the appropriate time to interrupt my lesson, we'll move on to these. The Grimshale Isles."

Another yellow light flashed along the curved collection of dots in the southeast. "The Grimshale Isles were formed so long ago, it's difficult to track their entire history, even with the extensive records kept in Havendom of all historical and geographic timelines. But, as I'm sure you might guess from the name, these islands are at the top of my list of places King Vaughn himself couldn't order me to explore."

A few students murmured in surprise at that. Raven frowned. *There's not much talk about the king in Brighton but I'm sure Bixby took that one too far.*

The short professor cleared her throat. Her huge eyes fluttered as her face turned almost as red as her hair. "Forget I ever said that."

"Hey, it was only a joke, right?" Henry called out.

"Mr. Derks, I—" Bixby shook her head and clasped both hands on the edge of her podium. "Of course it was a joke. But the Grimshale Isles are not. If it weren't for the Sea of Barden separating Threndor from those islands, I imagine even the Great Wall wouldn't be enough to protect us. Don't worry yourselves unnecessarily about that one. I am confident that Malenspire would deploy their own security measures against any attack from the Grimshale Isles. And that is where their employment of sea serpents comes into play."

"Professor?" Raven raised her hand.

"Yes, Miss Alby."

"What about the raiders?"

A surprised snort escaped from between Bixby's lips, which she then pressed tightly together as she stared at the redheaded witch. "What about them?"

"Have the other kingdoms on Threndor had any trouble with them in the past like we have?"

"I wouldn't call it trouble, Miss Alby. We've had the occasional band of miscreants to deal with, but the wall remains our greatest source of protection, even from them."

"What about the other kingdoms, though? Do they have walls?"

"We all came together during the Great War, and I'm sure the other kingdoms have enacted their own security measures for the safety of their people. But raiders are a far cry from anything facing our kingdom these days, I assure you. Now." Bixby clapped her hands and pointed at the table beside her podium. "I want each of you to come up here and take a roll of parchment paper. You'll copy both these maps on your own, and you'll be tested on the larger expanse of these continents and the details of Lomberdoon itself at the end of the week."

She flicked her wand toward the map and it separated itself to show both versions she'd illuminated for the class.

"Not another word of raiders or dragons or sea serpents, understand? The only thing I want to hear in this classroom is the sound of diligently scratching quills." With a final nod, she folded her arms and regarded them sternly.

The students rose morosely from their desks to head to the table covered in rolls of parchment paper. Raven stood to take her place in the slowly moving line, and Henry tapped her shoulder before he whispered, "So you switched from talking about the Swarm to bringing raiders up, huh?"

She glanced at Bixby, whose focus had turned to watch each student take their supplies from the table. "William said dragon trainers from out of town brought news about doubling down security because of raiders."

"What?" Henry hunched his shoulders and shrank into

himself when the professor darted him a warning glance. "That doesn't apply to us here, though, right?"

"I don't know. He said his dad was only overreacting. I thought I'd bring it up here but I guess that's another forbidden topic."

"Psh. I wanna hear more about sea serpents. How did we not know about that?"

Raven smirked and shrugged as the line moved slowly toward the table. "Beats me."

I bet there's way more out there in the world than anyone's gonna tell us here.

CHAPTER NINE

Her next class was weapons training with Professor Fellows, and the students streamed through the stone archway to enter the field beside the stables and the barn. Raven had raced ahead of everyone else after the monotonous conclusion to History of Magic and the laborious task of copying maps of the kingdom and beyond. *It's basically a given now that class outside means Leander's invited.*

She reached his pen and flashed the rune on her forearm at the gate. Orange light illuminated on both her access rune and the gate's latch, which slid aside with a metallic click before the gate popped open. He stretched his wings wide when she poked her head in. "Did I catch you in the middle of something?" she joked.

"Waiting for you."

"I got here as fast as I could. We're up with—"

"Weapons training. Yes, I know. Spare me the explanation."

Her mocking frown had little effect and she stepped

back to open the gate for him. "If I didn't know better, I'd say you knowing which class is next means you're excited about it."

"But you know better." He snorted. "The schedule you keep with these classes is monotonous and predictable."

"Yeah, well, how else would they get a horde of teen mages to remember where they're going and when?" She laughed and pulled the gate open fully so the massive red dragon could step onto the field.

He stretched his wings wide again and shook his head vigorously.

Raven pushed the gate into place but left it open a crack. "No smart remark for that one, huh?"

"You wouldn't appreciate it, anyway."

"Oh, really?" Smirking, the young mage folded her arms and stepped toward her dragon familiar, who now had his glowing yellow eyes focused on the crowd of first-years streaming toward them across the field. "Fair enough. At least you get out of that pen for a while, huh?"

"Is there any chance you'll put me back in it?"

She laughed. "What?"

"I'd much rather be in there than around what you call your peers." Leander swiveled his head toward her until their faces were merely inches apart. "Which we both know they are not."

Playfully, she nudged his face aside, turned to face the other students, and muttered, "Yeah, maybe keep those remarks to yourself too."

At the front of the milling students, Henry grinned and nudged Rory Davidian in the arm before he moved quickly toward Raven and Leander. The other young mages stopped a fair distance away from the pen and most of them stared at the red dragon they should have grown used to seeing out there.

"It never gets old, Alby." Henry hoisted his shoulder bag to a more comfortable position as he approached his friend. "You and your dragon. Awesome. Hey, any chance—"

"No. You can't pet me." Leander growled. "Stop asking."

"Okay, okay." He raised both hands with a little chuckle and took a few steps back. "I can admire from a distance."

"It's the best place to keep that head on your shoulders, too."

"All right, Leander. Be nice." Raven gave him a playfully warning look.

The dragon peeled his red-scaled lips into one of his more terrifying grins. "Like this?"

"Uh…" Henry scratched the side of his head and glanced at the other students. Rory's mouth had dropped open and stuck there, his owl familiar's head tucked under one wing as if she couldn't stand to watch. Murphy clutched a few textbooks to her chest and stared with wide eyes. "Yeah. Real nice, Leander. I'll go wait with everyone else."

"He doesn't mean anything by it, Derks."

"Yes, I do." The dragon closed his lips and uttered a low growl as Henry darted toward the other students waiting for Professor Fellows.

"Okay, that's enough." Raven pushed his head gently but firmly away from where it hovered beside her. *We have the trust thing down. Maybe I've skimped on the "get a trained dragon to settle" part.* "Henry's my best friend—my best human friend, okay? Cut him a break?"

"I did."

She snorted a laugh and shook her head as she caught sight of Professor Fellows stepping through the stone archway to join them. A few of the other students followed her gaze and shuffled uncertainly while they waited.

"I know, I know. I'm late." Fellows waved off the vacant glances of his students with an impatient gesture and his long gray hair fluttered behind him as he strode across the field. "Mr. Davidian, help me pull the weapons out."

Rory didn't seem to hear the request and he jumped when the man clapped a hand on his shoulder.

"Staring at dragons won't help you pass my class, kid. Show me your rune."

"Oh. Uh…" The boy raised his arm, Professor Fellows pointed at it, and the access rune on the boy's forearm glowed with orange light. "Cool."

"Yes, very cool, Mr. Davidian. Now shut your mouth and come with me. We're already late, and I'm not sure the rest of your classmates will wait so patiently if we take much longer." He paused and turned to sweep a finger across the students gathered beside the stables. "But you will wait patiently." With that, he spun and headed to the weapons shed between the barn and the stables, passing Raven and Leander on the way. The man's gaze flicked briefly toward the dragon before he inclined his head and tried to hold a smile back. "Miss Alby."

"Hey." Raven sent him a surprised glance and immediately looked at Murphy. The girl's textbooks almost slipped out of her arms but the near mishap fortunately pulled her out of her dreamy stare at the back of Professor Fellows' head. *She has it bad and I honestly don't get it.*

The class watched Rory flash his access rune at the weapons shed, which glowed orange and popped open in front of him. He turned to give his friends—Henry among them—a huge grin and two thumbs-up before Fellows pointed into the shed and muttered something none of them could hear. The boy stiffened and stepped inside.

Raven slipped her satchel off her shoulders and set it between the wall of Leander's pen and the slightly open gate. The other students did the same while they waited for Fellows and Rory.

"Hey, Raven," Bennett called, dropped his bag in a heap, and made Murphy stumble when it glanced off her leg.

"Ow. Hey." She frowned at him and set her books gently in the grass.

"My bad." Bennett turned to Raven and nodded. "Does your dragon ever—"

"Dude." Henry slapped the other boy's arm with the back of his hand and shook his head slowly. "Don't go there."

"What? It's only a question. You'd think that was allowed after her familiar's been here for weeks."

Leander snorted and turned away from Raven and the group of staring mages in training to amble a few yards away from them toward the far end of the field. He lowered himself to his belly and rested his head on his forepaws, his back to the entire class.

Raven chuckled. "I'm fairly sure that's your answer, Bennett."

"I didn't even get to ask!"

She shrugged and shook her head.

Rory's heavy grunt made everyone turn toward the weapons shed as he pushed one of the huge wheelbarrows overflowing with practice weapons. "Yeah, laugh it up. These things are much heavier than they look."

"It builds character, Mr. Davidian," Professor Fellows muttered behind him as he pushed the second wheelbarrow. "You can stop there beside the stables. That'll do."

The boy almost upended the entire wheelbarrow when he jerked to a stop, but he righted it in time and spun it sideways so the other students could access the weapons.

"All right, you all know the drill." The professor waved toward the weapons, stepped aside with a sigh, and ran his hand through his gray hair.

With a last smirk at Leander, Raven went to join the loosely organized line of first-years who selected their preferred weapons. Murphy didn't see her coming until she bumped shoulders with her friend.

"What—oh. Hey." The girl exhaled another dreamy sigh and returned to ogling their professor.

"Still pining over that one, huh?"

"Raven, I don't care what you have to say about it. I honestly don't care about anything else right now but this view."

She smirked and nudged her friend again. "It's a good thing you don't stare at Henry like that. You're practically drooling."

That effectively dislodged the girl's attention from

Professor Fellows, and she stared at her with wide eyes and hunched her shoulders. "What are you talking about?"

"Come on, Murph. A semester and a half of mage school. I can't be the only one who's noticed."

"Well, whatever you think you know..." Murphy flushed furiously and shook her head. "Keep it to yourself. Please."

"That was the plan anyway. Are you ever gonna say anything to him about it?"

She gave her friend a sidelong glance and smirked. "Are you ever gonna talk to Daniel Smith again?"

They both burst out laughing and stepped closer to the wheelbarrows. When they finally had their turn to select their practice weapons, only a few things were left. Raven sighed and took the dented, poorly balanced practice sword with a laughably dull edge. "Do you think they'd let me bring a real sword to school?"

"Do you have one?"

"Back at the ranch, yeah."

Murphy shrugged and scanned the wheelbarrows before she broke into a wide grin. "Oh, yeah."

She tossed a few wooden daggers into the other wheelbarrow and hefted the huge, dull ax before she let it fall to her side.

Raven chuckled. "You're getting attached to that war ax, huh?"

"What can I say? I'm a creature of habit." Murphy swung it dramatically as she gave her friend a haughty, confident smirk and headed toward the other students who waited with their weapons.

"You're gonna end up taking someone to the ground with that thing."

"That would be awesome, wouldn't it?" The girl raised the weapon and managed to aim it mostly in Teresa Reynolds's direction before she couldn't hold it up any longer with only one hand. "I might like fighting against her more than with her."

With another laugh, Raven lifted the practice sword and wrinkled her nose at the dent halfway up the blade. "I don't know, Murph. Fighting with someone you don't necessarily like all the time has its perks."

"Oh, yeah? Like you and Bella?"

Her gaze fell instinctively on Bella Chase, who'd taken a bo staff again and twirled it effortlessly through the air as she practiced a few forms. *Showoff.* "Something like that."

"Mr. Derks," Professor Fellows called through a stifled laugh. "Are you sure you don't want to trade your slingshot for an actual school-provided weapon?"

The boy retrieved another pebble from his pocket and settled it into the cup of his slingshot before he drew it back and aimed. "I'm good. Thanks."

"Is that so?"

Turning quickly, Henry aimed the slingshot at Fellows' head and fired. The pebble cracked against the wall of the stable beside the professor's head with a spray of splintered wood.

The man stopped laughing immediately and turned to look over his shoulder at the small hole in the wall. Calmly, he turned to Henry and inclined his head. "Point taken, Mr. Derks."

"Sorry." He grimaced and shrugged but tried not to

laugh when he heard the other students around him choking over their snickers and chuckles.

"Don't be. I egged you on and I'm glad to see you're as confident with that slingshot as I am wary of it." Fellows raised his eyebrows and nodded at the sheepish looking student before he straightened to address the entire class. "Let's get to work!"

CHAPTER TEN

"By this point, we've done considerable sparring one-on-one and in pairs." Professor Fellows paced across the field and his gaze scanned the students gathered near the other wall of the stables. They had grown restless with weapons in their hands. "And you've all strengthened your bonds with your familiars, which helps. Today, we'll step it up a notch by using specific attack and defense spells with a partner. Miss Alby, help me demonstrate."

"Okay." Raven gave Murphy a wide-eyed glance before she stepped onto the field to join their professor. A few yards away, Leander swiveled his head toward them and finally paid attention to what was happening.

"Are you familiar with any minor defensive spells?"

"I have more minor attack spells under my belt, actually."

Fellows chuckled and stepped away from her and the red dragon who rose to his feet behind her. "This is what I want each of you to practice today. A minor defense spell still strong enough to deflect most attacks if timed correctly. *Deflecto nocere.*"

Raven nodded and repeated the spell. "*Deflecto nocere.*" A tingling burst of magic rippled down her arms despite the fact that she hadn't cast the spell. *It doesn't feel like a minor spell to me.*

"Excellent pronunciation, Miss Alby. Casting it shouldn't be difficult for you at all." A broad grin spread across his face and his eyes crinkled at the edges. "And I have a feeling you're familiar with the minor attack spell we'll be working with this morning. *Recta impetum.*"

Fellows turned and aimed the spinning ball of bright-green magic into the field. It struck the grass with a muffled thump and dislodged clumps of dirt and grass on impact.

Dummy spells. No problem. She smirked. "Yeah, I've seen that one before."

She glanced at Bella and when their gazes met, the girl rolled her eyes and shifted her weight onto one hip.

"Very good. These are the spells you'll all work with today. And if you're able, try to join with your familiars' magic to give these attacks and defenses an extra boost."

Almost as if he had addressed Leander directly, the red dragon moved forward and turned smoothly to step behind Raven. She felt him approach and nodded at the professor. *Leander can go on all he wants about being bored out of his mind but he's ready for this too.*

"Now, Miss Alby, this is the part where you demonstrate defending against my minor attack."

"Got it." She straightened and watched him intently,

even when Leander snorted and she felt his hot breath blast against the back of her neck.

Fellows raised his hand and shouted, "*Clypeus corporis!*"

The whirling ball of green light barreled toward her and she opened her mouth with the defensive spell on the tip of her tongue. Before she could speak, Leander shoved her aside with his huge head and opened his mouth. Dragon fire streaked from his throat and burned the spell away before it continued to the weapons professor.

"*Sequantur flamma!*" Raven shouted as Fellows cast a shimmering white shield of light around his body. A few students screamed. The column of fire responded to her command, stopped in its tracks halfway toward her professor, and rolled into a massive fireball when she clenched her fist. She tossed her hand aside and the blazing sphere hurtled across the field. It careened in a long arc and buried itself in the grass beside the front gates of Fowler Academy with an explosive thud and a spray of dirt and grass.

She whirled and stared at Leander. "What was that?"

The dragon merely growled in response, but his yellow gaze was locked onto the weapons professor.

"*Solvere.*" Fellows waved his hand, and the shimmering white light around him vanished. He cleared his throat and chuckled. It didn't sound nearly as amused as his usual carefree laughter. "That was certainly not the demonstration I intended this morning, but it's an excellent lesson on the importance of staying on one's toes. Battle outside any training ground is equally as unpredictable. So." He clapped briskly and waved at the gathered students, most of whom stared in shock at him, Raven, or Leander. "Go on. Pair off and practice on each other using only the spells I provided."

She tilted her head at Leander and spread her arms in a gesture of irritation. "Seriously. What got into you?"

"Miss Alby, I'd like a word." Fellows nodded at her and stepped farther across the field with his hands clasped behind his back.

"Come on." She nodded for the dragon to follow and he did, snaking along behind her with his head lowered beside her hip. The professor spun to face them when they approached. "Professor, he didn't mean to—"

"Yes, he did, Raven. Your dragon most certainly meant to burn me to a crisp. And you responded quite admirably." He nodded and studied Leander with an uncertain gaze. "I'm willing to call the whole thing an excellent learning opportunity for all of us provided you both can reassure me that won't happen again."

Leander spread his wings and folded them against his back with careful slowness. They both stared at him and the dragon's head swayed from side to side on the end of his long neck. "I'm not in the habit of lying."

"Leander." Raven turned toward Fellows with wide eyes. "Yes, Professor. I promise it won't happen again."

"Hmm." The man bravely entered a staring contest with the young mage's dragon familiar, and he was also smart enough to break from that stare first. "I suppose it might be an unfair request to have a familiar give assurances as well as his mage, given that none of your classmates' familiars can speak for themselves."

The dragon uttered another low growl but a quick

warning glance from Raven cut it short immediately. *What's wrong with him?*

"Still, out of pure curiosity at this point," Fellows continued, "I should very much like to know why I found myself raising a shield against dragon fire in the first place."

"Professor, I'm—"

"You attacked her," Leander growled.

Raven turned toward her dragon with wide eyes. "What?"

"I know I said it clearly enough." The great dragon's head raised to hover beside Raven's as he stared at the man with unblinking yellow eyes.

Fellows cleared his throat. "I believe that's the definition of a magical demonstration."

"Leander, you know how this works." She frowned at him. "We've sparred out here with other students for weeks."

The dragon's gaze drifted briefly toward the rest of the class as the other students practiced with their given attack and defense spells. "This man is not a student."

Both the young mage and the weapons professor gaped in surprise at the huge red dragon. Fellows rubbed his hairless chin and tilted his head in thought. "Well, you've certainly proven the truth of what I've heard about a dragon's logic."

"That it's impossible to argue," Leander suggested.

"That's one way of putting it. Miss Alby, I'm well aware of the fact that you and your familiar have come a long way together in the last few months. If I take his concerns into consideration and choose other students for class demonstrations, can we agree that this little misunderstanding won't repeat itself?"

"There was no misunderstanding," her familiar muttered.

"Please don't say anything else," Raven whispered and nodded at Professor Fellows with raised eyebrows. "It won't happen again, Professor. I promise."

"Excellent." The man returned the young mage's nod and glanced at Leander again. "I don't usually find myself apologizing to students, but I'll make an exception here for you both. I should have been more aware of what your familiar is willing to do to protect you, Miss Alby. And I'm sure you're willing to do the same for him."

"Of course I am." She rubbed her palms down the sides of her pant legs.

"I know." He clapped and took a deep breath. "If you can find another student who's willing to spar with you during this class, do go on and continue the lesson. If not, I'm sure you'll have many opportunities to try your hand at these spells during your...extracurricular activities with Miss Chase."

"Okay."

The man smirked a little and tilted his head toward her. "Very well done with that fire manipulation, by the way. I didn't expect to see that either."

"Thanks." She tried to smile but it didn't quite come out the way she'd hoped.

He merely hummed in acknowledgment before he clasped his hands behind his back and walked away from them, his attention now returned to the other students who practiced the way they were supposed to. "Miss

Murphy, square your shoulders. A defensive spell is much more effective if you cast it in a confident position at the very least."

With a huge sigh, Raven turned toward Leander. She took his massive head in both hands and pulled it down gently until his eyes were a few inches below hers. "That's a mistake we really can't make again."

"You heard me, Raven. It wasn't a mistake."

"Okay, look. I know some things are more black-and-white for you. Sometimes, they are for me too and I totally understand where you were coming from. But Professor Fellows wasn't trying to hurt me."

"An adult casting attack spells on a student." Leander snorted. "He knew exactly what he was doing."

"That's the point, Leander. We're at a school, not on a battlefield. Forget about the fact that it was a professor demonstrating an attack spell on me. If you hadn't stepped in, I would have deflected it anyway. I felt that defense spell respond to my magic even before I used it."

"That's my point, little girl. You didn't have to."

Raven closed her eyes and ran her hand along the ridged scales on either side of her dragon's face. "We're arguing two completely different things here."

"Clearly."

Despite how much trouble they could have gotten themselves into, she couldn't help but laugh a little. "Let's clean the slate on this one, okay? Fellows said he wouldn't use me for demonstrations anymore, which is kind of a bummer but I understand why. It's not gonna do either of us any favors if you hold grudges against my professors. You're my familiar, Leander, and we're here to learn together. No more blasting fire at anyone unless you pick up that I want you to, okay? Please."

Leander assumed an innocent look. "How do you know I didn't pick up on that five minutes ago?"

The young mage rolled her eyes and nudged his head away playfully. "Nice try. We both know dragon fire didn't cross my mind even a little. I love that you try to protect me. Thank you for that but...tone it down a little. This is only a class."

"I understand." A low rumble rose from the dragon's throat. "You're angry with me."

"No, I'm not angry." She brushed a few strands of stray hair away from her face and turned to look across the field at the crater her dragon's fireball had left in the earth. "But I want us to have the best chance to make it through Fowler as a powerful war mage and her unstoppable dragon familiar."

"We might as well leave now, then."

She chuckled and darted him a sidelong glance. "You're full of jokes today, aren't you?"

"I wasn't joking."

"Yeah, I know you weren't. But we still have a long way to go." Raven stepped sideways and stroked her dragon's broad, glittering red shoulder. "And we'll have to work on knowing the difference between training and when I'm actually in trouble."

Leander stretched his wings again, maybe in agreement or maybe in irritation.

I'm sure he already knows that.

"So." Raven stepped toward the sparring students and lifted her practice sword to settle it against her shoulder.

She scanned her classmates' faces but none of them looked at her. Apparently, even Julia Knowles was willing to work in a group of three instead of partnering with Raven and her dragon. "I'd love the chance to practice these spells but it doesn't look like anyone's all that excited to practice with us."

"That's a bad thing?"

Rolling her eyes again, she headed toward Julia, hoping to talk her into being her sparring partner. "Come on, unstoppable dragon."

Leander uttered a few sharp, hissing bursts of laughter before he ambled after his mage.

CHAPTER ELEVEN

"All right. Time's up!" Professor Fellows pointed at the almost empty wheelbarrows beside the stables. "Weapons away, if you please, then you can skip toward your next class. We'll try this exercise again next time with something of a twist. Good work today, Mr. Jeder. You and Mr. Derks seem to have a handle on those spells."

The man headed toward the wheelbarrows and stopped beside them to watch each student who fell in line to return their training weapons.

Raven swung the practice sword at her side and sighed.

"Some demonstration, huh, Alby?" Henry stepped beside her, pulled the cup of his slingshot back, and aimed it somewhere across the field without anything in it to shoot.

"Yeah, it was definitely...unexpected." She turned to look over her shoulder at Leander, who'd curled in the grass a few yards away from the sparring students when they both accepted the fact that no one wanted to spar with them.

"Unexpected. Terrifying. Totally awesome!" Her friend nudged her with his shoulder. "I always knew you were quick on your feet but that fire spell was amazing."

She gave him a small smile. "Thanks. I didn't think I'd have to use it during an actual class, though. Or to keep Leander from frying our weapons professor."

"Nah." He waved a dismissive hand and shoved his slingshot into his pocket. "You saw that shield Fellows put up, right? He already had that one covered."

"Probably."

Murphy joined them and the giant ax swung at her side while Fritz darted between her feet. "Are you okay?"

Raven laughed. "I'm fine, Murph, but I wish I had a chance to practice those spells today like everyone else."

"You'll get a chance." The brown-haired girl took a swing with the training ax in both hands. Her companions leapt aside and laughed in surprise. "I'd be down to spar with you, but my arms are a little tired."

She grinned. "You can still swing that like no one's business."

"Yeah. That's probably the last time for today." Murphy met her friend's gaze and smirked. "I think Rory was more afraid of the ax than of any attack spell."

"People should be very afraid of you with that."

"I wouldn't fight you," Henry added. "That's for sure."

Murphy's eyebrows drew together in a little frown. "I'm not exactly sure how to take that."

"It's a compliment, Murph. Promise." He grinned at her and nodded encouragingly, and the girl almost dropped the ax onto her own feet.

"I gotta...put this back." Without looking at him, she

hurried to the end of the line of students returning their training weapons. Raven and Henry fell into place beside her so they could continue to talk.

He scratched his head before he tucked a croaking Maxwell under the flap of his messenger bag. "Have you heard anything from your grandpa yet, Alby?"

"Nope." She shrugged. "I went to the ranch yesterday, though. It's business as usual, I guess. Mostly."

Murphy frowned. "Mostly?"

"There's a giant hole in our living room."

Henry barked a laugh but it cut off when he saw she wasn't joking. "You're serious."

"Yeah. Deacon and Patrick will get right on it and it should be patched before my grandpa comes home, whenever that is. I'll probably still have to tell him about it, though."

"About what?"

"I'm fairly sure the Swarm broke into our house looking for that skull. You know, before Leander burned it out of existence."

He stared at her with wide eyes and his mouth slowly fell open.

Raven laughed. "I'm sure Maxwell's the one who's supposed to catch bugs in his mouth, Derks."

The boy's mouth closed instantly with a click. "You had the Swarm in your house?"

"Apparently. But they didn't find what they were looking for, did they? And now they're not looking for anything."

"Was it creepy?" Murphy asked.

"Only a pile of splintered wood and stirred-up dirt

below." She shrugged, not quite sure how to explain what she felt. "Now that the Swarm's taken care of, I'm not worried about anything that has to do with them."

Henry narrowed his eyes. "I sense a 'but' coming."

She laughed. "But I think there might still be something to worry about."

"It can't be as bad as the Swarm, though, right?" With a grunt, Murphy hefted the practice ax and settled the head on her shoulder as they moved toward the wheelbarrows.

"I don't know."

"And what exactly is this new danger that Raven Alby, war mage and dragon rider, is so concerned about?" Henry folded his arms and wiggled his head in mock indignation.

"Hey, Derks. You've mastered your Professor Gilliam impersonation."

He snorted.

"I'm not concerned so much as curious. I told you William was doubling down on security at Moss Ranch."

"Because of raiders." He rolled his eyes.

"But there's obviously something going on that has to do with raiders, right?" Murphy glanced at the moving line and took a few steps forward. "Bixby was very non-answery when you asked her about it."

"I think she'll be non-answery about almost everything I ask her now." Raven shook her head with a small smile. "I scared the crap out of her with that skull. Still, I wanna know about the raiders too. It feels important, what with the giant hole in the wall and William's dad getting warnings from a few other dragon trainers to buckle down and get ready."

"I'm sure we'd hear about an issue if raiders were trying

to get into the kingdom," Murphy added. She swallowed uncomfortably. "Right?"

"I hope so."

"That doesn't make me feel any better."

They all chuckled, and Raven nodded at her friends. "Have you guys heard anything else about it?"

"Nope." Henry gestured dismissively. "We're all happy campers at home with no worries at all. Except for maybe whether or not Norman can handle any chores on his own without hurting himself more than doing it right."

She snorted. "What about you, Murphy?"

"It's only me and my parents. And Fritz." The girl glanced at her familiar, who yet again stared at Maxwell's head where it poked out of Henry's bag. "Nothing beyond those flyers put up in the center of town."

"I already told you guys that's only automated stuff that comes through from way out there." Henry stretched his hand into the distance. "Hey, I bet we could pinpoint exactly where they came from now that Bixby gave us such a riveting account of the whole kingdom this morning."

"I already know where a few came from." Raven glanced over her shoulder at Leander to make sure he hadn't moved. *I trust him, but he's been a little antsy today.* "Some of those flyers had the same seal as Havendom."

"There ya go. They made it out here and we have a few warnings about whatever the capital wants people living way farther north to do."

"You don't think it applies to Brighton too, Derks?"

Henry wrinkled his nose and shook his head. "Probably not. I'm in William's boat. Too much overreaction and people trying to imagine trouble when there isn't any.

That's nothing new to you, though, is it?" He stepped behind Murphy to try to elbow Raven in the ribs.

She darted away and pointed at him as he laughed. "You gotta be faster than that, Derks."

"Oh, I'm fast. Maybe not redirect-dragon-fire fast, but I have my moments."

Finally, Murphy reached the wheelbarrows and unloaded the heavy training ax onto the almost overflowing pile of sparring weapons.

"Excellent." Fellows smiled at her with a nod and the girl almost froze. "Does anyone else have a weapon?"

"Oh. Yeah." Raven dropped the dented sword into the other wheelbarrow and gave him a brief smile.

"Then that's everything."

With wide eyes and another blush, Murphy turned away from their weapons professor and headed toward Raven and Henry again.

"Miss Murphy," Fellows called. "Since you're here, why don't you help me with these wheelbarrows? Two of us will get the job done much faster and easier."

The girl gave Raven a surprised look and blushed even deeper. "Uh…sure."

She headed toward the same wheelbarrow as Professor Fellows, then stopped short when he took the handles. It took a few seconds for her to remember the other one, and she jerked toward it and grunted when she lifted it.

"You got this," Fellows muttered with a little chuckle. "Don't think I didn't see you swinging that ax, Miss Murphy. You're stronger than you look."

"I'm, uh…thanks?" She darted her friends a mortified glance over her shoulder.

Raven merely grinned and waved her friend away before Murphy turned and followed her professor crush toward the weapons shed.

Henry tilted his head and frowned after them. "Is it only me, or did she get weirdly quiet and red all of a sudden?"

"Wow." She laughed. "For someone as smart as you are, Derks, you can be clueless sometimes."

"Don't forget freakin' skilled with a slingshot." He grinned. "We covered that one too, right?"

"Yeah, we covered it." She folded her arms and shook her head playfully at him. "Let's wait for Murphy, though. I have a feeling she might get lost if no one is here to walk her to the main buildings."

Henry stared at her and his brows drew together in confusion. "I don't get it."

"Well, it's not my place to explain it." She shrugged and watched Murphy struggle after Professor Fellows with the wheelbarrow.

The man pointed at the girl's forearm, which bloomed with an orange light before the identical glow illuminated on the door to the weapons shed. They stepped inside and a few seconds later, his sharp laughter spilled through the open door.

"Huh." Henry smirked. "I didn't think Murphy had the comedy gene."

Raven wrinkled her nose over a smile. "I think there's much more about her you haven't discovered yet."

He scoffed and copied her posture mockingly, folded his arms, and stuck one hip out to the side.

Fellows and Murphy stepped out of the weapons shed,

and the professor nodded for her to join her friends. The girl practically ran toward them, her cheeks blazing red and her eyes wide, but she was grinning.

"What was that about?" Raven asked and laughed at the dazed look in her friend's eyes.

"He...he asked me to help him with the wheelbarrows before and after every class for the rest of the year." While the girl walked dreamily toward the stable walls to retrieve her knapsack and loose textbooks, Fritz dropped to the grass a few feet away from them and rolled happily onto his back.

"And that makes you happy." Henry glanced at Raven and twirled his finger beside his temple. "That's like an extra job, Murph."

She slapped his hand away and laughed. "Did he tell you why?"

Murphy turned around to face them, her arms folded over her loose books and the ridiculously blissful smile still plastered on her face. "Yeah. He said he doesn't wanna break Rory and that I make a good wheelbarrow assistant."

Raven glanced at the weapons shed, where Fellows closed the door and ran a hand through his long gray hair. "He laughed loudly. What'd you say?"

The girl stared at her for a moment and the smile faded from her face. "I don't know." Before they could respond, she hurried across the grass toward the main buildings.

Laughing, Raven nodded toward Leander. "I gotta see to my dragon first. I'll catch up with you guys in a sec."

"Yeah, there's no way I'm buying her excuse." Henry hurried after the other girl, holding his messenger bag steady at his side. "Major points for deflection skills, Murph, but now you gotta spill it."

She strode quickly toward the dragon and gestured to him. "Come on. Let's get you settled in again, huh?"

He pushed himself to his feet and moved toward her, his neck bent low and his head swinging from side to side. "I had begun to think you'd forgotten I was still out here."

"What?" She laughed and waited for him to catch up so she could scratch the underside of his chin. "I never forget where you are."

When he didn't have an immediate reply to that, she gave him a curious glance and skipped toward the slightly ajar gate to pull it open the rest of the way. He stepped dutifully into his pen, his head still low in an oddly disconcerting posture she hadn't noticed before.

She stepped inside with him and folded her arms. "What's going on?"

"I disappointed you."

"Hey, we already cleared the air on that one." She waved dismissively, but when he turned in a few slow circles before he curled in the grass—all without looking at her—she frowned. "Leander?"

"Raven."

"Do you believe me when I tell you I'm not angry or disappointed?"

"I believe you believe it. That may not change what you actually feel."

"Oh, boy. Okay. I guess I underestimated a dragon's ability to be embarrassed by a simple mistake."

He snorted and flurried a puff of dirt and a few ripped blades of grass in front of his face.

Raven stepped toward him and knelt in front of his huge red head. "I'll sit here as long as I have to until you look at me."

Leander rumbled softly and after a long moment, shifted his yellow eyes slowly to meet her gaze.

"I'm not saying everything's okay because I don't want to hurt your feelings. You know that too, and I'm very sure we both remember how unaware I was of how you felt when we first met."

He snorted. "Unaware. Uneducated. Unprepared."

She laughed. "Yeah, all of the above. But seriously, as long as you don't try to protect me from a professor—again, which I appreciate in principle—we're all good. I don't hold it against you, okay?"

The dragon exhaled another breath sharply through his nose and studied her face. "I'm convinced."

"Oh, good." With another chuckle, she ran her hands along the sides of his scaly face and nodded. "You're doing well since we moved here, Leander. Try giving yourself more credit for that too, okay?"

"If you say so." He lowered his head and turned away from her to curl his long neck toward his side until she couldn't see his face anymore.

He's way more embarrassed than he wants to admit. All he needs is space and a little time.

With a deep breath, she nodded and pushed to her feet. "Okay. I'll be back after regular classes. Then, we're on Alessandra's time."

"Goodie."

"But after that—"

"Yes, Raven. Flying always makes me feel better."

She chuckled. "You beat me to it. That's what we'll do for the rest of the day, okay? And don't keep beating yourself up."

"I'm not," Leander muttered. "I think I'll take a nap."

"Right." She wiped the smirk off her face. "Enjoy it. You have a nice day for sleeping out in the sun."

The dragon rumbled in response.

And that's my cue to leave.

"I'll be back soon."

Raven slipped through the gate and closed it securely. The metal latch slid into place, and she returned to the stone archway across the field, pausing briefly to pick up her satchel and sling it over her shoulder. *We have the trust part down. I guess this is as good a time as any to show him I don't stay upset about anything for long.*

She caught up to her friends quickly enough where the students gathered in the main courtyard before their next class of the day. Murphy still blushed and shook her head as Henry tried to pry out of her what she clearly didn't want to tell him.

"Derks, I'd back off if I were you," she told him. "Murphy's much stronger than she looks."

"Ha. See, it's something like that, right?" He grinned at their red-faced friend. "Is that what you told him?"

"Why do you care so much?" Raven asked.

"Why? Seriously? The only way I make Fellows laugh is by pulling my slingshot out. Which isn't that funny when you think about it."

"Well, you proved your point." She raised an eyebrow.

"We can seriously drop this conversation now," Murphy muttered. "And maybe get to our next class instead."

"Yeah, sure, Murph." Henry gave the girl's back a slightly harder than necessary pat and her eyes widened. "I'm only messing with you. You know that, right?"

"It's kinda hard to miss." Despite not being able to look directly at him, the girl smirked.

"Everyone has their secrets, huh? Fine. But tell me one thing, yeah?"

Finally, Murphy looked at him and raised an eyebrow.

"You didn't say anything about me, did you?"

The girl burst out laughing, doubled over the books in her arms, and shook her head.

He glanced at Raven and shrugged. "Did I break her?"

She fought back her laugh. "I don't think so."

"Okay. I'll hafta check in about that later. For now, I'll... uh, show up early to class. I'll save you guys some seats." He eyed the other girl who was still doubled over and laughed with tears streaming from her eyes now. "Unless she ends up having to go to the infirmary for this." With a sheepish grin, he shrugged again and darted through the crowd, calling for a group of his other friends to wait up.

Murphy straightened, took a deep breath, and wiped the tears off her cheeks. "Oh, boy."

"Are you okay?"

When the girls looked at each other, she burst out laughing again.

"Okay." Raven couldn't help but laugh with her. "Now I'm really curious. My guess is Henry wasn't even remotely on your mind in that weapons shed. So what did you say?"

The laughter died surprisingly quickly before she gave her a sidelong glance and grimaced. "It popped out."

"Uh-huh."

"I told him I'd be his assistant for whatever he wanted, even without wheelbarrows."

When the blush returned full-force, she draped her arm around her friend's shoulders and tried not to laugh. "At least you got his attention."

"Oh, shut up."

Raven caught sight of Bella moving through the crowd of students toward her next class, Wesley wheeling in large circles above her head. "Hold on a sec, Murphy. Bella! Hey!"

The black-haired mage turned to look over her shoulder, then rolled her eyes and picked up the pace toward the main buildings. "Whatever it is, Raven, I don't have time for it right now."

"You might want to make some time, though." She jogged to catch up to the girl. "I found something I think you should see."

"Seriously, we're already stuck training together after school. Give me some space." Bella ducked into the front door of the building where most of the potions classes were taught and Raven stopped short.

"What's up with her?" Murphy asked.

She frowned and turned toward her friend with a shrug. "I don't know."

"Honestly, I was a little surprised she didn't drop her sparring partner to be yours instead."

"Well, I bet she's saving it up for our training with Alessandra this afternoon. That'll be so much fun."

The girl winced but couldn't help a little chuckle. "Better you than me. Good luck."

CHAPTER TWELVE

Connor Alby sat in the private receiving room and listened to Councilor Dandryce drone on and on about his list of reasons why his suspicions were completely unfounded. *If I can't get them to understand what we're facing, this whole meeting will be a waste of time. Maybe it already is.*

"We simply cannot upset the everyday routines of Lomberdoon's people on a hunch." The councilor spread his arms in the elegant armchair and inclined his chin to study him from beneath wildly bushy eyebrows.

"It's not a hunch," he replied and forced his voice to maintain its usual levels of calm and sincerity.

"It is when you come to us with very little proof."

"I have proof." He licked his lips and frowned as he thought carefully about what he said next. "More than a few pieces of it. My magic—"

"Yes, yes. Your magic's returned. You've said that more than once." Dandryce waved dismissively.

"And how can you be sure it's an actual return,

Connor?" Councilor Vanderbos leaned forward in his armchair and raised his eyebrows. "Have you considered the fact that what you experienced during the war was enough to subconsciously cloak your magic instead?"

"Yes, Mihael. I've spent quite some time considering all the possibilities. And I wouldn't have bothered to bring it up, but I received that letter—"

"War Mage Athena has been temporarily excused from these meetings for that very reason, Mage Alby."

"I realize that. But she shouldn't have been."

The other two of the four military leaders and royal advisors who'd agreed to have this meeting with him exchanged wary glances with one another. Councilor Artuse looked at her lap and clasped her hands together. Councilor Nerole sucked on his teeth and darted his gaze from Connor to Dandryce.

"Do you disagree with our methods, Mage Alby?" The man's bushy eyebrows raised and made the question sound much more like a threat.

"I mean no disrespect, Councilor, but I disagree with your methods about as much as you doubt the evidence I'm setting right under your nose."

"A spent wizard regaining his magic is evidence of only that and nothing else," Dandryce snapped.

"War Mage Athena thought there was something more at play," Connor added. He gazed slowly at the faces of all four officials seated around the receiving room with him. "I traveled all the way from Brighton to study the archives, nothing more. This meeting wasn't part of my plans, and I wouldn't have pushed to arrange it if the signal hadn't already been raised."

"The Endflame. Yes." Nerole leaned back in his chair and tossed his long black hair out of his eyes. "Which was raised south of Brighton and inside the wall, if I'm not mistaken."

"It was." Connor nodded. "The other Guardians saw it and sent the signal along. In Kemfiir, Azerad, and Morningstar City—"

"None of those Guardians have any idea why the Endflame was raised, Connor." Artuse spoke quickly and her lips pressed tightly together as she regarded him impatiently. Her eyebrows—as light-blonde as her shoulder-length hair plaited neatly along the back of her head—were oddly highlighted by her frown. "Or by whom."

He clenched his fists briefly and forced himself to open them again. "That's the whole point of the Endflame, is it not? To raise the alarm across the kingdom no matter what the danger or which mage is responsible for making that call."

"As I recall," Nerole added, "the number of veteran mages in and around Brighton is very low. And only two of you were shown the Endflame when King Reginald put it into play."

With wide eyes, he glanced in disbelief from one pair of skeptical eyes to the next. "Surely you're not inferring that I manufactured some kind of emergency."

Vanderbos spread his arms in a placating gesture that also seemed a little insulting. "We have to cover our bases, Connor."

"I agree. That's what I'm trying to do and that's why I called this meeting. The four of you have much more reach than I could ever hope to achieve on my own. We have to spread the word—"

"Of what? A potential danger somewhere in Brighton which no one can explain. The only other mage living that far south is Peter Eckling, and everyone in this room is entirely aware of his mental decline over the last few decades."

"If Peter's mental faculties have been dulled so much that you no longer trust him, then so have mine." Connor pushed himself back in his chair to keep from throwing himself at the king's officials. *How can they be so blind?*

"Honestly, Connor, that's what we originally thought." Artuse gave him an apologetic smile and hesitated before he continued. "We were all surprised that you left the peace and safety of your ranch—a very prosperous ranch, to be sure—to make the journey here. I for one can say that I'm more inclined to listen to you than if Peter Eckling had shown up on our doorstep instead."

"That is where I have to disagree with you, Tabitha," Dandryce interjected sharply.

"And I as well," Vanderbos added.

He shook his head. "I'm not sure how much clearer I can make this. My magic's returned for reasons I can't explain, and if Peter is the only other veteran down there paying any attention to what's happening beyond the wall, I trust his judgment. The Endflame was only taught to the best of us—the mages we trusted the most to do what had to be done when the time came."

"There are very few assurances against the faults of a naturally aging mind, Connor." Nerole shook his head slowly. "None of us could predict how long it would take, however unfortunate it is that Mage Eckling's mind has deteriorated faster than the rest of ours."

His gaze flicked toward the royal advisor with a flashing intensity. "Neither one of us are crazy old men."

"We never said you were," Dandryce added quickly and looked far more nervous now than Connor liked. "Admittedly, the news we've received over the last few weeks about the confrontation at Fowler Academy was startling and somewhat disconcerting, but all things considered, it was handled very well."

Of course it was. Connor took a deep breath. *And I'm sure Raven had something to do with it.* "Are you saying that because the Swarm has been eradicated completely, Lomberdoon has nothing to be afraid of anymore? Because that would be a dangerously shortsighted assumption to make, Edmund."

The man's bushy eyebrows twitched toward each other. "I'm merely suggesting that the timing of the first Endflame warning and the defeat of the Swarm, as close together as they were, bring any other potential threat under intense scrutiny, Mage Alby. We're already well aware of a few bands of raiders roaming the western border and we've known about gathering raiders for some time. I can only assume that is why War Mage Athena sent for you, in the first place."

"Brighton's not even close to the western border," he protested. "And if War Mage Athena sent for me about the raiders you've already seen coming, I don't understand why she's been prevented from seeing me."

None of the advisors and military leaders had anything to say to that, apparently.

Mage Alby took a deep breath and raised his hands in a peaceful gesture. "The Endflame could not have been sent to warn Lomberdoon of something you four have already discovered for yourselves. This is new. At the very least, we need to send scouts to the wall and even farther to either side than the only breach it has seen since it was erected."

"If the danger beyond the wall was severe enough to threaten our safety here," Vanderbos added curtly, "we'd have word from Sterlin Velt. Possibly even from Everwiel or the outer territories."

"I promise you, if we're waiting to get word from any of the other kingdoms before we take action, we will find ourselves as unprepared for the coming danger as we were for a second Swarm attack, no matter how much smaller it was in comparison."

"Mage Alby, you speak of this coming danger as a real threat, but you cannot tell us what it is, where it is, or where it's headed. Without that information, there's nothing we can do but wait."

"That's entirely false, Edmund." Connor frowned and shook his head. "Don't try to play me for a fool."

"That's not what I'm doing."

For a few seconds, the receiving room fell silent. He stared at the untouched goblets of wine the porter had poured for them at the beginning of this meeting. "I'd like an audience with King Vaughn."

"That is absolutely out of the question." Vanderbos shook his head and his bald pate glistened in the low light of the lanterns dangling from the wall sconces.

"Have you been promoted to First Advisor, then?" he asked.

The man cleared his throat. "No, but—"

"Then get me an audience with Advisor Jaldair." Without expression, he searched the other mages' gazes. *Give me one open door. Please.*

"Advisor Jaldair, I'm afraid, will not find your evidence any more compelling than we do."

"Will you allow me to see him or not?"

Dandryce shook his head. "I'm sorry, Connor."

"Fine." He took a deep breath and closed his eyes. *It looks like I'm running out of options. I can't keep all the secrets to myself anymore if I want to accomplish anything with these fools.* "What would you say if I told you that Peter Eckling was also considered a spent wizard?"

A few officials took in sharp breaths. Artuse gave Connor a sympathetic smile. "If your magic has returned, Mage Alby, it would be foolish of us to think that any other veteran of the Great War hasn't faced the same difficulties in accessing their magic and called themselves spent."

"Then perhaps you'll have an explanation as to how the nine-year-old boy I spoke to outside Azerad managed to lift me three feet off the ground when I startled him out of a nap."

The councilors stared at him in silence.

"And I don't mean physically, either," he continued. "It was magic, plain and simple. After the lad calmed, he invited me to his home for supper and begged me the whole walk there not to tell his parents what he'd done."

"A young boy wanting to avoid his parents' discipline is hardly proof of—"

"Because they didn't know." Connor turned his intense gaze onto Vanderbos now. "Because magic doesn't run in his family. Not since every citizen of this kingdom had the use of magic at their fingertips, and that's far longer ago than living memory can tell us."

"Don't play games, Mage Alby."

"This is most certainly not a game, Councilor. I was a spent wizard. I knew it the minute I cast my last spell and I remained that way until I cast another only a few months ago. If magic's returned to me and has come to claim a boy with no history of mages in his bloodline, who knows where else that magic is returning as we speak."

Artuse swallowed thickly. "You don't mean—"

"Yes, I do." Connor nodded stiffly. "It's always been a possibility and we knew this from the beginning. Especially after my daughter and her husband passed."

"Warnings from long-dead historians do not constitute certain knowledge," Nerole interjected.

"My granddaughter's parents may be gone from this world but that boy was no long-dead historian. Nor is Mage Eckling and nor am I."

Silence settled over the receiving room again until Dandryce cleared his throat. "I believe that concludes this meeting, Mage Alby."

"Edmund—"

"My decision is final, Connor." The man fixed him with a warning glare. "You may go about your business in Havendom as you intended but do not expect us to make ourselves available at your request again. Not unless you have concrete evidence that extends beyond you, Mage Eckling, and a nine-year-old boy outside Azerad." The man stood abruptly from his chair, gave him a brusque nod, and turned to open the wide double doors into the receiving room.

Artuse snatched the glass of wine in front of her and downed the contents in a single gulp before she followed her fellow councilor into the hall.

Nerole nodded politely and left without a word. When Vanderbos stepped toward Connor, the wizard stood from his armchair and met the councilor's gaze. "It's good to see you again, Connor."

"I'd like to say the same under different circumstances." Despite the lingering tension, he took the man's hand and gave it a brief, firm shake.

"I understand. Between you and me, these obstacles to looking into what may be ahead of us aren't confined to you personally. You've always done very well with finding whatever information you needed. Perhaps you can find something the rest of us have overlooked."

I already have. He gritted his teeth and nodded. "Please, Mihael. Tell me where to find War Mage Athena."

The royal advisor gave him a tight-lipped, apologetic smile. "I would if I knew where she had disappeared to. For all I know, she may have left the capital after sending whatever letter you received."

"I'm not making this up."

"I know." Vanderbos nodded firmly. "But you and I both know that recognizing the truth doesn't necessarily mean we have all the answers." With that, he disappeared into the hallway and left Connor Alby completely alone in the receiving room with all his frustrations.

I'll have to dig deeper and look farther. He glanced at the four remaining goblets of wine and shook his head. *If*

Raven were here, she'd no doubt come up with a plan to draw this all together in a way I never would have thought of.

That made him chuckle. "How ironic."

The man gathered the few scrolls he'd borrowed from the archives to support his point—which he hadn't had the opportunity to use—and tucked them under one arm before he strode out of the room. *I can't reach out to her until I know more. Until I'm sure. She needs to hear it from me personally.*

CHAPTER THIRTEEN

"Very good." Alessandra folded her arms and inclined her head as she regarded her students. "It's not much of an improvement, if I'm honest, but at least it's something. I expect you two to keep your heads screwed on tightly over the coming weeks, understand?"

"What's happening over the coming weeks?" Raven asked. She sent a confused glance at Bella, who only stared at their trainer with something between a scowl and a grimace.

"More of this, Miss Alby." The woman spread her arms to indicate the training they'd finished for the day. "And hopefully, a damn sight more of an improvement over today. You're dismissed."

Bella turned toward her satchel propped beside the stables without a word. Raven moved quickly toward Leander, who was already halfway toward his pen. He nudged the gate open with his head before he stepped swiftly inside. With a last glance at the other girl, she poked her head into the enclosure. "Are you okay?"

"Hurry if you want to catch her in time," he muttered and ambled toward the full basin of water beside his feeding trough. "I'll wait."

"I shouldn't be surprised that you already know what I want." She smiled at him. "I won't take long."

"I know."

She shut the gate firmly and spun to look across the field. The other girl was a fair distance away from the stable wall, but she jogged quickly and caught up. "Bella. Can you wait a second?"

Bella didn't slow or turn around.

With a heavy sigh, she ran in front of the other war mage in training and finally made the girl stop. "Please. I've tried to talk to you all day. Can you give me two minutes?"

"I don't have two minutes." The girl glanced at Wesley who wheeled above their heads.

Raven chuckled a little, then forced it under control. "Why not? Classes are done, training's over with, and now you're heading home, right?"

"Exactly. And I can't be late for that, either." Bella stepped around her and walked even faster toward the front gates of Fowler Academy. She deliberately chose a shorter path across the field than the route through the stone archway.

"Does your dad have you on a curfew or something?" She jogged to catch up with her and leaned forward a little to try to catch her gaze. *Why won't she look at me?*

"We're sixteen, Raven. Not ten." The girl yanked the straps of her satchel higher on her shoulder and raised her chin.

"So you can spare only a few minutes to hear me out. I found something in my grandpa's old journals—"

"Look." Bella stopped and turned fully to face her, her lips pressed tightly together in discomfort. "I said I don't have time for this right now and I've said it all day. I have way too much on my plate."

"Really?"

With a grunt of irritation, the girl rolled her eyes and kept walking.

"No, I only mean that you and I are literally in all the same classes and war-mage training. Unless you're taking some other secret class I don't know about. Then I'd probably ask you how I can get in on that too." She laughed softly, but her companion obviously didn't think it was very funny. "Hey, I know we're not best friends or anything, but are you okay?"

Bella stopped again and took a deep breath as she closed her eyes. "I'm fine." When she opened her eyes again, she didn't look directly at her but Raven thought she saw tears forming in her eyes.

"You're normally very convincing but not right now."

"I'll be fine, okay?" The other student shrugged her concern off and rolled her eyes. The tears retreated without a single one spilling over. "And that'll happen much sooner if you quit chasing after me trying to get me to do...whatever you're doing."

"I only thought you might want to hear about—"

"Not now, Raven, okay? I have to get home. Things are...weird. My dad and my grandparents are putting much more work into locking our property lately."

"Did they hear something?"

Bella finally met her gaze and shifted her weight onto one hip. "No. But they take Brighton's bulletin board very seriously, and they're kinda freaking out about all the new directives to double-down on safety measures and to be prepared. And they need my help for their rigid timeline of setting all this stuff up that—" She scoffed and shook her head. "I don't even know why I'm telling you all this but here's the deal. I have enough going on with their frayed nerves and trying to juggle all our classes and training with War Mage Cheerful back there."

Raven snorted and the corner of Bella's mouth twitched in response, although she still didn't smile. "Maybe reading some of the stuff I found is exactly the kind of distraction you need right now."

"Whatever you found in those journals can wait. I don't have it in me to sit and read stories with you on top of everything else, okay?"

"It's not reading stories, Bella. I found something in there about your—"

"Miss Alby. Miss Chase."

Both girls turned as Professor Worley moved briskly toward them from the stone archway off the school's main courtyard. Bella hissed a sigh. "Now what?"

"Maybe he wants to sing your praises after you got Wesley to stand on his hind legs for two minutes today," Raven muttered.

A small smile bloomed on the other girl's mouth but she shook her head and took a step away from her.

"I'm glad I caught you before you headed home, Miss Chase." The man approached them and his long dark cloak swirled around his ankles as he gave the young mages a gentle smile from within his wild black beard. "Head-master Flynn would like to see you in his office."

Bella's shoulders sagged visibly. "Can it wait until tomorrow?"

He stared at her in astonishment and uttered a sharp, surprised laugh. "I don't think so. And I assume neither of you needs an escort to find him."

"No, we don't." Raven smiled. "Thanks, Professor."

"I'm merely working overtime as the messenger." Worley chuckled and nodded briskly before he turned and strode toward the barn. "You'd better hurry. He's waiting for you."

"Oh, Professor Worley?"

"Yes."

"Could you tell Leander where I went? He tends to get a little nervous when I don't show up when I said I would."

"I don't have to step inside to talk to him, do I?"

She fought back a laugh. "Shout it from a couple of yards away. He'd probably prefer that."

"So would I." The man flashed her a quick grin before he laughed and spoke his next words in a dry tone. "I'll tell your dragon, Miss Alby."

"Thank you." Raven hurried toward the stone archway and paused when she realized Bella hadn't moved. She looked at the other girl over her shoulder and shrugged. "I guess the journals can wait but you can't say you don't have time for Headmaster Flynn, right?"

With a massive sigh, the student tipped her head back and glared at the clear blue sky before she stormed after her. Above them, Wesley uttered an agitated screech.

The girls increased their pace across the grass that had

begun to deepen into a lush green now that spring was well underway. The minute they stepped through the stone archway and into the main courtyard, Wesley swooped and landed gracefully on Bella's shoulder. Neither of them said anything until they walked down the hallway toward the huge winding staircase to the headmaster's private office and quarters.

"Do you have any idea what this is about?" Raven asked softly.

"No." Bella stepped past her to head up the stairs first. "But if you did something to get us in trouble again, I'm gonna lose it."

"Yeah, I don't know why he called for us, either." She pressed her lips tightly together to keep from laughing. "The only issue I've had lately was in Fellows' class this morning, and you saw the whole thing. So—"

"I'm not your babysitter," Bella whisper-shouted and her voice echoed surprisingly loudly against the narrow staircase's stone walls. "You could've gotten into anything without me knowing about it and you're obviously intent on dragging me into it with you—"

"Hey, wait a minute. I'm being totally honest. Maybe you did something and everyone assumes I'm involved. Did you ever think of that?"

"No. And I don't think that's occurred to anyone else in this school, either."

"What is that supposed to mean?"

"Oh, come on, Raven. I'd be lying if I said you and I aren't on the same skill level with classes or even our magic. But I'm doing this by the book. I want to graduate from this school and find a prestigious position in the kingdom as one of the best mages in Brighton, if not the entire kingdom. The only thing you want is to break tradition and be the center of attention while you do everything your way."

Their echoing footsteps punctuated the stunned silence that followed.

"That's not true."

"It's totally true and you know it."

Raven shook her head and frowned at the black, shiny hair that swished from side to side across Bella's shoulders. "I'm not trying to break the rules."

"Right. You merely cherry-pick the ones that don't apply to you and break them anyway."

"Okay, I get that you're stressed right now. I mean, more than usual—"

Bella scoffed.

"But seriously, don't you think you might be taking it out on me a little too harshly?"

The other young mage offered no reply as she continued briskly up the stairs. Both were breathing heavily now, and Raven wiped a thin sheen of sweat off her forehead with her forearm.

I can let that go. Silence is consent, right?

They reached the top of the staircase and Bella knocked firmly on the large, ornately carved door at the very top.

"Enter." Despite the thick door, Headmaster Flynn's voice boomed from inside the room and echoed a little in the stairwell too.

Raven waited a few steps below her companion so the girl could open the door from the second stair to the top. The door almost cracked against the stone wall but fortunately, the stressed young mage managed to catch it in time. She gave her a condescending look over her shoulder before they both reached the top of the stairs and stepped into the huge, circular room beyond.

"Headmaster?" Raven glanced around the empty-looking quarters as Bella sucked in a sharp breath of surprise.

Rider, Flynn's intimidatingly large, dark-gray wolf familiar, padded silently toward them from the left side of the room. His ears perked up when Raven couldn't hold back a small laugh any longer.

"Someone's a little jumpy," she muttered and smiled at Rider's dark eyes glinting with intelligence.

"I'm not jumpy," the other girl whispered. "I simply didn't expect a giant wolf to come out of nowhere and —hey."

The wolf had pressed his muzzle against the bottom of the young mage's knapsack and sniffed. From his perch on Bella's shoulder, Wesley stretched his wings and uttered a warning hiss.

"Do you keep dragon jerky in there or something?" Raven chuckled.

Bella gave her a quick glance, her eyes wide. "Yeah, actually." She leaned away from Rider and tried to shoo the huge beast away and prevent him from sticking his snout in her things. "Not for training. Only because Wesley likes them."

"That's fair enough." Raven grinned when the wolf stepped toward her next and his tufted ears twitched a little as he sniffed her open hand.

"It would be great if Headmaster Flynn were already here before he sent Worley to come fetch us."

Right on cue, a door opened in the back of the room—which had looked like another section of the curved wall at the top of the tower—and Headmaster Flynn emerged. The man dusted his tunic off with both hands and coughed a few times before he closed the door again behind him. He gave his beard a few quick tugs, turned toward the open door to his quarters, and saw the two young mages standing there in complete confusion.

"Ah, yes. Miss Alby and Miss Chase. Thank you for taking the time this evening to chat to me on such short notice." He nodded at them and walked quickly toward his desk. Rider moved to join him but turned to study the young mages standing in front of the open door. Bella stiffened a little and Wesley curled his tail tighter around his mage's neck.

Raven glanced at them from the corner of her eye. *There's no way she's actually scared of his familiar.*

"Now." Flynn cleared his throat and turned to open a drawer on the side of his desk. The long scar down the side of his face glistened in the magical light overhead, even through his scraggly beard. "I've asked you here for a very important reason. If you'll give me one moment..." He shuffled through a few loose leaves of parchment paper in the drawer, withdrew two, then chuckled and put the second in his desk again. "One is all we need, I suppose."

The two girls exchanged a curious glance as he put his thin-framed reading glasses on and scratched something on the parchment paper with his quill and ink.

"There. Now, as I'm sure you both are already quite

aware, because—ha. Well, the entire school has counted the days down, haven't we? Yes. Now, um…where was I?"

He's seriously distracted. Raven wrinkled her nose a little and tried to help. "We're both aware of…"

"Ah, yes. At the end of this week, the majority of students at Fowler Academy will kick off the spring break with a bang, I imagine." Flynn chuckled again and shook his head before he peered at the other scattered parchment papers on his desk. "It's very exciting to have an entire week away from academic obligations. But you two, fine young mages in training that you are, will do something a little different."

Bella leaned toward Raven without looking away from the headmaster at his desk and muttered, "I swear, if you got us both into some other kind of detention while we're on our spring break, I don't care what we have in common. I'll destroy you."

She closed her eyes. "I didn't do—"

"Excuse me. I couldn't help but overhear the word detention." The headmaster's eyes looked huge behind the lenses of his spectacles, which he quickly removed and tossed onto his messy desk. "That is quite the opposite of what's in store for you. I can assure you that much."

The girl clenched her teeth and muttered, "Great."

CHAPTER FOURTEEN

"Well, I can tell you two are riveted with curiosity so I'll get to it." Headmaster Flynn took one final glance at his desk, tugged his beard, then looked at them and sniffed. "Normally, the school reserves this opportunity for upperclassmen. But War Mage Barnasis has put in a good word for both of you and I'm inclined to agree with her when she says she believes you're ready. At the very least, it'll be another excellent exercise in working together."

Raven inclined her head a little warily and Bella asked, "What is?"

"Hmm. I keep forgetting this is a new experience for first-years. Every spring, Fowler Academy sends five students showing the most promise in multiple areas. Combat and the use of magic are two of those areas, yes. There's also diplomacy—as a general subject, I suppose. Only so much of that can be taught in class or learned through books, exactly like knowledge of the rest of the world. The two of you will be among these five students traveling to another city in the kingdom to represent your school in a...gathering of great minds if you will."

It took a few seconds for both young mages to fully grasp what they'd heard. Raven finally allowed herself to smile a little. "Are we going to the capital?"

"Not quite." Flynn clasped his hands in front of his waist and looked at Rider, who'd lowered himself to the floor and now watched the discussion with minor interest. "This year, the kingdom-wide collaboration, you might call it, will be held in Azerad. I know there's only so much Professor Bixby is able to capture during her lessons about the surrounding cities in Lomberdoon—"

"She had us copy a map," Bella interjected. "But she didn't tell us anything specific about the other cities."

"Really?" The headmaster responded with a little smile. "Well, I'm sure it was bound to be in a future lesson at some point but now, you get to discover all the nuances of Azerad for yourselves. I'd ruin the most exciting parts if I gave anything more away, but I will tell you that Azerad is far more like Havendom than Brighton. And during your week there, you'll have the chance to experience another part of the kingdom, network with mages in high places, and absorb what you can about the way things work beyond life as you've always known it in Brighton."

Raven glanced at Rider. "Shouldn't we be training, Headmaster?"

He gave her a patient, knowing smile. "Being a war mage isn't only about fighting with magic, Miss Alby. Not even from the back of a dragon. It's about leadership in this kingdom wherever it's needed, even if it takes you to new cities and immerses you in new customs you don't know anything about."

"Headmaster." Bella lowered her gaze to the floor, and a hint of color rose surprisingly in her cheeks. "I want to go. But my dad—"

"That's what this is for, Miss Chase." Flynn stepped around his desk and stepped toward them. "Call it a permission slip, only we're not asking for your father's permission. We're reminding him that he already gave it when you enrolled at Fowler Academy."

He winked and handed the parchment paper to her. She took it with a little nod and her eyes widened as she scanned the words.

"And before you ask, Miss Alby, I am well aware of your situation. I don't plan on writing one of those letters to myself, given that I am temporarily acting as your guardian until your grandfather returns."

"Okay." She licked her lips and stared at the headmaster, whose wide eyes glistened with excitement. "If we're gone for a whole week, though, I can't simply leave Leander—"

"Of course not, Miss Alby. All that's been taken care of as well. Azerad has a rather large dragon stable for our fine winged friends flying with dragon trainers and soldiers. Leander will be perfectly taken care of, I assure you. I assume it goes without saying, but just in case…if you get even so much as a bad feeling about the way your familiar is cared for there, I expect to hear of it immediately."

"Thank you." She grinned at him, who merely nodded in reply and pursed his lips.

"How will we get there?" Bella asked softly.

"Hmm. That is an excellent question. I'll let the how continue to be a surprise, Miss Chase, but you will be accompanied by the other three students selected from among your peers. For years, I've been the one to accompany Fowler Academy students on this little outing, but I think Alessandra's grown tired of country life." Flynn chuckled and shook his head.

"She's coming with us." This time, it wasn't a question from the girl but more a deflated resignation.

"Yes, Miss Chase. The two of you have spent considerable time with your combat instructor. I have no doubt you'll set an excellent example for the other students who join your traveling party."

Bella gave Raven a sidelong glance and wrinkled her nose.

I'm right there with you. A week holed up in close quarters with Alessandra isn't my ideal spring break, either.

"I believe that's everything." Headmaster Flynn's smile widened, although his gaze had begun to dart distractedly around the room again.

"Headmaster?" Raven steeled herself when he looked at her again and ignored Bella's curious gaze. *I don't care if she hears. This might be my last chance to ask.* "Have you heard anything about my grandpa?"

"Unfortunately, Miss Alby, I have not." He tugged his beard again. "But if I do, I'll be sure he knows where you've gone for the week and you'll hear all about it when you return."

"Right." She rubbed her arm a little self-consciously, then shook herself out of it and nodded.

"I don't mean to sound rude, young mages, but I have a fair amount to attend to this evening. If you'd be so kind as to close the door behind you on your way out, I would very much appreciate it. Rider's been a little...antsy today."

Bella whirled and headed quickly through the door and down the staircase. Raven stared after her for a second before she stepped out quickly onto the second step from the top to push the door closed again with a soft, muffled thud. The other young mage's footsteps echoed from below, and she skipped down the stairs two at a time to catch up. "Hey, wait up."

"What, Raven?" The other girl didn't turn. She seemed entirely engrossed in the handwritten note to her father from Headmaster Flynn.

"Did you know about this trip? Okay, not that we were going but that it exists?"

"No. But it makes perfect sense that they'd send us this year instead of all upperclassmen."

She paused for a second at the unexpected compliment and grinned. "Thanks."

"Don't thank me for the truth. Especially when it's obvious."

They reached the bottom of the staircase, and Bella didn't hesitate but strode purposefully down the corridor toward the assembly hall and the front doors to the main building.

"Well, now that you have the headmaster's permission slip," Raven added with a little chuckle, "you have a few minutes to hear me out about those journals, right?"

The girl gave her a hasty glance over her shoulder, her expression almost deadpan except for the tiny flicker of a smile at the corners of her lips. "When my dad sees this letter, I'll have to work overtime at home to get as much done as I can this week before we're gone for a whole week after that. No, Raven. I don't have a few minutes for your silly little stories."

"Oh, come on." She rolled her eyes and sighed, although another little laugh spilled through it. "Are you really gonna keep calling them stories?"

"Aren't they?"

The girls pushed into the early-evening sunlight, and Raven shook off a little chill at the sudden drop in temperature. "I'm fairly sure we didn't cast the Magic Meld and destroy everything that was left of the Swarm with a silly little story."

"Fine. Maybe there's something else worth my time in those old stacks of paper, but it'll have to wait. You can show me while we're camped out with Alessandra." Despite the fact that Bella still hurried across the main courtyard toward Fowler Academy's gates, both girls groaned at the prospect of spending so much time with their war mage trainer.

It made Raven laugh. "Good plan. I'll see you tomorrow, then, I guess."

"Whatever." Bella gestured dismissively, but as she passed through the school's front gates, she cast another hasty glance over her shoulder. She headed swiftly down the road and it seemed clear that nothing would stop her.

"I saw that little smile, Bella Chase," Raven whispered. "You're not as good at keeping up this whole frenemies act as you think you are."

For a few more seconds, the young mage stood in the

center of the empty courtyard before she turned in a slow circle to take in a sweeping view of the many buildings that formed Fowler Academy's campus, the tall towers and rows of windows, and the highest spire she'd climbed up and down again from Headmaster Flynn's quarters.

We'll get off these grounds for a whole week. This is gonna be so much better than going back to the ranch for spring break.

Raven spun on her heel and darted across the courtyard toward the stone archway leading into the field beyond. Her red braid streamed behind her as she ran, pumping her arms wildly to pick up more speed.

"Leander! You won't believe what we—oh." She skidded to a halt on the grass a few yards from her dragon's pen when she saw Professor Worley push to his feet.

The man chuckled and dusted the back of his loose linen trousers. "Don't mind me, Miss Alby. I believe Leander and I were about finished."

She glanced at the pen's gate, which was still locked, and frowned at her familiar-training professor. "Finished with what?"

A loud snort issued from inside the pen. "It seems not every human is a walking disaster. And not every professor is intent on attacking his students."

In an effort to not roll her eyes, she wrinkled her nose instead. "That again?"

Professor Worley folded his arms with the end of his wiry, bushy black beard tucked between his forearms and his chest. "Leander is an incredible conversationalist, which I'm sure you've known for quite some time."

Raven tried to fight a smirk and failed. "Yeah, he has his moments."

"You know, Miss Alby, I've seen you come out here every morning before dawn and every evening before lights-out since you two moved onto the school grounds." He inclined his head toward her with a knowing smile. "At first, I thought it was merely your admirable dedication to making sure your familiar had everything he needed."

"Great." Raven laughed and wished she could see Leander's face. "Did he say something about my dedication?"

From the other side of the pen's metal walls, the dragon's sharp, hissed laughter floated toward them.

"Not at all." With a knowing smirk, Worley glanced at the enclosure and the dragon neither of them could see. "But I think I understand why you spend as much time out here as you do in your classes. I'd heard dragons make excellent companions if one can get past all the teeth and fire first."

She burst out laughing and clamped a hand over her mouth. "For me, it was mostly about learning how to not get hurled around like a mouse with a new cat friend."

"I can imagine a few similarities between dragons and cats. And I mean that with the utmost respect, Leander."

"I expect nothing less," he responded with another hissed laugh.

"But you, Miss Alby, are most certainly not a mouse." The professor unfolded his arms again and nodded. "I'll see you both tomorrow in class. Thank you for the priceless entertainment."

For a moment, she thought the man had taken a stab at her in fun.

Before she could think of a response, Leander rumbled

appreciatively and replied, "Thank you for not being an idiot."

Chuckling, Professor Worley licked his lips and headed away from the stables and the barn toward the main court-yard, whistling cheerfully with his hands thrust in his pockets.

CHAPTER FIFTEEN

Raven watched Professor Worley until he was halfway across the field before she stepped quickly to the gate and unlocked it with her access rune. It popped open and she slipped inside. Leander was curled in the usual position in which he waited for her to join them within his much roomier dragon pen. She folded her arms and inclined her head as she regarded him with a teasing smile. "Did you have fun?"

"Fun and entertainment are not always synonymous, little girl." He raised his head and swiveled it a few feet to fix her with his glowing yellow gaze.

"You know what I meant."

"Are you not entertained?"

She snorted and shook her head. "I don't even know what happened. I asked Worley to tell you where I'd gone. I guess he took that request a step farther and stuck around for a little chat with a dragon, huh?"

"It was a natural progression." The dragon watched her intently as she stepped across the pen toward him, her hand outstretched in preparation to stroke his muzzle. Leander's eyes closed in pleasure when she finally ran her hand slowly down the scaled ridges between those eyes. "He did as you asked and then he sat to listen to what I had to say."

"About what?"

"Myself, mostly."

Another soft chuckle escaped her, and she continued to run her hands along the top and sides of his huge head. "He's the familiar-training professor for a reason, I guess."

"Yes, the man has a surprising knack for befriending animals of all types."

"And dragons."

"Of course, Raven." Leander opened one eye, which rolled sleepily in its socket before it settled on her. "A dragon is not an animal."

"I could've told you that. Great and powerful beast is the acceptable title, isn't it?"

"I prefer dragon." He nudged his muzzle against her hip and snorted.

"Noted."

"Did you know he has four familiars?"

"What?" Raven withdrew her hands and stared at her familiar in surprise. "How do you know that?"

"Beyond the fact that I could smell it on him?" The dragon lowered his head and curled slowly in the grass again. "He told me."

"Wow. I knew it was at least two. But four?" She swiped loose hair away from her forehead and took her usual position sitting against his warm, scaly side. "It has to take seriously strong magic to make the connection so many times."

"Or perhaps an above-average level of dedication."

"Well, yeah. That too." Raven laughed and leaned her head against his side before she jerked it up again and turned to look at him. "Did he tell you what his familiars are?"

"I didn't ask."

"Oh. That would have definitely been one of my first questions."

"Which is why we work so well together. Your mind is filled with far more things than I would ever waste my time considering."

With a surprised laugh, she nudged Leander's side with her elbow and gave him a look of mock insult. "I choose to interpret that as you and I making up for what the other lacks."

"And what do I lack, Raven Alby?"

"If I mention what happened with Professor Fellows, would that answer your question?"

"That was not a lack. Merely an overabundance of protective instinct."

She laughed again and the dragon swiveled his head toward her on his long neck. His eyes narrowed and he gave her as much of a smile as he could without fully exposing all his teeth. "I'm glad to hear you're feeling a little better about the whole...incident."

"I'll feel even better when we get out of this lidless dragon box and into the sky."

"I promised you a ride and we'll get there. But I have to tell you something first."

"Why you were called away to speak to the headmaster."

"Get out of my head, dragon." Raven shifted against him to get a little more comfortable and chuckled. "Save me from having to repeat it all if you already know what I'm about to say."

"The mage with four familiars told me where you were, not what you discussed."

"Oh." With a crooked smile, she stared at the sky, which still had at least a few hours of daylight left. "So apparently, we're going on a trip."

Leander grunted.

"To a big city to 'learn and practice diplomacy,' I guess."

"Then I don't understand why I have to go."

"Ha, ha." She thumped the back of her hand playfully against his ribs. "Flynn said he already has a place ready for you out there. In a whole stable of dragons."

"He didn't call it dragon school, did he?"

Raven shook her head and sighed. "I seriously doubt that's what this is. As far as I'm concerned, the only school you'll go to is this one, and it's as my familiar. And my friend. We're in this together."

"And you very much want to go to this…big city."

"Azerad. Yeah, kind of. I can only imagine what it would be like to see a place that's more like the capital than Brighton. That's what Flynn said—so many things to explore."

"So many things to make noise and stink." He raised his head to look at her with a distinct lack of enthusiasm.

"If you don't wanna go, Leander, I'll tell the headmaster we have to decline."

"What I don't want is for you to resent not having said yes." The great dragon nudged his snout against her ribs and snorted. "Perhaps you need to get off this patch of land for mages in training as much as I do."

"It would be a nice change of pace, huh?"

A slow sigh escaped his nostrils and heated the space between his face and the side of her torso.

"So, I know how dangerous it is to assume anything with you—"

"I go where you go, dragon rider. You should know that by now."

Raven wrapped her arms around his massive, scaly head and gave it a little hug. "I know, but I wanna make it clear that I'm not forcing you into anything. And that I never will."

"Yes, you've learned your lesson on that one."

She gave a long belly laugh and had to wipe the tears from her eyes once it settled. "You're not gonna let that one go, are you?"

"So far, it's the only complaint I have against you. Of course, you're much better now."

"That makes two of us." She leaned forward and pressed her forehead against Leander's for a few seconds before she drew a quick, sharp breath. "Okay. I promised you space and free range in the sky to clear our heads. It's time to make good on that."

Raven slapped the soft grass beneath them and pushed to her feet. Leander rose almost as quickly and leaned toward her when she stumbled to catch her against his broad flank. Chuckling, she patted his side and nodded. "Yeah. You go where I go. I like it."

"How lucky for you."

"Oh, come on. You're a lucky dragon too, you know that?"

"Indeed."

They walked together across the pen and she pushed the gate open the rest of the way and stood aside to let the great red dragon move with powerful, graceful steps onto the field. She closed the gate most of the way again and clapped. "Let's—"

Leander's wings burst to their full span so quickly, it buffeted a shock of cool spring air against her face and ruffled the hair that had sprung loose from her braid. When she shook her surprise aside, he had already crouched low enough for her to climb on.

She grinned at him and shook her hands out in anticipation. "Is there any chance you wanna try—"

"Do it, and we'll see."

Raven laughed again and bounced on the heels of her boots. "Very soon, I won't have to say anything to you, will I?"

"Not about this." Crouched like a winged red panther about to pounce on its next meal, Leander swung his head toward her and widened his eyes briefly. "I'm ready."

"Yep." She slapped a hand against the metal wall of his pen to help her focus before she sprinted the few yards between her and her dragon. *If he's joking, I'll hit his ribs face first.*

A second or two before she reached him, the young mage leapt toward the center of his back that was far too high to reach on her own. At the last second, Leander's head swung on his long neck and under the sole of her boot. The dragon's powerful boost was more than enough to center her squarely for the perfect landing atop his back.

"Yes! That—woah!"

He surged skyward and she lurched forward in time to wrap her arms around his powerful neck instead of sliding all the way down to the grass. In moments, they were airborne and climbed higher and higher as the wind hurtled past them in a chilly, breathtaking rush.

Raven threw her head back and uttered a long, crowing whoop. She clung to her dragon's neck as he cut an almost vertical path away from Fowler Academy and into the pale blue sky.

When he steadied, the young dragon rider pushed herself back to slide down the base of his neck and into her usual seat on his back. "That was awesome!"

"It could use some refining."

She laughed and tears streamed from her eyes as the wind rushed past and beneath them and fluttered along the rippling edges of the dragon's translucent wings. "That's a given, Leander. But for a first attempt, I'd say that was amazing. Especially because for a minute there, I thought I'd land on my ass."

The dragon craned his neck to look at her. "I would never let you fall."

"Of course you wouldn't. But it's not completely out of the question for you to try making your entertainment."

Leander snorted and wheeled aimlessly through the sky. "The thought's amusing. Maybe I'll save that for the next time you annoy me."

Squeezing her thighs tightly where she used to sit in a

saddle, Raven folded her arms. "That doesn't happen very often."

"Not in a long time." He flashed her an unsettling grin before he stretched his neck far in front of him and descended a little closer to the ground.

"You talk a big game, dragon." Raven chuckled and patted the base of his neck.

"I take even bigger bites."

You and me both. "Let's keep the biting down to an absolute minimum while we're in Azerad next week, huh?"

"So, one?"

"Ha! Zero, Leander. That's the minimum."

"How exciting." His tone—as best she could hear it over the wind that whipped past her—was low and flat. She felt the rumble of amusement in his chest more than she heard it.

The young mage straightened, spread her arms wide to either side, and closed her eyes. *I go where you go, dragon. Have at it.*

The minute he felt the intention from his mage, he dove with a burst of speed that almost lifted her from his back.

"Whoohoo!" The young dragon rider shrieked with joy and held on with her legs as her dragon familiar echoed her cry. He pulled out of his dive above the treetops of the forest that stretched for acres around Fowler Academy.

There is nothing better than only the two of us in the sky.

CHAPTER SIXTEEN

The next morning, after her usual check-in with her dragon and a quick stop at the buffet table in the common room of the girl's dorm, Raven hurried to the main courtyard with her satchel slung over both shoulders.

Most of the students had already gathered in the center of the square, where they jostled one another, practiced spells, and called to their friends before the start of their classes. She caught sight of Murphy close to the front gates and the girl bounced on her toes with a grin and waved enthusiastically at her.

Beside her, Henry stuffed an entire roll into his mouth and dusted his hands off. When he saw what his companion was doing, he looked up and noticed Raven in the crowd of students and mirrored the spirited greeting. His grin was almost a grimace around the sticky, half-chewed roll that puffed his cheeks out, but the sentiment was there.

She laughed and hurried to join them. "What happened?"

"What?" Murphy chuckled and wrinkled her nose. "What do you mean what happened?"

"You guys are in a better mood than usual."

He gulped his mouthful of roll, coughed a few times, and smacked his lips. "Hey, don't look at me. Murphy started it, and I had no idea it was contagious when I walked with her from the fountain."

The girl gave him a playful frown. "I'm not contagious."

He impersonated her huge grin with the eager wave and all the bouncing again, only he aimed it at her instead of Raven. "It feels so good to be this excited!"

Raven chuckled and folded her arms before she shared an amused glance with Murphy. "About what, Derks?"

"I told you Murphy started it." Henry slid his arm around the brown-haired girl and pulled her against him with a little shake. Murphy eyed her with wide eyes and unsurprisingly, couldn't hold back another blush. He didn't notice and laughed as he released her, put his hands on his hips, and straightened to take a deep breath. "Smell that morning air, am I right? And what's that? I caught a whiff of something…"

"I don't think you'll find any leftovers in the dorms," Raven replied with a smirk. "Sorry."

"Yeah, that's a bummer." He pointed at her and squinted. "But that's not what this is, Alby. What I smell on this fine day is the scent of…yes…it's *freedom*."

The two girls burst into such loud laughter, it echoed across the main courtyard full of students and made a few second-year witches beside them shuffle warily away.

"What are you talking about?" Raven asked through another fit of laughter.

Henry grinned and puffed his chest out. "Spring break, you guys. Come on! Don't tell me either of you can think about anything else besides a whole week of not having to do all this."

"We still have four days of school left." Murphy looked at him and shrieked another laugh. "Including today."

"And lemme tell ya, Murph, those four days might be the longest of my life. But when they're over, I won't get out of my hammock for a week."

Raven wiped a few tears from the corners of her eyes and released a long sigh. "Won't your parents put you to work?"

He wiggled his eyebrows and darted her a devious smirk. "Not if they can't find me."

"You're gonna pass this first year with flying colors, Derks." She patted her friend on the back and nodded sagely. "No doubt about it."

"I happen to be remarkably skilled at compartmentalizing. Call it a gift."

"If you say so."

Murphy glanced around the cobblestones at their feet until she found Fritz rolling in a patch of weeds that protruded through the stones a few yards away. "My parents will probably put me to work."

Henry turned around toward her and spread his arms. "You could tell them you have loads of homework. Or orders straight from Headmaster Flynn to not do any work over the break—fresh minds when we come back and all that."

"But make sure you don't tell them both of those priceless suggestions," Raven added with a grin. "You'll need to choose one."

"Nah, she'd find a way to make it believable even then. Wouldn't you, Murph?"

"I...guess." The young witch shrugged and gave Raven another confused glance above a skeptical smile.

At least she's not blushing.

"Attention, students!" Professor Gilliam's voice rang out over the noise of the young mages who milled around the courtyard. The dozens of independent conversations died down—although some continued in low voices—and everyone turned to the entrance of the main building.

Henry stood on his tiptoes and tried to peer over the heads in front of them. "I can't see anything."

"Isn't that what the magically projected voice is for?" Raven smirked at him and when he caught her gaze, he shrugged and stopped trying to see.

"Thank you," Professor Gilliam continued in her calm, commanding voice. "Before classes begin today, Headmaster Flynn has a very exciting announcement to make. Please make your way into the assembly hall in an orderly fashion—I said orderly, Mr. Sinclaire."

A few of the other boys at the front of the group laughed as the tide of students swept past the woman and into the main building toward the great hall.

"What about you, Raven?" Murphy nudged her friend with her elbow and raised her eyebrows. "You're probably the only one of us who doesn't have to come up with an excuse to not be put to work, right?"

Henry snorted. "Yeah, she'll sic her dragon on anyone who tries."

"No, that would only be if someone tried to put Leander to work. Then, he'd give himself the command." Raven chuckled and shook her head. "I'm not gonna spend the spring break here."

"So you are going back to the ranch, then."

"This is perfect," Henry muttered as they stepped into the main building at the end of the line. "It'll be like old times, Alby. You and me, running around and climbing the wall. You can come with us if you want, Murph."

"I don't think anyone's climbing the wall right now," Murphy replied. "Not with the giant hole they still haven't fixed."

"Or whatever." He shrugged. "We'll climb trees. Take it way back to the beginning."

Raven scrunched her face and exaggerated a grimace as she stared intently at the stage on the other side of the assembly hall while the rest of Fowler Academy's student body took their seats. "It sounds like fun, Derks. But I'm not going home, either."

"Okay." Henry tossed his arms up and let them fall against his thighs with a smack. "I'm out of ideas." Maxwell uttered a startled croak from where he peered over the edge of his mage's messenger bag, and the boy winced. "Sorry, buddy. I got a little caught up there."

"Well, you definitely won't expect what I'm about to tell you." The three young mages took their seats in the second to last row and lowered their heads so she could share her story without drawing too much attention. "Headmaster Flynn called Bella and me to his office last night."

"Damn, Alby. You get called there more than Percy and he hasn't done much to stay away from there either."

She raised her eyebrow at him with feigned irritation. "Well, I don't try to get called there all the time. It just happened."

"What'd you and Bella do to each other this time?" Murphy asked. Henry immediately choked and snorted chuckles followed before all three of them snickered in the back of the assembly hall.

"Nothing. We've been working things out, I guess, which looks more like not doing anything to each other."

"Uh-huh."

"Actually, Flynn wanted to tell us in person that we're going on a secret trip to Azerad with three other students. Normally, it's an upperclassman event, but Alessandra thinks Bella and I are ready to go this year."

"Woah…" The confusion slowly bloomed into an awed grin on Henry's face.

"Are you serious?" Murphy's mouth dropped open.

"As long as the headmaster isn't a huge fan of practical jokes before the spring break, then yeah. And Leander's coming too."

"I don't get it." He grabbed both sides of his head and his fingers slipped through his already disheveled hair. "You get to do all the cool stuff, Alby. As a first-year."

Raven shrugged and gave him a conspiratorial smile. "I guess when you're trying to break tradition by being a war mage and a dragon rider and have a dragon familiar, it kinda spills over into everything else, huh?"

"No kiddin'."

"Wait, so what are you guys supposed to do in Azerad?" Murphy asked.

"I don't know. Something about—"

"Good morning, Fowler Academy." Headmaster Flynn's firm, far-reaching voice filled the assembly hall from the stage. He didn't need Professor Gilliam's voice-enhancing spell. "I have a quick announcement today because I know all of you are itching to get to your classes and start another fine day filling your minds with useful knowledge during your journey to becoming recognized mages."

A few soft chuckles rose in response, followed by a few hesitant whispers from other students as Headmaster Flynn swept his gaze slowly across the full room. He only paused his gaze for a second or two on a young mage's face before he continued to the next, but the corners of his mouth turned up in a small, secretive smile.

"Or perhaps that itch is coming from all your pent-up excitement about finally making it to the spring break."

"Woo!"

"Yes, thank you, Mr. Jeder. Excellent demonstration."

The gathered students were a little more generous with their laughter now.

Flynn cleared his throat. "Those of you who have already completed your first year at this prestigious mage academy most likely know what to expect of this announcement. First-years will be pleasantly surprised to hear they have this to look forward to in the years to come as well.

"Next week, five of your fellow students will leave the relative peace and quiet of Brighton to embark on a journey farther into the center of the kingdom—this year, it will be to Azerad."

"Holy crap, Alby. He's gonna say your name next, isn't he?"

"Probably." Raven leaned back in her seat and watched the headmaster intently.

"There, they will be joined by five other student representatives from each of the two other mage academies in Lomberdoon, Mandrose Academy and the Ziel Institute. And this, of course, is where the annual Tournament of Mages will be held."

A rustle of murmured surprise filled the assembly hall, and she gaped.

"Tournament?" Murphy whispered.

She darted her friend a sidelong glance. "He failed to mention that part."

"All right. Yes. Very exciting." Flynn raised both hands to signal for silence. "Your professors are all eager to see this competition take place."

"Clearly," Henry whispered and nodded toward the professors lined up against the right-hand wall. Both Fellows and Worley smirked as they studied the students' reactions. Gilliam's lips were pressed tightly together. Bixby nodded furiously but looked entirely confused. Dameron scowled, but that wasn't out of the norm for him.

Raven snickered and shushed her friend.

"For different reasons, of course," the man continued with a little chuckle. "Unless the rules have changed and I haven't yet been made aware, the winning school receives a whole new supply of magical textbooks and one teacher receives a complete overhaul of their classroom supplies. Yes, Professor Dameron. I know you've had your eye on a new set of glassware for your potions classes."

Dameron flicked his gaze toward the stage and the scowl melted fractionally from his face.

"In all seriousness, though," Headmaster Flynn continued, "this is an exciting time for both Fowler Academy and those five students selected to represent this school at the event next week. Perhaps even for the rest of you, should any of you decide it's worth your time and curiosity to return to the grounds during the spring break to take part in a little...spectatorship."

Henry scratched his head. "I swear, the guy talks in riddles more often than not."

She shot him a playful frown. "Really?"

"Well, do you know what the heck spectatorship means?"

"Not yet."

"Who gets to go?" one of the upperclassmen shouted.

"Mr. Ashworth." Flynn stared at whoever was seated in the front row. "I would never forget such an important piece of this fun puzzle, now would I?"

The boy's friends laughed and jostled him in his seat. The headmaster raised an eyebrow and raised his chin to gaze at the students again. "These five students have been selected—and have agreed—to participate in this year's Tournament of Mages. Miss Rodenmeyer and Mr. Hutton, both in their third year. Mr. Smith, in his second year."

"Which one?" both Daniel Smith and another boy Raven only knew as Charlie shouted in unison. Most of the students in the same middle row burst out laughing.

"I'm sure you could work that out on your own," Flynn replied, "but I'll alleviate the headache. Mr. Daniel Smith will attend."

Daniel grinned and shook his head as his friends

pushed him around in his seat, elbowed him, and slapped him on the back. "Cool."

Raven sank a little lower in her chair. "Not cool."

"Huh. That choice is even more confusing than you, Alby."

She glanced at Henry and rolled her eyes. "Yeah, thanks."

"And finally, our last two students selected for this grand adventure to Azerad may not come as much of a surprise to any of you. Miss Chase and Miss Alby, two of our outstanding first-year students."

A collective gasp of surprise filled the great hall and quickly filtered into whispers and a few laughs and what sounded like confused mutters. Daniel Smith turned in his seat and scanned the faces behind him. When he found Raven, his lingering smile faded and he spun quickly without a word.

"That's gonna be so awkward," Murphy muttered.

"You've heard the rumors too, huh?"

Henry wrinkled his nose. "It's hard not to when it's all the guy can talk about. He opens his mouth for two seconds, and every time, it's, 'Like, when Raven and I—'"

"Okay, Derks. Cut it out." She shook her head and couldn't help but laugh. "The whole situation is ridiculous."

"We both know he's simply full of crap," Murphy added with a reassuring nod.

"At least I have my friends on my side, right?"

"Totally."

"Duh." Henry bumped his shoulder into hers. "We're with you every step of the way, Alby. Rain or shine. Swarm or no Swarm." The two girls snorted. "School or—oh.

Okay, with the exception of next week. We'll be with you figuratively."

"That's exactly the kind of support I need, Derks. I knew I could count on you."

"Settle down, please," Headmaster Flynn commanded. Some of the more distracted students jumped in their seats but the side conversations ended quickly. "I'm not quite finished. The last part of this—which I want you all to hear before you scramble to pack as much knowledge into your brains and then allegedly not use them at all for a week—is this. While classes at Fowler Academy are not in session during the spring break, anyone who wishes to view the Tournament of Mages taking place inside Azerad's city walls is welcome to return to the school grounds. Over the last several years, we've worked with the professors and headmasters of the other two schools to perfect the use of a large-scale calling spell. This means students residing in Brighton during the tournament have the opportunity to watch all of it unfold in real time from right here."

He pointed sharply at the stage beneath his feet and nodded.

"Will there be food?" The force of Henry's shouted question startled him out of his seat. The assembly hall burst into uproarious laughter, and even Professor Gilliam cracked an amused smirk.

"Thank you, Mr. Derks," the headmaster responded. "You may bring whatever you like. However, Fowler Academy is not in the habit of running its own inn and I don't believe any of your professors are interested in spending their well-deserved break catering to strapping young men with gaping chasms for stomachs."

Now, most of the professors joined in the laughter, and Henry gave the headmaster a goofy little salute before he settled in his seat once again.

"Thank you all for your time and what little attention you had to spare this morning." The headmaster clasped his hands behind his back and nodded. "Now, get to class."

The assembly hall exploded with the sounds of the many students shifting out of their seats. They slung knapsacks, satchels, or large bags over their shoulders, muttered about the tournament, and laughed.

Henry stared at the stage, lost in his own little world as he formed his own plans for coming to watch the event in this very room in less than a week.

"Remember what you said on our first day here?" Raven asked and fought back another burst of laughter. On the other side of Henry, Murphy doubled over and laughed silently as her shoulders shook over her lap.

"You mean the part about keeping a low profile?" He turned toward her and grinned. "I gave up on that a long time ago, Alby. It comes with the territory."

"What territory."

"Being your best friend." He gave her shoulder a playful punch, lurched to his feet, and ran down the quickly clearing aisle between the chairs to get out of her reach.

CHAPTER SEVENTEEN

Getting through a day of classes after the surprise reveal in Headmaster Flynn's announcement was harder than Raven expected. When her last class with Professor Worley ended, the excitement radiating off the other students about being able to see the Tournament of Mages—and about two first-years making the cut—had infected her too.

Bella took it much better. The normally haughty young mage smiled through the entire day, including once at Raven. She didn't stalk off in a huff after Worley's class finished either.

I'd be even more confused if we didn't have training with Alessandra right after this.

Henry hurried toward her, holding Maxwell tenderly in both hands. "I still can't believe it, Alby."

"I know."

"You get to fight in an actual competition against other mages from other schools."

She turned and gave him a sly smile. "I think you might be a little more excited than I am."

"Of course I'm excited! My best friend, Raven Alby the dragon rider and war mage in training, broke the record for the youngest student at Fowler Academy to be sent to one of these events. I didn't even know the Tournament of Mages existed until this morning."

Laughing, she shook her head. "I haven't done anything yet, Derks."

"Yeah, that's kinda the point."

Murphy joined them, holding Fritz in her arms after her familiar had been involved in a slightly more aggressive than usual scuffle with Teresa Reynolds' ferret familiar. The barn cat looked exhausted and so did his mage. "That might not be completely true."

Henry glanced at her and laughed. "Which part?"

"What? Oh." A self-conscious smile spread across Murphy's lips. "The part about Raven being the youngest."

"Huh." Raven tilted her head and her gaze found Bella again, who was in the middle of animated conversation with Teresa and two more of their friends. The girl grinned. "Does anyone know when Bella's birthday is?"

"Finding out wasn't a top priority on my to-do list, Alby." He shrugged.

"Right. It doesn't matter anyway, does it?" She shrugged. "I'm simply happy to be one of the first-years chosen to go on this trip next week."

Murphy raised an eyebrow. "From where I stand, you don't exactly look happy."

"What?"

"More like resigned acceptance. See?" The brown-haired girl pointed at her and uttered a soft laugh. "You're grimacing."

"I am excited." Raven plastered on a smile that looked as forced as it felt, and they all laughed. "And surprised. A little hesitant. Confused."

"What's there to be confused about, Alby?" Henry asked and ran his hand down Maxwell's bumpy back. The toad blinked slowly in enjoyment. "Everything Flynn said this morning was damn clear to me."

"It was." She squinted across the field at Bella on the other side of the barn and the stables. "I'm confused about why he didn't tell us last night in his office that we'd be fighting. Or sparring, I guess. Whatever. He made it sound more like this was a diplomatic mission and we would get experience as future war mages. Nothing was said about having to compete against other schools so Fowler Academy can get new textbooks and an updated set of glassware."

Her friends responded with short, choked-back snorts.

"At first, I thought he was serious about that," Murphy added and tossed her dark hair out of her eyes. "But I think he might have been joking. It's kinda hard to tell with Flynn."

"Tell me about it." Raven's focus remained on Bella. *If I can catch her being her regular tight-laced self for a second, this wouldn't be so weird.* "Maybe I'm even more confused about why Bella's so..."

"Happy?" Murphy offered with a grin.

"She has a point, Alby." Henry nodded toward the girl

and her circle of chatting friends. "Miss Chase has you beat in the looking-happy department."

"And it's weird, right?"

As if they'd planned it, her two companions tilted their heads, frowned in consideration, and nodded.

"It's kind of creepy, honestly," Murphy replied.

Henry squinted. "Like the other shoe's about to drop at any minute."

Raven nodded. "I know she has her moments. It's the all-day smiling and chattering that's throwing me off. She didn't even send Wesley after Leander once during Worley's class."

All three friends turned slowly toward the far end of the field opposite the school's main courtyard. Leander had taken his usual pre- and post-class position in the grass, curled in a loose ball of dragon with his head turned away from the gathered students enough to look like he almost wasn't paying attention.

I know better.

"At least he didn't try to attack her," Henry added.

"That's never happened." She raised an eyebrow at her friend. "And it won't. We worked it out after the whole Fellows thing yesterday."

"Okay, I know breathing fire at a mage professor without warning might be generally frowned upon—"

"Might be?" Murphy asked and darted him a skeptical glance with wide eyes.

"But you gotta admit, Alby, it was cool."

"Didn't we go over that yesterday?" Raven huffed a small laugh and shook her head. "Sure, the dragon fire and the magic were cool. The overall situation wasn't."

"Well, hey!" Henry spread his arms, balanced Maxwell perfectly in the palm of one hand, and grinned. "Now you can put all that stuff to good use in Azerad. That overall situation is perfect for dragon fire and magic that the rest of us haven't even read about yet."

She smirked and lowered her chin. "I didn't read about the fire-manipulation spell."

He studied her face for a few seconds and leaned toward her. "If you tell me it came to you in a dream, Alby, I'm gonna have to take back everything I told Bennett about his ridiculous theory."

Murphy snorted. "Which is?"

"That dreams can tell the future." He wiggled his eyebrows and cupped his other hand over the top of the toad's back again. "Which is ridiculous. Okay, sure, maybe it was possible, like, centuries ago. And maybe one or two seriously powerful mages can still do it. But it's not something anyone can do. Unless Raven Alby tells me right now that I'm full of it."

With a small smile, she shook her head. "Not a dream, Derks. My grandpa taught it to me before Leander passed his dragon trials."

"Phew." He mimed wiping sweat from his forehead and nodded. "Then I'm off the hook on having to eat my words."

"I'm happy to help, Derks."

He offered her a goofy little bow over his upturned boot. Maxwell protested with a loud croak and tried to leap from his outstretched hand. "Woah!" He caught his familiar, stumbled forward, and shook his head. "Nice try, buddy. I thought we'd moved past the jumpiness already."

The toad's throat swelled and shrank, and Murphy took a sideways step away from him. "Sorry. It might be Fritz again."

The barn cat in her arms stared intently at Maxwell, his amber eyes already narrowed, and one of his ears twitched.

Henry studied them warily and stepped farther away. "I like you, Murph. We're friends. But if your cat tries to eat my familiar, we might have problems."

"He's not gonna eat your toad, Henry." Another soft blush rose on her cheeks, but she managed to laugh through it. "Maybe he only wants to make friends. Did you ever think of that?"

"Nope. I never heard of a cat who kills things to earn its keep making friends with one of those things. Namely toads."

"There aren't any toads in our barn."

"And why do you think that is?" He leaned toward her and raised his eyebrows.

Murphy frowned and glanced at the roof of the stables beside them.

They're gonna start an actual fight if this goes on much longer.

"All right, guys," Raven intervened with a hesitant laugh. "Things are obviously different with familiars. You've both had enough training to keep them under control, so it's not really—"

"Well, I've seen mice in the barn," the other girl interjected and completely ignored her friend's attempt to cool things down a little.

He scoffed. "Or maybe Fritz discovered he likes the

taste of toad better and let a few of the other helpless creatures slip under the radar."

"Do you know how much damage a few mice can do?" Turning away from him, Murphy looked over her shoulder and directed her frown to Henry now as she hunched protectively over her familiar in her arms. "You seem determined to blame Fritz for something that hasn't even happened yet."

"Guys—"

"Murph, I'm not blaming him for eating Maxwell." Henry held his hands a little more firmly around his familiar until only the toad's wide, glistening eyes could be seen. "I'm saying that for weeks, that cat has eyed this toad like he's already been put in a dinner bowl next to a saucer of milk."

"Well, maybe this cat only wants to get that toad's attention, Henry Derks! Did you ever think of that?" Her shout carried clearly across the field. The other students who hadn't yet left the barn and stables for the day stopped their conversations to turn toward the normally quietly cheerful Murphy. Most of them returned to whatever they were doing fairly quickly, but a few continued to stare in surprise. The girl wouldn't look at them and the blush on her cheeks deepened to an alarming shade of red, although she held Henry's gaze.

Raven glanced from one to the other and bit her bottom lip. *That's as close as she's ever been to simply coming out and telling him.*

Henry's wide-eyed gaze traveled slowly to the bristling barn cat in Murphy's arms. Then, he looked at Maxwell, whose sides were heaving now, and sighed. "No, actually."

MARTHA CARR & MICHAEL ANDERLE

When he looked at Murphy again, Raven was surprised to see the young witch still staring at him without flinching or a hint of backing down.

Someone's been working on her confidence.

"I didn't think about that, Murph." He raised and lowered his eyebrows. "But you can't blame me for thinking your cat's hungry when he stares at Maxwell like that all the time, can you?"

"No." Murphy swallowed. "But I can blame you for jumping to conclusions and not even considering the other possibilities."

"Huh." He held the toad against his chest and scratched his ruffled hair with the other hand. "Well, maybe there are other possibilities. Maybe we'll let them work it out for themselves. Right?"

"As long as you promise not to step in before they do that."

"Yeah. Sure." Henry glanced at Raven, frowned a little, and turned to head toward his shoulder bag, which he'd placed against the stable wall.

Raven sighed quietly and moved slowly toward the other girl. "Are you okay?"

"I don't know." The brown-haired witch gave her friend a sidelong glance and shrugged. "I guess I'm simply fed up with being written off."

"Right." Leaning toward the girl, she whispered, "That wasn't completely about Fritz and Maxwell, was it?"

Murphy stared at the grass in front of them and her eyes grew wide and worried again. "Maybe…I'm starting to think all that went over his head anyway."

Wrinkling her nose, Raven glanced at Henry as he ducked his head under the strap of his shoulder bag and tucked Maxwell safely away inside it. "I don't know, Murph. I'd give him a little more credit. It's kinda like—"

"If you say that what happened between me and Henry is anything close to whatever kind of weird friendship-slash-competition you have going on with Bella, I might hit you."

She laughed and shook her head. "I was gonna say it's kinda like training a dragon."

"He's not a dragon."

"True." They both chuckled a little. "But he's far more complicated than he looks. Most of the time."

Her companion rolled her eyes but her small, slightly embarrassed smile remained.

Both girls looked up again when Henry approached them. Murphy's jaw practically fell open when he held her knapsack out toward her.

"I'm sorry for being a jerk."

"I...uh... You..."

Fritz leapt from her arms and landed gracefully in the grass before he wove between her legs and rubbed against each foot.

Henry gave her a crooked smile, nodded at her knapsack, and lifted it a little. "I had no idea how heavy this was when I decided to pick it up."

"Sorry." She lunged forward and all but snatched it out of his hands. Without looking at him, she strapped it hurriedly over her shoulders and nodded.

With a chuckle, he adjusted his shoulder bag and looked

at Raven. "You're kinda ruining my apology and peace offering, Murphy. I don't know what you have to be sorry for."

"I was kind of a jerk too, I guess. Apology accepted and thanks." The last came out of her in a rush of almost jumbled words and she could only look at him for a split second before she glanced anywhere but at his face again.

"Are we good?"

"Yep!" Murphy hurried to the end of the field and the road leading to Brighton's town center. She jerked to a stop and looked at Raven over her shoulder. "See you tomorrow, Raven."

"Have a good night, Murphy." She gave her friend a little wave and turned to Henry with raised eyebrows. "Nicely done, Derks."

"Hey, I'm not so full of myself that I can't apologize." He shrugged and double-checked Maxwell's safety again while Fritz darted across the grass after his mage. "I hope she doesn't hold it against me."

"I doubt it."

"Anyway. See you tomorrow, Alby." He clapped his best friend on the shoulder and grinned. "Happy war mage training."

"Yeah, thanks. It's the perfect opportunity to look for Bella's other dropping shoe." She laughed and shook her head. "See you tomorrow."

"Hey, Murph!" Henry raced across the field after their friend, his usual playfulness completely returned. "We could practice the whole friends thing on the walk, huh? I'll plop Maxwell out of my bag and they can do their thing."

Raven couldn't hear what the girl said in reply, but he spun and gave her a thumbs-up.

She smiled and returned the gesture, then headed toward Leander. *At least they cleared something up. That was rough.*

CHAPTER EIGHTEEN

By now, only two of Bella's friends were left in the field and they said their goodbyes to her before the other students set off toward the stone archway across the grass. The smile Bella had worn all day didn't fade, even when it was only the two of them left.

When Raven reached Leander, he raised his head and turned it on his long neck to face her. "I've always loved that you and I can talk to each other. Watching my friends argue about their familiars made me even more grateful."

The dragon responded with a low rumble and stretched one hind leg. "Because I can speak for myself."

She laughed. "Yeah, that's part of it."

"And the other part?"

"Uh...I guess it forces me to be honest too."

"You've never had a problem with being honest." He nudged her with his snout and released a heavy breath. "Stubborn and infuriating, perhaps, but I haven't heard you lie."

Raven rubbed the top of his head and shook her head as

she smiled at her huge red dragon familiar. "We're basically the same on the inside, aren't we?"

His only reply was to snort and push to his feet.

With another laugh, the young mage turned toward the stables, where Bella stood alone and fed something to Wesley perched on her shoulder. "Alessandra's usually out here by now. Come on. We might as well get ready for training and I wanna see if I can find out why Bella's still so smiley."

Leander rumbled agreement and followed his mage across the grass toward the stables.

The other girl looked at them as they approached. Her smile wavered only a little, but it was replaced with curiosity this time instead of irritation.

"So." Raven shrugged and put on her best friendly face. "It looks like you're super-excited to go on this trip next week."

"Of course I am." The frown Bella bestowed on her was playful and she laughed. "Don't tell me you're having second thoughts about it."

"Me? Definitely not." She pushed her long red braid over her shoulder so the side of her neck could get some air. "I'm ready to go and it'll be a good experience."

"Yep." The girl raised her eyebrows. "Why are you telling me what both of us already know?"

And a hint of the normal Bella returns.

"I'm making conversation." Her smile widened. "Did you find out any more about what we'll do at the Tournament of Mages?"

"No. I'm sure whatever Flynn didn't tell us is supposed to be what we find out on our own."

"Fair enough."

An uncertain silence hung between them, and Bella raised an eyebrow. "Raven, why are you looking at me like that?"

"Like what?"

"Like you've never seen me before."

Behind his mage, Leander stretched his wings to half their span and settled them against his back again.

"Honestly, I've never seen you this excited before."

"And it's weirding you out, isn't it?" The girl smirked and gave her a sidelong glance.

Raven couldn't help but chuckle softly in surprise. "Yeah, you basically nailed it."

"I'm simply glad to see all my hard work has paid off. I didn't expect anything like being chosen to go to Azerad and I didn't even know about the Tournament of Mages."

"Neither did I."

"But it's a serious chance for us to make waves. I mean…" Bella glanced briefly at Leander. "You know how big a deal this is, right?"

"I thought I did when Headmaster Flynn told us last night." She shrugged. "Now, I'm beginning to think I don't know what we'll get into next week."

"I think the only thing we need to know is that it's so much more than sparring with other students." The girl tossed her black, wavy hair away from her face and smirked. "Obviously, having the chance to beat older students from other schools in a match in front of everyone has its own perks."

Raven fought not to laugh. "Obviously."

"And then there's the city—all the people and the dignitaries from everywhere else who'll be there to watch us. They'll scout for new talent, Raven. This is probably the biggest opportunity we'll have to be seen by the ranking mages throughout the kingdom. If they like what they see, we have a ticket out of Brighton as soon as we graduate from Fowler." Her smile widened a little and she looked pert.

"Out of Brighton." She stared at her.

"Oh, come on. Don't tell me you want to stay here forever to be a goat rancher who happens to cast spells and rides a dragon." Bella folded her arms and shifted her weight onto one hip. "That would be a complete waste."

"I wouldn't call it a waste. And I wasn't exactly planning on being a goat rancher after we graduate, either."

"Well, it's all about who you know and where you are. Like your grandfather."

She frowned. "What?"

"He was one of Lomberdoon's most powerful mages. Everyone knows that. But now, he's a spent wizard who hardly ever leaves his goat ranch and no one cares about who he was or what he did before that."

Although she knew this was merely Bella's terse way of laying out the facts, Raven's hands closed slowly into fists at her sides anyway. *I can't even argue and tell her Connor Alby's not a spent wizard. I have nothing.*

"He rode a dragon too, didn't he?" her companion continued. "But it's all in the past now because he decided to stay here."

"You know he did that because of me, don't you?"

Bella shrugged. "Well, yeah. It's great that he stuck around to raise you. But he didn't ever try to leave." She shook her head with a little shiver. "I can't even imagine spending the rest of my life in Brighton. I want to get out and see the cities. Maybe even make it all the way to the capital one day. Who knows?"

She continued to talk, but Raven had stopped listening after the part about Connor Alby sticking around to raise his orphaned granddaughter. *I know he doesn't resent me for that. But she makes it sound like it wouldn't have been anyone else's first choice.* With a frown, she turned the thought over in her mind.

"Wouldn't it?"

"What?" She startled and looked at the other young mage with wide eyes.

"See, that's why I don't have many heart-to-hearts. Everyone ends up tuning me out."

"No, it wasn't you," she added quickly. She didn't want to offend the other girl, who'd finally said more than a few short, clipped sentences to her at a time. "Sorry. I was distracted."

"Whatever. It's fine. You caught me on a weird day." Bella shrugged and turned toward the stone archway off the main courtyard with a sigh. Alessandra appeared a second later and stalked toward them across the field in her gray military uniform. "Finally."

"It took her long enough." Shaking off the rest of her thoughts about Connor and the surprisingly new idea of leaving Brighton in the future, Raven chuckled wryly. "After all the time she's spent drilling the necessity of punctuality into us, you'd think she'd be better about it herself."

The other girl snorted. "Right? She's at least fifteen minutes late."

Alessandra raised her chin as she joined the young mages in the center of the field. "There is a slight deviation in our schedule this afternoon."

"No problem." Raven stuck her thumb over her shoulder toward the larger expanse of open grass behind them. "It's time to get to it, then, right?"

"Not quite yet." Their trainer put her hands on her hips and glanced at Leander, who stood behind his mage. "The students selected to participate in the Tournament of Mages next week have all been asked to meet in the great hall for a few preparations. I came to fetch you."

Bella turned toward her fellow student with wide eyes.

Raven spread her arms. "Consider us fetched. I assume Leander's not invited to this one."

The woman inclined her head, completely unamused. "I believe an invitation indoors would only be an insult to your dragon, Miss Alby."

With a hasty glance over her shoulder at Leander, she nodded. "You're probably right. I'll meet you guys there, then."

"We'll wait." Alessandra raised an eyebrow and didn't move an inch, her hands still on her hips as if Raven and Leander were about to be berated for something.

"Okay." As she glanced from Bella to their war mage trainer, Raven fought a laugh and tried to copy the woman's seriousness. She turned toward the stables and Leander's pen. Without a word from his mage, the great dragon turned with her and followed her swiftly across the grass. When she felt they were safely out of hearing range, she leaned toward him and muttered, "Sorry about all the back and forth."

"I don't mind. That elder in the jumpsuit was right."

She snorted and raised her access rune toward the gate. "About what?"

"An invitation would have been insulting."

"I know. She could have been a little nicer about it, though." The gate opened with a metallic click, and she pulled it toward her as she stepped back.

The dragon snorted and headed into the enclosure, his tail swishing through the grass behind him. "I prefer frankness over false charm."

"You know, I've picked up on that over the last few months." She took a few steps inside with him and folded her arms with a broad grin. "Maybe I have a problem with bristling personalities."

Two sharp, short hisses escaped the dragon's mouth as he spun in a slow circle and settled into the grass to wait for her return. "You seem perfectly comfortable with yourself. And me."

That caught her by surprise and she laughed. "That's different. You and I worked together to figure things out, bristling or otherwise. You smile more than she does."

"No one else knows that." Leander lowered his head halfway to his forepaws and regarded the young mage with an expression of exaggerated patience.

"Are you trying to tell me to not judge a war mage by her grumpy disposition?"

The dragon closed his eyes and finally lowered his head all the way. "I'll be ready when you return."

"Good." Raven's smiled widened, and she shook her

head at her obstinate dragon. *He hands out more dangling pieces of wisdom than any human I know. William was right. Dragons are way more complicated than people give them credit for.* "It shouldn't take us too long to do…whatever we're doing. I'll get you out of here in no time."

"Good." His sigh made the grass flutter wildly in front of him.

The mage slipped out of the pen and shut the gate firmly behind her. She hurried toward Bella and Alessandra, who stood a few feet away from each other with their arms folded and watched her take care of her dragon familiar. *It's not surprising those two couldn't find much to talk about. I wonder if that'll change on our trip next week.*

When she reached them, she clapped and rubbed her hands together. "Ready when you are."

Their trainer turned quickly on her heel and led the way toward the stone archway despite the fact that both young mages knew exactly where they were going.

Bella fell in beside her fellow student and lifted the last small sliver of dragon jerky toward Wesley perched on her shoulder. He wolfed it down like he hadn't eaten in weeks and emitted a small puff of thin, light-gray smoke.

"Does she seem grumpier than usual?" Raven muttered.

"Not really." The other girl darted her a sideways glance. "But I'm not interested in exploring the inner workings of War Mage Alessandra Barnasis' mind."

She laughed but managed to keep it low. "I bet it's a steel trap in there."

"Yeah, the kind that probably doesn't open again."

They smirked and followed their trainer toward the main building and into the assembly hall.

CHAPTER NINETEEN

Everyone else had already gathered in front of the stage by the time the three entered the room. Jessica and Cooper huddled together at the far corner of the stage and spoke in low voices. Daniel Smith spoke animatedly to Professor Gilliam, who looked entirely bored by whatever story he was telling her. In front of the center of the stage, Headmaster Flynn and Professor Worley were engaged in a low-toned conversation. Worley chuckled, and when he looked up to see the new arrivals, the other man followed suit.

"Ah. Now, our party's complete." The headmaster nodded at Alessandra before he offered Raven and Bella a satisfied smile he hadn't shared with their trainer. "Right this way, please. We'll get this completed and everyone can go back to their usual evening routine."

Daniel stopped talking mid-sentence and turned to look at Raven. She gave him a small smile of acknowledgment, but that only made him spin away from her again.

This is gonna be a tense trip for him if he keeps doing that.

The five students fanned out in a semi-circle around Headmaster Flynn and Professor Worley. Gilliam and Alessandra stood at the side to watch without a word.

"This, ladies and gentlemen, is the final preparation we make until the day the five of you pack and ship off to Azerad." After he'd looked each of them in the eye with a thin smile, Flynn stepped aside and gestured toward the stage beside him. A large wooden box—with delicate gold handles on each side, two gold latches on the front, and a thin line of gold trim around the edges and every seam—rested at the edge of the stage.

"What is it?" Cooper asked with a curious nod.

"Exactly." The headmaster glanced at Worley, and the familiar-training professor took one step toward it before he undid the latches gently.

The lid opened smoothly and silently on its hinges until the professor had opened the entire thing into three sections. Either side rose on hinged levers to sit six inches above the center of the box. All the students leaned in a little closer to have a better look.

Daniel Smith tilted his head and frowned. "A big metal ball."

With a smirk, the man reached into the box and pressed a button hidden in one of the interior walls. A series of clicks came from within the device and accelerated into a soft flutter until the metal sphere in the center split apart and ejected a small square mirror on the end of a thin lever. Two doors in the elevated sides opened to reveal a matching set of lavender crystals the size of Professor Worley's thumb.

"Cool."

"Yes, Mr. Smith. It's very cool." Headmaster Flynn chuckled. "For about...oh, I'd say the first decade of my time as Headmaster, give or take a few years, the process of transmitting these annual tournaments involved significantly more spellwork than is necessary now. Sethvarin was gracious enough to donate one of these magnificent pieces of machinery before you. Mandrose Academy got it first, mind you, but we soon made replicas. As of now, we call it the Periview. And it's quite simple, all things considered."

"How does it work?" Raven leaned forward and tilted her head from one side to the other in an effort to get a better view of the metal sphere in the center and both crystals raised on either side.

"That is an excellent question, Miss Alby. Although I do hope it was posed in unbridled fascination and not because you expected me to skip that part." He met her gaze, and one side of his mouth twitched in a half-smile and squished the long scar that ran down the side of his face.

She couldn't fight back a little smirk before she returned her attention to the box.

"To put it simply—"

"The mirror projects whatever image comes through from the other side of the spell," Bella continued and ignored Headmaster Flynn's incredulous gaze as he leaned away from her and scowled. "It's probably like a giant calling potion, except there's no potion with this one. Those are harboring crystals. The spell is cast in multiple locations at roughly the same time, the crystals bind with each other, and that's how anyone here can see what's

MARTHA CARR & MICHAEL ANDERLE

happening wherever the other Periviews like these are activated."

Cooper forced a cough. When she didn't look at him, he turned to Jessica and exaggerated rubbing the tip of his nose.

"That is an admirable assessment, Miss Chase." Flynn glanced at Professor Worley, who merely folded his arms and leaned against the edge of the stage beside the box with a chuckle.

"But I have no idea what we have to do with it." She frowned and leaned toward the Periview for a closer look. "None of us will cast the projection spells. Will we?"

"No, you will not." Flynn cleared his throat and smiled. "But you will be a part of it, in a way. Each of the three schools in this competition has its own device like this one, and a fourth will be used inside Azerad itself. That is where the spell starts, Miss Chase, and in order to more accurately focus the viewing through these devices, the spell must be tied to each of the participating students as well."

"Why?" Jessica asked, her brown eyes wide with curiosity.

Professor Worley chuckled again. "There were...transmission issues a few years ago. Without the focus, those who arrived at their schools to watch the Tournament of Mages found themselves connecting directly to students at the other two schools. Occasionally, the direction backfired and projected eager spectators from outside the competition into the center of the sparring ring. That was in...Morningstar City that year, wasn't it?"

"I've always admired the clarity of your memory, Professor Worley." Flynn gave the man a warm, closed-

178

lipped smile and returned his attention to the gathered students. "The transmission works best when it's directed only one way—namely, from the hosting city to the schools —and focused on each of the competing students. I highly doubt that any of your peers would be interested in watching Governor Irlish's chief of staff scratch his sweaty armpits for half an hour at a time."

Daniel and Cooper snorted in unison.

"So what's the missing piece?" Bella asked.

Raven looked at the other first-year mage from the corner of her eye. *She doesn't like that she can't work it out completely.*

"You already have it," Headmaster Flynn replied. He raised his forearm and tapped the underside of it with his finger.

The girl's eyes widened, and she pushed the loose sleeve of her shirt up to expose the access rune on her forearm. "That's it?"

"That's it, Miss Chase. No plucking hairs or spitting into vials."

Professor Worley tugged on his beard and tried not to laugh. "One year, we used a few drops of blood."

All the students turned toward him with shocked expressions. Cooper went a little pale at the mention of blood. "Are you kidding?"

"Maybe."

"Thank you, Professor." Flynn gestured with his hand toward Worley as if to brush him aside and shook his head. "None of that is even remotely relevant anymore. All we need is your access rune. So, step up to the Periview one at a time and show your rune exactly as you would to any of the other locked doors in this school to which you've been given access. Once that is done, we can call this meeting at an end and I can return to the bowl of squash soup that has undoubtedly grown cold in my office."

At the far corner of the stage, Alessandra uttered a low, dry chuckle. Beside her, Professor Gilliam smirked and pressed her fingers against her lips.

Bella stepped forward immediately to be the first in line. With a frown that was more curious than concerned, she raised her exposed access rune and turned toward the headmaster. "Where?"

"The mirror, if you please." Flynn lowered his head and gestured toward the Periview with an amused smile.

The black-haired first-year moved her arm to center the reflection of her access rune in the small square mirror. It glowed a bright orange, as did its reflection, before the mirror emitted a bright white flash.

"Excellent, Miss Chase. Thank you."

The girl glanced at everyone else in the assembly hall like she'd only now realized they were there, then stepped away from the stage and let the next student take her place.

Cooper stepped forward as eagerly as she had and brandished his rune at the mirror. After the brief orange glow and another white flash, he moved away and Jessica followed. When she was finished, Raven stepped toward the box on the stage as Daniel did the same. They almost bumped into each other, and she did everything she could to not burst out laughing. "Oh—sorry. I guess we—"

They both shuffled forward and back at the same time before she finally gave up and did laugh. "Go ahead."

He lurched forward without a word or a glance at her and flashed his rune at the mirror. As soon as the white light receded, he shoved his hands into his pockets and walked along the edge of the stage to avoid looking at her altogether.

We're gonna have to address that sooner or later.

Her lips together, Raven approached the Periview and raised her forearm. A small, itching tingle spread down her forearm when the mirror flashed at her. *That's new.* She rubbed it as she stepped away from the stage and let her hands fall to her sides.

"And voila!" Headmaster Flynn spread his arms dramatically. "Thank you for your time, young mages. Now you may go."

Professor Worley chuckled and stepped toward the Periview to begin the process of closing all the doors and hinged layers.

Alessandra stepped forward to catch her trainees' attention. When the two girls looked at her, she nodded toward the doorway into the assembly hall and marched away without a word. Jessica and Cooper resumed their hushed conversation, and Daniel Smith made sure he was the first student out of the room.

Raven and Bella left the assembly hall side by side, and the redhaired mage absently rubbed her forearm again. "That was a little anticlimactic."

"It would've been much better if I'd thought of the access runes," her companion muttered. "Why didn't that occur to me?"

They stepped into the hall, and Raven gave the other girl a sidelong glance. "Don't beat yourself up too much.

The rest of us couldn't have guessed even a tiny part of what you did."

Bella's head whipped up quickly, and she flashed her companion a fiery glare. "I wasn't guessing."

"Okay. Still."

"No, not 'still.'" The girl sighed and wiggled her lower jaw sideways in frustration as she shook her head. "I should have thought of that."

"The tournament hasn't started yet, Bella." She offered her a reassuring smile. "I don't think they'll count it against you for not knowing exactly how to work a device none of us have heard of."

"That's not the point." The mages in training stepped out of the main building and into the afternoon light. Bella's heavy, irritated footsteps sounded even louder out there on the cobblestones of the center courtyard. "I had enough time to put it together and I still missed the most important piece."

"You're being a little hard on yourself, don't you think?"

"Not when I know what I'm capable of. It doesn't matter that they keep that a secret from the rest of the school. Information's useless if I only have half of it."

Raven glanced at Alessandra who strode beneath the stone archway in front of them and she frowned. "Wait. What do you mean they keep it a secret from the rest of the school?"

"Seriously?"

"Yeah. I'm allowed to ask that, right?"

Bella looked at her again, this time in surprise, and nodded. "Sure. It's obvious, though."

She couldn't help herself when a laugh escaped her.

"Okay, pretend I'm not nearly as observant as you are at any given second of the day."

"I don't have to pretend." The girl didn't say it as a direct insult but merely as a statement of fact she assumed both of them already knew. Raven puffed her cheeks and pretended to sigh to cover another laugh. "Daniel, Jessica, and Cooper already knew about the Tournament of Mages as upperclassmen but none of them had seen that Periview before or knew how it works."

"Okay…"

The girls stepped beneath the archway and moved across the field. Wesley launched himself from Bella's shoulder and glided ahead of them.

"Which means that box is kept somewhere else where none of the students will see it when they come back to the school to watch the competition in Azerad. It's probably to keep everyone away so some smartass like Percy doesn't try to mess with the transmission as some kinda joke."

Raven put all the pieces together in her head after that and raised her eyebrows. "Wow. I didn't even think about that."

"Clearly." Bella took another glance at her fellow war mage trainee and smirked.

"You know, I wonder if Lomberdoon needs any mages who could double as a spy."

Her companion barked a laugh. "What in the world are you talking about?"

"You." She turned toward the other mage as they neared the stables and grinned. "Bella Chase would be an excellent war mage spy."

CHAPTER TWENTY

The rest of the week blurred past in a series of classes, studying, training with Bella while Alessandra barked her usual confusing instructions at them, and evening flights with Leander. By the last day of school before the spring break, Raven was more than ready to take a break from the normal routine.

She always looked forward to familiar training with Professor Worley. This was partly because she and Leander were able to work specifically with their connection as more than a mage who also rode a dragon, and partly because of the way he interacted with Worley after their little chat a few days before.

"Don't think I haven't noticed," she muttered as she held the gate open for her dragon to emerge from his pen.

"To what are you referring, little girl?" He gave her a quick glance with hooded eyelids as he moved gracefully through the aperture.

Raven laughed. "That you made a friend at Fowler Academy."

"Incorrect. You and I were already friends before we moved in."

Closing the gate most of the way, the mage turned to face her dragon with a coy smile. "I'm talking about Professor Worley."

Leander snorted.

"Okay, obviously not as close a friendship as we have—"

"He's tolerable." The dragon raised his head and walked toward the first-year students who had gathered outside the barn for the last class of the day.

Shaking her head, she caught up to him and patted his broad, powerful shoulder. "It's okay if you like someone other than me, you know."

"When I actually like someone, Raven, you'll be the first to know."

She chuckled and folded her arms as they came to stop a few yards away from the rest of the class. *I see right through that dragon act and he knows it.*

Henry and Murphy hurried across the field toward the barn. Fitz pounced after Murphy a few feet at a time, most of his long leaps surprisingly in sync with Maxwell's toady hops through the grass. Raven laughed, watched her friends, and returned the wave when they both raised their hands in greeting. She stepped away from Leander so she could meet them without encroaching on the dragon's personal space.

"Seriously, Alby." Henry stopped, bent forward, and propped himself with his hands on his thighs to catch his breath. "I don't know how you do it."

"Me neither." She glanced at Murphy, who was

breathing as heavily but didn't seem quite as winded. "What did I do?"

"Phew." He straightened and put his hands on his hips long enough to take in a slow, deep breath before he gestured toward the field. "We have all our classes together and you somehow make it all the way out here after Gilliam's class before anyone else. Leander's already standing there, and you didn't even break a sweat."

Raven chuckled and shrugged. "Maybe it's easier to get around when I don't have to wait for my familiar to catch up."

"Which is something you'll never have to do anyway," Murphy pointed out.

She caught her friends' glances and nodded behind them to Fritz and Maxwell. The barn cat sat on his haunches, his black-and-white tail flicking from side to side across the grass. The toad made a short leap closer to the other familiar. Both animals sat almost motionless—other than Fritz's tail and Maxwell's swelling throat—and watched their mages intently.

"It looks like the decision to let them work it out on their own was successful, huh?"

Henry turned to look at them and chuckled. "Today, at least."

"It took a little trial and error, honestly," Murphy added with a shrug.

"How come I'm hearing about this trial and error for the first time now?" She tried to give her friends a look of mock insult, but it failed completely and she ended up laughing anyway.

"Probably because he was embarrassed."

Henry looked at Murphy with wide eyes and exaggerated looking entirely shocked. "Me? Embarrassed? Come on, Murph. You know I don't do that."

The girls chuckled, which made him smirk as he stuck his hands in his pockets.

"Why would Derks be embarrassed?" she asked. "Hypothetically."

"Oh, I don't know. Maybe because the only one of our familiars who had issues when we finally let them work it out was his."

His gaze shifted quickly toward Raven, his expression deadpan. Then, he grinned and gave a sheepish shrug. "That part's not hypothetical, either."

"I would love to hear what kind of issues your jumpy toad has." She folded her arms and looked eagerly from one of her friends to the other.

"Okay." Henry stepped back and nodded toward Fritz. "I gotta give credit where it's due. Fritz is apparently one barn cat who doesn't like the taste of toad."

She burst out laughing. "You can't stop there!"

"He licked Maxwell," Murphy said through her laughter. "Fritz. Not Henry."

"Yeah, we already knew that was a thing."

Henry pointed at her, then wagged his finger from one girl to the other. "I've only kissed Maxwell, thank you very much. I know Professor Worley said a good lick helps with healing magic and maybe one day, I'll get there."

Raven wrinkled her nose. "I hope not."

"Neither of them liked that little experiment." Murphy shook her head and studied the seemingly well-trained familiars behind them. "Fritz was done after that, but Maxwell apparently had more to say."

"I still don't get it."

Shooting her an exasperated glance, Henry brought one hand up and down again in a tall arc before he smacked it into his other hand. "Maxwell pounced on the cat's head in protest."

"Okay, wait a minute." Murphy pointed at him. "You can call it protest all you want. It was clearly an attack. Not a very effective one, but still."

He pumped a fist in the air and grinned. "Protest."

"Oh, my God." The girl rolled her eyes. "So now Raven gets to be the tie-breaker on this one."

The redheaded mage stared at her friends with wide eyes and spread her arms in a noncommittal gesture. "I'm not sure I wanna be involved."

"It's simple, Alby." Henry jerked his thumb toward his chest. "You'll side with your best friend no matter what, right?"

"That's not how this works," Murphy said curtly, turned to Raven again, and nodded. "So. Fritz licked Maxwell and surprised them both. Then Maxwell jumped on Fritz's head—not once but twice—and shoved my familiar's face into a mud puddle in the middle of the road. Attack or protest?"

She burst out laughing and clutched her sides as she doubled over. Her friend raised her eyebrows at Henry with a smirk, and the young wizard folded his arms.

"Don't worry, Alby. Take your time. We'll wait for the verdict." He wiggled his eyebrows at the other girl and she snorted.

When she finally caught her breath, she had to wipe a few tears from the corners of her eyes. "Oh, man. I don't know if that's funnier to imagine or to see in person."

"You have a vivid imagination, Alby. Make your choice." Despite his efforts, he couldn't make a very convincing serious face.

"Sorry, Derks. I gotta side with Murphy on this one."

"See?" Murphy widened her eyes at him and grinned. "It was a toad attack."

"Definitely an attack," she added through another round of chuckles.

Henry squinted at them both and glanced at the two familiars who remained perfectly still in the grass. "Honestly, it's a win-win either way. Either Maxwell knows how to defend himself, or he made the first move and whipped that barn cat into shape."

"Yeah, okay." Shaking her head, Murphy met Raven's gaze and rolled her eyes playfully.

"And either way," Raven added, "you guys don't have to worry about your familiars beating each other up anymore, right? It looks like they got to the friendship stage fairly quickly."

Right on cue, Maxwell took another small leap closer to Fritz's forepaw. When he uttered a loud croak, the cat jerked his head down to eye the toad and leaned away a little.

Raven and her friends had another good laugh at that, and Henry slung his arm around Murphy's shoulder. "Everyone's learning how to make it work, huh, Murph?"

The dark-haired witch looked at Raven with a knowing smile, and the blush rising in her cheeks wasn't nearly as noticeable this time. Murphy glanced at Henry and shrugged playfully from beneath his arm. "It's a start, I guess."

"She guesses." Henry tossed his hands in the air and shrugged at Raven. "Baby steps."

"You gotta start somewhere." Raven studied Fritz and Maxwell again and pursed her lips. *My friends aren't fighting, so it's something. It doesn't look like Murphy's spilled the beans yet. And it's none of my business.*

"Speaking of baby steps." He whirled and scanned the field, the rest of their class, and the barn beside the stables. "Where the heck is Worley?"

"What? How did you go from baby steps to a hairy professor who could be part giant for all we know?"

"That wasn't an instant association for you guys?" He put on a good show of looking confused before he grinned at Raven and pointed at his temple. "It's a masterpiece up here, Alby. I don't wanna hurt you by walkin' you through it."

"Ha! Thank you so much for sparing my sanity."

The loud, growling sound of Professor Worley purposefully clearing his throat came from somewhere behind the barn. The entire class stepped toward the edge of the building to look for him. Finally, the man emerged from the thick woods that hemmed the school grounds, lifting his boots high to step over a few small shrubs that grew at the edge of the grass.

"I did not expect that," Henry muttered.

"Ditto," Murphy added.

Raven pressed her lips together as every student in the class watched their familiar-training professor brush twigs, leaves, and a few burs off his loosely flowing tunic and trousers. "I think the professors are as ready for the spring break as we are."

Henry snorted. "Oh, yeah? You think he lost his mind on the last day and went running around in the woods to blow off steam?"

"I don't know what to think."

Worley looked up from his clothes and froze when he noticed each of his first-year students staring at him in confused amusement. "Great. You're all right on time."

"It looks like we were early."

"Thank you, Mr. Jeder." The professor chuckled and tugged quickly on the bottom of his tunic. "I may have lost track of time."

"A common mistake when hiding from his class in the forest," Henry muttered. "Weren't there vagreti panthers in there a few weeks ago?"

Raven elbowed him in the arm and choked back a laugh when he flinched and chuckled.

"So." Worley clapped his hands together and headed briskly toward the class. "Let's get to work. I have a feeling all of you will enjoy this exercise. This is the last class before the spring break, people. Let's make it count."

Murphy looked at her and raised both hands, her fingers crossed. "At least it's not a hike through the woods."

"Yeah, I'm already going on one field trip."

CHAPTER TWENTY-ONE

"Mr. Cotton. Miss Knowles. Feel free to make jokes about my arrival on your own time." Professor Worley grinned at the students he'd called out as he stopped on the open field. "I'd be lying if I said I didn't want you to pay attention. In less than two hours, mages, you're free for a week. I know you can give me that."

A few of the other students laughed at that. Raven and her friends shared curious glances before their professor continued with his lesson.

"After so much time spent honing and strengthening your connection with your familiars, I'm sure you've noticed by now that a familiar much prefers to be in close proximity to their mage, if not directly beside him or her."

A startled squeak rose at that, and everyone turned toward Elizabeth, who stood a few feet away from the gathered students. She glanced up from where her bat familiar Iggy clung to the front of her shirt, saw everyone looking at her, and simply didn't care.

Worley chuckled. "Or clinging to their mage, in Miss Kinsley's case. On the other side of that, a strong bond with our familiars naturally increases our sense of ease and comfort when they're with us."

Raven glanced at Leander, who lay in his usual position away from the class. His huge red head rested on his forepaws and his red scales glinted like fire in the sunlight. *We already know that part.*

"What you may not know," the man continued, "is that it is, in fact, possible to send your familiar away from your physical person without losing that sense of connection. Some familiars can go farther than others—and I should know. I have several."

"We've only seen one, right?" Murphy whispered.

Henry shuddered. "That snake."

"He has four," Raven added. Her friends looked at her with wide eyes.

"You've seen them?"

"Nope. But that's what Worley told Leander."

He snorted. "See, that's a connection my head doesn't make."

"I'll tell you later."

"Keep in mind, young mages, that the range your familiar is capable of reaching when they leave your side is not a reflection of how closely connected you've become. They're like us in that way. Everyone's a little different. But some of you may be quite surprised to discover how far your familiars are capable of going."

From his perch on Bella's shoulder, Wesley uttered a curious screech. The students turned to look at him and found the firedrake crouched and staring at the sky.

"Woah," Rory Davidian exclaimed. "Look at the size of that."

Everyone else followed suit and stared at where a massive bird wheeled in slow, lazy circles above them. Even Leander's curiosity was piqued, and the dragon raised his head for a quick glance before he settled it onto his scaly paws.

"There's nothing new about a bird," Murphy muttered.

"Not one almost as big as a dragon," Raven countered, and they smirked.

Professor Worley produced a thick leather glove—she thought she saw him take it out from under his arm—and slid it onto his hand while he talked like his entire class hadn't been distracted by a large avian. "With the right intention behind it, considerable focus on your connection, and more time practicing, you can train your familiar to go farther and farther away from you. Think of it like stretching a muscle, if you will. Eventually, it becomes second nature. And if you're really dedicated—which I expect each and every one of you to be—you can teach your familiar to relay images of what they see with their eyes when they're not with you."

"Wait, what?" Henry jerked his head down from staring at the bird soaring overhead and shut his open mouth with a click.

Raven's eyes widened. *That got my attention too.*

"Take Gresh, for example." Without looking away from his students' faces, which showed a range of expressions from confused to rapt, eager attention, Professor Worley raised his arm to shoulder height, his elbow bent at a ninety-degree angle.

The huge bird above them uttered a piercing screech and dove.

"Shit. Maxwell!" Henry ducked into a crouch and scanned the grass at his feet. His toad familiar jumped toward him as the young wizard bent to scoop him up with both hands.

"Derks," Raven whispered and nudged him with her elbow. "I think you're good."

"What?" When he looked up, he followed her awed stare to see a gigantic hawk perched on the thick leather glove that reached almost to Professor Worley's elbow.

The tawny bird's wings fluttered a little, stretched wide, and folded against its sides. The professor favored his students with a small, knowing smile beneath his wild black beard. "Gresh goes much farther than most if I do say so myself."

"That's your other familiar?" Erin asked.

"One of them, yes." The man glanced slowly at Gresh, who cocked his head at his mage for a brief moment of eye contact before the great bird turned his head toward the class to look at the students.

A low murmur of surprise rippled through the first-years.

Professor Worley nodded. "He's been gone for three days, which isn't unusual for him. He's been hunting. I could spend hours regaling you fine young mages with all the things I've seen during that time. But most of it would bore you, I'm sure."

"You can see through his eyes?" Raven asked breathlessly.

The professor turned his dark-eyed gaze on her and nodded once. "I can, Miss Alby. It's the closest I'll ever get to experiencing flight."

When he winked at her, Raven couldn't help a tiny smile in response. She didn't miss the brief and fleeting glance he darted at Leander behind the gathered class. *No wonder those two get along so well.*

"Now today, you will all have your first taste of sending your familiars away from you," Worley continued. "The first step is to practice with distance in small increments. If you push too far, you may end up traumatizing the bond with your familiar. That is a massive step backward in how far each of you has already come this year. Over time, you will grow more accustomed to releasing your familiars for longer distances if that's something you wish to improve in the future. Not everyone's cut out for that kind of separation, which is perfectly fine. I'm merely here to give you the tools and guidance to start experimenting. Keep in mind that I do fully expect all of you to put at least a little of your well-earned free time over the spring break into practicing this exercise with your familiars. Once school resumes after the break, we'll work on more specific intentions with this."

"When do we learn to see what our familiar sees?" Bella called quickly, her eyes wide with determination and excitement.

"That comes much later, Miss Chase. When you and that firedrake are ready for it, you'll know. Are there any other questions before we begin?"

"Can your familiars see what you see?" Rory asked from

somewhere near the back of the group. His voice broke at the end of the question, and everyone else turned to look at him. The kid had gone a little pale and looked like he might be sick.

Worley chuckled. "That may be possible eventually, Mr. Davidian. Yes. But that particular skill is much more difficult. And judging by the look on your face right now, I assume this will reassure you when I say that no familiar may enter your mind unbidden. The act of a mage sharing their own mind and specific images—yes, some may even call it their thoughts—must arise as a direct intention from that mage with an incredible and oftentimes exhausting level of focus."

"Can you do that?" Elizabeth muttered. The question was loud enough for the entire class to hear and Worley no doubt heard it as well.

His gaze darted toward the stoic young witch and her bat familiar for a fraction of a second before he smiled at no one in particular and headed toward the gathered students. Everyone stepped away to allow him space down the middle of the group. They jostled each other and stared at the giant hawk perched on their professor's arm.

When he'd stepped out into the field far enough away from his class, the man turned and nodded. "Now, spread out. Take as much space as you need out here to make your familiar comfortable and start by sending them away from you a few yards at a time. When they've reached their limit, you'll know."

The students scattered across the field and their familiars trotted, hopped, scurried, and fluttered behind them while others were held tightly in their mages arms or perched on their shoulders.

Raven caught Elizabeth's gaze as her roommate turned to step away from their classmates. She nodded toward Professor Worley, who was busy staring into Gresh's amber eyes again, and the other girl shrugged. Her deadpan expression didn't change.

He definitely heard her question. Why won't he talk about it?

"It's a dangerous thing to start doing, if you ask me," Henry muttered as he stroked Maxwell's bumpy back.

She turned toward him with a smirk. "Why's that?"

He made a face of mock insult. "Did you learn nothing from the Great Toad-Cat Debacle?"

She laughed and glanced at Murphy. "Honestly, Derks, I didn't think that was supposed to be a learning experience for me specifically."

"What I'm talking about, War Mage Alby," he said with a wiggle of his head, and the premature title made Raven snort, "is that being so far away from our familiars doesn't sound like a smart idea. If Maxwell's hopping down the road toward the center of town while I'm still here, who's gonna be there to stop a snake or a bird or one of those kids near the mill who like to torture small animals?"

"Aren't they the same age as us now?" Murphy asked and tried to cover her frown of horror at the thought.

"Sure, the ones we know." He shrugged and Maxwell croaked from the safety of his mage's cupped hands. "There are always more, though, aren't there?"

"Henry Derks." Raven folded her arms and feigned surprise. "Your flair for the dramatic has kicked up a notch in the last week."

"It's easy for you to say. Your familiar's a dragon. And it's not drama when it's a valid concern, Alby." He pointed at her and cocked his head, but the hint of a smirk shone through his attempt to look serious. "Some of us have familiars who are fairly low on the food chain out there."

Murphy glanced at Fitz who was seated patiently at her feet. "Not all of us."

He ignored her. "And what about the animals everyone else is afraid of, huh?" Henry gestured toward Professor Worley with a flippant wave before he lowered his voice. "If I'd seen Worley's boa constrictor slither around somewhere with no mage walking beside it, I would've tried to cut its head off."

The girl burst out laughing. "You would not!"

He grinned. "Okay, fine, Murph. I'd take my slingshot out."

"And hope you can fire it faster than that snake can strike, right?" Raven laughed with her friends. "But then you'd have a pissed-off boa constrictor coming after you."

"Hey, I'm fast enough." Henry patted his pants pocket where he kept his trusty slingshot and a constantly replenished supply of pebbles and stones in various sizes. "Trust me, Alby. I'd keep slinging away until it either backed off or stopped moving."

"She, Derks." She smirked at him. "Worley's boa familiar is a she and her name's Vastra. Remember?"

He scoffed and waved her off. "That's only one snake."

"So your point," Murphy added when she recovered from laughing so hard, "is this is a useless exercise because some familiars will either be confused as prey and eaten, or taken for dangerous beasts and attacked by young wizards with slingshots?"

Henry stared at her for a moment before a wide grin spread across his face. "You nailed it, Murph."

The girls rolled their eyes dramatically. Murphy shoved him in the shoulder and he stumbled away from her.

"Wow, Murph." He laughed and rubbed his arm. "Careful. All that heavy battle-ax lifting has taken your shoves up a notch."

The girl ignored the jest and stepped away from her friends. Fritz walked close behind her. "I'm gonna let you worry about that familiar issue all on your own. Maybe Raven can talk some sense into you."

"Only sometimes," Raven called in response and delivered a joking punch into his shoulder.

"Woah. Hey." He stepped away from her and couldn't hold back a laugh of surprise. "You might punch me again for saying this, Alby, but I'm sure Murphy's got you on strength right now."

"Maybe only when it comes to you."

Henry tilted his head in confusion and frowned at her. "I have no idea what that means. It's a weird sensation."

"Don't worry about it." She glanced around the field, where their classmates were getting comfortable enough with their personal practice bubble to start sending their familiars farther and farther away. "I have a solution to your problem, though."

"Which one?" He laughed when she darted him an exasperated glance.

"The one about prey and terrifying beasts as familiars."

She grinned. "It's simple. Don't send Maxwell anywhere there's a possibility of him getting eaten, snatched, stepped on, or...tortured."

"Huh." The young wizard glanced at the toad and nodded. "I think we've got that covered. I don't know where else I'd—oh!"

"That looks like your epiphany face, Derks."

"Because it is. It woulda been nice to know this was possible three weeks ago. But if it ever happens again—which it probably will because, you know, it's you—"

"Me? I don't follow this at all."

"Professor Gilliam turned Maxwell and me away from the infirmary more than once when you were in there after the Swarm, Alby. Maybe more than four or five times." He shrugged with a devious smirk. "But whenever you're back there—"

"If I am sent back to the infirmary."

"No, I'm very sure it's when. You've always been prone to getting hurt, Alby. Even when we were tiny."

She pointed at him. "Only in kickass ways."

"Sure." They both laughed, and Henry lifted Maxwell to his face to stare into his toad's glistening eyes. "Yeah. We're gonna practice the hell out of this little trick, Maxwell. And the next time Raven Alby needs us, you'll slip into wherever they won't let both of us in and use some of those healing-toad properties."

She burst out laughing, and when he looked at her with a goofy and genuinely eager grin, it set her off all over again. "I guess I'd better work on preparing myself for a toad on my face the next time I get knocked out for a few days."

"I've found my motivation, Alby!" He turned away from her and headed onto the field to find a place to practice. "You wait. Maxwell and I are gonna master this!"

"There is not a doubt in my mind," she muttered with a smile.

CHAPTER TWENTY-TWO

Raven watched her best friend a little longer before she focused on Leander.

The huge red dragon lay exactly where he'd settled on the grass before Worley's emergence from the woods. Her classmates had given him a wide berth when they chose their practice areas. She grinned and headed toward him.

"I assume you heard the whole explanation of what we're supposed to work on right now."

He raised his head and stared intently at her as she approached. "Every word. And each of them as useless as handing me a plate and a set of silverware."

She chuckled and stroked his muzzle as he raised his head even higher to meet her touch. "Because we've already had months of practice being away from each other?"

"And I could sense you from Moss Ranch the minute I agreed to be your familiar, little girl."

"I know. There's so much we can do that most people can't."

He responded with a low rumble of agreement and closed his eyes, enjoying her fingers' attention on the top of his head.

"Still, the rest of it's cool to think about." Raven looked toward the center of the field where Professor Worley stood watching his class.

Gresh had given up his perch on the man's gloved arm and now stood in the grass beside his mage, over two feet in height and up to Worley's knees.

"It's almost like you can read my mind already, Leander."

"I cannot."

She chuckled. "So you keep telling me. But it could be fun for us to practice sending images to each other, right? Like when we can't be together."

"We always can." Leander opened his glowing yellow eyes and the one closest to her rolled slowly to examine her face. "You mean when we're not."

"Right. That feels more accurate."

"It is an idea, at the very least."

With a smirk, Raven patted his neck a few times. "But you're talking about it, which I'm reasonably sure means you're not entirely against the idea."

The huge dragon didn't reply.

"I see what you're doing there."

Another rumble rose in his throat, and he nudged her hip with his massive head.

"We'll learn how to send messages to each other," she muttered. "That's another promise. Now that I know it's possible, it's one more goal within reach."

"Even if it weren't possible, dragon rider, we would do it anyway."

She looked at her dragon familiar and grinned. "Hell yes, we would."

Out in the field, Gresh uttered a long, shrieking call and flapped powerful wings before he rose into the sky again to wheel above the Fowler Academy grounds. Professor Worley watched the great bird for a few seconds. When he looked down again, he caught her gaze and headed toward her and Leander.

"I think I probably know the answer already," Raven told him, "but I have to ask. You have Vastra and Gresh. What are the other two?"

A slow smile spread across the professor's lips, mostly hidden behind his wild beard, but his eyes twinkled in amusement and crinkled at the corners. He looked directly at Leander. "I can't say I expected you to not share our previous conversation, Leander. At least in part."

The dragon lowered his head toward the familiar-training professor and pushed gracefully to his feet. His translucent wings stretched wide with a little shiver before he folded them against his back again. "That is a foolish expectation."

Worley chuckled softly. "Don't I know it. Miss Alby, I'm sorry to disappoint you, but as far as I'm concerned, it would be unfair of me to talk to you personally about my other familiars before the rest of your first-year class has a chance to discover that for themselves—much in the same way they met Vastra and Gresh."

"Well, I'm not that disappointed." She shrugged. "It's what I thought you'd say. I can wait."

"Then we're on the same page." He nodded and drew the thick leather glove from his hand before he tucked it under his arm. "I realize that our exercise in class today is something of a been-there-done-that situation for you two."

Raven glanced at Leander, who lowered his head until it hovered over her shoulder. She patted the outside of his muzzle. "Kind of."

"I've thought about it for a few weeks, now, Miss Alby. There may be a way for us to approach more of an... advanced lesson plan for you and Leander as far as familiar training goes. If that's something you'd be interested in, of course. I wanted to ask you first before I took the idea to Headmaster Flynn."

With a grin, she leaned away from her dragon a little to meet his gaze. "What do you think?"

"I think you've already decided."

She snorted and ignored the man's little chuckle at the dragon's response. "Not out loud."

"Then say it."

The young mage looked at her professor and nodded. "We're in."

"Excellent." Professor Worley's smile widened. "It might take some time to set up but I have a good idea of where to start."

"Thank you, Professor."

"You and Leander are doing very well here, Miss Alby. Most of the professors, including me, aren't used to seeing so much potential wrapped up in one student and one familiar. And none of us make it a habit to let that potential go to waste if at all possible and especially in a first-year intent on bending tradition to achieve the impossible."

"Most people say 'breaking tradition.'" Raven narrowed her eyes at him and smiled in curiosity. *He's trying to get at something. I know it.*

The professor shrugged. "I hardly think that one foot in Connor Alby's legacy and the other in your mother's constitutes breaking anything, to be honest. Keep in mind, though, that it's much harder to bend something as far as you want it to go if you don't already know the breaking point."

Leander released a quick sigh and his hot breath fluttered the loose hairs around her face. She nodded. "I'll keep that in mind."

"I'm sure you will." He glanced briefly at the other students and tilted his head from side to side. "I wish there was more I could offer today as an exercise that might be challenging for either of you."

"That's okay. It's not really something new for us."

"And that might change if Headmaster Flynn agrees to my proposal of more advanced training."

"Right." A laugh of surprise escaped the young mage when she realized what that might look like. "I have classes, war mage training every day, and now, advanced familiar training. This'll be interesting."

"The decision's entirely up to you." Worley shrugged. "But I can promise it won't cut into your daily flight schedule." He nodded at Leander. "I know how important that is."

"Yeah, it is." Raven ran her hand down the glistening

scales along the dragon's long neck. "We appreciate it. Thank you."

"Don't thank me yet." The man released a full-belly laugh and turned to head toward the other students so he could offer tips and advice. "I still have to find out how what I know and teach applies to a dragon."

"You could probably simply blow everything up to an epic scale, and that might work." She fought back a laugh as her joke dawned on the man and he snorted.

"We'll see."

"Oh, Professor?" she called. He looked over his shoulder at her and raised his eyebrows. "How do we start practicing with sending images?"

"Keep doing what you're doing, Miss Alby. You'll get there." That was the end of the conversation as his attention turned toward Tessa and her butterfly familiar. "Miss Hambridge, I recommend a gentler approach than shouting the same command over and over at that butterfly of yours. It seems like more of a distraction."

Not wanting to stare at Tessa's quick blush as the girl shut her mouth to listen to their professor, Raven turned toward Leander again and shrugged. "Well. I guess we kind of hang out and wait for the rest of the class?"

"Riveting."

"I'm sorry, Leander. I had no idea how complicated things would become by going to mage school."

"By being yourself, Raven." The dragon lowered his head to nudge her side again. "That makes everything less complicated."

She grinned and wound her arm around his neck for a

brief pat before she released him. "That's a great way to look at it."

"Of course it is. It's my way of looking at it."

"Yeah, you have an excellent outlook on everything." Raven snorted and shook her head. "Do you think we could work out how to send images like that on our own?"

"Probably."

"Okay. We'll give it a try, starting...now." The young mage caught his face with both hands and directed her dragon's head gently so he looked directly at her. "Stare into my eyes. And think about...something."

She squinted and studied her familiar's glowing yellow eyes while she fought against the urge to blink. After twenty seconds, Leander snorted a heavy breath through his nostrils and into her face.

"Hey!" The young mage waved her hand rapidly to dispel the hot air and snorted too. "Ugh. Whiff of dragon feed right to the face."

He pulled his head away from her and looked out across the field. "I win."

"What do you mean you win?" She chuckled and waved her hand in front of her face again to dispel the smell. "We were focusing."

The huge dragon's scaly red lips peeled back for one of his smaller, more devious grins, and he gave her a sidelong glance before he returned his gaze to the field. "I thought it was a staring contest."

With a sharp sigh, Raven tossed her hands in the air and feigned exasperation. "It's never a dull moment with you. What do I have to do to get you to take this part seriously?"

"As long as you don't throw yourself at me and shout

commands like when we met, little girl, I'll get there eventually."

She threw her head back and laughed, then folded her arms and turned to watch the other students practicing with their familiars, all of whom had been chosen long before she chose Leander. *We really did make that connection faster than anyone.* "Yeah, we'll get there."

CHAPTER TWENTY-THREE

When their last class before the spring break ended, the first-year students lost all sense of control where they gathered outside the stables and the barn. Leander's wings twitched outward, and he stepped back quickly with a snort as the field echoed with shouts of triumph, laughter, and friendly jests that exploded from Raven's classmates.

"Woah." She laughed and watched the chaos. Rory Davidian and Mike Jeder collided with each other in their eagerness to snatch up their satchels from against the stable wall.

"Watch it, Rory!"

"Dude, your head's like a rock."

They both grimaced and rubbed their heads, but the minor setback didn't stop them from clapping each other on the back as they walked toward the stone archway, still laughing.

"Henry! You comin'?" Rory turned to gesture for Henry to join them.

"Yeah, yeah! Just a sec. Don't start that new rain spell without me."

"It's only conjuring a little water."

"Whatever. I gotta see it with my own eyes." He pointed at his friends in warning, then jogged toward Raven. Maxwell hopped quickly behind him and kept up fairly easily.

She patted Leander's shoulder and left him safely beyond the whirlwind of students who raced to retrieve their packs and leave the school grounds for nine days of freedom. "So what are you gonna do first now that the spring break's officially started?"

Henry ran a hand through his disheveled hair and glanced toward the main courtyard. "First, I'm gonna watch Mike totally mess that spell up."

"I'm not sure anything you do on the grounds counts as the start of break."

"It does for me, Alby. He's been telling people all week that he tweaked it a little to make it awesome."

"Uh-oh." She glanced at the other two boys who disappeared under the stone archway. "Didn't Gilliam already give him a warning about tweaking?"

"Yep. You heard Rory, though. Mike's head's like a rock." He wrinkled his nose and glanced at Maxwell. The toad didn't move at all when Murphy and Fritz joined their little circle.

"That was a crazy class." The brown-haired mage exhaled a heavy sigh and shook her head. "I thought Fritz was gonna claw my face for sending him around the stables."

"Not from behind the stables."

Murphy met Raven's gaze and folded her arms. "No. Once he came back. How far did you and Maxwell get?"

"It's hard to tell." Henry shrugged. "I tried to get him to come say hi to you and your dragon, Alby. He got halfway there before Rory's owl flew over him and bam, the toad hops right back into my arms. Now I'm starting to wonder how all this stuff Worley teaches us works."

"With practice," Raven suggested with a little chuckle.

"Yeah, ha, ha. Okay, we learned to help them overcome their natural instincts before we started this today, right? I thought that was some kinda building block, you know? You cover that and it's locked into place and you level up to the next thing."

"You gotta expand your mind, Derks." she said and when the two girls met each other's gazes, neither one of them could hold back a little laugh. "I think it's about keeping everything we learned in your head at the same time so Maxwell doesn't get confused."

"He wasn't confused." He frowned at them. "Only terrified of being eaten."

"Oh, boy." Murphy glanced at the sky. "But he wasn't."

"Yet." Henry looked at the barn cat seated at his friend's feet and nodded. "I'm not talkin' about you, Fritz. You're cool."

"It looked like you guys did well, though," Raven added.

Murphy regarded her curiously. "How do you know?"

"Leander and I had a perfect view through the whole class." She shrugged and had to laugh a little sheepishly. "There wasn't much we could do out here that we haven't already done before."

"Perfectly, I bet."

"Well, thanks, Murphy." With a grin, she glanced over her shoulder at her dragon familiar. "Most of the time."

"It looks like all the time from where I stand." The other girl forced back a laugh. "If we ignore the whole part about trying to burn weapons professors alive."

"Yeah, we can ignore it completely."

They shared another laugh at that, then Henry stepped toward Raven and opened his arms. "Well get in here."

"Oh…" She stepped toward him slowly until he wrapped her in a huge, tight hug. "Woah. Little tight, Derks."

"That's for luck." He released her and clapped his hand on her shoulder. "You have war mage training and then, you're shipping out to Azerad tomorrow. You might need some luck."

She rolled her shoulders after his giant squeeze and sighed. "I'll take what I can get."

"And don't think for a minute that we won't be here to watch every single match," Murphy added. She opened her arms to give her a hug, and Raven shrugged before she stepped into her friend's embrace. "You'll win every single one of them. I know it."

"Thanks, Murphy."

"Oh, crap. I gotta go." Henry scooped Maxwell up and took a few hurried steps toward the main courtyard. "Mike has patience issues."

"Don't let me stop you."

"Hey, Alby. Go win us some new textbooks, huh?" He darted away from his friends and headed toward the stone archway.

"I'd better go too," Murphy muttered. "I'm kinda used to walking into town with only Henry now."

"How's that going?" Raven grinned at her friend. *It looks like she has that blush under control too.*

"Well, minus the parts where he starts word-vomiting about Jenny Connors, we have a good time. And at least he doesn't blame Fritz for everything that happens to his toad anymore."

Laughing, she nodded. "That's a start, I guess."

"Or whatever." With a self-conscious chuckle, the girl turned slightly and waved goodbye. "You're gonna kick ass at the Tournament of Mages, Raven. Then you'll have to come back and tell me all about the stuff in Azerad we won't get to see."

"I'll make a list. Have a good break, Murphy."

Her friend hurried across the field after Henry while Fritz pounced and occasionally sprinted short distances after her.

Raven turned and jumped back, her arms flailing. "Woah! Jeez, Leander."

A hissing laugh escaped him.

"Do I need to practice extra hard on listening for your sneak attacks now, too?"

"If I don't want you to hear me, little girl, no amount of practice will change a thing."

"Oh, yes." She rolled her eyes with a little smirk. "That is very encouraging, dragon. Your unwavering support is invaluable."

"I know."

They stood and stared at each other until she finally had to laugh. "It kinda feels anticlimactic, doesn't it? The spring break is now officially here and it's business as usual for us."

"Until tomorrow."

"Right." She caught sight of Bella standing a few yards away from the stables, her neck craned to watch as Wesley darted toward her from the sky. "As soon as Alessandra gets here, I guess we're back at it."

She wandered toward the other girl as the firedrake landed on his mage's shoulder. "How'd you guys do in Worley's class?"

The other young war mage in training turned toward her with a slightly irritated expression. "As well as we always do. Wesley could have flown across the field and to the other side of the main buildings if I'd wanted him to."

"I don't doubt that at all."

"I merely didn't want to make everyone feel bad by doing it for fun."

Raven smiled. *What happened to the competitive showoff?* "Yeah, I know the feeling."

Bella tossed her long dark hair over her shoulder and looked across the field at the stone archway. "Mostly, I didn't want everyone to rush at me with questions about how to get to where Wesley and I are with sending him away."

There it is. I can let that one go. Fighting back a laugh, she gave the other girl a nod of understanding.

"I already have enough on my plate right now," her companion continued. "And I'm not a professor."

"Not yet, right?"

Her companion scoffed and rolled her eyes. "Teaching is the last thing I want to do. I told you, I'm getting out of

Brighton when I graduate, Raven. Getting sucked in to be a professor, even of a prestigious mage school, is not in my plans."

"Okay." *She's a little more on edge than normal.* "Different strokes, right?"

"Sure." Bella spun quickly to face the archway into the main courtyard. Alessandra finally decided to make an appearance and now strode toward them with her usual expressionless efficiency. "I hope she doesn't plan to keep being late all the time once we leave tomorrow."

"We have two full days before the tournament officially starts, don't we?"

"We do. But what happens when we're supposed to follow her to go somewhere in Azerad and she doesn't show up to get us?"

Raven laughed and spread her arms. "We both know that wouldn't be an issue for either of us."

A small smirk flickered across the girl's lips before it disappeared. "True."

"This is such a waste of time," Alessandra grumbled as she approached them. Her dark-gray military uniform swished with every quick stride. "When we return from Azerad, we'll find a different way to meet. Or, at the very least, a better way to communicate if we're not all out here at the same time."

The two girls exchanged a sideways glance. The other young mage looked as confused as she felt. "We're ready when you are—" Raven began.

"Training's canceled." The trainer glanced from one trainee to the other with no expression at all. "And I had to walk all the way across the school for two seconds to tell you that before doing it all over again."

Cranky war mage trainer. Not a good combo. She shrugged. "At least it's a nice day."

The veteran war mage clicked her tongue and looked around the open field like even that disappointed her. "It'll be a better day tomorrow. You two have the rest of the afternoon to yourselves. You're expected to be packed, dressed for travel, and standing at the front gates by sunrise tomorrow. Understood?"

"No problem."

Bella glanced at Fowler Academy's front gates. "How will we get there?"

"Miss Chase, I'm not in the mood to explain to you what you'll find out soon enough for yourself. Now, if you'll excuse me, I have to prepare my things to return to civilization." She glanced at the two girls, offered a half-assed smile that looked more like a grimace before it disappeared a second later, and spun sharply to march toward the main courtyard.

"Woah." Raven sighed and shook her head. "Flynn wasn't kidding when he said she was done with country life."

Bella raised one shoulder in an apathetic shrug. "Can you blame her?"

"You don't like living in Brighton, do you?"

"It's not about what I like, Raven. It's about opportunity, and Fowler Academy's about the only opportunity Brighton can offer mages like us."

She narrowed her eyes. "And you're not worried about leaving your family or missing them while you're gone? I don't mean this week at Azerad. I mean when you're a famous war mage spy traveling all over Lomberdoon and between kingdoms."

For a few seconds, Bella stared at her.

She's gonna hit me or something.

Then, the dark-haired witch burst out laughing. Wesley responded with a startled squeak and stretched his wings before he settled on her shoulder again. "You really think I'll end up being a spy."

Raven grinned. "It's not impossible."

"Think bigger, Raven Alby. Much bigger is where I plan to be when I get out of here." The girl moved quickly to the stable wall to pick her knapsack up and slung it over her shoulder. "And don't forget, bigger has more than enough room for two of Fowler Academy's best war mages, right?"

"Wow. Is that an invitation for me to join you in your quest for greatness?" She folded her arms and raised an eyebrow. Despite trying to tone it down, her smile continued to grow.

Bella stepped past her and set off toward the far end of the field and the road to Brighton's town center. She turned to walk backward and spread her arms dramatically. "Please. We both know you don't need an invitation for anything. Neither do I."

She spun away, and Raven finally allowed herself to laugh. "See you bright and early, Bella Chase."

"I wouldn't miss it."

In less than a minute, the girl's quick stride took her past the front gates and her figure diminished rapidly beyond the trees that lined both sides of the road.

"Bella Chase is in a surprisingly good mood. I guess

there wasn't another shoe after all." She shook her head and turned slowly, prepared for another sneak attack by her dragon, but Leander hadn't moved from where she'd left him beyond the end of his pen. *He's only trying to keep me on my toes. It's kind of annoying.*

With a little chuckle, she strode quickly across the field. *And here's another chance to test our theory. He'd better be right about feeling everything I want to do before I do it.*

With a little sigh to bolster her courage, the young mage burst into a sprint toward Leander and ran faster than she'd dared to before they knew exactly what they could do. She didn't expect the huge dragon to race toward her with his head stretched low in front of his muscular body to streamline his speed.

There will be one massive collision if we don't nail this.

Raven pushed herself to go faster. With barely a few yards left between them, he pivoted his entire body and spread his wings in a burst of air and translucent red light. His long, sharp claws dug trenches into the grass as he spun, and she leapt toward his back before he'd even turned his side completely to face her.

They timed it perfectly.

One dark work boot was lifted by the red dragon's powerful, scaly head, and she landed in a crouch atop his back at the exact moment that he surged into the sky.

"Yes!" she screamed, both hands and feet pressed firmly against the ridges at the base of her dragon's long neck. She stared at the sky and his neck gave her the perfect angle to see exactly where they were headed. Up, away, and anywhere they wanted.

"That was amazing!" She laughed and uttered another

loud, drawn-out whoop as she balanced herself against the dip and rise of his muscles that pushed them higher and faster. "I know I said that the last time, but this one's a new record."

Leander's only response was a shrill, warbled screech as he extended his wings fully to soar and level them out of their ascent.

My thoughts exactly.

She slid out of her crouch to sit astride her dragon's back, and the second she settled, he plunged with surprising agility. The laugh she attempted was forced down her throat by the wind that rushed up against them. She shut her mouth and blinked away the streaming tears while she watched the ground grow larger and closer below them.

Leander pulled up in a smooth motion and flapped his giant wings a few more times to lift them up and over the tallest tower at Fowler Academy. She pumped a fist in the air and shouted in triumph again.

We have all afternoon to do whatever we want. More than enough time for a visit to Moss Ranch.

Without a single word from his dragon rider, the dragon wheeled and set a new course around the outskirts of Brighton to take them south.

CHAPTER TWENTY-FOUR

Three hours later, Leander landed gracefully in the field at Fowler a little beyond the edge of his pen. Raven leapt from his back and tried to smooth the hair that had come loose from her braid.

"Oh, forget it. This thing's done, anyway." She pulled the tie free and only had to shake the mostly destroyed braid out before her long red hair fell in waves around her shoulders. With a quick shake of her head, she blew more strands out of her eyes and glanced at her dragon familiar. "I might have to come up with a better way to keep my hair back."

"Or not." He turned his head away from her and scanned the field and the forest at the edge of it with only partial interest. "I hope your mane isn't your first concern."

"Lions have manes." She patted his shoulder as she stepped past him toward the pen. "And maybe Professor Worley."

A short, quick hiss escaped her dragon as he fell into step behind her and swung his head from side to side.

"And it's not my first concern, by the way. Since you don't even have hair, allow me to educate you."

"Oh, do." Leander's voice fell entirely flat, and she chuckled as she flashed her access rune at the pen gate.

"Imagine flying up there in the sky exactly like we did for the last few hours. You have the wind in your face, your wings spread, total freedom—"

"Raven."

She pulled the gate open and waited for him to step inside first. "I know you know. I'm painting a mental picture." *Very soon, that might not even be necessary either.*

He snorted and ambled into the enclosure as his wings twitched to readjust themselves against his back.

"The flight's perfect. Everything you wanted." She stepped inside behind him and pulled the gate almost closed. "And then, what's that? Something caught your attention? You turn your head to look and you get this instead!"

The young witch rubbed her hands frantically around her hair and tossed it into her face in a massive red mess. She sputtered and tried to spit out the pieces that had found their way into her mouth.

Leander sat on his haunches and stared at her.

"Yes. Even the hair in the mouth, Leander. That was a perfect demonstration." She blew at the locks of hair that almost covered her entire face.

"Cut it off."

"What?" Raven's mouth fell open in silent laughter before she ran both hands through her hair a few times to restore it to some degree of neatness. "I can't cut my hair off."

"Why not? Is that where your magic comes from?"

She rolled her eyes and gestured dismissively. "You're being ridiculous. I can't cut off my hair simply for convenience because…" Slowly, she slid her fingers through a bright red lock and glanced at it. "It's part of who I am."

"On the outside. It's rather useless if you ask me."

"Uh-huh." She headed toward him with a smirk and stopped in front of his large head where it loomed over her, even when he was seated. "Well, I didn't ask you. And for a dragon who's never had hair, I can't expect you to completely understand, can I?"

"Yes, you can." Leander lowered his head until his scaly snout was a mere two inches from her small, round nose. "I understand perfectly."

"Oh. Thank you."

"And I stand by my suggestion to cut it off."

She snorted and swatted his face away. The dragon rumbled low in his chest and turned away from her to make his usual slow circles before he settled in the grass.

"I'll get your dinner. Be right back."

"Wait."

Raven had only taken one step and she returned to him immediately. "Is everything okay?"

"That's what I'm asking you."

With a little frown, the young mage leaned away from her dragon and studied him in confusion. "I'm fine."

"You're disappointed."

"I don't have anything to be disappointed about. So I'm not sure—"

"Because the dragon trainer wasn't home to see us off."

For a few seconds, she simply gaped at her giant familiar. Finally, she exhaled a huge sigh and lowered herself to her knees in front of him. "I can't keep anything from you, can I?"

"Less and less every day."

She ran her hand from the tip of his snout all the way up between his eyes, then gave the top of his head a gentle pat. "Yeah, I guess I am a little disappointed about that. His dad said he'd pass our message along, but having someone else tell William, 'Goodbye and wish me luck,' for me isn't exactly the scenario I had in mind."

"A little lacking in conversation."

Raven chuckled. "Ernie Moss isn't the best conversationalist anyway, Leander. And he was busy putting all the finishing touches to that shed. Man, did you see it?"

"I saw all of it."

"Human figure of speech, dragon." She chucked the side of his scaly jaw with a loose fist, and he settled his head on his forepaws and watched her intently. "So Ernie barely had time to listen to me explain and I doubt that he'll remember half of it by the time William gets back. I honestly can't remember a time when William Moss left the ranch for emergency supplies when it had absolutely nothing to do with dragons."

"The man was scared."

"Who, Ernie? Yeah, exactly like William said. It's hard to imagine being that worried about something without any proof that it'll actually happen."

Leander's tail whispered across the grass as he swung it from one side of his body to the other. "Raiders."

"That's what I've heard. William's dad didn't seem too keen to talk about it—or talk at all."

"He'll get your message, Raven." The dragon snorted and closed his eyes for a few seconds before he opened them again.

"You sound awfully sure of that."

"I am. It's hard to forget a dragon rider war mage landing her dragon without a saddle at one's front door."

Raven chuckled and nodded. "Yeah, we are unforgettable, aren't we?"

"Fairly."

"Only a little." The banter made her smile grow, and she sighed with resignation. "So William will hear at least part of what I told his dad and hopefully, that part explains why we won't make regular visits during the spring break. Still, it would have been nice to tell him in person. That will have to wait until we get back from Azerad." She slapped her hands on her thighs and pushed to her feet. "What we need to focus on now is getting ready for our grand adventure tomorrow."

"Yes, a grand adventure of leaving relative solitude and one perfectly roomy pen for a crowded city and a whole stable of dragons. I simply cannot wait."

"Hey, tell me how you really feel." She spread her arms and stepped backward across the pen toward the gate. Leander merely stared at her with his glowing yellow eyes and didn't move an inch. "It'll be fine. I promise. Headmaster Flynn said everything you need has already been taken care of there, and I'll check on you every morning and night like I have done here. It won't be a whole week of us having to stay away from each other."

"No, we'll have to try to stay away from everyone else."

She laughed and paused at the open gate. "Or you could

look at it like this. Leander and his war mage rider get to spar with a few other students who have no idea what they're in for. If that doesn't get you excited, I don't know what will."

"We'll see."

"We sure will." Raven pointed at him, and he gave her an amused rumble in reply. "Food time."

After she'd fed her dragon, made sure he had everything he needed, and said goodnight before their early start the next morning, she hurried across the field toward the main courtyard. *Now that there's nothing else to think about, I'm excited about this trip.*

Her satchel felt light enough on her back despite carrying most of her supplies from her classes, and she turned right with a little bounce in her step toward the girls' dormitory. Before she'd made it halfway there, muffled crying caught her attention.

She glanced around, but no one was there. *Crying on the first real night of the spring break? I don't care who they are. That can't be good.*

Concerned, she hurried around the last of the large buildings used for classes and the front of the girls' dormitory came into view. Her eager pace slowed when she recognized Professor Gilliam and Professor Dameron who stood in conversation with Jessica.

"I understand that it's highly upsetting, Miss Rodenmeyer," the woman muttered and frowned with her hands clasped in front of her. "There's always next year. And we most certainly will not mark this against you."

Jessica cried even harder and buried her face in her hands.

"We should speak to them ourselves," Dameron snapped.

"Professor Dameron." Gilliam shot him a stern glance that clearly conveyed what little was left of her patience. "Please. That won't help anything."

"I disagree. After all the planning and preparation? After Miss Rodenmeyer's put so much effort and dedication into this? I have half a mind to ride out there myself—tonight—and give them a piece of my mind."

Jessica sniffed, lowered her hands, and looked at the irate bald professor who only taught upperclassmen. "Really?"

"As a—"

"No, Miss Rodenmeyer," the woman interjected and silenced her fellow professor. "Not really. It seems Professor Dameron shares your frustrations but I'm sorry. It's not our place to argue their decision."

"I really—" Jessica caught sight of Raven who walked hesitantly toward the dorms. The girl swallowed quickly and spun to hurry away from watching eyes. She went the long way around the other side of the main buildings to avoid her—or Raven being able to look at her.

The two professors turned slowly and the bald man released a frustrated sigh. "It seems my original decision comes into play after all." He gave his colleague a gruff frown before he turned away as quickly as Jessica had and strode through the center of the main buildings toward wherever he slept on school grounds.

Raven finally approached the front doors of the dormitory and studied Professor Gilliam's reaction. The woman stared at nothing between the rising stone towers in front of her and nibbled on her bottom lip. "Is everything okay, Professor?"

The question tore Gilliam out of her thoughts, and she turned to give her a tight, grim smile. "Miss Rodenmeyer will be perfectly fine, Miss Alby, if that's what you're asking."

"She looked very upset."

"Yes. She did." A tiny frown of confusion crossed the woman's face before she stepped aside and gestured toward the dorm's front door. "I suggest you head to your room and get as much sleep as you can tonight, Miss Alby. You have a long day ahead of you and an early morning tomorrow."

She shrugged. "Sunrise isn't that early."

Professor Gilliam seemed completely baffled by that, but she plastered on another forced smile that looked a little more genuine and nodded. "Good night."

"Good night, Professor." The young mage opened the front door and slipped inside but held it open behind her enough to peer through the crack for another glance at her professor.

With her back turned toward her, Gilliam wrapped her arms around herself as if she stood in the winter chill instead of the pleasantly cool spring evening. One hand raised to pat the hair coiled into a neat bun. After a long moment, she shook her head and moved quickly across the grounds toward the main building.

Raven let the door fall shut behind her and frowned. *Nothing about the last few minutes felt right. I hope Jessica can work things out before she has to compete.*

A yawn broke free from nowhere, and she finished it with a sigh and shook her head. "It's not even dark out."

With a quick turn, she wandered across the common room toward the wide staircase in the back and up to her room for the night. *The sooner I get to sleep, the sooner we can head out in the morning for a real adventure.*

CHAPTER TWENTY-FIVE

"Where the hell is Durik with that ladder?" Vorlen hissed as he crouched at the base of the great wall surrounding the kingdom of Lomberdoon.

"He's comin'." Len sniffed, raised his forearm from where he'd propped it on his bent knee, and rubbed the back of his hand under his nose. "I can hear him mouth-breathing from a mile away."

"Will you hurry it up? You good-for-nothin' stick in a shirt." The other man rose slowly from his crouch and searched the darkness outside the wall. It was almost impossible to see as far as he wanted, but now that they'd heard of the Swarm being eliminated for good, there wasn't much out there to be afraid of in the unnamed lands between kingdoms. *Well, there is, but it happens to be us.*

The dangerously thin Durik huffed and puffed closer. He struggled beneath the weight of the slightly uneven ladder they'd cobbled together from what wood they could find about three miles north of there. "I got it. I got it. You don't think you coulda grabbed this one for me, Vorlen?

Maybe one freakin' time? You got twice as much muscles as I got."

"Everyone has twice as many muscles as you, moron," Len quipped.

"Hey, watch it with that thing," Vorlen snapped and ducked in the dark as the even darker outline of the crooked ladder swung toward their heads.

"Shut up and help me stand this thing."

The two men begrudgingly helped their skinny comrade stabilize the hulking, poorly built ladder against the wall. They stepped back and Durik wiped his forehead. "Why didn't we do this a long time ago?"

"You really are a moron." Vorlen shook his head. "There aren't any lookouts stationed around here."

"What? Did we take all them out already—ow." The emaciated man flinched from Len's slap to the back of his head and scowled. "What'd you do that for?"

"I'm tryin' to smack some brains into you."

Vorlen allowed himself a long, irritated sigh. *If we don't find a ranch or a farmhouse or something on the other side of this wall, I'll kill him.* "All the lookouts went to the giant damn hole in the wall. Remember? That's where they think the danger is."

"The hole?"

The two men exchanged wide-eyed glances in the dark. "I'm gonna kill him," Len muttered.

"I'm way ahead of you," the other man declared curtly.

"Oh, that hole in the wall." Durik shook his head vigorously. "Yeah, yeah. I know the one."

"So does half the damn continent." Vorlen turned to scan the darkness again before he peered north along the outside of the wall and nodded. "That's why Riley's joining up with Tiberius Nash. They figure they have enough hands together to defeat this fancy little kingdom in here so we can take whatever we want."

"Wait, Tiberius Nash?" Durik balked. "The Black Thief Tiberius Nash?"

"I swear, Durik. I'm about this close to burying you head-first near that bush over there. Alive."

"I heard Nash's coming our way with some kinda magic," Len muttered.

Vorlen glanced at his friend and narrowed his eyes. "Like a mage turned dark or somethin'?"

"Dunno. Magic is magic, right? It doesn't matter where it comes from."

"Huh. Maybe." He looked at the long length of the ladder that ended about three feet short of the top of the wall. "Did you bring that rope?"

"Yeah, Sid's got it with him."

"Good." The leader of this relatively small raider band turned north along the wall and stuck two fingers in his mouth for a quick, sharp whistle. Two dozen of his best moved swiftly across the grass toward them. He caught Len's gaze and grinned. Spit glistened on his stained teeth between the gaps of all the others he'd lost over the years. "I tell you what, though, men. I don't give a damn about magic. Not when I can grab whatever I want with my own two hands."

The man jerked his long, wickedly sharp dagger from its sheath at his belt and lifted it for his men to see. The blade caught the moonlight perfectly and he gave a low, devious chuckle.

"You tell Sid to come up behind me with that rope." Vorlen stuck the dagger between his teeth and climbed to the top of the crooked ladder. It was easy enough to pull himself up over the edge, and when Sid joined him on the wide lip of Lomberdoon's protective wall, they anchored the rope and lowered the rope down the other side and got to work.

Two dozen raiders followed quickly and made little noise in the dark of night. They were close to putting the first piece of Kendril Riley and Tiberius Nash's plans into motion.

The band of raiders rappelled down the other side of the wall one by one. When two dozen pairs of scratched, torn, worn-bare boots landed, Vorlen signaled them forward and they strode across the grass.

A mile inside the great wall on the southeast border, the raiders overwhelmed the barn, stable, shed, and small farmhouse of a man named Harry Farden and his wife, Genevieve. In their early seventies, the couple prided themselves on how healthy and young-feeling they'd managed to stay by raising pigs and chickens on their piece of land that was comfortably big enough for the two of them.

Harry awoke to see a sneering man missing many of his teeth looming over him with a knife, but he was too slow to defend himself or even raise the alarm. Genevieve never woke at all.

After that, the fat sow and her piglets made considerable noise, but there was no one to hear them.

Almost thirty miles north along the wall, the second band of a few dozen raiders did very much the same thing.

These targeted the small mining town of Turnbrook Hill and the fight, at least, was much more eventful. Despite resistance, every man, woman, and child in Turnbrook Hill met their end before the raiders took what they wanted from each barn and house and store shed.

Five miles east of Pelinor, a third band stalked through the forest inside Lomberdoon's great wall. Two-thirds of the kingdom's troops had been sent to the hole in the wall south of Brighton for added protection and waited for the attack that hadn't yet come. None realized that it wouldn't come—not there, at least.

CHAPTER TWENTY-SIX

R aven woke at her usual pre-dawn hour the next day and was instantly alert, her eyes wide without even a trace of early-morning blurriness.

"This is it," she whispered.

On the other side of the room, Elizabeth shifted in her bed and grunted softly. For some reason, the girl would only travel home that morning.

It wouldn't be fair to wake her roommate, so she hunched her shoulders with a little grimace and attempted to be far quieter than usual as she moved around and dressed. Today, she made sure to slip her dark jacket on over her plain traveling clothes—the weather would warm up quickly, but at least she'd have a jacket. And more importantly, she'd have her mother's pin with her as she navigated what waited for her in Azerad.

Her grandfather's oilskin bag had been packed for a week-long trip for days now, and she slid it out from under the bed to hoist it over her shoulder. *It's so much lighter than when I moved into the dorms.*

Fortunately, the doorknob didn't squeak when she turned it.

"Kick some ass, Raven."

The other girl's low, scratchy voice made her jump, and the oilskin bag over her shoulder almost made her fall when its weight shifted. "I tried so hard not to wake you," she whispered.

Her roommate rolled over in bed and smacked her lips. "You didn't."

Laughing silently, she slipped into the hall and pulled the door closed gently behind her. "See you soon."

It clicked shut and the young mage hurried down the third-floor hall, anxious to get out into the fields. *It's still dark out so we have more than enough time for our normal morning chat.*

She didn't allow herself to run until she'd reached the bottom of the stairs, where there was no one around to hear her footsteps pounding across the common room.

Later, leaned against Leander's flank while he curled around her in the grass, Raven looked at the sky and took a deep breath. "Sunrise. Are you sure you don't wanna eat any more before we head out?"

The dragon snorted. "I've had enough."

"Okay. We should probably get going."

His only response was to raise his head and haul himself slowly to his feet so he gave his mage enough time to do the same without falling.

"I don't think you have anything to worry about, Leander."

"I'm not worried."

Raven approached the gate. "This'll be good for both of

us. Besides, dragons aren't meant to only roam one small town and a couple of ranches—and sometimes over the wall."

"Ah, yes. A large city is much better suited for a dragon."

The gate clicked open and she pushed it aside swiftly. She turned to grin at her dragon over her shoulder as he ambled after her onto the field. "I know you'll find something that makes this whole thing worth it for you."

"I already have, Raven."

She stopped but he continued to walk across the grass toward the front of the school. *I swear that sounded like an annoyed sigh.* With a hushed chuckle, she swung the gate closed again, heard the lock click, and scooped up the oilskin bag and slung it over her shoulder.

"What are you looking forward to the most?" she called as she hurried after him.

"Not the city." Leander spread his wings before she caught up to his side. She stopped short to avoid clotheslining herself on those outstretched wings and rolled her eyes as he folded them against his back again. "You're looking forward to this."

"Of course I am. Okay, maybe not as much as Bella, but I have a feeling she's excited about the whole thing for two heaping handfuls of reasons she hasn't bothered to share with me."

"Your excitement makes it worth it for me."

"Oh, come on." Raven laughed a little and fiddled with the strap of the oilskin bag on her shoulder. "I love the sentiment, don't get me wrong. But that can't be the only thing."

"It can. It is."

With a deep breath, she rolled her shoulders. "Never underestimate a dragon's loyalty, huh?"

"Especially mine."

"Because you're my familiar too. I know."

Twin puffs of steam burst from Leander's nostrils when he snorted. "Because my loyalty wasn't trained into me by someone who wanted to control it. I gave it freely."

The young mage grinned at her dragon as they moved across the field. "That's right. So did I."

"Eventually."

When her laughter died down, they'd almost reached the edge of the wall surrounding Fowler Academy's main buildings.

Leander stopped short even before she saw why. "I'll stay here."

"What's wrong?" She tried to peer around the edge of the wall and only caught a glimpse of Alessandra's dark-gray uniform sleeve as it moved toward the gates.

"Nothing yet. The horses will have more to say about it if I come any closer." He dragged a forepaw through the grass and exhaled a quick, heavy breath. "At least I'm downwind."

"Horses?"

He swung his head toward the road a dozen yards ahead of them. "See for yourself."

"Uh-huh." Raven moved forward to the edge of the wall. When she skirted it, sure enough, there were horses.

Professor Worley stood outside the gates, holding reins for two horses in each hand. They were already saddled and ready to go, waiting patiently beside the man who had enough of a connection with animals to have chosen four of them as his familiars. He blinked heavily and rocked a little on his feet, his wild black beard sticking out in all directions exactly like his hair.

Alessandra finished hitching a fifth horse to a cart a little smaller than Deacon's delivery wagon. She straightened, patted the mare's flank, and turned to see Raven standing a few feet away from where the grass met the dirt road. "Miss Alby. You're also early."

"Well, you didn't say how long after sunrise." The young mage shrugged and dropped her bag onto the grass with a thump.

"I assumed sunrise and arrived ten minutes before that." Bella stepped down the road to get a good look at Raven, her arms folded with a smirk.

"It's good to be prepared." Raven gave the other young mage a quick smile, then searched the area near the front gates. "Has no one else arrived?"

"Not yet," Worley told her groggily. He turned and nodded toward the main courtyard past the gates. "But they're coming."

Daniel Smith and Cooper walked lazily across the paved area, their eyes still heavy with sleep and their bags dangling from limp arms. Professor Fellows walked behind them, shook his head, and grinned. Headmaster Flynn and Professors Bixby, Gilliam, Dameron, and Ambrose shuffled through the front doors of the main building. Flynn was wide awake and walked briskly across the courtyard toward the front gates with wide eyes and an eager smile. Despite the fact that all the other professors looked like they'd been pulled out of bed seconds before, they'd at least remembered to change out of their pajamas.

When they reached the front gates, they spread out to the side and lined up with Worley, though they gave him and his four gentle horses generous space. Fellows joined them with Daniel and Cooper, and when the weapons professor saw the headmaster's clothes, he barked out a laugh. "Were you too excited to change out of the night-gown, Headmaster?"

Flynn drew the thick gray house robe closer around his middle and the long hem dragged behind him in the dirt. "I'm decent, Professor Fellows. Thank you."

A few of the others chuckled, and the humor seemed to wake them up a little more.

Raven searched the faces and raised her eyebrows. "Where's Jessica?"

She didn't miss the scathing glare Dameron directed at Gilliam, exactly like he had the night before.

"Unfortunately, Miss Rodenmeyer is unavailable this morning," Flynn said quietly. "But I believe—"

"She's coming." Professor Gilliam nodded at the head-master. She turned, possibly to go to the girls' dorm, but stopped with a nod. "Ah. There she is."

Bella took a sideways step closer to Raven and muttered, "That's not Jessica."

"Nope."

The other girl who made her way toward the front gates was an incredibly tall, thin third-year with two blonde braids that hung to her waist. She carried a small, tightly packed bag in either hand and her bright gaze studied each person who waited for her arrival.

"As it turns out, Miss Delaine was thrilled by the opportunity to accompany the rest of you to Azerad this morning instead."

When the tall girl passed Professor Dameron, the man nodded curtly without any change to his perpetual frown. Anika nodded with a tiny smile.

"Do you have any idea what happened?" Bella whispered.

"Not really. But I saw—"

"All right, listen up." Alessandra folded her arms and studied the faces of the young mages about to embark—three wide-eyed, attentive witches and two wizards falling asleep on their feet. "It's a full day's ride from here to Azerad, so you'd better wake up now and start paying attention. I don't find accidents very funny, and setbacks in our schedule don't make me happy."

Raven choked back a laugh. "This is worse than when we're training with her."

Bella rubbed her mouth to hide the smile she otherwise couldn't conceal and whispered, "I'm starting to think it's because she likes us."

Both first-year mages chuckled quietly until the woman had launched her large bag into the back of the wagon.

"Each of you has your own mount. I don't care if you don't know how to ride. Professor Worley assured me the horses know the route and have few problems with new riders. As long as you don't try anything stupid while you're in the saddle, you should be fine."

"We all have to ride?" Bella asked and studied the surprisingly patient horses beside Professor Worley. "On a horse?"

"That's what I said, Miss Chase. Yes."

"Who gets to ride in the cart?" Cooper asked and squinted in an attempt to see better through his early-morning-wakeup fogginess.

Alessandra turned her head quickly to look at the third-year student, and her mouth opened with a little smack. "Me."

"I'm not a horse person, though." Bella focused on the animals across the road and grimaced.

Worley chuckled and spread his arms. The horses beside him didn't flinch when his hands passed under their heads. "It's merely another learning opportunity, Miss Chase."

"I can ride." Anika cocked her head and stepped forward to place her small bags in the cart.

"There you have it. This one's figured out how things work." The veteran war mage nodded toward the cart. "Everyone's things in the cart. Let's go. The sooner we get out of here, the sooner we can all put our feet up in Azerad."

Raven picked up her grandfather's oilskin bag and joined the other students who had begun to load their things into the back of the cart. "Alessandra?"

"Miss Alby."

"Four horses. And I have a dragon."

The veteran war mage regarded her impassively. "That is an inspiring observation."

She ignored her trainer's prickly attitude. "I'm saying I'm very sure Leander won't agree to walk down the road all day behind or even in front of a cart and a group of horses. Not only that, I have no idea how to get to Azerad, even if we're flying."

"Yes, Miss Alby. You and your dragon will be flying this morning. But not alone."

The sound of buffeting air rose from the north side of the school grounds before a massive shadow soared over the small field where they'd held the spring gala a few weeks before. The dragon who cast the shadow glided swiftly across the courtyard and over the school wall again into the huge field behind Raven. She only caught a brief glimpse of the huge creature and its single rider before it disappeared from view to land.

"That was remarkably well-timed." Alessandra cocked her head. "Do you have any other questions?"

"Yeah." Cooper turned toward the horses beside Professor Worley and wrinkled his nose. "How do you get on a horse?"

The man laughed and his booming voice echoed into the stone courtyard behind them. "I'm happy to help with that, Mr. Hutton."

"Okay…"

"But make it quick, will you?" Alessandra darted the man a blunt glance before she turned toward Raven again. "Your escort awaits, Miss Alby."

"Oh. Okay. See you guys in Azerad, then."

"We're looking forward to seeing all of you compete in the Tournament of Mages," Headmaster Flynn added, although his gaze lingered on Raven a little longer than on the others.

Bella grimaced again and muttered to her, "I have to ride a horse."

"And you'll master it like everything else you do." She smiled as the girl stalked begrudgingly across the road to join the other students, who approached Professor Worley's horses hesitantly.

CHAPTER TWENTY-SEVEN

Before Raven could turn away and slip across the field, her stomach grumbled ferociously. Professor Fellows chuckled but made no comment. She clapped a hand over her belly and glanced quickly toward the girl's dorm. *There's no time for breakfast with two dragons waiting.*

"Alby."

She spun toward Alessandra, caught off guard by hearing Henry's nickname for her pop out of her trainer's mouth.

The woman tossed an apple at her and she caught it with both hands and jerked her chin up. "It's the most important meal of the day."

"Right. Thanks." She raised the apple in farewell, turned, and raced as fast as she could into the field without looking panicked.

Leander hadn't moved from where she'd left him, but he'd raised his head high enough to make it look like he was stretching. He hadn't turned to look at the strange new dragon who stood only a few yards away from his pen, either.

"You didn't say anything about an escort," he rumbled.

"No one else did either until about thirty seconds ago." Raven patted the underside of his outstretched neck and peered around him at the new dragon. "It'll be fine. There can't be too many rules for traveling by air, right?"

"I'm less concerned by rules than by a dragon I don't know."

"I get it. So we may as well introduce ourselves now and get it over with, right?"

His expression disgruntled, he lowered his head and studied her with his glowing yellow eyes. "If we must."

She gave him a reassuring nod and smiled. "Come on, then."

Behind them on the road, a horse nickered before one of the boys uttered a startled shout. Worley's laughter boomed louder than any of the other professors who joined him. "Well, that's one way to sit a horse, Mr. Hutton. I'm not sure it's the most efficient, however."

Raven took a deep breath as she and Leander walked to the pen and their new dragon and rider escort. *I'm so glad I'm not stuck on a horse. And I would have had no problem with it six months ago.*

The rider had already dismounted and busied himself with checking the girdle around his dragon's underbelly. The bright blue dragon swiveled her head to peer at them, and the man straightened when he noticed. "Good morning."

"So far." Raven smiled, but she could already feel the tension coiled inside Leander. She rubbed his broad shoulder reassuringly. *Easy, dragon. They're only here to help.*

That seemed to be enough. He puffed out a cloud of steam and lowered his head until it hovered over her shoulder again.

"My name's Bert." The dragon rider stepped forward with his hand extended.

She tossed the apple into her other hand before she shook his. "Raven Alby."

"Yeah, I know who you are, kid." He smirked and ran his tongue around the inside of his mouth like he'd just finished his breakfast. "You and that big red made enough of a name for yourselves in Nadine with that competition win. Anyone with a dragon has heard about what you pulled off that day, even if they weren't there."

"Huh. Thanks." She tilted her head slightly toward the big red's head over her shoulder. "I'd stick with calling him Leander, though."

"Absolutely." Bert smiled at him with raised eyebrows and waited for the massive dragon to say something. After a few silent seconds, he shrugged and turned to gesture behind him. "This is Evelyn."

"Nice to meet you, Evelyn," Raven said with a nod that might have been half of a small bow as well. The blue dragon turned slowly to face Leander and the young mage head-on.

"It is my pleasure, Raven Alby." Her voice was surprisingly gentle and smooth.

You can't judge a dragon by its voice, either. That's a soldier's patch on Bert's uniform.

"Well." Bert nodded toward the stables as Evelyn

253

lowered herself to her belly. "As soon as you have Leander saddled, we'll be on our way."

The man stuck his foot into the stirrup of his dragon's saddle and she grinned. "No, we're good."

He froze, one foot lifted comically high while the other remained firmly planted. He gazed from her to her dragon familiar a few times before a tiny smirk lifted one side of his mouth. "Nice try. Go on, Raven. It's a shorter trip to Azerad for us than for the rest of your friends, so they'll expect us before the others."

Without waiting to be sure the young mage headed into the stables for said dragon saddle, Bert jumped and swung his other leg over Evelyn's back. By the time he looked up again, Raven was already situated at the base of her dragon's long neck. Leander turned a few steps to the right to give the soldier and his blue dragon a better view. He swiveled his head toward Bert and Evelyn and gave them a fearsome dragon's grin.

"Ready when you are." Raven grinned too.

The man raised an eyebrow and leaned forward over his dragon's neck. "You seein' this, Evelyn?"

"I am." The blue dragon's eyes narrowed at the young mage and her familiar.

"Yeah, I'm seeing it too. It wasn't a joke, apparently."

She wouldn't let her smile fade but she leaned over Leander's neck to mutter, "They don't believe us."

"That is not my problem."

"Well, it's gonna be if you—no!" Bert reached out instinctively toward the crouching red dragon as Leander's wings whipped out to their full span. "Don't even think—"

The red dragon launched into the sky and barely

cleared the blue dragon and her rider before he climbed steadily higher and away over the forest. He turned only slightly north and slowed to let their escort catch up.

Bert looked over his shoulder to watch the dragon and shook his head in amazement. "She's only a kid."

Evelyn stared at the two who soared high above them. "She looks like a dragon rider to me, Bert."

He snorted and snatched her reins in his hand. "You can keep your opinions to yourself for now. I need to come up with a plan for how the hell to handle something like a mage academy student who thinks she's too good for a saddle before she falls out of the sky."

"As you wish." The blue dragon waited for her command and soared into the air to join the child with more control and confidence of her winged mount than either Bert or Evelyn had seen to date.

Raven caught her breath through the rush of crisp morning air through her hair and her clothes. She leaned forward over the dragon's long neck. "They're not gonna be very happy about that one."

"Are you telling me it was the wrong choice, Raven?"

"Definitely not!" A laugh burst out of her, and she turned to see her escort gaining on them quickly while Leander soared with a draft. "I'm merely making sure we both know what to expect."

"I don't expect much of anything from those two. They didn't take us seriously."

"True. I think we've made our point, though." Despite the more serious tone in her voice, she couldn't hide a satisfied smile. "Can we go easy on them until we get to Azerad?"

"Easy." He twisted his head to look at her. "Fine."

"Thank you."

Evelyn glided beside them, reduced her speed to keep pace with the huge red dragon, and seemed to have accepted the fact that they flew without saddle or harness. Raven forced herself to pretend she hadn't noticed the man's disapproval, but she couldn't keep that up for very long. When she turned her head slowly to look at Bert, he scowled at her.

"That's an incredibly dangerous decision you've made, mage. Some might even call it stupid."

Raven raised her eyebrows. "That's an incredibly judgmental opinion, soldier. Some might even call that stupid too."

Leander snorted, and she felt his rumble of amusement through his warm scales.

Bert shook his head and had to stare straight ahead to gather his thoughts again. "Here's the deal, Raven Alby. You and your dragon follow me and mine and do exactly as I say until we get to Azerad, with no more fancy tricks and no more showing off. Beyond how very sad it would be to see a student of Fowler Academy fall out of the sky on my watch before the Tournament of Mages even started, it would bury me in reports and guard duty outside some governor's bedchamber for the next six months. I'm sure you don't care about the latter, but neither of us wants the former either."

"This isn't my first time flying," she called in response. Her smile widened when Evelyn turned her head to fix the young mage with icy silver-blue eyes. *They have no idea what to think of us.* "And it's not our first time flying without all that gear either. And look how much time we saved already."

The man sighed with frustration through loose lips and shook his head again. "I don't want any more surprises either, understand?"

"Don't worry. You'll escort us safely into Azerad in no time. And if anyone asks, I'll make sure to tell them how cheerful and accommodating you were."

Running his tongue around the inside of his mouth again—this time in irritation—the man lifted Evelyn's reins gently and called loudly enough for the young mage to hear, "Stay close. This isn't a flight over Brighton to your grandfather's ranch."

"Excellent."

He gave the reins a little flick and the blue dragon banked her wings to turn a little farther to the north.

Leander followed suit with perfect timing. Raven gave the other rider a sidelong glance, then lifted the apple in her hand and took a huge, crunching bite. *It's a nice day for a ride. This'll be fun.*

They stopped only once about three hours later. Bert pointed to a huge, empty pasture coming up on their right. It was located about a quarter of a mile east of the main road they'd followed northeast for the last hour and a half. "It's time to take a break."

"Already?" She turned to him and grinned.

The man nodded at the pasture and didn't look anywhere near pleased about it. "We're landing. If you two aren't on the ground with us inside a minute, you can find your own damn way to Azerad from here. Evelyn holds the second-highest record for speed in Lomberdoon's Third

Division Fleet. You wouldn't be able to catch up to us if you tried."

Raven raised her hands in surrender. "I'm not trying to argue with you. We'll land, no problem."

"Good." Bert and Evelyn descended immediately from their high altitude and turned right as they passed beneath Leander and his young mage.

"Go ahead and—"

"I know." Leander soared a few more seconds, then curved his long neck to look at her. "I would catch up to them."

"Of course you would. Even if you didn't try." She patted his scaly hide. "Go on."

The great red dragon wheeled in a tight circle as he dove so they joined their escort in the pasture coming in from the north. Bert didn't dismount until he saw all four of Leander's massive clawed feet land gracefully in the short grass. Satisfied, he swung his leg over the saddle and dropped to the ground. "Half an hour. The dragons get a rest and we get to stretch our legs."

"It sounds good to me." Raven stood on Leander's back before she vaulted nimbly into the grass. She brushed her hand along his shoulder and muttered, "How are you doing?"

"I could've kept going."

"I know. I think the break was more for them." She nodded toward Bert, who swiftly and deftly undid the girdle on his dragon's saddle and slid it easily from Evelyn's back. "They also flew out to meet us and must've left in the middle of the night if they came from as far as Azerad. Or farther."

"They look fine to me."

Evelyn stretched her wings slowly while her rider slipped a lead over her neck before he stroked her muzzle. The lead was incredibly long, and the blue dragon barely seemed to notice.

"Except for that, maybe." His tone rumbled with disapproval.

Raven nodded. "We're definitely the outliers when it comes to the kind of training you've had and how much we trust each other."

The red dragon sighed in exasperation. "I'm going for a walk."

"Yeah, okay."

Leander nudged the young mage in the back of her shoulder, which made her laugh as he stalked past her across the short grass, his tail weaving from side to side behind him.

She exhaled a heavy breath and moved toward Bert and Evelyn. "Is there anything we're supposed to do while we're here?"

"Rest, mostly." The man turned his head slowly to follow the red dragon's slow meander across the pasture. "Does he get to do that often?"

"As often as he likes. We have an understanding."

"Huh."

Ignoring the humans' conversation, Evelyn pawed the ground a few times before she turned in a slow circle and curled a few yards away from her rider.

Raven smiled at the glistening blue scales running in darker tones along the raised ridges down Evelyn's back.

That's the general shape of a dragon resting, all right. "How long have you two been flying together?"

"A little over two years. It took a lot of time and patience to get where we are—" Bert realized who he was talking to and the fact that Raven and Leander most definitely had not been flying together for even a quarter of that time. "I bet the magic helps make a connection with that dragon of yours, huh?"

"Actually, being a mage only had a tiny bit to do with it. You can't train a dragon with magic, that's for sure."

"Hmm. Where did you—"

The clop of dozens of hooves above the rolling rumble and creak of slowly turning wheels carried toward them from the main road. The man walked closer, left yards of slack in his dragon's lead, and peered through the opening in the trees.

"Is everything okay?"

The man cocked his head. "It sounds like the military to me."

"What?" Raven stepped beside him and waited for whoever it was to come into view.

The noise of the large military caravan preceded the actual party itself by a few minutes. Eventually, an entire contingent of officers on horseback, drawn wagons, soldiers marching on foot, and a few pack animals made their slow, steady way down the road, heading south.

A few of the horses snorted when they sensed the two dragons close by, but they were trained well enough to not act on their surprise. "That's a large number of soldiers," she commented.

Bert nodded. "And supplies."

"Are they sending more down to the wall south of Brighton? That hole's been there for three weeks and hadn't been touched the last time I saw it."

"Maybe." The man scratched his chin and inclined his head thoughtfully. "Mostly, they're going around to make sure everyone's doing what they're supposed to be doing. It can't be too safe when there's a giant hole in the wall and raiders on the loose."

Raven forgot about the long, loud caravan of troops sent from one city or another—maybe even the capital itself—and turned to stare at him. "So there are raiders."

He darted her a sidelong glance. "There are always raiders. This is only a precaution."

"It looks like a very big precaution to me."

Bert smirked and gave her a small, apathetic shrug. "It's a very big hole in the wall."

CHAPTER TWENTY-EIGHT

The half-hour passed faster than Raven expected and she and Bert mounted their dragons and took to the sky for the second half of their journey. The man didn't say another word about her decision to ride without a saddle, and Leander didn't make any more challenging comments, whether or not their escort could hear him.

They flew high over rolling hills and swaths of dark, thick forests. A wide, swiftly rushing river crossed their path below and churned with white foam as the ground rose in altitude and became a little rockier. To the east, Raven caught a glimpse of an encampment of brightly colored tents erected beside one of the rockier, more jagged faces of the Mountains of Jared. The range cut much farther west than she'd thought, but this was the farthest away from Brighton she'd ever been.

Things are different the farther north we go. Even the mountains.

At midday, they reached the outskirts of Azerad and the smaller homesteads set up along the city's outer border. It looked very much like Brighton until she looked ahead of them and saw the rising spires and raised tiers in well-manicured circles ringing the five massive towers at the center of the city. Azerad had its own wall as well, but even from that high, it was obviously much lower than the great wall around all of Lomberdoon.

I could climb it in two moves.

"This is where you two need to pay attention," Bert called beside them. "Things can get a little dicey with the traffic in and out of the city so stay close. It's easier to get distracted up here with all the people and the noise but we're heading directly to the stables first."

"It's only for dragons, right?"

The man gave her a pert smile and nodded. "There's a whole level only for dragons. You'll be fine as long as you follow my lead."

Raven nodded and patted the base of Leander's neck. "We're almost there."

"It smells like we're there already."

A few minutes later, they followed Bert and Evelyn over wide stone walkways laid through the city center. Buildings were everywhere, those in the residential quarter crammed so tightly together she could hardly see the stone streets between the long rows of houses. The marketplace looked a little more spread out, but the best part was the wide, sweeping terraces that jutted in multiple levels around the center group of fantastically high towers.

"Those have to be twice the size of the tallest tower at Fowler. Maybe three times." Raven looked over her shoulder as Leander wheeled past the tall structures on Evelyn's heels. She glanced directly below them and noticed that the terraces were a complicated network of paths leading into meticulously manicured gardens of various shapes, sizes, and bursting colors. "This is beautiful."

"There's no natural space," Leander muttered.

"Which is why they have the gardens, I bet."

They passed over the curving verandas and followed their escort to a higher level of jutting terraces behind the main group of towers in the center of the city. In front of them, Bert leaned sideways a little and pointed at one of these levels before his dragon descended toward it to land.

"And there are dragon stables," she added. Her eyes widened as they descended behind Evelyn. "With many more dragons than I expected."

Before they landed, the air filled with snorts and scratching and a few shrieks from the other dragons who interacted with each other and their trainers and even the few soldiers who'd been selected to fly with a dragon as sentries over the kingdom.

Leander landed swiftly beside the blue dragon as Bert dismounted and kept his hand firmly around the reins of her harness. Raven stayed where she was for a few seconds to take in the two long rows of dragon stables down the center of the terrace. When she saw a thin, gruff-looking man move toward them with a scowl, she leapt quickly off the red dragon's back and stood beside him with a hand planted firmly on the warm scales of his muscular shoulder. "Try to be nice. Or at the very least, try not to be frustrating. No one looks all that happy to see us."

"It's better if I don't say anything at all, then," her dragon replied with a snort.

"Yeah, that might be the best option."

The scowling man gave Raven and her unsaddled dragon a thorough study, his nostrils flaring, before his gaze veered toward Bert. "What is this?"

"The student from Fowler Academy and her dragon," the man replied flatly.

"I see a child standing beside a huge red beast without a single piece of tack—no saddle, no halter, and not even a lead. What the hell am I supposed to do with that?"

"You don't have to do anything," Raven said, stepped toward the man, and extended her hand. "Raven Alby. This is my dragon familiar Leander."

He glanced briefly at her hand and his mouth twitched into an irritated sneer before it morphed into a scowl again. "Did you ride from Brighton bareback like that?"

"Absolutely." She grinned and kept her hand extended for that handshake. *I won't back down from this. If I do, I would be simply a child with a dragon.*

Bert darted the young mage a sympathetic frown. "Raven Alby, this is Marcus Ferth, dragon stablemaster."

When Marcus realized the introductions had been formally made, he stepped toward Raven with a grunt and took her outstretched hand. It was a limp shake and more of a quick grab before he practically flung her hand out of his. "We have a stall set up for that dragon of yours, girl. Whatever you're trying to prove by flying bareback, I don't want anything to do with it. I know I have an extra lead around here somewhere—"

Leander snorted and shook his head vigorously before he drew it back and away from Raven and the stablemaster.

She didn't have to look at him to know what he was thinking. "No lead, Marcus. I'll take care of it, thanks."

"No lead?" The man's scowl intensified and he aimed it at Bert. "How the hell am I supposed to get that big red where he belongs without any way to control him?"

The soldier's mouth dropped open, and the young mage stepped toward Marcus Ferth while she fought to not clench her hands into fists. "You don't need a way to control him and we won't need any leads. I appreciate you setting a place up for Leander while we're here but beyond that, I'll take care of the rest of it."

"No, you will not." Marcus tapped his chest. "My stables means my responsibility. You're a student from Fowler, which means you have enough of your own situating to get done. A guard is waiting to show you out of here and to wherever you're supposed to be so get going."

A low, rumbling growl rose from Leander's throat. Most of it was covered by the sounds of other shrieking, stamping, snorting dragons and a few of their voices in soft conversation, but it was loud enough for both men to hear. The stablemaster glanced at the red dragon and pursed his lips.

"I won't simply leave Leander here without making sure he has what he needs." Raven fixed Marcus with a determined expression and waited for him to look at her. "That's a promise I made him, and you won't have to worry about a dragon who doesn't use a lead. Trust me, you don't even want to try to put one of those on my dragon."

He raised an eyebrow. Behind Bert, a soft hum of curiosity rose from Evelyn and she tilted her dazzling blue head to study the young mage.

"Fine." The stablemaster nodded at Bert. "You know the routine, man. I'll leave you to see to yours."

"Much appreciated." The soldier led Evelyn away by the reins of her harness. When they passed Raven and Leander, he stopped and gave the young mage a brief nod. "You didn't make me regret it, mage. I'll give you that much."

"Thanks for the escort."

He glanced at her dragon, nodded, and led Evelyn down the wide avenue between the two long lines of stables.

"Hurry up, then," Marcus grunted. "I have more than my fair share of work for the next few days before this damn Tournament of Mages. Let's go."

Raven glanced at Leander and nodded. The huge dragon lowered his head until it hovered over her shoulder again and muttered, "Thank you."

"You don't have to thank me at all." She winked. "And you're welcome. Ready?"

Her familiar snorted in reply and they followed the man quickly down the rows of stables and away from the walkways that connected the dragon terrace to the main buildings and the towers of Azerad. Dragons of every size and color peered at them from their stalls, which had enough room for a fully grown beast to turn in a few circles, lie down, stand, or take a few steps and not much else. Raven and Leander both heard the conversation rising behind them, and it came directly from the other dragons.

"Nothing. Not even a lead."

"What did that girl do to him?"

"I smell…what is that?"

Raven put her hand on Leander's shoulder to comfort

them both. *We've always stood out. Now it's even more obvious. Still, it's not a problem.*

Marcus led them to the end of the stables and gestured to an empty stall on the left. "This one's been set aside for you." The man studied Leander intently and sighed. "I was given specific instructions so your familiar has the largest pen on the end with a decent view and only one neighbor. It was cleaned yesterday and should be fine."

"Thank you."

"Does he eat dragon feed too or do you have him on some kinda special—"

"Dragon feed." She nodded and hoped Leander took the hint to not start making jokes about eating only large barn-yard animals and the occasional stablemaster. "I can come out here to see him whenever I want, right?"

"Yep." The man scratched his head. "I heard about that too. As long as you don't try anything funny with the other dragons in my stable, I wouldn't care if you climbed into that stall with him and stayed the night. Is that it?"

"Yeah, I think we're set." She gave him a grateful smile.

The stablemaster glanced at Leander, shook his head, and hurried away through the stables again, muttering about little girls with no concern for the right way to train a dragon.

"Well, it looks like this is it." Raven stepped toward the stall door and pulled it open swiftly. *This is smaller than the pen at Moss Ranch.* She turned to look at her familiar's glowing yellow eyes and shrugged. "It's only a week."

"And I'll be out most of the day once the matches start." The way he said it sounded like he was trying to reassure his mage instead of the other way around.

"Exactly. And I'll be here as often as I can. I don't know what the tournament is gonna take or even what I'm supposed to spend the rest of my time here doing. But morning and night, at the very least, I'll be here."

"And I'll be fine." Leander ambled into the largest dragon stall at the end, which at least had enough room for him to turn and face her as she closed the door gently between them. He sniffed the air and poked his head out of the stall to look down the long lines of stables, both of which were mostly full.

"Is there anything else I can get you?"

The dragon's head swiveled toward her. "Not while we're here."

"Okay. But so we're on the same page, I'm getting kind of a nervous vibe from you. It makes sense but if I can help, I will."

"I'm not nervous, Raven." The dragon withdrew his head into the stall so he couldn't be seen unless someone stood directly in front of him. "I've been alone on a ranch, separated from the other dragons without a clan. I prefer being alone at your school. This is—"

"Definitely different."

"There are at least two dozen beasts in here, little girl, all of them so close to each other and still alone. I'm the only one who hasn't had the dragon trained out of me."

Raven glanced quickly down the line of enclosures and stepped closer to the stall door. "Careful. That might not make you any new friends."

"I'm not here to make friends, Raven."

"Right. Neither of us is here to make enemies, either."

Leander snorted. "Enemies are at opposing ends of the same abilities. I won't have any here."

She released a slow, quiet sigh and couldn't help but chuckle. "I think you might be right. If I'm not back here any earlier, you're the last stop I'll make before I turn in for the day. I promise."

"I know." The great red dragon poked his head out over the top of the stall door enough for her to hold his huge head in both hands and press her cheek against the side of his powerful jaw.

"We have a real chance at this competition to make waves, Leander, and open our options. Thank you for coming with me."

"If I have nothing to thank you for, dragon rider, neither do you."

Raven stroked his long neck as far as she could reach and gave it a little pat. "Fair enough. See you soon."

"Indeed."

The young mage stepped away from her familiar's stall, gave him a little wave, and turned to stride down the avenue between the stables. She had to crane her neck to see the top of the tallest tower in the sky ahead of her. *He'll be fine and I'll know if he's not.*

Dragons, soldiers, stable hands, and trainers passed her with only brief glances and a few nods as she made her way toward the walkways off the dragon terrace. Most of the people efficiently going about their business didn't notice a redheaded teenager walking alone through the organized chaos. The dragons, though, turned to watch her as she passed.

It feels exactly like the first time I stepped onto a field full of dragons. Only those couldn't fly and these are all trained into obedience.

Marcus turned toward her from where he'd snapped orders at a few boys around her age and pointed toward the walkways. "The guard with the green badge on his chest. Don't keep him waiting."

"Thanks." Raven raised her hand to wave at the stable-master, but the man had already focused on more important things. She sighed wearily and rolled her shoulders. "Here we go."

Grandpa would tell me to simply be myself. It's the best advice to follow if it came from my dragon too.

CHAPTER TWENTY-NINE

The guard who guided Raven away from the dragon stables didn't say a single word when she told him who she was. He simply studied her for a moment, scratched the side of his head, and nodded for her to follow.

He took her down a complicated series of walkways and paths carved out among the different levels of over-hanging terraces. They passed one with a massive circular pool, the water as clear and as blue as the spring sky. Once they had moved clear of the bustle of soldiers, incoming visitors, and dragons flying low toward the stables, the guard opened a low gate at the end of one path that was there more for aesthetics than to keep anyone out. They passed the gardens and she was fascinated by the multiple terraced levels bursting with flowers of every color, pruned hedges forming intricate mazes, and flowering orchards.

I need to get back here and into those gardens. She took a deep breath through her nose and sighed. *They'll have the best smell I'll find here, probably.*

Finally, the guard stopped at a large, plain wooden door set in the side of one of the thick stone buildings and pulled it open. He waited for her to step in first, let the door shut behind him, and stepped past her to lead the way again.

"So, what's this building called?" Her voice echoed in the enclosed space. Her newest escort didn't say anything. "I didn't see people out in the gardens. Are they off-limits or is everyone simply busy?"

The man turned the corner and opened another door before he led her up a short staircase.

Raven pressed her lips together and gazed at the clean walls around them. *I guess he has orders to not talk to me too. I wonder why.*

They walked down another corridor lined with smaller wooden doors with brass rings for handles, and the guard stopped at one on the right before he pushed it open. He gestured inside and when she caught up with him, he stepped across the hallway and clasped his hands behind his back.

"Oh, wow." The young mage peered into the opulently decorated room with an empty fireplace, finely woven rugs across the stone floors, two armchairs, two writing desks on either side of the room, a small washbasin in the back, and two beds. She turned toward the guard and raised her eyebrows. "Guest quarters, I'm guessing."

He nodded once but didn't speak.

"For me. Okay. Uh…thank you. This is great."

With another nod, he pivoted swiftly and marched down the hallway to attend to his next duty.

Raven chuckled in genuine confusion and shook her head. "It wasn't something I said, I don't think, but he got his point across just fine."

She stepped into the lavish room and pushed the door closed gently with a soft thump. In the silence, she turned and gave herself a minute to explore. "Two beds. I bet I can guess who Headmaster Flynn told them to put in the same room with me."

That made her laugh again, and she moved toward the bed on the left side of the huge room. *Sharing a room with Bella won't be that bad. We've both changed a little since the first day of mage school.*

As soon as she sat on the soft, delicately embroidered comforter and considered the fluffy-looking pillows with a heavy sigh, a swift, sharp series of knocks came from the door.

"Oh. Um, come in?"

It opened and a woman maybe ten years older than her wearing a smart plain uniform and a crisp apron pushed a narrow cart into the guest room. "Afternoon."

"Hi." Raven grinned at the woman with ruddy cheeks, hazel eyes, and plain brown hair twisted into a bun on top of her head.

"I've brought food for you, miss, if you're hungry."

"Yeah, actually." She pushed off the bed and crossed to the woman and the narrow wooden cart on wheels. "Now that you mention it, the only thing I've eaten today is an apple."

"Oh." Her eyes widened. "And you traveled all this way on an apple?"

"Well, no." The young mage chuckled. "I traveled on a dragon."

For a second, the woman looked entirely confused until she caught the joke, allowed herself a sharp laugh of surprise, and shook her head. "I heard you were the student from Fowler with the dragon familiar, miss. No one said a thing about your sense of humor."

"Honestly, you're the first person who's given me a chance to use it. And you can call me Raven."

"Very well, Miss Raven."

She chuckled. "Honestly. Only Raven is fine. What's your name?"

The woman lowered her gaze with a soft smile and shut the door behind her gently before she rested both hands on the handle of the cart again. "Jocelyn, Mi—Raven."

"It's nice to meet you, Jocelyn." She put her hand out, and Jocelyn laughed self-consciously before she took the young mage's hand. It was a brief shake—more like her lightly wiggling the visitor's fingers—and the woman wiped her hands on her apron and pushed the cart toward the armchairs in front of the empty fireplace. *Like she's not supposed to shake hands with anyone. That can't be right.*

"The other students are slowly making their way into the city. Those from Fowler Academy too, but I think they'll be here a few hours later than the rest."

Raven joined the woman at the armchairs and forced herself not to stare at the heaping tray of food revealed beneath the domed lid. "Did something happen?"

Jocelyn looked at her and seemed startled for a moment

before her expression settled. "No. Brighton's much farther from Azerad than the other two cities with mage schools. Fowler Academy's always last to arrive at the Tournament of Mages."

"Oh." Finally, the young mage let herself study the meal in front of her—two chicken thighs, peeled oranges, bread and butter, a bunch of grapes, and tiny bright-red strawberries. "That looks amazing."

"It's only a snack, I'm afraid, but it's enough after a day of traveling."

"Definitely more than enough. Thank you."

The woman dipped a little curtsy and rubbed her hands on her apron again. "Once everyone arrives, you'll be summoned to the opening ceremony in the ballroom. I imagine everything else you need to know will happen there."

"Great. I'll see you then."

"Oh." The woman chuckled with ill-concealed embarrassment. "No, I only serve the food. Someone else will come to take you where you need to go."

Raven stared at her, then smiled because she couldn't immediately think of anything to say. "Sounds good."

"Is there anything you need while I'm here?"

The young mage's stomach growled hungrily and she glanced at it in surprise. "Only something to eat and you already covered that."

Jocelyn laughed again. "I'll let you get to it, then. Welcome to Azerad, Miss Raven. And good luck at the tournament."

"Thanks." With a grin, she waited until the woman had slipped quickly and quietly out of the guest room before she practically threw herself at the cart and the tray of food. She ate one of the chicken thighs in under two minutes. With a handful of orange slices clutched in greasy fingers, she took them with her as she turned and explored the rest of the room.

It's definitely nicer than anything in Brighton. The only guest rooms we have are at the inn, and I don't think they even come close to this.

She caught sight of the two large trunks against the wall, each of them pushed toward either bed to show where they belonged. Raven popped another orange slice into her mouth and sighed. She looked at the pieces in her hand and smiled, then chewed slowly. "I bet they grow these in one of those orchards out there. That's where I really wanna be right now."

After studying the rest of the room—which didn't have any interesting secrets—the young mage sat on the bed she'd claimed, kicked her shoes off, and lay back slowly to sink her head into the pillows. "Okay. I can wait here for a few hours alone and with nothing to do. Man, this bed is nice."

Five minutes after she'd finished the oranges, Raven fell asleep.

The door to the guest room burst open and jolted the young mage from her nap. Raven sat quickly, scowled around a yawn, and tried to remember where she was. Bella Chase stood in the doorway and swept her glance around the room. When she saw her fellow student seated on the bed, she took a deep breath and exhaled a heavy sigh. "Of course."

"Yeah, I'm not surprised, either." She rubbed her eyes and spun her legs to dangle her feet over the side of the bed.

"Excuse me." A man in a navy-blue uniform stepped into the room when the other girl moved aside. He deposited both their bags on the floor barely inside the door and nodded. "Someone else will come to take you to the opening ceremony. Evening."

Without waiting for a reply, he stepped into the hall and pulled the door shut behind him.

Raven frowned. "Have you noticed that everyone here seems to only have one job. Like, forever."

Bella dusted her pants off and gave her a disbelieving glance. "That's how the bigger cities work."

"Really? It kind of seems like a waste. Many of the people I've seen today are capable of doing more than one job."

"Right, but if they don't need to, why do more?" When the girl realized her companion still didn't get it, she laughed and shook her head. "There are way more people in a big city, Raven. If everyone only has one job, they can give jobs to more people. And in a place this big, no one wants to hear that the person who's supposed to serve them dinner was caught up mucking the stables out and is gonna be a little late."

"Huh. Is all that part of your diplomatic-mage plan?"

Bella shrugged. "I read it in *Life of Lomberdoon.*"

"So you read history books in your spare time. I see."

"No, I read current information about what the rest of

the kingdom's like. I told you I'd be prepared for this, didn't I?"

"You sure did. Extra-prepared." Her mouth dry and uncomfortable, Raven stood and crossed the room to the cart near the armchairs. She poured herself a glass of water from the silver pitcher, paused, and offered it to Bella instead.

"Thanks."

She poured herself another and they both stood and drank in silence until their glasses were empty. "How was the trip?"

"Long. Smelly. My butt hurts."

The way she said it drew a laugh.

With a smirk, the girl set her glass on the tray and gave her fellow mage a sidelong glance. "And I had to listen to Daniel and Cooper make crude jokes for almost four hours straight."

"Is that all?"

"Well, Alessandra almost bit their heads off after that. I never thought I'd be grateful to have her around on an all-day road trip."

"She has her uses."

They shared another laugh, and Raven popped another orange into her mouth.

"I need to change." Bella turned toward their bags. "This room doesn't have a bathroom, does it?"

"Nope. There is a washbasin in the back, though."

The girl made a face and dragged her bag to the right-hand bed. "I guess it'll work."

"And then we'll be summoned to the ballroom." Raven

snorted. "Do you have any idea what this opening ceremony's about?"

"It's kind of self-explanatory, isn't it?" Bella set out a fresh set of clothes and changed quickly.

"I guess. I'm ready to get out of this room, though. That's for sure." *And I think I know a little more about how Leander feels.*

CHAPTER THIRTY

Half an hour later, a completely different man arrived to take them to the ballroom. *He looks more like a scholar than a guard. Whatever.*

The two girls followed him quickly down the halls and through a huge maze of corridors and entryways neither mage could fully grasp. Every hallway looked the same, and their escort moved too quickly for them to get their bearings. Finally, he left them in an empty receiving room, bowed, and disappeared. The doors on one side of the room were propped open to admit a little light and a fresh, cool breeze.

Raven sighed and took a deep breath.

Her companion frowned. "This is not a ballroom."

From the hall on the other side, two more Azerad employees led Anika, Cooper, Daniel, and Alessandra into the receiving room. The students nodded at each other but weren't given a chance to say anything before one of the escorts cleared his throat.

"They're waiting for you inside." He turned the handles on the second set of double doors and pushed them into the massive room beyond. With a bow, he stepped away from the group and into another hall.

All the sound from the ballroom spilled into the receiving room—polite conversation, laughter, clinking glasses, and hurried footsteps. The room was full of people, most of them dressed far more formally than anyone had bothered to tell the students from Fowler Academy.

"This is night one," Alessandra muttered and straightened her fresh change of clothes. The woman looked stoic and unapproachable in a white riding shirt, black jacket, and straight gray pants. "Your job is to mingle with the other students. All of you. Mandrose Academy on the right, the Ziel Institute on the left. They'll only stay that way if you don't start playing nice and at least pretend like you're making friends before you kick their asses in the tournament. Go on."

The students shared hesitant glances, and Raven leaned toward Bella. "It's not much of a pep talk."

"She wasn't trying to encourage us. That was more of an order."

The girls smirked and stepped into the ballroom together. Cooper, Daniel, and Anika followed closely, and the veteran war mage smacked her lips. "As long as they don't embarrass themselves tonight, we'll be fine."

There is no way I can remember all these names after only one night. A little later, Raven tried not to let her gaze wander as the short, muscular second-year from Ziel Institute rambled on and on about an award he'd won. It might have had something to do with mage school, but he spoke so quickly, it was almost impossible to identify one word from the other.

"And apparently, it earned me a place in the tournament here in Azerad. Can you believe that?"

"Wow." She plastered a polite smile in place.

"Yeah, it's great. I might—"

"I didn't do anything to get here," Daniel Smith interjected, stepped toward Raven, and shrugged at the short kid.

"Ha, ha. Nice try." The other student poked his own chest with his thumb. "I've practiced for this competition my whole life. I always wanted it. Now, I'm here."

"That's cool."

Raven gave Daniel a sideways glance and wanted to roll her eyes. *Here we go again. And he's avoiding me while standing right there.*

"Yeah, it's way cool." The short kid stuck his hand out. "What was your name again?"

"Daniel Smith."

"Terry Monart."

They shook, and Daniel ran a hand through his dark hair. "I'm serious, though. Awards and stuff are cool, but I was honestly surprised when our headmaster called my name out to be here this year. It's not really my thing."

"Well, you must've done something. They don't let simply anyone compete in these events."

She turned her head and noticed Bella listening intently to a boy and girl beside Cooper, her eyes narrowed as she nodded slowly and took in every word. The other students were grinning. *Bella looks like she's stockpiling things to use against them.*

Now that her attention was no longer required, she started to turn away from the conversation she didn't find interesting in the least but Daniel stopped her.

"Not like Raven, though. She's done more than any of us will in the next couple of decades, probably."

She glanced at him over her shoulder and smiled. "Not really. I'm merely being myself."

"Oh, come on." He caught her shoulders and guided her back to the conversation. "Go on. Tell Terry about your familiar."

The other boy's eyes widened and she wanted to laugh at the way he had to look up, even at her. "Are you the one with the dragon familiar?"

With a tiny smile, she raised her hand and shrugged. "Guilty. Excuse me."

"Wait, wait, wait. Don't go yet." For the first time in weeks, Daniel looked her in the eye and flashed his brilliant smile as he nodded in encouragement. "You gotta tell them what happened with the dragon trials."

"We only—"

"Hold on." Terry turned to the other students from Mandrose Academy and shouted, "Hey, you guys! It's the dragon rider. You gotta come hear this!"

The three other boys and one girl didn't waste time but scurried toward them to listen to Raven Alby's grand tales of how she mastered an obstinate dragon and made him her familiar, all as a first-year mage student.

She shook her head. *I gotta out of this.* "It's not all that exciting."

"Naw, she doesn't wanna make the rest of you guys feel bad," Daniel added.

"Did you really find your dragon in the wild and command him right there as your familiar?" The girl with huge brown eyes and a short bob stared eagerly at her.

"What?" Raven laughed. "That's not what happened."

"Told you." Terry nudged the girl's shoulder and rolled his eyes. "She stole an egg and raised that dragon from day one."

"Nope. Wrong again." She glanced at Daniel, who chuckled and gave her a quick shrug. "I don't know where the heck you guys hear this stuff."

"Uh...everywhere?" one of the other boys told her.

"Well then, everyone has things all mixed up."

"Go ahead and tell 'em, Raven." Daniel nodded and turned toward the other kids. "This is seriously the most kickass witch you'll ever meet."

She frowned, not quite sure why her fellow student had initiated this. "Okay, I'm only gonna tell this once. My friend's dad owns a dragon ranch in Brighton. He told me about a stubborn dragon he had to pen alone because he couldn't train him. The dragon trials were coming up, Leander had to go through them, and if he failed, he'd have his wings clipped."

"That's your dragon? Leander?"

"Yeah. He came with me too."

A round of startled gasps and awed whispers came from the students gathered around her, their numbers swelled by two more kids from the Ziel Institute.

"So, what? You're a better dragon trainer than the dragon trainer?"

"Not really."

"Did you have to use magic?"

"No."

"I bet she used a whip. My cousin's friend trains dragons and says the only way to train 'em is to give 'em a good—"

"Okay, stop!" Raven's voice echoed a little in their area of the ballroom, but the conversation from all the adults continued as usual. The young mage glanced at Bella and the other two kids from the Ziel Institute. The dark-haired mage glared at her now and only partially paid attention to the other students' animated discussion. *Great.* "Look, I spent a ton of time with Leander. I had to forget about what I wanted so I could earn his trust. We became friends first, I helped him pass the trials, and then I asked him to be my familiar."

"Technically, they didn't even go to the trials," Daniel added with a smirk and puffed his chest with pride. "They went to the competition in Nadine and won first place so they skipped the trials completely."

"It worked out," she muttered. *It's so like Daniel to talk me up when I simply wanna get out of this conversation.*

"I heard you fly your dragon without a saddle or harness or anything," one of the other students added.

Raven opened her mouth to reply, but Daniel cut her off and pointed at the kid who'd spoken. "No, that part's true. Wait until you see her do it in person. It's the best thing you've ever seen."

"How is that even possible?"

"Won't you fall?"

"If you can't control a dragon with a saddle and reins, how do you make sure he won't throw you off?"

"I need water," she murmured with a tight smile.

She turned away and moved as quickly as she could across the polished ballroom floors toward the banquet tables lined against the opposite wall. *I think there's a new Swarm in the kingdom. Mage students and their dragon questions.*

A round of laughter exploded behind her before Daniel shouted, "Raven! Wait up!"

Oh, boy. She stopped a few feet away from the tables set with more food than she could imagine, but he had to walk around her so they could look at each other.

"Is everything okay?" he asked.

"Yeah, but I needed a break from that."

"From what?" His smile didn't waver at all and he looked over the top of her head at the other students who now no doubt created even more rumors about Raven Alby and her dragon. "They're totally impressed—and intimidated. That'll help when the matches start."

She folded her arms and waited for him to look at her. When he saw her raised eyebrow, he frowned and returned her stare a little warily. "What?"

"We have a few other things to talk about, don't we?"

"Uh…" He chuckled and ran his hand through his hair again. "I'm not sure what you're talking about."

"We can start with the part where you told everyone at Fowler that we made out before the spring gala."

He gulped.

"And then there's the fact that you've avoided me completely since that night. I wouldn't mind if I didn't know that you tried to hide so I wouldn't call you out on it. Now, I'm beginning to think you're trying to make up for it by painting a ridiculously inflated image of me right before the Tournament of Mages, which I don't need anyone to do for me, either. Put it all together, and it feels like you're using me to make yourself look better."

Daniel's mouth had fallen open as she spoke and he gaped at her for a few seconds. Finally, he shut his mouth, laughed, and scratched the side of his head. "I guess you got me."

"I think so, yeah. And I think we should probably clear this up right now before it goes on any longer."

"Yeah…" With a shrug, he leaned toward her and tilted his head. "Look, I'm sorry. I…uh, I say weird things when I don't know what else to say. I like you, Raven, so can we please…start over?"

She pressed her lips together and studied his sheepish smile and the concerned frown that dragged his eyebrows together. *At least he's not trying to deny it.* "I don't know what to start over with, Daniel. We never started anything in the first place."

"Well, almost, right?"

Biting her bottom lip, Raven took a deep breath. "Maybe. I don't know. You asked me to the gala and I left halfway through to save the school from the Swarm, so—"

A laugh burst from him, and he shook his head. "Man, that sounds as crazy as all the other rumors about your dragon."

"Yeah, but that one actually happened." She couldn't help but laugh with him. Daniel seemed to run out of things to say as he stared awkwardly at nothing in the loud, bustling ballroom. *He's trying, though.* "Okay."

"Okay?"

"Before you say weird things, okay. We can start over. I'm not sure what that means, but I'm willing to forget the whole kissing rumor and the fact that you've run away every time you've seen me in the last few weeks. But don't keep doing either of those things, all right?"

The second-year's flashing grin returned with full force and his blue eyes twinkled. "Cool."

Raven snorted a laugh. "Yeah."

He leaned toward her like he used to before their interrupted date, and she leaned away a little and flashed him a quick look that stopped him coming closer. "That makes me feel much better. And I'm sorry."

"Apology accepted." She smiled in response. "So about—"

"Attention! Attention, please, everyone!" A thin man with wiry shoulders stood at the very back of the ballroom with a crystal glass in hand and clinked a silver knife against it until the room fell silent. His wiry gray hair fluttered around his head when he turned it to gaze at the mingling guests.

"Mages, dignitaries, professors, students, honored guests, and whoever else my wife invited," the man called. The adults chuckled politely, and the man offered them all a thin smile. "First, allow me to welcome you to Azerad, home of the Tournament of Mages this year."

A few students in the back cheered and quickly fell silent.

"I'd like to give a special thanks to these esteemed

guests with us tonight." He gestured toward a group of people who stood off to the side, all of whom looked politely bored with the whole affair. Each nodded in acknowledgment when he listed their names one by one, where they came from, and how they were important.

Raven closed her eyes. *Don't fall asleep. I seriously wish Henry and Murphy were here with me. At least we'd find something interesting to talk about while this guy blabs on.* She almost jumped when he clapped and the loud crack echoed through the marble-floored ballroom.

"Now, this next address is for the students participating in this week's competition. We're honored to have you here for the Tournament of Mages. You've all looked forward to this, I know, but before we begin, I want to offer young, impressionable minds the opportunity to learn about Azerad and all it has to offer. Tomorrow is for you to do with as you will. Stay in your rooms, explore the city, and eat as much of our renowned cooks' meals as you can."

A stout man with a huge belly beside the banquet tables lifted a heel of bread from his mouth and cheered.

"Excellent," the speaker continued with a smirk. "Feel free to move about the governor's estate as much as you like. Please remember that if guards are posted anywhere, that means you're not allowed entry."

The man laughed for the first time at one of his jokes and a fair number of the adults joined him. Raven glanced at Daniel, who laughed a little too but looked completely confused.

"That concludes the announcements for the opening ceremony. Friends, guests, and competitors, may I extend

Governor Irlish's warm greetings to you all. Enjoy the rest of your stay in Azerad." He vanished into the crowd and the conversation picked up where it had left off. From somewhere on the left side of the ballroom, a four-string quartet struck a lively tune that sounded more like Professor Fellows' magical band at the gala than something that belonged in a ballroom like this.

Daniel turned toward Raven and grinned as, predictably, he leaned toward her again and into her personal space. "Are you hungry?"

It's funny how many times he's asked me that. "Um…" She glanced around the ballroom and realized that the students from Mandrose Academy watched her intently. *Like they're about to pounce and make me answer their questions.*

She darted him a hasty, distracted smile. "Not really. I ate before we were brought here."

"Okay. Well, anything else you wanna—"

"I think I'm gonna head to my room and get a good night's sleep."

"Yeah, awesome beds, right?"

"Sure." She moved away from him toward the double doors into the receiving room. "See you tomorrow."

"Bye, Raven." Daniel Smith grinned after her and she felt his gaze on her back the entire time. *It might've been simpler if he continued to avoid me the whole time.*

Alessandra stepped in front of her before Raven reached the ballroom entrance. "What's going on?"

"I'm tired." She kept her expression neutral. "The ceremony's over, right?"

The veteran war mage studied her with an unreadable expression, then shrugged. "I wish I could slip out unnoticed like that but there are…expectations. Someone out there should be able to take you where you wanna go. Resting is a good idea, Miss Alby." The woman pointed at Raven and almost winked. "Get ready for the big matches."

"Definitely. Thanks." She stepped through the doors and into the receiving room. *This will be an interesting week.*

CHAPTER THIRTY-ONE

As her trainer had said, one of the hired guides in the hallways out of the receiving room was more than willing to show Raven through the governor's estate—that looked more like a castle, she'd long since decided. This time, she was led directly outside to walk the pathway that curved in a wide circle around the base of the city's center. Access pathways to all the different terraces branched off every dozen yards or so.

"It's much easier to get somewhere if you go outside first, isn't it?"

"I can't rightly say, miss." Her guide looked about the same age as Jocelyn. "I know those hallways inside as well as I know these paths out here. But it is a good deal easier to see where you want to go and how to get there when you don't stare down a tunnel walled in on both sides."

"That's what I thought."

It took them ten minutes to wind their way around the outside of the building before they climbed a staircase to the upper level. "The stables are directly ahead. I'm happy to take you the rest of the way if you like."

"It's a straight walk, right?"

"It is."

"I can handle it from here. Thank you."

"'Night, miss." The man bowed and spun smartly to return to his post.

Raven wrinkled her nose and muttered under her breath as she passed the other branching terraces and continued to the stables. "Miss and bowing and a different person for everything. They have a weird way of doing things."

When she reached the dragon terrace, the entire row of stables on her right was illuminated by the sunset and those on the left were cast in their own shadow. She stepped onto the platform, walked down the wide avenue in the center, and gazed politely at a few dragons who poked their heads out of the stalls. *Politely but don't stare. It's kinda weird that no one else is out here right now.*

"You're a mage," one slender green female muttered on her right.

The young mage inclined her head. "Hello."

"I saw you come in on that red," a male honked on her right. His startlingly un-dragon-like voice almost made her laugh but she forced it down.

"Yep. That was me. His name's Leander."

"I'm called Jethro."

"Anansi."

"Malechi."

A few more dragons called their names out as she passed their stalls, although most of the few dozen beasts remained silent. They all watched her with the same intensity, however. She merely nodded, smiled, and muttered, "Hello," and "Nice to meet you."

A massive brown dragon knocked against the door of his stall and grunted as he stared at her with glowing yellow eyes.

"Mm-hmm." Raven nodded and increased her pace until she reached the end of the stables.

"This is sooner than I expected," Leander rumbled from inside the last stall.

When she stepped to the shoulder-height door that penned him in, she found her dragon familiar curled in his usual ball against the back of the stall.

"Me too, actually." She unlatched the door and slipped inside with him before she closed it firmly again behind her. "I honestly thought this trip was supposed to be more exciting."

"And so far, it is not." He raised his head a little to look at her, then lowered it onto his forepaws.

"So far, yeah." The young mage settled beside him with her back against the dragon's side. "We'll see what happens. Hey, at least you get a nice view of the sunset from here. Or I guess what's being lit by the sunset."

"More dragons. Hurray for me."

"You know, there are worse things you could be looking at right now."

"Name one."

Raven chuckled. "A group of mage students ogling you."

Leander responded with a low rumble. "True."

"Have you at least talked to any of them?"

He grunted. "Why would I do that?"

"Maybe to say hi. I don't know. It might be cool to hear about where other dragons come from, what they've seen, where they're headed—"

"I don't think any of these dragons are interested in philosophical discussions, Raven."

She turned her head to look at him and his long neck curved inward so he could face her. "Why not?"

"They only want to ask questions about you."

"Huh." A silent laugh rocked her body against his side and she shook her head. "You know, I had the same experience inside that…castle thing. Apparently, there's a rumor going around that I trained you with a whip."

"You were smart enough to realize your mistakes before taking it that far. They clearly know nothing about dragons."

"Right. But that seemed to be the topic of the day. I'd had enough of it."

Leander's sigh was one of long-suffering. "Now you know how I feel about these dragons. None of them are worth sharing what I know about you, Raven."

"That's such a nice thing to say. In a roundabout way."

"You're welcome."

She laughed and rested her head against his side with a huge yawn. "Woah. I don't get it. Half a day of flying and the rest of the day spent doing nothing, basically. I have no idea why I'm this tired. I even took a nap."

"Change, little girl." The dragon shifted on purpose to bump her away from him. "Sleep. I'm not going anywhere."

"Good. Hey, did they feed you yet?"

"Yes." Leander raised his head and tilted it at her, his

eyes narrowed. "My neighbor has disgusting eating habits, even for a dragon."

Laughing, she pushed to her feet and ran her hand along his scaled head when he raised it toward her. "I'm not even gonna ask about that one."

"Yes, I'd prefer that too."

She gave his head a quick hug and another pat, then turned and unlatched the gate. "I'll be back in the morning."

"I know."

Raven turned and forced herself to move quickly down the avenue and back toward the walkways skirting around the towers. *It's harder to leave him in here overnight than anywhere else.*

Once again, the dragons poked their heads out of their stalls, whispered their names, or beckoned the young mage to step closer so they could smell her scent better. She looked straight ahead, reluctant to engage any of them. *That'll only make things harder for him once I'm gone.*

The sounds of dragon voices and huge, shifting bodies in the stalls grew louder. A few of the beasts grunted or snorted. Someone's back leg clawed the rear of their stall. A few dragons uttered soft rumbles of acknowledgment when she passed, and while they were quiet individually, each one added to the rising racket of dragon sounds that followed her down the avenue.

A piercing shriek split the air, followed by Leander's loud roar of, "Quiet!"

The other dragons fell silent immediately, and she smirked as she stepped off the terrace and onto the walkway. *That's my dragon, all right.*

CHAPTER THIRTY-TWO

The next morning, Raven stretched lazily beneath the quilt covering her and mumbled a protest. When she forced her eyes open, early-morning sunlight streamed through the window beyond the foot of her bed. "Woah."

"Look who finally decided to wake up." Bella sat on the edge of her bed, fully dressed, and tied the laces on her boots.

"Yeah, wow. I can't remember the last time I slept this late."

"Probably when we were in the infirmary."

She snorted. "That was different. This is a normal day and I'm not sick or injured."

"Well, I've been up for an hour." The girl stood and pulled the hem of her light sweater down. Behind her, Wesley hopped across the bed his mage had already made neatly and cocked his head at her. "Someone brought breakfast in already. It's near the chairs. I covered it again, but the rolls are probably cold by now."

"You could've woken me for breakfast, you know." She

scratched her head, ran a hand through her sleep-tangled locks, and attempted to brush them out that way.

Bella turned to her and raised an eyebrow. "I tried. You sleep like a rock, you know that?"

Laughing, she nodded. "Yeah, I've been told that once or twice."

"It's impressive. But now that you're up, I guess it saves me from being asked where I was when I get back. I'm not really into leaving notes before I go somewhere, by the way."

"Um..." She rubbed the sleep out of her eyes and yawned. "I wouldn't have expected you to leave a note."

"Good. I saw a shop for spell-enhancing charms on our way in yesterday, and I'm very sure I'll be there for the whole morning if not all day."

"Okay." Slowly, Raven pushed to her feet and shuffled across the room toward the tray of food on the wooden cart. *Sharing a room sure does make her more willing to share her plans.* "Please tell me that's orange juice."

The girl nodded. "It's really good."

"I bet." She took the single full glass on the tray and gulped half of it in one breath. "Wow. That's even better than—"

"The orange juice at Fowler? Yeah. I was a little disappointed to find that out. I thought we were drinking the best at lunch and now there's something even better in a city I won't be able to see again for... well, probably until after we graduate."

"But at least you'll have a whole day at a shop full of... what were they again?" Raven lifted the silver lid on the tray and took one of the rolls first for a huge, hungry bite. *These aren't bad. Can't beat Brighton's, though.*

"Spell-enhancing charms," Bella muttered. "You're not awake yet, are you?"

"I will be after I eat all this. Thanks for saving it for me. There's so much here, though. Are you sure you had enough?"

"I had my own tray, Raven." The girl tilted her head and regarded her with a pert little smile. "Apparently, all we have to do is leave these in the hall when we're done."

"Huh." She glanced at her roll. "Didn't you say you covered it again?"

Bella headed toward the door with a smirk. "I wanted to see if they sent you anything different for breakfast."

She almost choked on her next bite of roll. "Did they?"

"No."

"Oh, hey. This is the perfect time, now that I think about it."

Bella exhaled a heavy sigh and glanced at the ceiling. "Not really. I'm trying to leave."

"Trust me. You'll want to hear this." Raven washed the roll down with more orange juice, then went to her oilskin bag she'd placed on top of the trunk beside her bed. "I've been trying to tell you about these journals, right?"

"Really, Raven? Is it that important right now?"

Once she'd jerked her bag open, she turned to look over her shoulder and raised an eyebrow. "I found a ton of stuff about your mom, so... You tell me."

"Wait, really?" Bella's shallow irritation vanished completely and she took a few steps toward the end of the room before she stopped to look at the door. "What does it say?"

Raven removed the journal she'd been trying to read and held it up. "I don't know."

"Then how do you know my mom—"

"When I found her name, I stopped, okay?" She opened the journal, rifled through the yellowing pages, and located the leather bookmark. "There's a whole list of war mages in here and each of them gets a page or two about everything they did for the kingdom, what they worked on, how they changed things."

"Only a page?"

She laughed. "That's your question? Some of them have one or two. There was even a page about both our moms. They did a lot together."

Bella studied her from head to toe and folded her arms. "That doesn't surprise me, honestly. It would have six months ago but it makes sense now."

"Yeah." Raven carried the book to her companion, her finger in to hold the page. "But actually, both Vanessa Chase and Sarah Alby have more than one or two pages written about them."

When she opened it to the page she wanted and turned the journal, Bella's eyes widened and she swallowed. "You didn't read any of this?"

"Nope. It felt like something you should do first."

The girl's gaze didn't stay on the open journal for more than a few seconds at a time. "We can look at it later, right?"

"Oh, totally. Between matches during the Tournament of Mages."

Bella snorted. "We have all day, Raven. And all night too since we're here for a week. I really want to find this shop."

"Okay. We can look at it later. When you're ready. At least now you know what I've been trying to show you all week."

Making a face at the other mage, Bella took one last glance at the journal and spun away. "That would have been another distraction I didn't need. This week, I have way less to focus on." She opened the door to their guest room and paused. "Thanks for telling me."

"Sure." Raven closed the journal and grinned. "Just make sure that if you find anything about my mom, you'll let me know too."

"Ha. My grandparents weren't war mage dragon riders storing important mage documents for decades. I probably won't find anything."

"Well, it's the thought that counts, right?"

Bella chuckled and raised her eyebrows. "See you later."

"Good luck with the charms."

The door pulled firmly shut and the young mage headed out for her first shopping spree in Azerad. Raven tucked Connor Alby's old journal under her arm and went to the breakfast cart again. When she lifted the lid, the thought of Bella Chase inspecting her private meal made her wrinkle her nose. *She'd better not have licked any of it.*

When she'd finished breakfast and dressed in her plain work clothes—which were still all she had—she slipped out of their guest room and headed down the hall. *I remember how to get to Leander's pen from here.*

Except that when she reached the end of the passageway where she expected to find the wooden door onto the walkway outside, she encountered another hall-way. This one was much wider and had two soldiers stationed outside a huge door on the left. "Huh. I must have gone left one turn too soon."

"Excuse me." A man in dark clothes and a half-cape carrying a thick shoulder bag at his side brushed past her in the hall. Before she could say anything, he shouted, "For Governor Irlish! Urgent message for the governor."

The soldiers glanced at the messenger without a word, and the man pulled a large, folded piece of parchment paper from his bag and waved it around like he thought the guards couldn't see him.

That's the seal from the capital again.

Squinting, she tried to hear the messenger's rushed conversation, but he was so out of breath that the guards probably couldn't hear him, either.

"Go on." One of them nodded for the man to enter.

"Thank you." He disappeared into the room and she decided to stroll casually past to explore a little.

The guards had turned to watch the man they'd let enter. Raven caught a glimpse of an opulent room on the other side of the door lined with bookshelves. Sunlight streamed through a domed glass ceiling to illuminate a huge desk in the center of the room. Behind it sat a man with dark hair and a black mustache. He stood when the messenger approached and accepted the letter with a small frown of confusion.

He doesn't look too happy about that urgent message.

The guards turned and saw the young mage move at a snail's pace past the study. "Keep moving."

They stepped together and blocked her view as the man

behind the desk looked up and saw her there. One of the guards caught the iron rings on both doors and pulled them shut quickly.

She glanced from one to the other and smiled despite the fact that both muscular men stared at her with no expression whatsoever. "What is the quickest way out to the dragon stables?"

One of the men rolled his eyes and gave her curt directions. Both watched her leave.

By the time she finally found her way to the dragon terrace, Marcus the stablemaster was already neck-deep in feeding a few dozen dragons their morning meal. The air was filled with snorts, grunts, and impatient quips from the dragons who grew hungrier by the minute as they waited for their turn to be fed. The man had three other stable hands helping him, but they weren't fast enough for the dragons' liking.

She was halfway toward the end of the stables when Marcus turned, saw her, and held his hand up. "No, no. Not now, mage."

"I'm only coming to check on Leander. I won't get in your way."

"This isn't the time for a little girl to be around a horde of hungry dragons at feeding time, got it? Get on your way. You can come back when things settle a little."

Raven folded her arms and frowned at him. "I won't go near any of the other dragons."

"It doesn't matter. Go on."

She sighed belligerently. *He's not gonna go back to his work until he sees me leave.* "Fine."

"Later. Go on."

She turned, hurried toward the walkway, and turned right like she meant to wander to some other part of the estate. When Marcus and his stable hands returned their full attention to dumping huge sacks of feed into each stall, she darted around the other side of the stables and hurried along the back of it toward the very end.

No one keeps me from my dragon. She reached her destination and poked her head over the little window in the side of his stall, which was apparently only available on either end of the stables. A smile bloomed on her lips when she saw Leander curled tightly in the corner, his eyes closed and his breathing slow and even. *Now I get to sneak up on him.*

The minute she opened her mouth, his eyes snapped open and his gaze settled on her. "I heard you the minute you came around the other side."

Her shoulders sagged as she curled her fingers over the edge of the window. "Damn. I really thought I had you."

"Not today, little girl." He raised his head slowly, glanced through the front of his stall, and turned toward her. "He told you to leave."

"Yeah, I'm not really in the habit of taking orders from grumpy stablemasters who don't understand what you and I have goin' on."

"That's an excellent choice."

"They're making their way down here quite quickly, though. I don't know how long I can stay."

Leander sighed with ill-concealed impatience. "Go if you have to go. I'll be fine."

"You keep saying that." She chuckled softly. "It doesn't stop me from wanting to check in on you. How's it going?"

"The dragons here are very quiet."

Raven fought back a laugh. "It doesn't sound like it to me."

"I don't mean vocally, Raven. They don't have much to say about anything at all other than food and the next time they get to wear a saddle. And you."

"That doesn't seem so bad."

The dragon shifted his hind legs and glanced out the front of his stall again. "They're quiet as if they've been threatened too many times for making natural sounds. For thinking or feeling." He sighed when he saw her confusion. "I'm starting to think your flyboy trainer friend had far more tact than those who trained these dragons. They seem…empty."

"Oh. That doesn't sound very good."

"No."

"Has anyone said anything about you?"

Leander closed his eyes. "I heard two trainers imagining what they'd have to do to me if I broke free and they couldn't use a lead."

"Are you serious? That's ridiculous."

"They had no idea what they were talking about."

Raven grinned at her dragon familiar and nodded. "Of course they don't. Hey, if any of those trainers or other riders try to mess with you, feel free to mess back."

He looked at her again with a rumble in his throat. "I don't need your permission for that, Raven."

"You definitely don't." She peered around the corner of the stable and jerked her head back. "Those guys move fast. I'd better get out of here. It's a good idea to stay out of trouble if I'm gonna represent Fowler Academy while we're here. I'll come back later, okay?"

"Whenever you can. I'll be right here. Sleeping. Counting down the minutes until I get out of here."

"Okay. Breakfast is almost here. Bye, Leander."

He closed his eyes and settled his head on his forepaws again. She ducked around the back of the stables and headed toward the end of the dragon terrace and the walkways that would take her farther into this weird palatial environment everyone called the governor's estate. *I'll have to ask William about dragon-training methods. It sounds like someone might be hitting the train a little too hard or maybe in the wrong ways.*

CHAPTER THIRTY-THREE

It was easy enough to make her way off the estate and into the city itself, where the rest of Azerad's citizens worked, lived, slept, and went about their daily lives. Despite her anticipation, Raven didn't stay out there for long.

"Hi. Excuse me." She smiled at the fourth person who'd actually looked at her when she addressed them. The man scowled at her as they walked toward each other. "I'm looking for this shop that—"

With a grunt, he strode past her and disappeared into the milling crowds along the narrow alleys and streets that wound through the city. From a higher story in one of the long rows of what had to be small homes built on top of each other, someone shouted a long string of profanities. Whoever they yelled at sent a verbal attack in return, and a woman seated in a chair beside a staircase to the stoop looked up and hollered, "Cut it out! We've been listening to your crap all morning!"

She stepped away from that side of the street and

pushed through the crowds. *I've had enough of this. I'd be that cranky too if I was crammed in a city this size with so many other people.*

Only one young mother with a baby on her hip gave the young mage a genuine smile, and when her baby echoed the expression, it gave Raven a chance to take a breath. "Busy morning, huh?"

The mother nodded slowly. "There's always something going on. You're not from here, are you?"

"No." She chuckled. "Brighton, actually."

The woman laughed in surprise and her baby tugged at the strands of long brown hair that peeked out from beneath her mother's cap. "Well, no wonder you look like you've been chased by a bear. Go take a walk through the gardens." She nodded toward the upper-level terraces that stretch over the city marketplace and residential quarter. "Instant peace. I can promise you that."

The young mage gazed at the underside of the terraces, which were plain-looking and had no more decoration than the stone streets beneath her feet. "Anyone can go up there?"

"Whenever they want. As long as they keep the shenanigans down and don't hurt the gardens themselves. Of course, more people would be in those gardens now if it wasn't such a haul up so many stairs."

Smart move, I guess.

"Thank you." Raven made a goofy face at the baby, who laughed and reached for her red hair before she passed them and started toward the central towers. "Have a good one!"

The mother used her child's hand to wave at the

redhaired teenager who darted away from them. She huffed and shook her head. "All the way from Brighton. What's a girl like that got business in Azerad for?"

She took the staircases to the governor's estate two steps at a time until she was about halfway. From that point, she had to pace herself. "Phew. These were much easier going down."

Eventually, she reached the first layer of circular walkways around the central towers and took a minute to catch her breath. She wiped away the stray hair stuck to the sweat on her forehead and cheeks and turned left toward the southwestern group of gardens that jutted from the main buildings like large, round tree branches.

The first garden was filled with rosebushes beginning to blossom with a maze of pathways that wound through the trimmed bushes. She took a deep breath and sighed. "That smell is amazing. There's no shade, though."

The second garden terrace was positioned slightly above the first and looked more promising—small, narrow, neatly trimmed trees meant more for shade and aesthetic than for fruit. *Not an orchard. Definitely shady.*

Raven climbed the last short group of five stairs to the second level and strolled toward the next circular garden hanging over Azerad's bustling life below. A tall arch served as a narrow entrance and the remainder of the attached terrace was blocked off by hedges pruned to look like horses in various action poses. The archway itself was covered in vines and bursting with flowers already for this early in the spring. "Perfect."

She stepped beneath the arch and into an entirely different world. Birds chirped within the thick foliage on tree branches. More pruned hedges—these in the shape of tall birds like storks, herons, and cranes—lined the main footpath leading into the trees. It branched off somewhere in the distance, and she heard the burble of water from a fountain up ahead.

"Yes." She took a deep breath and closed her eyes. "This is—"

"So much quieter?"

Raven's eyes flew open, and she spun to where Daniel Smith stood behind her with his hands in his pockets and grinned.

She regarded him a little cautiously. "Well, I was going to say better, but yeah. Way quieter too."

"And cooler." He chuckled and wiped his forehead as he gazed at all the trees that formed another arch over the walkway. "It's not that hot out yet—unless you're running up endless stairs two at a time."

Her mouth dropped open. "You were watching me?"

"Trying to keep up with you, actually." He scratched his head and stepped toward her. "You're fast, Raven. I'll give you that."

"Compliment accepted." She smirked at him and started walking. The young wizard didn't miss a beat and kept pace beside her as if they'd walked through this garden together for years. "So you're not a big fan of the city down there either, huh?"

"For the most part, no, if I'm honest. It has a few redeeming qualities."

"Oh, yeah? Like what?"

Daniel chuckled. "I found a really good meat pie. The next guy over was selling the same thing but I thought it was better to buy one from the two kids helping their aunt than from the sweaty man next door missing half his hair. On his head, at least."

Raven laughed when the wizard exaggerated a little shudder. "Good choice."

"I thought so. And I found you down there."

She looked quickly at him and raised an eyebrow. "Your pickup lines might need a little work. I'm not part of the city."

"Well, no. But I thought it was a good transition." He gave her his flashing grin and moved closer as they walked. "It's almost impossible to figure out where you're going inside that..."

"Estate?"

He snorted. "I was gonna say weird castle, but yeah."

"It is weird. Everything here is—like the whole city's trying to be something it's not. Or only half of it managed to turn into something different."

Daniel squinted at her and lowered his head. "What do you mean?"

"I don't know. It's simply a feeling." With a shrug, Raven gave him a quick smile and slowed as they approached the fountain in the middle of the garden.

The young mages stopped to stare at the carved figures at the fountain's center. She tilted her head and studied it carefully. "I might be wrong, but that looks like two naked guys doing handstands."

"Uh-huh." His head tilted in the opposite direction. "So those two other streams of water... Those are coming from their—"

"Okay." She clamped her hand around his upper arm to

keep him from saying anything else. "Which way do we go now? Left or right?"

Slowly, he looked at her arm on his bicep and wiggled his eyebrows.

Raven jerked her hand away and looked at him from the corner of her eye. "I have no preference."

"I'll go wherever you want, Raven."

Despite the fact that he sounds like Leander, he's getting much smoother. She couldn't help but smile at that as she nodded to the left and turned in that direction. "It's probably a giant circle, anyway."

"Uh-huh." The young wizard followed with his hands in his pockets and the grin that brought out his dimples.

Raven slowed to let him catch up with her. When he didn't reappear at her side, she turned and almost shouted in surprise. She would have fallen onto the path if he hadn't slipped one arm around her waist, cupped her cheek with the other hand, and drawn her toward him. It didn't play out as well as it could have with her still so off-balance, but the next thing she knew, his lips were on hers. She tried to find her footing, tripped on one of his shoes, and pulled away from him so she wouldn't fall.

"Um…" She stared dumbly at him, then smiled at the ground while she tried to find the right words.

"Sorry." Daniel chuckled and ran a hand through his hair. "Bad timing?"

"Do you mean sneaking up on me for a surprise kiss or, like, my life in general?"

Clearing his throat, he stuffed his hands into his pockets and shrugged. "Both, I guess."

They shared another self-conscious chuckle, and she

nodded. "Okay. First, I'm not a big fan of being snuck up on. Leander's the only one who manages to do it, and he's a dragon, so...I can't hold it against him."

"Huh. I didn't know dragons could be so quiet."

"I didn't either until he started thinking it was hilarious to surprise me like that." Raven shrugged. "And I have a thing about appreciating my personal space."

"You kinda have to make an exception for that when you kiss somebody, though, right?" He stepped toward her and bit his bottom lip as he stared into her eyes.

He's really laying it on thick. It's better to be honest now than be caught up in something I'm not sure I want. I learned that lesson with the gala.

"Well, that leads me to the second half of the bad timing." She took a deep breath and spread her arms apologetically. "I have so much going on right now, you know? This whole Tournament of Mages is only a tiny piece of it. I'm trying to balance all of it at the same time, and I'm not ready to...do anything serious with anyone. Right now."

Raven pressed her lips together and waited for his response. *That was gentle enough.*

Daniel continued to smile and his gaze roamed her face. Finally, he nodded and looked away, his head lowered. "Yeah, okay. I can't expect a girl with her own dragon to have much free time."

She shrugged with a little chuckle. "It's a process."

"I bet. Can we... I mean, we can still hang out, though, right?"

"Sure. We can still hang out."

He leaned toward her again and pulled his hands out of his pockets. "But nothing serious."

"Right. And that has to be good enough." *Is he about to try again?*

Daniel's blue gaze did fall to her lips, but he stopped leaning in and simply said, "Cool."

She laughed at that and covered her mouth. "Yeah. Cool."

The young wizard stepped back and spread his arms with a goofy little bow. "I accept your terms, Raven Alby, as long as you don't stop talking to me completely."

She wrinkled her nose and pointed at him. "You don't have to worry about that. You were the one avoiding me, remember?"

Daniel threw his head back and laughed, and his hands went into his pockets as they began to walk down the curved path again. "That was stupid of me, honestly."

"A little."

"Yeah… Don't worry. I don't make the same mistakes twice."

Raven grinned at him and bumped her shoulder against his. "You know, that's one of my top three rules too."

CHAPTER THIRTY-FOUR

Connor Alby glanced up and down the hall before he slipped out of the guest chambers he'd been given and made his way down the dark corridors beneath King Vaughn's royal chambers. *If I find I've wasted my time on this entire endeavor, I'll— No. I won't give up, will I? I'll keep looking until I find the truth. Or until it finds me.*

He'd memorized the crudely drawn map one of the porters had slipped under the door to his chambers, and he took each turn exactly as instructed. *This is insane. Sneaking around in the king's castle like some teenager headed out to meet a girl in the barn.*

The veteran dragon rider shook his head but kept moving. *Not a girl tonight, though. A woman a little older than my Sarah would be, and she's the only person in this damn city who isn't blinded by a false sense of security.*

Finally, he reached the narrow, unmarked door that could have led to any servants' quarters and opened it quickly to slip into the room beyond. It shut behind him with a soft whisper of wood under layers of dust, and he turned to study a small anteroom that hadn't been touched in decades. Lit torches flickered in iron sconces on the stone walls and cast dancing shadows across every visible space. A plain wooden table stood in the center with only two chairs. The seat on the far side of the table was empty, but a cloaked, hooded figure sat stone-still in the chair closest to the door, their back turned toward the old man.

"The past ignites the future," Connor muttered. When the figure didn't move or offer a response, he frowned. *My memory's fine. That's the exact phrase she said to use.*

"The future holds our fate." The voice was low, cautious, and barely more than a whisper.

Holding back the sigh of relief he wanted to exhale, he moved quickly across the room and rounded the table to finally see the figure's face. The black hole within the raised hood showed him nothing. "As far as I know, we're alone," he muttered. "If you're the one who sent me that map, I'd very much like to see your face."

Black-gloved hands raised slowly to pull the hood back from the figure's face. The woman seated before him was slender and pale, and she stared appraisingly at him before she settled an almost violet gaze on the old man's gray eyes. "Sit, Mage Alby. We have much to discuss and not nearly as much time as I'd hoped."

Connor pulled out the squeaking, wobbling wooden chair and sat across the table from War Mage Athena. *This is the woman King Vaughn's entire council cast out just like that?*

His unblinking stare made her glance self-consciously at the table, and her auburn hair cut just below her chin fell in a shimmering curtain around either side of her face. She dusted off a section of the table with her gloved hand and focused on him.

"War Mage—"

"All right, Connor. We can leave the formalities out in the hall and you can call me Kyree. At least while we're sitting here." Her smile was thin, strained, and carried as much trepidation and as he felt with the same kindling hope beneath it.

"I received your letter," he muttered.

"Obviously. I'm sorry I couldn't be more convincing to the council before you arrived."

"Don't apologize for that." Connor scowled quickly but forced himself to calm and look her in the eye. "What I want to hear from you is why it's taken over a month for us to have this meeting."

"Hmm." Kyree Athena's thin smile twitched. "The king's trusted advisors have kept a rather close eye on me. It's a wonder my letter even reached you at all."

"Are you a prisoner here?"

"Trust me, if I wanted to leave the impenetrable safety of our monarch's unending hospitality, I'd be long gone."

"From what I've heard of you, I'd say I believe every word of that." He chuckled wryly. "As it turns out, what I've heard of War Mage Athena is as frustratingly little as what I've managed to find of you in Lomberdoon's histories."

"Yes. Well, I suppose there's a reason for that as well." Kyree folded her gloved hands and settled them in front of her on the table. "Because I believe, with all my being, that magic is, in fact, returning to the people of our great kingdom and even those living beyond it. Quickly and very possibly with consequences we can't begin to understand. Not alone, at any rate."

"I feel the same." Connor nodded and leaned back in his chair. "You're looking at a spent wizard who is quite unmistakably not spent at all."

The woman's eyes widened briefly and she leaned forward. "We do have much to discuss. Would you like to start, or shall I?"

The veteran dragon rider gestured toward her with a nod. "Please. I've spent the last month scouring this maze of a fortress to prove to myself that you exist and you're more than a story whispered behind doors closed and locked for the night. Tell me what you know."

"As you wish."

CHAPTER THIRTY-FIVE

The next morning, the two girls followed a spindly older man in a neat black tailcoat through the governor's estate.

"This is it." Bella glanced at Wesley perched on her shoulder, and the firedrake screeched eagerly. "The start of the Tournament of Mages. Now we get to show them what we can do."

Raven smiled at the other young mage's short, confident pep-talk to herself and her familiar. *It sure would be nice to head out to the competition* with *Leander. I'll get him soon enough.*

When the older man opened the door on a higher level of the estate than their guest room, the sound of the cheering crowd waiting for them outside struck them instantly. Raven grinned. Bella raised her chin and squared her shoulders toward the arena set up for this year's event.

"Over there, if you please," the man said with a little bow and gestured to the right.

"Thank you." Raven smiled at him, and the girls stepped

out onto the massive overhanging arena three times the size of the dragon terrace.

On their right, Alessandra and the other students waited for them in a portion of the stands that surrounded the entire perimeter of the terrace. In the center, an obstacle course had been erected within the arena—walls to climb, hoops to send spells and familiars through, platforms to jump, and training dummies everywhere.

Raven leaned toward Bella and muttered, "I bet those dummies down there aren't anywhere close to Alessandra's at Fowler."

The other girl snorted. "I bet you're right. We're so overprepared."

Their trainer gave them both a curt nod when they reached the group representing Fowler Academy. The crowd of dignitaries, landholders, city representatives, and Azerad's honored guests applauded as the last two mage students joined them. The loudest cheers and whistles came from the people of Azerad themselves—those who'd braved climbing all the stairs to see young witches and wizards battle each other for this year's prize and the honor of winning.

The veteran war mage nodded across the circular arena toward the stands on the other side. "Mandrose Academy is over there, straight ahead. The Ziel Institute is at three o'clock. Watch and absorb as much as you can, mages. Each school teaches slightly different techniques. If all of you learn theirs before they learn ours, we have the advantage."

The two girls filled the empty spaces between Alessandra and the rest of Fowler Academy's competing students. Raven found herself standing between Bella and Daniel.

He smiled at her, and after feeling his gaze on her for a full fifteen seconds, she finally looked at him. "Hi," he said quietly.

She gave him a small, closed-lipped smile. "Hi."

Immediately, she returned her attention to the arena as the announcer walked into the middle of it. *As long as we don't distract each other today, we're fine.*

A woman in a scarlet dress joined the wiry man with crazy gray hair in the center of the arena and muttered a spell before she pointed her wand directly at the man's throat. Raven leaned toward Bella and whispered, "They have their own mage."

"Of course. Every major city has at least one. Probably more. Where did you think they all go after graduating from one of the schools?"

She shrugged. *Out to war like my mom and Grandpa. I didn't think about serving an actual city.*

With the mage's spell, the announcer's voice boomed across the arena terrace. "Welcome, ladies and gentlemen, to this year's Tournament of Mages!"

The crowd went wild again, and he raised his hands with a chuckle to quiet them.

"Before we begin, I'd like to explain why this year's competition is especially unique. Of course, we have fine young witches and wizards from each represented school. Mandrose Academy, the Ziel Institute, and Fowler Academy." Each group of students cheered for their school, but their voices didn't come close to the noise the crowd raised. "And special recognition goes to two students this year who've shown exemplary mastery over their abilities in magic, working with their familiars, and combat training. For the first time in recorded history, two of our competing mages were selected to attend this tournament in their very first year at Fowler Academy."

Oh, great. Here it comes. Raven glanced at Bella, but the other girl was preparing herself to meet the grand announcement with a proud smile.

"Bella Chase and her firedrake familiar Wesley, and Raven Alby with her dragon familiar Leander."

The crowd picked up a cheer but it was immediately drowned out by an earsplitting screech from below. Raven turned over her shoulder to see the dragon terrace immediately below them, overlapping by a few yards. She could see the end of the stable where Leander was kept and she grinned.

He's cheering too.

When his dragon call filtered into a low roar, the crowd in the arena terrace went wild, shouted, whistled, and stamped their feet. She grinned and raised her hand in a small wave.

Daniel glanced behind them too, saw the dragon stables, and shook his head. "That is so cool."

She chuckled. "Yeah. It kind of is."

"Now that's out of the way and without further ado, I officially open this year's Tournament of Mages. Our first match is between Anika Delaine from Fowler Academy and Terry Bolton from Mandrose Academy, here with the fox familiar Maritsa and the warthog familiar Rudy, respectively."

The crowd erupted in cheers, and Anika turned from

the end of the line of Fowler students to smile thinly at Alessandra. Her fox familiar trotted swiftly behind her as she passed her fellow students to clear the stands and head toward the center of the arena. Directly across from them, Terry and his warthog did the same.

Daniel chuckled. "This'll be interesting. She has, like, two feet on the guy."

"Well, it's not a height competition."

He snorted and shook his head, and she smirked.

"Take your places now, young mages. Over here, thank you." The announcer stepped out of the arena, followed by the mage directing his voice with her enhancement spell. "The rules are simple. Use anything on this course to your advantage. Points will be deducted for any undue physical harm that was not a direct result of your opponent failing to deflect a spell or otherwise counter an attack. Basically, don't hit your opponent while they're already down. On my count, you will begin."

The announcer counted down, and the first match started.

"*Adsulto protentia!*" Anika shoved both hands forward and Terry catapulted away.

"*Auferetur,*" he shouted, and a white light bloomed beneath him to slow his descent and land him gently on the arena floor. He settled squarely on his feet, and the crowd burst into cheers again.

"Do we have any idea yet where Mandrose Academy's specialty lies?" Alessandra muttered and watched the two war mages in training from the corner of her eye.

"Defense." Bella stared at the arena and watched intently.

"Hmm. Perhaps. Keep watching."

Alessandra's vague answer didn't affect the girl at all. She nodded but was already certain she'd given the correct answer.

I wouldn't have even made a guess after seeing only one spell. Raven smirked at the black-haired witch beside her. Wesley peered over Bella's shoulder, his lithe neck stretched to its fullest extent to watch the match with the same intensity. *Overprepared. She wasn't kidding.*

The sparring students circled each other in the arena and exchanged spells in a series of attacks. Terry's assault spells were erratic and poorly aimed compared to Anika's, but he had impressive control over deflecting or at least protecting himself against her much stronger attacks.

He had moved the fight onto the platforms of various heights, which forced his opponent to climb after him if she wanted to stay within an accurate range. When he reached the tallest platform, a huge bell dinged from somewhere in the stands.

"Excellent work, young mages," the announcer boomed. "A fine opening match. You may return to your places with your schools, and the judges will calculate your respective points for this round."

Cheers, shouts, and encouraging whistles filled the arena terrace once more while the two combatants returned to their groups. Anika grinned when she walked through the stands past Alessandra, her cheeks flushed only a little. The trainer nodded, and when the girl passed Raven, the redhaired mage leaned forward and muttered, "That was great."

"I know."

Daniel and Cooper each patted the girl on the back before she settled into place beside them.

Two minutes later, the announcer stepped into the arena again and spread his arms. "The judges have reached their final tally. For Terry Bolton and Rudy from Mandrose Academy, thirty points!"

The kids from Mandrose Academy cheered with the applauding crowd, clapped their first competing mage on the back, and jostled him enthusiastically. The short, muscular kid smirked and folded his arms.

"And for Anika Delaine and Maritsa from Fowler Academy, forty-two points!"

The crowd went wild, and Anika looked down the line of her fellow students with a smirk. "I knew it."

"Well done, Miss Delaine." Alessandra nodded at the girl and the corner of her mouth twitched in as close to a smile as she'd ever displayed.

"Now, we'll break for a short time and the second match will begin shortly thereafter." The announcer nodded at the stands, smiled as the cheers died down, and stuck his hands on his hips. "Don't go too far, now. We won't be long."

The governor's staff had put together an early lunch for the honored guests and the competing students, although the rest of the crowd and any citizens coming from the city streets below were expected to bring their food with them. Most of them did.

The meal was served at the base of the stands at the far end of the arena terrace, and Raven found a seat as close to the edge as she could get. It gave her the best view of the dragon stables below and Leander's stall on the very end.

She nibbled a slice of buttered bread once she'd finished a large slice of ham and a few grapes.

Bella Chase surprised her when she came to sit beside her and look over the edge of the terrace beside her. Wesley hopped after her and snatched up the tiny pieces of ham his mage tossed for him. "We know a little more of what we're up against, at least. Once we see the way the Ziel Institute uses magic, we'll have a much better chance."

"Aren't our chances already high enough with the first win?" Raven smirked at the other young mage.

"Not necessarily. Obviously, the scoring is on a points system. We score points for the school as a whole, and not every student gets to fight each other. But the two or maybe four highest-scoring students get to spar in the final match against each other, and the school with the most overall points wins."

She nodded. "So even if someone loses, they could still add enough points to win the entire tournament."

"Right. Forty-two is a decent score." Bella glanced over her shoulder to reassure herself that Anika couldn't hear them. "I plan to double that, at least."

"Really?" She took another bite of bread and gazed out over the city. "Where'd you learn all this stuff about the tournament? We only found out about it a week ago."

With a smirk, the girl tossed two more pieces of ham to Wesley, who gobbled them out of the air. "I read. And I asked a few people in the city yesterday. I ended up walking around the market until dinner."

"And the crowds didn't bother you?"

"Not at all. It's kind of refreshing, actually."

Raven choked out a laugh. "Refreshing. All those people

crammed together down there? I couldn't handle it for more than half an hour."

"How'd you spend the rest of your day, then?"

A warm flush rose unbidden to her cheeks. "Walking through the gardens."

"With Daniel Smith?"

She turned toward the other girl with wide eyes. "Where did you hear that?"

Bella shrugged and smiled. "I heard it in passing somewhere."

"I seriously hope it wasn't in passing from Daniel."

"Nope."

That's a relief. "I don't know how you can spend so much time in a crowded city like this. It's nice here but down there, it gets...cramped."

"I like the people." When Raven darted the other mage a disbelieving glance, Bella shrugged. "There are many people to talk to and get opinions from. That's what I mean. Especially when they don't know every single person living around them or on the other side of the kingdom and everything about all their neighbors' lives. It's too hard to find any privacy in Brighton. Everyone talks."

"Ha. You know, I was thinking the exact opposite." With a little shrug, she touched the red and silver pin on her jacket. "I guess it's the goat-rancher in me."

"I'd hope that's the only thing you take away from growing up on that ranch if I were you." Bella tossed her hair out of her eyes. "You have so much more potential than a goat-rancher."

"Yeah, you too."

The girls snorted together and shared a soft laugh. *I'm not even surprised anymore that we've reached this point.*

They fell silent for a few seconds before Bella took a deep breath. "So I've watched the other students from Mandrose Academy and the Ziel Institute. I think I have them fairly well pinned-down to know which one of us has the best chance of scoring more points against them."

Raven's eyes widened. "How can you have that worked out already? We've only watched one of them fight."

"It's based on their reactions." The girl shrugged and watched Wesley climb into her lap. "There's way more to learn from a person's automatic reactions than from what they practice showing everyone else—or hiding from everyone else."

"Wow. I'm officially impressed."

"You should be." Bella launched into a brief summary of the ten other mages from the competing schools, and she tried to absorb as much of it as she could.

This is what Headmaster Flynn was talking about. Bella has the diplomacy part all figured out.

CHAPTER THIRTY-SIX

The second match was between two students from Mandrose Academy and the Ziel Institute, then Cooper was called next to fight a girl from the Ziel Institute who was smaller than both Raven and Bella and had a scorpion familiar.

"That says enough about her right there," Raven muttered as the third match began.

"Maybe. If she uses the scorpion's independence and stealth the right way." Bella's eyes never left the arena below the stands.

Cooper won forty points for Fowler Academy against the witch and her scorpion familiar's thirty-nine points for the Ziel Institute. Only three matches were scheduled per day, and the announcer called the final tallied points for each school before he dismissed the spectators and the competing mages.

"It looks like we're still off to a good start," Raven said as the students and the governor's honored guests filtered out of the arena and into the estate castle. The rest of the citizens who'd come to watch stayed longer on the terrace, conversing and laughing and enjoying themselves above the bustle of city life below them.

"Well, we have eighty-one points and the Ziel Institute has seventy-nine." Bella studied the tall, lanky boy from the Ziel Institute with pasty-white skin and a mop of black hair falling into his eyes. "We'll see. I bet that one's the strongest mage of his team."

"The one with the vulture hopping after him?" She raised an eyebrow. "We haven't seen him fight yet." *He looks like the boy version of Elizabeth.*

"I told you we don't have to see them fight to figure them out. And I think he'd be the best choice for you to go up against."

She laughed. "What makes you think that?"

"Well, for starters, he's way too sure of himself."

"You know many people are probably saying the same thing about us, right?"

Bella waved off the comment. "Sure, but our confidence is totally founded. Think about it. He's overestimating himself and that vulture familiar makes the rest of it crystal-clear."

Raven squinted at the boy and his familiar before they disappeared inside the castle ahead of them. "Other than eating carcasses, I'm not sure how that applies."

"But that's exactly it—in a figurative sense, of course. Applied to magic." The girl stared at her and finally grew too impatient to wait. "That student is overconfident and will strengthen his magic with his familiar's ability to 'clean up,' so to speak. He'll wait for you to make a mess of a spell or two, maybe for Leander to make some kind of mistake, and then he'll attack when he thinks you're weakest. That's when he'll throw everything he has at you and he won't go all-out before that."

"Huh." Raven nodded as she considered how much sense that made. "That's an amazing analysis."

"Thank you."

"So why am I the best one to fight him?"

Bella gave her a sidelong glance and smirked. "Because you don't make messes in a fight, Raven. Not when it counts. He'll spar with you at half-capacity for the whole match, waiting for the perfect moment to unleash what he can really do, and you won't give him an opportunity before the bell ends the match."

Her mouth fell open, and she laughed in surprise. "I think you might be right."

"Of course I am."

"That's incredible, Bella. How did you learn to do that?"

The black-haired mage shrugged as they slipped inside the castle doors and followed the moving crowd into the ballroom again. "It's something I've always been good at. Second nature, you know? I got a perfect read of you the day we met. So far, I haven't been wrong."

I like that explanation for first-semester Bella better than thinking she hated me.

Raven grinned. "You keep raising the bar for compliments, you know that?"

Bella shot her a glance and rolled her eyes. "You keep raising the bar for earning them. I guess."

They stepped into the huge ballroom again, which was set up for a much more formal dinner than their opening ceremony the day before. The center of the room was filled with highly polished tables and intricately carved chairs, each of them set with fine china and silver for the no-doubt exquisite meal they'd be served.

Raven's eyes widened when she saw how the room had changed. Beyond the tables, glittering strands of magical lights swooped beneath the vaulted ceiling. The hors d'oeuvres tables were already piled high with foods she didn't recognize, and the governor's staff glided between guests with trays of crystal glasses filled with either gold, pink, or a dark-green liquid, all of them bubbling softly. The same four-string quartet played in the far corner and this time, their music selection felt more fitting to the scene.

Daniel stepped beside her. "It feels like a totally different world, huh?"

She turned to look at him and gestured acknowledgment with her hand. "Kind of. It might not be a world I belong to, though."

"Nah. You belong everywhere you go, Raven." He winked at her and she couldn't help but laugh.

"What about you? Are you a fan of the fancy dinner parties and all the excitement around watching a group of mage students battle each other for points?"

He pressed his lips together and frowned in thought. "Well, as far as fancy dinner parties go, I might be a little less against them if I wore the right clothes."

They both looked at their normal attire worn for school, traveling, and sparring in a new city. She snorted.

"Yeah, it would've been nice if someone bothered to tell us about the dress code."

"Honestly, I don't think anyone cares." Daniel leaned toward her and pointed at the gaggle of dignitaries gathered around the announcer with the wild gray hair. "Those are the real guests of honor. We're only here for entertainment."

"How do you know that?"

He raised an eyebrow, then chuckled. "Okay. Come with me for a little stroll around the room. You'll see what I mean."

Raven joined him and they wandered past the tables set for dinner and the lavishly prepared dishes of tiny morsels on the long buffet tables against the wall. They smiled and nodded at the various guests, dignitaries, and people of importance coming in from the other cities around Lomberdoon. He touched her arm when they neared a group of two men and a woman who spoke in low tones. Each of them had a glass of one of the sparkling drinks in their hand, and none of them paid attention to the teenagers who slowed a few feet away.

"I've traveled to these little games for the last seven years," the woman said and gestured with her bubbling drink, "and every year, I find myself surprised enough to agree to go to the next year's competition."

"Well, the two first-year mages are definitely a surprise," one man replied.

"A surprise, sure." The woman took a demure sip. "But hardly worth noting. I'm looking for the best mages from each school, not the youngest. The ones who show the most promise overall are the ones I'll reach out to personally."

The second man smiled and tossed his drink back with a quick jerk of his head. "It's almost impossible to imagine what two first-years have to offer. I assume their head-master wanted to reward them in some way for being the best of their class, but that doesn't mean a thing when they're matched with students who've studied and trained for this twice as long, at the very least."

Daniel tugged on Raven's arm a little, and they moved past the trio of fancy aristocrats who still didn't notice that they'd been overheard.

"Okay," she told him. "I have a much better picture of why we're here. Thanks."

"Hey, these people have no idea what they're in for once you get out into that arena. Don't let the doubters get to you.'

She smiled as she glanced around the room. "It's not getting to me. I'm even more excited now to prove them wrong."

He laughed. "Of course you are. That's what makes you so dangerous."

"So what?"

"Uh...so amazing." He flashed her his winning smile again and they broke into laughter.

Most of the other students had gathered into their own groups. They stood away from the adults who obviously wanted nothing more to do with them than gauging their abilities in a match. Raven caught sight of Bella in active conversation with a tall, dark-skinned man sporting a curling mustache and wearing a monocle.

As she and Daniel circled the room, she glanced constantly at the other girl. The black-haired mage spoke softly with a constant smile and engaged the man's full attention, then she spread her arms and raised her chin. The dignitary threw his head back and boomed a laugh, which made several of the other honored guests turn with interest toward the first-year student Bella Chase. Throughout the opening hour before dinner was served, she entertained any of them who came to listen to what she had to say.

She was born for this kinda thing. Raven smiled and accepted one of the clear bubbly drinks from Daniel that were only handed out to the students. *I can't wait to show them what I was born to do.*

About half an hour after she'd finished dessert, she slipped away from the dinner party to visit Leander. The dragon terrace was mostly quiet again and completely free of Marcus the stablemaster and his team. She moved quickly in the darkness and ignored the calls from the other dragons. This time, hearing their voices reaching out toward her brought a little shiver down her spine. *He was right. They kind of sound like ghosts.*

When she reached his stall, Leander was already on his feet and peered over the door at her. "How's it going in here?"

The dragon grunted. "Nothing's changed."

"Well, that's better than a turn for the worse, right?" Raven glanced over her shoulder at the other dragons who stretched their long necks out of their stalls to stare at her. "I think I know what you meant about these others being a little off somehow."

"I said empty."

"I know. Hang in there a little longer, okay? Only four more days and hopefully, we'll be out of here the day after the tournament ends." She turned toward him and patted the side of his muzzle. "That was a nice addition to our announcement this morning, by the way."

Leander uttered a low rumble, but it didn't last as long as it normally did. "I did it for you."

"Only me? Because I know everyone else heard it. They loved it."

"I don't care what they heard, Raven. I felt you wanting me there with you."

"And you called out your support." She ran her hand down his long neck and leaned toward him to press her forehead to his. "I can't tell you how much I appreciate that."

"You don't have to."

"Just wait, Leander. The second we get called up to fight in whatever matches they have planned for us, you'll be out of here and up there in that arena with me. We'll show everyone how wrong they were to think we don't know what we're doing."

"That is a marginally satisfying idea."

She chuckled. "You know, part of me hopes that it's mostly only the people here in Azerad who think that way about us. But I have a feeling it might get worse in the bigger cities if we ever end up going to them at all."

"Not if we make a big enough statement here."

Leaning away from him, Raven stared into Leander's glowing yellow eyes and grinned. "I think you're right. I've already realized that this whole Tournament of Mages isn't really about the students. Still, this might be the perfect chance for us to show the rest of the kingdom how fierce a first-year mage and her dragon can be."

"Even from Brighton."

She winked at him. "Especially from Brighton."

CHAPTER THIRTY-SEVEN

On the second day of the Tournament of Mages, the first match was held between students from Mandrose Academy and the Ziel Institute. Mandrose Academy's mages erupted in celebration when the girl from their school won their first match so far with fifty points, despite the fact that their total score still came in last.

"The only reason she won that is because the other girl from the Ziel Institute attacked her again without letting Mandrose Academy recover," Bella muttered.

"No hitting your opponent while they're down. Right. She doesn't look too hurt, though."

"It's the principle of it. I'm not a fan of that rule. Points deducted for unnecessary harm. The best mage should win hands-down anyway."

Fighting back a laugh, Raven leaned toward her fellow mage and muttered, "Even if you don't throw attacks when whoever you fight is down, you'll still win. But be careful about where to draw the line."

"I'm always careful," the girl retorted but she sighed and shrugged. "It's good to have a reminder, though. Thanks."

She frowned as the students walked quickly to their places in the stands. "Those were fairly advanced spells I haven't even heard of. Have you?"

Bella shook her head, but she smiled and leaned closer to speak in a low tone. "It doesn't matter. These guys didn't use the Magic Meld, so we have that on them."

The girls shared a private smirk over that and waited for the next match to be called.

The announcer stepped into the middle of the arena with Azerad's mage beside him, this time wearing an emerald-green dress as she pointed her wand at his throat. "Ladies and gentlemen, we'll take a slightly longer break before the second match of the day. It looks like we're, um…relocating to a much larger arena to facilitate the next match between Marcel Kent with his vulture familiar Dolores and Raven Alby with her dragon familiar Leander."

Bella smirked. "Told you."

A shout of surprise and excitement rose, mostly from the citizens of Azerad who'd come to watch. The governor's honored guests glanced at Raven but didn't show much of a reaction.

She exhaled a quick breath. "Okay. It's time to get that dragon."

"I think you have more than enough time." Bella nodded toward the announcer, who'd spun to face the gathered judges in the stands and looked a little upset. He waved his arms to gesture at some of the terraces that jutted from the castle walls above them.

"I guess they weren't as prepared for me and Leander as they want everyone to think, huh?"

"They haven't even said where we're moving to." Her companion shrugged.

"Miss Alby." Alessandra beckoned the young mage with a curt wave.

She leaned toward Bella before she moved past her. "Wish me luck."

"You don't need it. But good luck."

As she followed Alessandra out of the stands and toward the walkway around the castle, she tried to ignore the whispers of surprise. A little nervously, she shook her hands out and steeled herself for her first real match as a war mage in training. *And a dragon rider. That's the best part.*

When they reached the walkway, her trainer folded her arms and nodded toward the dragon terrace below them. "Go ahead and get him now. Once that bumbling announcer decides where to move the match to, someone will direct you."

"Okay." The young mage turned down the walkway.

"Miss Alby."

"Yeah."

A tiny smirk lifted on only one side of Alessandra's mouth. "Give that boy and his buzzard hell."

After a quick nod, Raven turned and raced along the path toward the closest staircase to the level below. She sprinted past the stablemaster when she reached the dragon terrace, shouting, "We're up, Marcus! You don't have to do anything. I got it."

The man opened his mouth to tell her to slow as she ran down the avenue between the stables. He clamped his mouth shut again a second later and shook his head, then grumbled about energetic teenagers.

She skidded to a stop outside Leander's stall and hooked her hand around the edge of the open frame to stop herself. Then, she thumped her forearms on the top of the half-door and grinned. "We're—"

"Fighting next. Yes."

"Let's get you out of here, huh?"

He looked up from his curled position on the stall floor and said flatly, "I thought you'd never ask."

"No, you didn't. You knew this was coming." Laughing, she unlatched the door and pulled it open.

The second the door moved, Leander pushed himself to his feet faster than she knew he could move and thundered out of the stall and into the wide avenue.

"Woah!" Raven ducked beneath the full span of his wings that unfurled from his back with a violent burst of air.

The huge red dragon stretched his neck toward the sky and uttered a piercing screech.

His mage clamped her hands over her ears and had to wait for the other dragons in the stables to quiet after their calls in reply. She stood and lowered her hands. "Wow. You were really cooped up in there, huh?"

"That was obvious." He kept his wings spread wide as he turned to face the avenue leading toward the castle.

"You could've said something. Now I feel kinda bad—"

"Don't feel bad, Raven Alby. I agreed to this. Be ready to fight."

She grinned and stepped toward him. The dragon's

wings shuddered a little when she patted his shoulder. "We're both ready."

"So let's go."

"Uh...they had to move the tournament to a different arena—to accommodate a dragon and everything. We're still waiting for someone to come tell us where we're supposed to go."

Leander's wings clamped against his sides with another burst of air. He snorted and fixed her with one narrow yellow eye. "That's a disappointment."

Raven chuckled a little and forced the rest of it down. "Yeah, it would've been great to hop on and take off outta here, huh?"

The dragon lowered his head and stared down the avenue, watching intently for the sign of where they had to go. "At least I'm out of that box."

"Right." She turned to stare in the same direction and folded her arms. "We're gonna blow them all away."

They ended up waiting for half an hour to hear about where they'd hold their match. She spent the time talking Leander out of taking off and going for a ride until someone got the tournament organized again.

"It's against the rules," she muttered for the twentieth time.

"Which neither of us cares anything about." He paced restlessly behind her and stared at the walkway attached to the edge of the dragon terrace.

"You said we need to make a statement. I agree. Breaking the rules in a city we don't know, especially at the Tournament of Mages, is most definitely the wrong statement."

The dragon snorted and raked steel-like talons across the stone floor of the terrace, raking huge chunks of it away in his agitation. Sparks flew.

Raven glanced at his forepaw and fixed him with a firm look. "That might be the only thing you can get away with right now."

"Not if we forget about statements."

"Raven Alby!" A guard moved quickly toward them between the stables and raised his hand to catch her attention. "They're ready for you."

Leander turned quickly to step protectively beside her, and she nudged him with her elbow. "This is it."

The young mage stepped forward to meet the guard, who caught his breath and nodded. "I'll take you to the new arena."

"Where is it?"

He turned and pointed much higher and farther past the original arena terrace. "Two more levels up from the last one. It's the overflow landing for incoming dragons, the only place they could find that wasn't already in use for—"

"Thanks!"

Without even thinking about what she did, Raven spun away from the guard and raced toward the edge of the dragon terrace. At the same time, Leander launched into the air and wheeled in a tight circle above the stabled dragons.

"Wait! What are you—" The guard stumbled forward to reach her as the stables erupted with excited shrieks and growls from the other dragons, all of whom watched a private show.

Raven Alby had already leapt off the edge of the terrace.

Her dragon dove and swooped cleanly beneath her and the young mage landed in a low crouch on the glistening ridges of his back.

"Yeah!" Dragon and rider shared shrieks of victory as he climbed higher toward the new arena terrace for their match. "Boy, am I glad you got the hint on that one!"

He beat his wings a few more times. "I knew you would do that before you did."

"And you timed it perfectly."

A low rumble followed before he swiveled his head to glance briefly at her through one eye, then raised his forepaw and pinched his talons together swiftly. "Plan B was to catch you with these."

A laugh burst out of her, and she steadied herself on his back as they rose higher. "Maybe don't talk about the fact that you even had a plan B unless I'm sitting down or we're about to land."

A few sharp hisses escaped him and he looked forward again to glide left around the outside of the governor's estate toward the new arena.

He knew exactly what he was doing. It looks like I did too.

"I think it's that one above us. Right there."

Leander turned away from the castle and made another wide loop to circle again.

"Okay, what are you—" An idea that didn't feel like her own popped into her head and she blinked. "Were you just thinking about—"

"Yes, Raven."

"It's perfect." She steadied herself on her dragon's back and when the dragon caught a draft to soar toward the castle walls, she stuck one boot behind her and rose slowly to her feet. Her arms raised out at her sides for stability, the young mage grinned. *This is gonna be good.*

He slowed as they approached the underside of the new arena terrace and flapped his wings in slow, heavy beats to lift them directly beside the edge of the massive platform that projected from the castle. Her head came into view over the edge first, and her grin widened as she and her dragon rose steadily beside the arena.

"Hey, look!" Terry shouted and pointed at the dragon rider with bright red hair standing on the back of her red dragon.

A collective exclamation of surprise and awe rose from the other students and especially from the crowd. The dignitaries all turned in their seats to watch the promising first-year student break more than a few records with her newest stunt.

"She doesn't have a saddle!" someone shouted, and everyone went silent while there was still a chance for the worst to happen.

Leander rose a few yards higher than the tallest rows of last-minute seating around the terrace, then swooped gently toward the center of the arena to land. Raven's boots settled on the thin layer of dirt as his feet touched down. She straightened and looked at the spectators with wide eyes.

The crowd exploded at once in cheers, claps, screams, and whistles, all of them twice as loudly as they had for any of the impressive performances already given by the other competing students. A little laugh escaped the young mage, and she turned in a slow circle as Leander folded his wings and circled behind her, watching where she watched. *This is as satisfying as I thought it would be.*

She found the students from Fowler in the stands beside Alessandra, all of them staring at her in various stages of surprise. Cooper and Daniel pumped their fists in the air while Anika stuck two fingers in her mouth and whistled. With her arms folded, Alessandra gave Raven a closed-lipped smile that lasted longer than one second and inclined her head. Even Bella was smiling and shaking her head. Raven spread her arms with a little shrug as she met the gaze of her fellow war mage in training. The girl rolled her eyes, took a deep breath, and cupped her hands around her mouth to shout, "Raven and Leander!"

Both Daniel and Cooper stopped cheering and leaned forward to shoot Bella matching baffled looks.

She turned toward them and her smile faded when she raised one shoulder in a careless shrug. "What? That was awesome."

"Ladies and gentlemen!" The announcer and his attending mage stepped into the center of the arena toward Raven and her dragon. He grinned from ear to ear with his arms spread wide. "I've seen many entrances, young dragon rider. That one most definitely hits the top five."

Leander snorted and lowered his head to her ear to mutter, "Number one."

"We can let him have his moment." When the announcer approached close enough to hear her in return, she nodded at him. "Thank you."

"It's well deserved, young dragon rider. Well deserved." The man turned distractedly to address the spectators again, his voice cracking across the massive new arena three times the size of the last and understandably without the same obstacle course. "Marcel and Dolores. Come take your places for our second match of the day and we'll begin."

The pale, lanky boy from the Ziel Institute rose in one swift, fluid motion and made his way down the stands. His vulture took flight behind him and made the spectators in the lower rows duck their heads and brush windblown hair out of their faces. Finally, the next two competing mages faced each other in the center of the huge arena, and the announcer stepped back.

"Now, for the purposes of this match, I've been asked to apply an extra rule. There's no real precedence for a competing mage and a dragon familiar, but we have to start somewhere." He chuckled, joined by the dignitaries' soft, slightly amused laughter. "No setting your familiars on your opponent for physical attacks. I believe that goes without saying for a dragon, but that vulture's talons don't look particularly harmless, either. Raven and Leander, while flight is not strictly prohibited, neither of you may fly beyond the reach of Marcel's spells. And no dragon fire, of course. Ha, ha."

While the man and the governor's honored guests laughed again, the citizens and other students glanced at each other and a few nervous chuckles suggested anxiety rather than amusement.

Marcel stared at her and didn't react at all to the mention of fire.

He knows we'll follow the rules. Or he has a great poker face.

"Is that understood?"

Both young mages turned toward the announcer and nodded.

"Excellent. On my count, you may begin." The gray-haired man stepped quickly toward the edge of the arena and counted down.

The second the last word left the man's mouth, Marcel lunged and shouted, "*Morsus!*"

A glittering yellow light darted toward Raven and ballooned into a massive attack.

"*Deflecto nocere!*" She deflected the first assault and the yellow magic hurtled vertically into the sky. *I finally got to use that one. It's a good thing it worked.*

Leander uttered a low growl, and the vulture landed a few yards away from her mage. Raven and Marcel circled one another and put more distance between them in the arena. *Bella was right. He's waiting for me to be sloppy. Good luck, Marcel.*

CHAPTER THIRTY-EIGHT

In the assembly hall of Fowler Academy's main building, the professors and students who'd come to watch the Tournament of Mages through the Periview cheered Raven on as if they sat in the stands in Azerad themselves.

"Unbelievable!" Henry shouted and pumped his fist in the air. "Did you see that freaking magical net she tossed at him? I didn't even know there was a spell like that."

Beside him, Murphy laughed and leaned forward to get a better view.

The image in the shimmering light projected like a window in mid-air above the empty stage panned wide to show Raven and Leander, who raced side by side away from the boy from the Ziel Institute. He'd cast a dozen projected copies of his vulture familiar, and all of them flew in pursuit of the mage and her dragon as Marcel fired a few more attacks after them.

"These other students have so many cool spells under their belt," Murphy added. "I don't even know how—"

"Woah!"

"Look at that!"

"Go, Raven!"

The girl had leapt atop Leander's back with a boost from his head, and the dragon took off a few yards into the air, veered away from Marcel's attacks at the last second, and wheeled in a steep turn to return to their opponent. The copies of the vulture vanished and the real familiar settled on the ground to watch the dragon and his rider.

"Man, they're getting good with taking off in action," Henry said, dropped into his seat in the front row, and held his head with both hands.

"Yeah, Derks. It's like they practiced or something."

"You know what, Percy?" He turned in his chair and made a face at his friend. "I came here to watch Raven and Leander compete, and you should be paying attention to that—"

"Woah."

"Hey, what happened?"

"Uh, Headmaster?"

Henry spun as the magically projected image flickered and sputtered with a bright light above the stage. It flared with a brilliant flash and vanished.

"What'd you do, Derks?"

Henry looked at his finger with wide eyes. "I only pointed, I swear."

Headmaster Flynn stood from his seat at the far end of the front row and walked to the stage. He looked back once to shoot Worley a knowing look, and the familiar-training professor stood as well.

"Get it back on."

"Raven was about to cast another spell."

Flynn raised his hands toward the much smaller group of students than when school was in session and gestured for them to quiet. "Mr. Derks is entirely innocent in this scenario, I assure you."

"See?" Henry turned and jerked his thumb toward his chest. "Innocent."

Murphy rolled her eyes with a little smile.

"Now, if you'll all be so kind as to wait patiently while Professor Worley and I leave to assess the situation, we'll have the images up in no time. And I do mean patiently. Thank you."

The headmaster hurried to the other side of the stage and stooped to mutter something in Professor Gilliam's ear. She nodded and leaned back in her seat as Flynn and Worley left the assembly hall quickly.

"Great." Henry folded his arms. "By the time they have their fancy spell fixed, Raven's match will already be over. That's the only one I cared about."

"Way to show some school spirit, Henry."

"Oh, come on. Don't tell me you think anyone else from Fowler is gonna fight a match as exciting as that." He started to point at the front of the stage again but stopped himself and folded his arms hastily.

"Maybe Bella," Murphy said.

He turned toward her while the other gathered students began their own conversations. "Okay. As much as I get a little itchy giving Bella Chase credit, you're right. She and Raven have almost the same chances at the best matches ever."

The young witch lowered her head and sent him a sidelong look. "They've trained together for weeks. I'm sure they're on the same level by now. They kind of always have been."

"Huh." He frowned at the empty stage before a huge grin spread across his face. "Raven has the bigger dragon."

Murphy burst out laughing. "Raven has the only dragon."

"And what's a firedrake, huh? I saw something in some textbook laying around. *Magic in Nature* or something like that."

"You do know how to read!"

Henry snorted. "Murphy, I gotta hand it to you. You've improved your comeback game."

"Why, thank you." She smiled at her lap and for once, didn't blush furiously.

"What was I talking about? Oh, yeah. Tiny dragons. That's basically what the book said. Firedrakes are like miniature dragons with lower intelligence and without the ability to speak."

His companion wrinkled her nose. "I don't even want to think about what Wesley's voice would sound like if he could talk."

"Probably...squeaky."

They both laughed, and Fritz jumped onto her lap. The cat stretched his body across her thighs and extended a paw to pat Henry's leg a few inches away from where Maxwell sat motionlessly. The toad croaked, and Murphy shook her head. "Before you say anything about a cat not knowing its own strength around a toad, let me tell you that Fritz can be—"

"Nah, I'm not worried about it, Murph." Henry swung a

casual arm over the back of her seat and propped his ankle up on the opposite knee. "Maxwell isn't either. We're past that."

She shrank a little where she sat, painfully aware of his arm around the back of her seat and his foot almost touching her thigh. She felt the heat rise in her cheeks and frowned. *Not now, Murphy. You're fine. This is normal Henry and it doesn't mean anything else.*

"Man, I wish I knew where Flynn and Worley went to fix that spell and—"

The doors to the assembly hall were thrust open before the headmaster and the familiar-training professor stormed inside. The students all turned in their seats to see both men frowning as they moved swiftly down the side aisle. Headmaster Flynn went toward the center of the stage while Worley stooped to mutter something to Professor Gilliam. Her eyebrows raised and she stood.

Professor Fellows rose from his seat as well and approached the headmaster. "Was it the crystals?" he muttered, hiding his expression and his voice from the students. "I checked them two days ago, but they might be—"

"No, Travis. The crystals were performing fine."

"Were?"

Flynn glanced up to meet the professor's gaze and inclined his head slightly. "In a moment." He stepped aside and clasped his hands behind his back. "It seems we're having magical difficulties this afternoon."

A round of groaned protests rose from the students.

"I know, I know. We were all very much looking forward to watching Miss Alby's match as well as our other representative mages. Unfortunately, there's nothing more to be done today as your professors and I need more time to reassess the magical connection with Azerad."

"So we have to miss the other match today too?" Teresa Reynolds called from the back.

"Correct, Miss Reynolds." The students groaned again. "I'm sorry. Some things are out of our control. You'll have to wait until your fellow students return from Azerad to tell you all about what we've missed. Please gather your things, if applicable, and those of you not staying in the dormitories may remove yourselves from the grounds. After all, this is our spring break as well." Flynn finished with a thin smile and nodded as he watched the disgruntled young mages rise from their seats to file out of the assembly hall.

Henry followed Murphy down the row and leaned to whisper in her ear as they walked up the aisle toward the doors. "Now I'm really glad I didn't do anything simply by pointing. Otherwise, Percy would be waiting outside to punch me in the face the minute I stepped outside."

She snorted. "No, he wouldn't."

"He already tried last week. Okay, yeah, it was about something totally different. But look at this, Murph. He tore a hole in my shirt before I got away."

"And you still haven't patched it, I see." She tried not to laugh. "What'd you do to him last week?"

"Uh…a little accident with a slingshot. No big deal."

When all the students had left the assembly hall, Headmaster Flynn heaved a heavy sigh and rubbed his temple. He glanced in turn at Professors Worley, Fellows, Gilliam, Bixby, and Dameron. "I would appreciate it if you would all come with me to the weapons shed. Each one of you needs to see this. Professor Worley, please lead the way."

Gilliam and Bixby exchanged worried glances, but no one else said a word as they followed the giant bearded professor out of the main building, beneath the stone arch at the side of the main courtyard, and into the field beyond.

The weapons shed looked completely normal, and Professor Worley pointed at the door with a muttered spell. A soft orange light flared on the lock with a click.

"The shed was open when we found it," he muttered. "And so was this."

When he pulled the door all the way, the professors gathered around the neatly stocked weapons shed and stared. Directly in front of the two wheelbarrows of practice weapons, exactly where they'd left it, was the Periview. Someone had opened it so forcefully that one of the side platforms had been ripped halfway off its hinges. The tiny square mirror was broken and dangled from the lever in the center of the device, and both purple amplifying crystals lay on the floor of the shed, one of them with a jagged crack down the center.

"Who would do this?" Professor Dameron demanded indignantly.

"Clearly someone who didn't want us to see what was happening in Azerad," Flynn replied firmly.

"And who has access to open the Periview in the first place?" Bixby asked.

"Only the students whose runes were activated before they left for the tournament." The headmaster clasped his hands behind his back and turned to Professor Fellows. "Which students have regular rune access to the shed?"

Fellows pursed his lips and rubbed the bottom of his hairless chin. "Rory Davidian. Anne Marie Murphy. Jessica Rodenmeyer and Leon Burgess."

Professor Dameron hissed a sigh. "Dammit."

Flynn turned his attention to the bald professor and lowered his head. "Victor, Eleanor, did we deactivate Miss Rodenmeyer's rune once she revealed she could no longer participate in the Tournament of Mages?"

Professor Gilliam gaped at him for a moment before her lips twitched into a grimace when she realized what this meant. "Oh, no."

"Is that your answer or an exclamation of regret?"

"We didn't deactivate her rune, Headmaster," Dameron answered for her. "Jessica still has access."

Headmaster Flynn's usually calm eyes blazed as he glanced at each of his staff in turn. "Find her before it's too late."

"I'll ride to her family's farm," Professor Fellows offered.

"I'll get you a horse," Worley told him and spun to head to the stables. "Give me five minutes."

Flynn addressed the other three professors, his mouth set in a grim line as he flexed his jaw. "The rest of us will scour the grounds. This incident occurred less than fifteen minutes ago. She can't have gotten very far."

"Yes, Headmaster."

The alumni scattered briskly across the field to search the grounds for the student who'd apparently opened the Periview and destroyed its connection. The headmaster sighed and returned to the main courtyard. *Wherever you are, Miss Rodenmeyer, stay strong. Don't lose hope.*

Behind the barn, Jessica whimpered quietly when the raider who held the knife to her throat pressed the blade's tip a little more firmly against her skin.

"Ah, ah, ah," the man warned. With his filthy hand clamped around the second-year mage's mouth, he gave the girl's jaw a warning little squeeze. "You keep your mouth shut, girlie. As long as you do that, you might survive this little get-together, eh?"

She took quick, desperate breaths through her nose and tears streamed down her cheeks.

"Aw…" The raider clicked his tongue and leaned closer to whisper in her ear. "We ain't here for you. Now you keep doing what you're told and when I take you home, your ma and pa might still be breathing."

CHAPTER THIRTY-NINE

"*Recta impetum!*" Raven launched the hurtling column of green attack magic Professor Fellows had taught them the previous week. It cracked against Marcel's defensive spell, and she launched another. The boy sneered at her but couldn't release his next defense fast enough. He dove aside and her second attack grazed the edge of his shoulder.

His vulture hissed and surged toward Leander, who only had to flap his powerful wings once before the rush of air tumbled the bird out of her dive.

They're both getting tired. And there's no leftover mess to clean up. She grinned at her opponent and raised her hand with a deep breath.

The bell rang several times to signal the end of the match, and she exhaled the breath she'd almost used to shout another spell in a sharp hiss.

"Excellent work, both of you!" the announcer called. "That was an impeccable display of both offensive and defensive magic, young mages. Raven Alby and Marcel Kent, ladies and gentlemen."

The crowd applauded and cheered a little, but they all waited to hear which of the mages had earned the highest score in their battle.

"Competitors, return to your places while our esteemed judges tally your points."

Raven waited for Leander to join her before she led him with a hand on his shoulder toward the edge of the arena. They stopped well away from the first row of the stands, and she gave his shoulder a gentle pat. "You were amazing."

"We were amazing," he muttered and lowered his head to brush his muzzle softly against the back of her head. "That is an interesting choice. A carrion-eater."

She chuckled. "Well, everyone has their own tastes. Ha."

The dragon rumbled and lowered himself slowly to the floor of the arena. To the spectators, it looked like her familiar was settling to rest after an exciting match, and it also allowed the viewers in the front rows to see the judges without a giant dragon blocking their view.

That's exactly what he wants them to think. It looks like Leander has a diplomatic streak too.

The wait for their scores wasn't as long as they expected. The announcer stepped beside the Azerad mage two minutes later and gestured expansively. "A unanimous decision speeds things up somewhat, doesn't it? Mages, you've received your total points from the judges. To Raven Alby and Leander, a total of one hundred and thirty-seven points." A few cheers came from the crowd, but most people remained silent to hear the rest of it despite the announcer's projected voice being much louder than any of the applause. "And to Marcel and Dolores, one hundred and…"

The packed stands held a collective breath.

"…twenty-nine points!"

Shouts and cheers and thrilled whoops of encouragement filled the air.

With a grin, Raven looked at Leander and raised her eyebrows. "We won."

"So I heard." He tilted his head to look at her with one eye and winked.

"Congratulations to both of you. Those are impressive scores, without a doubt." The announcer raised his hands to quiet the stands. "Now, as you're aware, we'll take another break. The third and final match of the day will take place on the lower level in our original arena. Please make your way there and we'll resume in half an hour."

One or two errant shouts of, "Raven and Leander!" issued from the crowd and the young mage merely responded with a little wave. Those who had come to watch the Tournament of Mages vacated their seats to filter gradually toward the other arena.

"Maybe one day, they'll start chanting," she muttered.

"Is that what you want out of this?" Her dragon snorted. "A chant?"

"Well, no. But it would be kinda nice to hear our names called out a—"

A bloodcurdling scream rent the air, and everyone looked toward the source of it, which appeared to be one of the high open windows within the closest tower. Someone inside shouted a command, and the brief clash of steel on steel rang out before the noises cut instantly.

The guards on the walkway off the new arena terrace sprinted toward the closest door into the governor's estate, and five more scurried up the stairs from the lower levels to join them.

Alessandra landed on the arena floor beside Raven and her boots thumped into the dirt.

"What's going on?" the girl asked.

"Stay here with the others. Wait until I return." The veteran war mage broke into a jog across the terrace until she joined the governor's guards who hurried inside.

Nervous conversation rose from the spectators, who'd all paused on their way out of the arena to watch what would happen next. The announcer took a deep breath. "Everyone, please stay calm. Whatever it is, we'll wait for word from Governor Irlish. If a match is postponed today, rest assured, it'll be made up for tomorrow."

That didn't do much to reassure the citizens of Azerad, most of whom huddled together and stared at the open window. Everyone looked frightened and unsure.

Wesley swooped from the stands in front of Raven a second before Bella hopped down and stopped beside her fellow mage. "Did you see anything?"

She shook her head. "I have no idea what's going on."

Daniel, Cooper, and Anika joined them a few seconds later.

"That sounded like swords, didn't it?" Cooper asked.

"Yep."

"I wonder who screamed."

"Well, I guess we'll find out."

They only had to wait for a few minutes before a large, scowling guard stalked across the huge area toward the judges' table on the far side. He moved quickly and completely ignored the citizens and spectators who asked him about the occurrence in the tower. The announcer met the man halfway and they spoke in low tones before the guard turned away and the wild-haired man nodded at the Azerad mage. She amplified his voice again, and he clapped sharply.

"There is nothing to worry about, ladies and gentlemen. Everything's under control and taken care of, but our gracious Governor Irlish has decided to postpone the third match and end the tournament for the rest of the afternoon. We will resume tomorrow with four matches to look forward to. Thank you, everyone. We'll see you then."

He cleared his throat before the mage had a chance to deactivate her spell, and everyone in the arena jumped or ducked or clapped their hands over their ears. The man looked furious, but he turned and plastered on a smile for the esteemed dignitaries and guests gathered at the far end of the stands.

"So that's it." Raven folded her arms. "They're trying to cover something up."

"Obviously." Bella squinted at the tower but was distracted when Alessandra emerged from the door on this level and met her students' gazes. She raised both hands to shoo them off, turned, and headed down the curved walkway.

"It looks like we've been dismissed," Daniel muttered.

"Is anyone hungry?" Anika asked and glanced hopefully at all four of her fellow students.

Cooper shrugged. "Yeah, I could eat."

"I want to know what's going on," Bella said and leaned toward Raven.

"Yeah, I'm right there with you." She turned toward Leander and nodded.

"Yes, I know." The dragon pushed to his feet, and a rippling shudder passed across his scales. "The dragon comes out of the box, and the dragon goes back into the box."

"It's only for three more days."

"Let's go." He boosted her onto his back and she was already seated at the base of his neck when Bella and the others turned.

"Meet me at that door," Bella said and gestured toward the entrance Alessandra and all the guards had used.

"No problem." She nodded and Leander spread his wings with a little snort before he became airborne.

They swooped and veered around the outside of the tower toward the dragon terrace. He landed on the edge and she leapt off without bothering to look for Marcus or the stable hands. She went directly to his stall and opened it for him. "I'll be back tonight—probably even sooner since we don't have any other matches today. But I have to see what's going on inside. Something doesn't feel right."

The dragon ambled into the stall and turned to face her. "I agree. Be careful, Raven."

"I always am." She closed the door behind him and wound her arms around his huge head. "Way to show them what we can do back there. You were fantastic."

A soft, purring rumble rose from his throat. "That was only the beginning."

"Oh, yeah. I know." With a final stroke along the ridges

between his eyes, she nodded and turned away to race between the stables on her way to meet Bella. *These people didn't think things through when they built all these stairs.*

By the time she reached the approach to the right door, Raven's hairline dripped with sweat and she was breathing heavily. She grasped the lapel of her jacket to shuck it off but stopped herself. *I can't toss it down out here.* Irritated, she ignored how hot she was and walked on.

Bella and Daniel waited for her at the door. He had his hands in his pockets and stared silently at the large second arena and the open space beyond. Wesley perched on his mage's shoulder over the girl's folded arms, and she perked up when she saw Raven approaching.

"That was fast."

"Well, we kinda cut the travel time in half with a one-way flight."

"Hey, Raven." Daniel grinned at her. "I didn't get a chance to congratulate you on the match. That was incredible."

"Thanks. It was a good fight." She nodded at the other girl. "Are you ready?"

Bella flashed her a pointed look and opened the door. They slipped inside and Daniel followed with a confused frown. "Wait. Where are you guys going?"

"Well, we're allowed to go wherever we want in the estate, right?" The dark-haired mage shrugged and decided to lead them down the hall to the right. "I bet we can find out something else about what happened if we pretend not to be too curious."

"Hey, I don't know if that's such a good idea right now." He scratched his head doubtfully. "It's serious enough for the governor to cancel the last match. Shouldn't we go somewhere else where it's safe?"

Raven sighed. "Bella, hold on."

The girl released an irritated breath and stopped. She spun and put a hand on her hip. "What?"

"Only a second." She turned to Daniel and smiled. "You can come with us if you want, but we're going to do a little exploring to see what we can find. Whatever happened in that tower wasn't supposed to happen. Maybe we can help."

"Raven, that's what the guards are for."

"Well, yeah. But Alessandra went to help them. She's not part of the governor's staff. I don't think she's from Azerad, either. If she can jump in to lend a hand, so can we."

He stepped toward her and lowered his head to mutter, "You could come with me. It's much safer. Maybe friendlier too." His gaze flickered to Bella.

Raven raised an eyebrow. "What do you mean by that?"

"I mean… I guess I don't understand why you'd rather go somewhere with Bella than with me. Everyone knows you hate each other."

The other girl scoffed and stepped quickly toward them. "We don't hate each other." She glared at Daniel, caught Raven's hand, and tugged her down the hall. "And mind your own business."

He frowned but a surprised snort escaped him anyway.

Trying not to lose her balance, Raven turned to look over her shoulder and called to him, "I'll find you later. We won't be too long."

The girls hurried down the hall and when they were far

enough away out of earshot, she scratched her head and glanced at Bella. "You didn't have to step in like that but I appreciate it."

"Don't mention it." Her companion peered intently down the hall and searched for any recognizable features or at least another stairwell or door. So far, they hadn't seen any. "Besides, people need to stop talking about whatever you and I might or might not think about each other. It's none of their business."

"I totally agree with you there." She smirked and tilted her head a little cheekily. "It's good to hear you say it out loud, though. We don't hate each other."

"I said don't mention it, Raven. Seriously."

CHAPTER FORTY

.

Henry and Murphy walked down the road toward Brighton's town center after being released from the assembly hall. "You know what, Murph? I found something the other day that made me think of—" He reached toward the flap of his shoulder bag, only to discover it wasn't there. "Crap."

"What's wrong?"

"I left my bag at school."

She walked a few steps farther before she realized he'd stopped behind her. "Hey, you can get it tomorrow. You are coming back tomorrow, right?"

"Yeah..." He grimaced and looked over his shoulder toward the school. "I have stuff in there I want to keep on me. And it's kind of Maxwell's safe place when he gets tired, you know?" He scooped his toad familiar up with both hands. "Like now, for instance. I'd put him in there at this point. The walk home's much longer for a toad."

"Okay."

"Go on without me. If I don't catch up, I'll see you tomorrow."

"Uh…I think I'll come with you." Murphy retraced her steps and glanced around the forest on either side of the road.

"I can get my bag by myself, Murph."

"I know." She shrugged and folded her arms. "But I don't wanna walk home by myself. That was a little weird back there. Flynn and Worley didn't look too happy about whatever they found."

"Yeah. And both of them are generally happy guys."

"Maybe I'm a little freaked out. I'll come with you and wait for you to get your bag."

"Freaked out by an angry headmaster, huh?" He chuckled and nudged her with his shoulder. "Don't worry about a thing, Murph. I'll protect you."

"Very funny."

They hadn't gone very far from the school and reached the gates in time to see Headmaster Flynn and all their professors gathered outside the weapons shed. Henry frowned. "You know, it's a given that professors like being at school, but party time at the weapons shed is the last thing I expected."

"It doesn't look like a party." Murphy tilted her head and watched Professor Worley stalk away from the shed toward the stables. "They all look upset now."

"Yeah, well, what are you gonna do? Flynn told us, didn't he? It's spring break for the professors too, so we'll slip into the assembly hall, slip out again, and—what the hell?"

"What?"

"Shh." He peered up at the side of the tallest tower rising from the main building, tapped Murphy's shoulder, and pointed as he whispered, "No sudden movements, got it?"

"Oh, shit," she muttered quietly as her eyes widened.

A man in tattered rags with a huge knife clenched between his teeth had climbed a quarter of the way up the tower. The rough stones provided perfectly strong handholds, and he was so intent on reaching the open window into Headmaster Flynn's quarters that he paid no attention to anything else.

Henry stepped forward quietly, placed Maxwell on the ground, and slid his hand into his pocket. *Even if I wasn't sure that's a raider, I know a dude with a knife isn't supposed to climb the school.* His fingers curled around his slingshot and he brought it out. Slowly, he crouched to pick up a particularly jagged stone from the courtyard and pressed it silently into the slingshot's cup. With a deep breath through his nose, he stared at the raider on the tower and focused his aim.

The slingshot lifted in a blur. Murphy didn't see the cup draw back or the rock launched before the raider shouted in pain and surprise. A bright red stain bloomed on his temple, and the man plummeted.

"Gotcha!" Henry shouted.

"What a shot." She caught up to him as he raced toward the raider.

He loaded another stone into his slingshot and aimed it at the man who groaned on the cobbled stone. "Professors! Headmaster! Over here!"

Through the stone archway, they saw the professors

and headmaster Flynn already racing toward them. Gilliam reached them first and stared with wide eyes at Henry. "Mr. Derks, would you care to tell us why you're—oh!" She saw the raider on the ground and grimaced. "Headmaster?"

Flynn ran toward them, assessed the bleeding outlaw on the ground, and looked at Henry. "I've heard about your aim with that weapon, Mr. Derks. Where was he?"

He pointed and the staff glanced at the tower.

The headmaster sniffed and gestured toward Bixby. "Professor Bixby, I trust you to keep an eye on this vagabond for us. Where there's one, there are sure to be—"

"Look out!" Murphy shouted and extended her hand to the stone archway. "*Recta impetum!*"

A green light surged from her hand and caught a second raider squarely in the chest. He catapulted away with a cry, and the dagger he'd attempted to throw at Headmaster Flynn clattered against the outer wall of the main building instead.

A horse whinnied and snorted, the sound almost as piercing as a girl's scream immediately after.

"Help! Somebody, hel—" Her voice cut off, and Flynn, Gilliam, and Dameron sprinted through the archway. Henry and Murphy followed closely and their familiars bounded at their heels.

Three more raiders had emerged into the field, sneering and chuckling madly as they tried to make their escape. Two of them had nocked arrows to their bows and trained them on the group that raced toward them. The third had his arm around Jessica's waist and his dagger pressed to her throat.

The horse whinnied and reared as Professor Worley

tried to calm him and pulled firmly on the reins. Professor Fellows ran from behind the wall around the main buildings and slowed when he saw the situation.

"What are you waiting for?" demanded the raider who held Jessica hostage. "Go on!"

Both filthy, reeking men loosed their arrows. Flynn and Dameron deflected them with quick spells while the horse whinnied and bucked again.

Three more arrows were loosed from the woods by three more raiders who ran toward them and nocked again. The battle on the field escalated. Henry and Murphy held their own alongside the professors and unleashed spells at the snarling raiders who retaliated with arrows. Professor Fellows surged forward to enter the fight from behind the raiders. He struck one of them with an attack spell and the other turned to him to fire more arrows.

The man with a knife at Jessica's throat tugged her farther out into the field. She finally struggled free from his nasty hand over her mouth and screamed, "Headmaster!"

Flynn whirled toward her and the raider stopped, straightened, and pressed the dagger into the girl's skin. "Don't even think about it, scarface."

The headmaster tried to move slowly toward them, but the raider clicked his tongue and shook his head. "I mean it, I ain't got nothin' to lose by cuttin' her right here."

Spells and arrows and a few more daggers careened across the field. Henry was far more accurate with his slingshot than the raiders were with poorly balanced bows, but it was enough to keep him busy. Flynn let the other professors fight the raiders while he focused on the student under his care held hostage by the lowest-level criminal. "Let her go."

"No. See, this is my ticket outta here. Your little kid shot my man out of the air. I ain't stickin' around."

"If you let her go now, the consequences won't be as severe as if you don't." From the corner of his eye, Flynn saw Miss Murphy sneak off and double back in a wide circle toward the open weapons shed. *Keep him talking. Give her time.* "And I would love to know what in the world your man was doing climbing toward my office."

"Ha! You would, wouldn't you? No!" The raider grasped Jessica even tighter and she cried out and sagged against his arm around her middle. "I told you not to move any closer. Her blood might be on my hands soon, but it'll be your fault."

The sounds of battle behind him had already faded and fortunately, the other professors had bound the raiders they'd overpowered with magical rope and what served as gags. The men shouted muffled protests, but their words were garbled and incomprehensible.

"Your men are finished and I have mages," Flynn added. "Give it up."

"Uh-uh. I got reassurances, see? I got—" The raider grunted, and his dagger thumped onto the grass before his eyes rolled back in his head and he crumpled. Jessica lurched forward and raced to the headmaster, her eyes wide and terrified.

Behind the fallen raider, Murphy lowered the giant training ax and sighed. "I've wanted to try that for a long time."

"Thank you, Miss Murphy. That was very much appreciated." Flynn nodded.

"Sure. Thanks for keeping him occupied." With a shrug, she slung the ax over her shoulder and walked toward the professors and the bound raiders without a second glance at the man she'd whacked on the back of the head.

"Wow, Murph." Henry grinned while he still aimed his slingshot at one of the magically bound raiders in the grass. "Way to go with that ax."

"It's growing on me."

Professor Fellows raced toward the unconscious raider and proceeded to bind the man as quickly as possible. After he'd led Jessica gently to the professors, Flynn returned to those who knelt in the grass in front of Dameron and Gilliam as Worley left the horse—now calm and reassured—in the stables and came to join them. Gilliam took the crying girl aside and guided her to the center courtyard.

The headmaster's lips twitched as he glanced from man to man. "Now. Which one of you would care to tell me what you didn't want us to see in Azerad?"

The other professors muttered quick spells to ungag the raiders, and the closest one to the headmaster spat at the man's feet. "It doesn't matter anyway, old man."

"What didn't you want us to see?"

"The same thing that's happening here is happening everywhere else," the raider snapped with a sneer. "And by the time you see the rest of us, it'll be too late."

Flynn's eyes widened, and he lowered his chin to stare at the reeking man in the grass for a moment. "Thank you very much." He stepped away, glanced at Professor Dameron, and nodded. The professor muttered another spell and the bound raiders fell unconscious in the field, although none of them would have a massive bump on their head like their leader.

The headmaster stopped in front of Henry and Murphy and nodded. "I have some emergency call potions to utilize. But I want to thank you two now before I run out of time. Mr. Derks. Miss Murphy. Thank you for your bravery and perfect timing. I believe you've had a hand in saving the entire kingdom. Excuse me."

With a brisk nod and a grim smile, he strode past them toward the stone archway en route to his private room in the tallest tower.

Henry turned to look at Murphy with wide eyes. "Did he say we—"

"Saved the kingdom? Yeah." She grinned. "No one's gonna say a thing about your slingshot after this."

"Only good things, Murph." He glanced at Maxwell at his feet, lifted his slingshot, and gave it a noisy kiss. "Only good things."

CHAPTER FORTY-ONE

In their shared room that night, Raven opened her grandfather's old journal and turned to the page she wanted. "I'm glad you asked about this tonight."

Bella sat on the edge of her bed and shrugged. "Well, it'll at least be a distraction from the disappointment of not finding anything. I don't know how that's possible. Someone is attacked in that tower, guards run everywhere, and there's literally no sign of what happened."

"Maybe it only means they have great security here."

The other girl glanced at her, narrowed her eyes, and chuckled wryly. "If they have good security, Raven, whoever screamed up there wouldn't have found herself in a position where screaming was necessary."

"Okay, maybe you're right. But we didn't find anything, so here. Distract yourself." She held the journal out toward the other young mage and nodded. "It's the perfect time for it, right?"

Bella studied it a little warily, took a deep breath, and accepted the old leather-bound yellowed pages with both hands. "Fine. Seriously, though, if this doesn't show me anything I don't already—"

A bellow rose from the hall outside their room and was immediately followed by more yells and the loud thud of boots on stone. Something thumped against the ceiling above them, and more hollered commands and harsh, sharp shouts of warning came from outside. Raven turned toward the window. "What's that?"

"How am I supposed to know?" Bella placed the journal on her bed, Wesley landed on her shoulder, and both girls hurried to the window on the other side of the room.

Raven drew the curtain aside and they peered out at dozens of soldiers who ran in neat lines down the walkways surrounding the castle. The clash of steel weapons was fainter and farther away but unmistakable. So was the fierce roar of more than one dragon. "Something's wrong."

"Obviously. Do you see anything—ah!"

The girls leapt away when a sneering, dirt-smeared face appeared in the window. The raider chuckled and stuck his tongue between his teeth seconds before an Azerad guard put an arrow in his back. He fell from the wall, screaming, and the sounds of combat swelled.

"Raiders in Azerad." Raven spun away from the window. "And I know one of those dragons is Leander. I have to get to him."

"Yeah, there is no way I will let you go out there—"

"Bella, I have to!"

"I was gonna say by yourself, Raven. At least let me finish."

"Sorry. Come on." She opened the door and the girls almost rushed head-first into a huge group of soldiers who sprinted down the hall to reach the fighting. They waited for the last of them to pass and jogged after Azerad's fighters. "We can follow them outside and get to the dragon terrace on our own after that."

"I hate this castle."

"Right?"

The girls moved quickly and followed close enough behind the guards to keep up but not too close to draw attention to themselves. They stopped when the last of the soldiers hurried through an outer door and into the chaos outside. The noise faded abruptly when the door shut again, and Raven turned to Bella with a nod. "Ready?"

"Are you kidding? Come on." The other girl led the way toward the door and shoved it open before both young mages stepped out into the night. Torches bobbed and weaved on all levels of the governor's estate. Soldiers clashed in combat with raiders—more raiders than Raven knew existed—and everywhere, bodies fell as combatants surged toward each other and entered the fray.

"This way." She tugged her companion along the walkway toward the dragon terrace. They stayed close to the wall as the soldiers rushed past and none of them paid any mind to two young mages who snuck through the danger. "Turn right and down these stairs."

They descended the staircase to the lower level as fast as they could. Wesley uttered a warning shriek, and Bella glanced up. "Watch out!" She caught Raven by the shirt and shoved her against the wall of the castle as a flailing, flaming, screaming raider fell from above them. He landed on the stairs where Raven had stood seconds before, then toppled over the side to one of the lower levels.

She peered over the edge of the stairs and grimaced. "Ouch. Hey, thanks."

"Yeah, well, we'd better be careful about falling debris from here on out, right?"

"Azerad definitely wasn't built with that in mind."

The girls raced on and paused only to avoid the wild swing of another raider's massive, heavy sword before an Azerad soldier kicked the man in the back and hurled him over the edge of the walkway. He nodded at the young mages and ran ahead to find another opponent.

Finally, they reached the dragon terrace and Raven darted forward. She didn't see the man hunched beside a crate of dragon feed in the middle of the avenue. He stood suddenly, his grin exposing stained teeth, and raised a bow to aim its arrow directly at her.

"*Adsulto protentia!*" Bella shouted. The force of her spell thrust him aside. The arrow went wide, the bow flew from his hand, and the raider pounded against the door of the stall that belonged to the silent but deadly brown dragon.

"Wha—aah!" The raider struggled to free himself, but it was difficult with a dragon's massive jaws clamped around his shoulder and half his chest. The other dragons roared and screeched their excitement. They beat against the stalls as the brown dragon jerked the raider into the stall with him. The man's screams cut off abruptly, followed by a sickening crunch and a ripping sound.

"Okay. Be careful around dragons in a battle. Got it." Bella nodded and frowned at her companion. "What are you doing?"

"I'm getting weapons." She crouched beside the crates of dragon feed and lifted a long dagger to show the other girl. "It looks like the guy took something of everything and stockpiled it. Here."

"Great. Thanks."

While Bella hefted the blade to test its weight, Raven lifted a mostly full quiver, shrugged, and slung it over her head and shoulder before she darted toward the raider's abandoned bow. "This is an Azerad bow. It has the seal and everything. It'll be good enough."

She stood and ran down the avenue to Leander's stall with the other girl on her heels. They had almost stopped outside the stall when the air blazed with brilliant flashes of green and blue. Alessandra stood in an open doorway on one of the upper levels and launched attack spells left and right as raiders swarmed up staircases, down walkways, and across terraces.

"Raven." Leander snorted and lowered his head.

She looked away from Alessandra and nodded at him. "Yeah. Let's do this."

"You're letting him out?"

"I don't care about the rules right now."

"I was asking more to make sure you were doing that because it's what I'd do."

"Oh. Then, yeah." She unlatched the door and yanked Bella aside as Leander burst through and almost ripped the door off its hinges. His wings spread wide, and he lowered his belly to the ground before he boosted Raven up with his head. Once she sat securely at the base of his neck, she squeezed tightly with her thighs and leaned down to offer Bella a hand. "Get on."

"What?" The girl stared at Leander staring at her.

"I won't leave you here by yourself. Take my hand."

"Raven, you don't have a saddle."

"You rode a horse on the way here. It's like that. Squeeze with your knees and hold onto me."

For the first time, Bella Chase looked terrified. After a moment, however, she gritted her teeth, nodded, and took Raven's hand.

"Step up," Leander told her and lowered his head beside her foot.

The girl sighed a little nervously, set her boot on the dragon's ridged head, and shouted in surprise when he lifted her up and onto his back behind his mage. Wesley wheeled above them and screeched. "I can't believe I'm doing this. Okay. So I squeeze with my knees and—ahh!"

The dragon practically plunged over the edge of the dragon terrace and Bella screamed as she clutched her arms around Raven's waist and squeezed.

"Okay, watch that dagger, huh?"

"Oh. Sorry." Bella dared herself to open her eyes and she held on with one arm while she lowered the knife in her other hand. "Oh, boy."

"Are you okay?"

"Yeah, I'm only…uh, riding a dragon." The mage gulped as Wesley followed closely as the huge red beast soared around the outskirts of the castle.

"You'd better get used to it fast. And keep your eyes open—literally." She glanced over her shoulder as much as she could without throwing her companion off balance. "An extra pair of eyes comes in handy."

"Yeah, no problem."

Leander took them higher until they had a full view of the chaos below. The cacophony of battle rose toward them. Swords clashed with swords, fallen men screamed, commands were bellowed, and the dragons' roars raised to a crescendo, punctuated by the flares of spells cast by Alessandra and the two mages who served Governor Irlish. A horde of the ragged, vicious outlaws in rags was locked in battle with Azerad's soldiers where they fought in the huge last-minute arena they'd set up for Raven and Leander's match.

She only had to think about joining the fight there and the dragon banked and descended toward the arena terrace. Bella squeaked and tightened her arm around her waist. "Do you know that voice projection spell Gilliam uses all the time?" she asked the girl.

"Yeah. Totally."

"Use it and when I say the word, tell the soldiers to fall back."

"Got it."

Leander swooped under the arena terrace to give Bella more time. She muttered the spell and tapped her throat, and the great dragon turned away from the castle again to lift them above the largest arena. They glided in a wide circle again, and Raven nodded. "Now!"

"Soldiers! Fall back!" The girl's voice cracked against the stone of the arena terrace and the thick outer walls of the castle. Everyone looked up from the fighting as the great red dragon circled toward them and descended at a sharp angle. They echoed the cry to fall back, and the last of the soldiers untangled themselves from the snarling, laughing raiders moments before Leander unleashed a massive column of fire.

"*Sequantur flamma!*" Raven stretched toward the flames

and rocketed them onto every raider who still stood in the area. Their screams drowned out the other sounds of battle, and a handful of raiders flailed so wildly that they stumbled over the edge and fell, shrieking and enveloped in flames. The others didn't last long after that.

The dragon uttered a triumphant screech and the soldiers they'd saved from another grueling battle raised their weapons and cheered.

"Great work," Raven told Bella as the dragon climbed higher to circle the tallest towers again.

"Yeah. That was awesome." Wesley fluttered beside them and echoed Leander with a small shriek of his own.

When they reached the west side of the governor's estate, more shouts and screams issued from below in the city itself. Out in a field within the much lower wall around Azerad, the city's people fled from a group of raiders who tried to escape across open ground. *And we'll stop them.*

Feeling her intention, the dragon leveled out and headed toward the far western quarter and the field. The raiders sprinted toward a tower built into the outer wall above a drawn portcullis. *That's not gonna happen, boys.*

"Bella."

"Yeah."

"We'll land directly behind those raiders, got it? That's where you get off and close in on them from behind."

"And what will you do?"

"Leander and I will head them off at that tower. If they're smart, they'll try to turn back. You'll be there and we'll eliminate them together."

"Raven Alby."

She glanced briefly over her shoulder. "What?"

"You have skills with battle plans. I'll give you that."

With a grin, she nodded and moved her fingers toward Sarah Alby's pin on her jacket. "So did my mom."

The terrified people of Azerad had practically cleared a path for the escaping raiders, and they all looked up from where they'd scattered across the fields to see the massive dragon descend from the dark sky and land ahead of them.

Bella leapt down and landed squarely in the grass. "I got this, Raven."

"Yeah, I know. Let's show these assholes what real war mages can do, huh?"

Leander launched immediately and skirted about three dozen fleeing raiders to head them off at the gate. Bella tightened her hold around the dagger and trudged after them, while Wesley flew above her head.

"Right there." Raven pointed although she didn't have to. Her familiar followed her lead perfectly and glided over the outer wall of the city before he circled. He descended and hovered beside the walkway on the top of the wall, which was too narrow for him but wide enough for her to vault from his back and land perfectly.

The dragon immediately swooped to the tower behind where she'd landed and a little to her right. She scanned the raiders who raced toward the gate as he landed on the tower with a crunch and his huge, deadly talons grated and scratched against the stone. Sparks flurried before he gained a firm hold on his perch and stared at the running criminals.

"Wait!" Raven darted him a quick glance. "They have hostages."

MARTHA CARR & MICHAEL ANDERLE

"I see." Leander screeched, and every single raider heading toward them skidded to a halt in the grass.

Two women and a boy a few years younger than the mages struggled in the grasp of three sneering and seriously pissed-off raiders. The thin woman with long brown hair that fell over her shoulders screamed when she saw the dragon on the tower.

That's the same scream from the tournament.

"Let them go," Raven shouted.

"What are you gonna do, little girl?" One of the first in line drew his sword and gave her a devious grin. "Your dragon's useless if you want to save these pretty little things we're taking with us. Governor Irlish's wife, her personal maid, and… Well, the boy was there so we snatched him anyway."

"Please!" the younger blonde woman shouted and struggled against the man's hold on her upper arms. "Help us!"

The mage stepped forward with one foot and propped it against the rising stone beside the wall's walkway. Calmly, she drew an arrow from the commandeered quiver at her back, nocked it, and drew back to aim the weapon at the raider in the front. "I said let them go."

"Screw you and your dragon," yelled a man with an eyepatch that even in the dark looked stained and a little damp. "We have our ticket out of here with these three. There's nothing you can do to—"

Raven switched her aim and loosed the arrow. It pierced the defiant raider through the throat and he choked, gurgled, and collapsed. The other outlaws hissed and cursed at her, but she ignored them as she nocked another arrow and aimed at the man in front again. *I wanted the gut. I should aim a little lower next time.*

"You don't have enough arrows in that quiver to kill all of us, you little brat!"

"True." She didn't move her gaze from her target, even when she grinned. "But I didn't come alone."

Thinking she meant her dragon, the raiders glanced at Leander perched on the tower. His yellow eyes glowed like torches in the night. "You won't unleash your dragon on innocent—"

Wesley uttered a startling screech seconds before Bella unleashed her first attack. "*Adsulto protentia!*"

The force of her spell was enough to hurl half a dozen raiders off their feet and careen them into the men in front of them. Shouts followed, swords were drawn, and Bella Chase finally had the chance to show what she could do.

Green and red attack spells surged from the black-haired mage's hands to strike raiders left and right with deadly precision. Raven saved her arrows for the men who moved toward the other mage while her companion was busy attacking others. She nocked, drew, and loosed again and again to find her targets every time and fell one raider after another at the girl's feet.

Bella had to step back to avoid the bodies, but it didn't matter. The raiders were penned in with no way out and no real way to fight back. A group of them separated to try running south instead, and Leander unleashed his dragon fire on them without any prompting at all from Raven.

"*Sequantur flamma!*" She stretched toward the spray of fire and delivered it to the retreating vagabonds before she nocked another arrow. Screams and shrieks resulted and quickly petered out. The men who hadn't met a fiery death retreated a little, trapped between a dragon and two very skilled mages.

Wesley swooped toward the center of the group and unleashed his stream of much more controlled flames. It mostly caught the raiders' hair on fire, but it was enough to do real damage while Bella continued to launch her spells at the stragglers.

Finally, the young mages had whittled the group of fleeing criminals down to five—the three securing the governor's wife and the other hostages, plus the apparent leader and another man with a long knife in either hand.

"We won't give these up!" the raider who clutched the boy declared belligerently. "You're done. Let's go." He hauled his captive with him, who shouted and kicked and put up an admirable fight.

Wesley dove toward the man with outstretched talons and clawed his stained, dirt-encrusted face. The blinded raider shrieked and batted wildly at the darting firedrake. He stumbled toward Bella and knocked himself out cold when he met the stone wall face-first.

Raven put an arrow into the man with two knives and a second later, the bastard who'd led his little band out there to escape screamed as her next arrow quivered where it protruded from his foot.

"You little—shit!" He hopped frantically and clawed at the man who held the governor's wife. His arm came down on her captor's shoulder and the second raider stumbled. The woman wrenched herself free from his grasp and ran toward Bella.

The third man holding Mrs. Irlish's maid chuckled at

the plight of his comrades, then jerked the blonde woman closer against him and grinned smugly. "It might be I'm the only one getting outta here at all."

With a snarl, Leander launched from the top of the tower and swooped beneath Raven as she leapt from the wall. She landed squarely on his back, and when the great dragon touched the grass between the charred corpses and the three raiders holding one final hostage between them, she already had another arrow in her bow. The tip was aimed perfectly at the center of the snarling raider's forehead. "I won't miss from this close. Let her go."

The man glared at her with narrowed eyes but finally shoved the maid away. She stumbled toward Leander, shrieked, and pivoted to run toward her mistress and the boy.

"Go on," Bella told them. "Get to safety. We'll handle the rest of it."

"Thank you," Mrs. Irlish whispered before she hurried with the other hostages across the field and toward the governor's estate.

The leader of the band of raiders that had now dwindled to three jerked the arrow from his boot with a howl. He flung the arrow aside and spread his arms dramatically. "Are you happy now? No hostages. Tit for tat, right? Let us out through that gap, and we'll disappear."

"I'm sure you'll disappear anyway," Raven muttered and maintained her aim at his forehead.

Bella stepped toward them, her hands raised and ready while Wesley landed on her shoulder. "I think a freezing dungeon is more appropriate."

The raiders glanced from one mage to the other and

scowled at their determined expressions. Before they could respond, a few shouts issued from the other side of the field. A group of soldiers raced toward them, and the cornered raiders spun in the only direction left to attempt to flee north along the wall.

Leander's dragon fire erupted from his jaws. Raven shifted on his back to keep her balance as he leaned forward and incinerated the fleeing men. At such a close range, he didn't need her help for a direct wash of flame, and the men had no time to scream before they lost the ability to do so.

When the column of fire died, the dragon snorted twin plumes of dark-gray smoke.

"Okay…" She removed the arrow from her bow and replaced it in the quiver. "That was also an option."

Wesley screeched on Bella's shoulder and delivered his own much smaller fireball into the grass where nothing more remained of the raiders than a few piles of ash. His mage turned her head to shoot him an exasperated glance. The firedrake met her gaze for two seconds, then launched himself into the air to flutter around her head.

Raven leapt from Leander's back and took inventory of the raiders they'd eliminated in only a few minutes. The guards finally reached them and stopped a safe distance from the massive red dragon and the smoking piles of remains. They caught their breaths, and one of them sheathed his sword. "It looks like you girls handled yourselves well."

Bella spun to face the man and folded her arms. "Mages. Don't call us girls."

The man nodded curtly without so much as a hint of a smile. "Yes, ma'am."

"Did the governor's wife and the other hostages reach you all right?"

"They did. Some of my men led them into the estate, and the fighting has died down to merely gathering a few battered prisoners smart enough to give up. With all due respect, Mage, I think it's best if you keep your dragon away from those. Governor Irlish wants them interrogated."

Raven almost laughed at the formal address. *It doesn't have my name after it, but it's a good start.* "No problem."

Bella nodded at her companion and headed toward the soldiers. "I'll go back with them."

"Are you sure?" She gestured toward Leander, who lowered his head and swiveled it toward the girl to flash her a dragon's grin.

"Uh...yeah. I think one ride on a dragon is enough to last me until the end of the year. At the very least. Good work, Raven. Leander."

The dragon lowered his head in a subtle bow, and his mage grinned. "We couldn't have done it without you and Wesley. Your timing was perfect."

"I know." Bella wiggled her eyebrows and whirled to step past the soldiers toward the towers at the center of the city. "Come on, then."

They jerked to attention, marched swiftly behind her, and occasionally glanced at the firedrake wheeling above their heads.

Raven sighed heavily and swiped loose hairs away from her face. She caught her long red braid and pulled it over her shoulder to give it a quick inspection. "Look at that. A tighter tie was all I needed."

"Yes, Raven. Your hair is the greatest achievement of the night."

Laughing, she slung the bow over her head and shoulder to rest against her back with the quiver and returned to him. "There were so many big wins today, Leander. But it's important to celebrate the little achievements too."

She paused when her gaze fell on the fallen bodies around her and the multiple piles of burnt raiders. A lump caught in her throat, and she swallowed it and forced it to remain unacknowledged.

"They would not have stopped if you'd given them the chance," Leander rumbled.

"I know but it doesn't make this any easier to look at. I have a feeling I'll see this for a while after tonight."

"Not as long as you would if you refused to acknowledge it now, War Mage. At least you're looking now."

"Yeah." She opened her clenched fists and nodded. "If a war mage title is in my future, I guess I'd better get used to this. You're right."

"There is nothing more to see, Raven. Let's go." He lowered his belly to the grass and gave her a boost with his head as she climbed onto his back.

The young mage gazed over her dragon's scaled head when he turned toward the center of Azerad. She squared her shoulders. *Do the right thing when it's most important, however and whenever that is. I'm trying, Grandpa.*

Leander leapt skyward and skimmed a few feet over the field before he ascended sharply. The night had fallen and become quieter now that the battle was over. A few soldiers still moved through the city streets as they soared overhead, and the same situation prevailed at the center of the city around Governor Irlish's estate.

"It's gonna be a little hard to go back to the stables for another three days, isn't it?"

He snorted. "Something tells me that silly little tournament will not continue."

She smirked. "Great minds think alike, dragon. After this, the Tournament of Mages is pointless. Honestly, I'll be happier if we are sent home tomorrow."

"Me too."

CHAPTER FORTY-TWO

Two days after the raider attack on Azerad, Raven, Bella, Henry, and Murphy stood in a line in front of Headmaster Flynn's desk in his living quarters that doubled as an office. The headmaster took a deep breath and looked up from the rolls of parchment paper with a gentle smile. "Thank you all for taking the time out of your busy schedules to meet me this evening."

The young mages chuckled a little nervously.

Henry shrugged. "Okay, I'm probably missing dinner right now—ow."

Murphy elbowed him in the ribs and he grinned at her as he rubbed his side.

"I'll make this as short and to the point as possible, Mr. Derks. Thereafter, if you like, you may join a few of your professors and myself in the common area outside the assembly hall for a meal. I believe it will be ready for our enjoyment by the time we're finished."

"Oh. Yeah, that sounds great." He nodded and shoved his hands in his pockets.

MARTHA CARR & MICHAEL ANDERLE

"Excellent." Flynn clapped briskly. "Of course, the ladies are also cordially invited. Now, let's get to the point of this meeting. I asked the four you here because I want to personally thank you. Of course, you may think you already know why—and yes, defeating ruthless murderers and thieves on your own without any previous battle experience is a worthy feat. But I don't believe any of you have been made aware of the full scope of the effects your actions have had on a broader scale."

Murphy bit her lip. "Oh, boy."

"That's a precursor to positive news, Miss Murphy, I assure you."

The other students laughed a little, and the girl grinned and folded her arms. There was no trace of a blush on her cheeks.

"In fact, it starts with your efforts yesterday, Miss Murphy, as well as Mr. Derk's initiative and impressive aim."

Henry raised his chin and wiggled his eyebrows as he cast Raven a sidelong glance. She smirked and shook her head.

"It's quite possible that we would never have become aware of the dangerous and unfortunate situation in which Miss Rodenmeyer found herself over the last few days if the two of you hadn't returned to school grounds when you did. To be perfectly honest, part of me doubts we would have even found those raiders on the property before it was too late for everyone. But we did thanks to you two."

Bella and Raven stared at Henry and Murphy. "You fought raiders here?"

402

Henry shrugged. "Well, almost directly below us."

"He shot a raider off the outside of this tower," Murphy added with a chuckle, "and I clubbed one on the back of the head with my favorite sparring ax."

"Oof."

"Which also conveniently released Miss Rodenmeyer from her captor's arms and delivered her to the safety of Professor Gilliam's." The headmaster smiled at his students and cleared his throat so they'd all turn to face him. "It doesn't take much to get the information one needs from a raider. Reading between the lines is fairly easy, even when those lines are vague threats and misdirection. These criminals took Miss Rodenmeyer and her family hostage and threatened their lives to compel her to help them break into the weapons shed to tamper with the Periview. Unfortunately, we lost the connection with Azerad's replica and consequently, most of your first match, Miss Alby. I do hope you'll recount it for us in full detail over dinner.

"I digress. The fact that a relatively uneducated band of raiders snuck into this school to dismantle a magical device and cut off our connection to Azerad gave me a hunch that they did not want us to see a planned attack in that city. One raider's useless threat confirmed it. I sent word immediately to Governor Irlish and told him what had happened. He explained that his wife had come down with a sudden illness and things were a little chaotic at the time.

"I suspected that he didn't want me to worry about having sent five of this school's brilliant students to his city for the Tournament of Mages, which was why he hid the fact that his wife had been attacked not half an hour before by a single raider within his own home. I therefore took the liberty of alerting as many of my contacts as I could reach on such short notice. Miss Alby, your friend William Moss the dragon trainer was one of them."

"Really?" Raven wrinkled her nose with a confused smile. "What did he do to help?"

"The better question is what didn't he do." Flynn folded his hands in front of him. "Mr. Moss and the dragon—Teo, I believe—delivered messages to the three closest cities and a few other small townships in record time. They were able to get word to the capital about the issues I predicted in Azerad. The message spread in a matter of hours, you understand, and William delivered one final message to the troops gathered at the breach in the great wall. They received their orders to return to their posts and prepare for a massive incursion of raiders. Whole contingents mobilized across the entire expanse of Lomberdoon, and the majority of the raiders inside the kingdom walls have been dealt with already."

"What about the rest of them?" Bella asked with wide eyes.

"Unfortunately, there a number who slipped through the net, Miss Chase—a few escaped raiders we couldn't reach in time. And this is where you and Miss Alby performed the unthinkable in Azerad, as I understand it."

The two girls shared a knowing glance. On the other side of Raven, Henry whistled and muttered, "I can't wait to hear this one."

"You two were the final, instrumental piece that allowed us to work as one across the kingdom at large and quite far beyond it, to be perfectly honest."

"What?"

Headmaster Flynn's smile widened. "Beyond having eliminated an impressive number of infiltrating criminals who scurried across Azerad, as I've heard it told, the two of you were the only ones who thought to look beyond the governor's estate. In rescuing Mrs. Irlish and the other two hostages at that western gate, you enabled Lomberdoon's warning to Sterlin Velt and Everwiel regarding the larger threat of oncoming raider parties revealed by a few of the criminals interrogated that night."

Bella frowned. "I don't understand."

"I don't hold it against you, Miss Chase. When you have all the pieces, you're remarkably skilled at putting them together. These pieces simply aren't common knowledge." Flynn spread his arms apologetically. "Azerad possesses the strongest model of the Periview in known existence. At times, it has been used to communicate with the governing bodies of Sterlin Velt and Everwiel when necessary. Governor Irlish would most certainly have agreed to hand his Periview over or even destroy it himself had those raiders successfully taken his wife out of the city. And, I imagine, the surrounding kingdoms, as well as our own, would have been quickly overrun. But that was not the case. With his wife tucked safely in their bed, the governor made the connection to the other kingdoms' leaders and advisors with a warning of the threat they also faced. The last I heard, both their militaries made quick work of the largest band of united raiders in living memory."

The headmaster leaned forward and smiled at the young war mages in training who stood in front of his desk with startled expressions. "All because you two worked together to face a threat even you did not fully understand. Three kingdoms owe their lives to the four of you. I'm sure we'll think of something to commemorate that."

The huge, circular room at the top of Fowler Academy's tallest tower fell silent. On the floor at Henry's feet, Maxwell croaked loudly and startled Flynn, who jumped a little in surprise.

Henry chuckled at his toad familiar. "You can say that again."

The students burst out laughing, and Flynn allowed himself a good chuckle with them. He gestured toward the door and took a deep breath. "That is all for this little meeting of ours. You're free to enjoy the rest of the spring break. All four nights and three days of it before classes resume. Please do feel free to join us for dinner. It's a special occasion, however private."

"Thanks, Headmaster."

"I'm starving."

"Henry…"

The four heroic young mages turned silently to move out the door after Bella pushed it open and led the way down the stairs.

"Miss Alby, I would like a few more minutes of your time before you join your friends if you please."

"Oh. Uh…sure." Raven leaned toward the stairwell and muttered, "You guys go on. I'm staying for dinner, obviously, so I'll be down there in a short while."

"Don't take forever, Alby!" Henry waved before he hurried behind Bella and Murphy to descend the winding staircase.

She turned slowly to face Headmaster Flynn and nodded. "If this is about the whole riding without a saddle thing, or me taking Leander out of the stables in Azerad to fly around the city, even though it helped save three kingdoms... I know I'm breaking many rules here. But I promise it's all for good reasons—"

"Let me stop you right there, Miss Alby." The headmaster cleared his throat and fought back a chuckle. "I didn't ask you to stay behind so you could receive your own private lecture."

Startled, she took a deep breath, exhaled, and frowned. "Okay..."

"I thought this might be of a more personal nature for you and I simply did not wish to cross a line by announcing it in your friends' presence. I'll leave that decision up to you."

The young mage swallowed and stepped toward the desk. "You heard something about my grandfather, didn't you?"

"Even better." Flynn smiled at his desk and removed a folded piece of parchment paper from beneath the scattered piles of other documents. "I received a letter from Connor Alby. Two, actually. And one of them is addressed to you."

Raven's heart fluttered in her chest. *Finally.* "What does it say?"

The headmaster shrugged and offered her the folded missive. "I have no idea. I'm not in the habit of reading student mail, Raven, even when it's addressed to one of my most astonishingly capable students."

With wide eyes, she took the last few steps to his desk

and accepted the letter. It was stamped with an unbroken sigil from the capital stamped in bright-red wax. "Thank you."

"It's the least I can do. Of course, this has nothing to do with what you've done for this school and Brighton and far beyond Lomberdoon over the last few weeks. But it's a letter with your name on it."

"It's honestly the best news you could give me right now." She rubbed her hand over the unbroken wax seal.

"I'm glad. Now, if you don't mind, I'll hurry to the first floor to alleviate these hunger pains. Doing so in good company can't hurt much either." With a knowing smile, Flynn stepped around the awestruck young mage and nodded. "Feel free to take your time here. When you're ready, I would still very much like to hear about your single match in the Tournament of Mages. I imagine the tale will be quite riveting."

"If you want riveting, Headmaster, maybe you should summon Daniel Smith to the school and have him tell it."

Headmaster Flynn responded with a loud, booming laugh and headed out the door to descend the staircase. "We shall see, dragon rider. Or is it war mage?"

"We could start a whole new order," she replied with a smirk. "I kinda like the sound of dragon mage."

"Hmm. It's something to think about, most definitely." With that, he hurried down the stairs and disappeared from view.

She waited another minute and couldn't bring herself to do more than stare at the unbroken seal on the letter from Connor Alby. Finally, she flipped the folded parchment paper and grinned. *"War Mage Raven Alby*, huh?" Thanks for the status boost, Grandpa."

Raven slid her finger slowly beneath the fold in the letter and broke the wax seal. With a deep breath, she unfolded the parchment paper covered in her grandfather's unmistakable handwriting and began to read.

A day later, Raven stood beside the newly fortified stables on Moss Ranch, her arms folded as she watched William tack up another board against the back of a stall one particularly upset visiting dragon had kicked out of place three days before.

"I still can't—ow." He shook his hand out, glanced at his thumb, and hissed a sigh before he hammered the last few nails in. "I still can't believe you went to Azerad to help Fowler Academy win a Tournament of Mages prize and ended up saving the governor's wife, the entire city, Lomberdoon, and two other kingdoms all in the same night."

"Hey, you know me." She spread her arms extravagantly and smirked. "I'm all about breaking records."

He turned and shook the hammer at her. "I thought you were breaking tradition."

"Well, someone told me how bending tradition works, and I think I like that definition a little better."

William laughed, pounded the final nail in, and stood from his crouch. He took a step back and nodded. "That oughtta hold until the next rowdy beast I lend a stall to for the night." He flipped the hammer in his hand, hooked the head over the top rung of the low fence outside the stables, and turned. "So what's next for the great War Mage Dragon Rider Raven Alby."

"Jeez, that's a mouthful."

"Well, you gotta find something catchy, whatever it is."

She smirked. "What do you think of Dragon Mage?"

His head tilted thoughtfully, he wrinkled his nose. "Nah. That sounds like a dragon casting spells. And lemme tell you, Raven, if that ever happens, I don't care how much of a black mark it puts on my reputation. I will take off my dragon-trainer hat, toss it into the mud, and maybe stomp on it a few times. I'll call it an entire life well-spent before I move onto something that won't make me completely lose my mind."

Raven burst out laughing and he couldn't help but chuckle with her.

The dragon trainer removed his wide-brimmed hat to wipe the sweat off his forehead, then jammed it over his long blond hair again. "I'm serious. Dragons have enough power as it is."

"Can you imagine Leander with magic?"

He thumped both hands against his chest, spun in an exaggerated circle, and staggered against the fence post. "Let me die, please."

"I thought more along the lines of hilarity with a side order of chaos, but death probably isn't that far off the mark."

Slowly, he opened one eye and raised an eyebrow as he smirked at her. "You know him better than anyone. Could he handle his own magic?"

"You mean beyond terrible strength and epic flight and

breathing fire?" Raven shrugged. "Yeah, I'm sure Leander would be fine. He'd have me to show him how it works."

William pushed away from the fence and pointed at her. "And that's exactly why I decided to quit worrying about you altogether, Raven."

"You mean it wasn't because of all the times I told you not to worry about me?"

With a small, thoughtful smile, his gaze fell to the trampled grass and dirt between them as he stepped toward the young mage. "I realized you and Leander have each other's backs no matter what. You made that very clear. So, yeah, I had to come to that conclusion all on my own before I decided not to worry about you." He bit his lip, and his gaze raised slowly to meet hers. "It doesn't mean I don't think about you."

Oh, man. What am I about to step into right now?

She hesitated but smiled at him, and for a few seconds, she thought he'd step closer, at the very least. Maybe even all the way.

"But..." He clapped and turned away from her to head down the fence surrounding the dragon field, where all Moss Ranch's trained beasts milled around with their respective clans. "You completely changed the subject and didn't actually answer my question."

With a little sigh, the young mage chuckled and joined him in his leisurely stroll. "Sorry, William. Remind me again what question that was, exactly."

"What's next for Raven Alby, Title To Be Determined?"

She snorted and offered a little shrug. "I honestly have no idea. But if I had to guess—and it's literally only a guess —I'd say I'm headed for some kind of secret appearance with a group of veteran war mages going behind King Vaughn's back to prepare us all for the eventual return of magic for everyone. Possibly."

William stopped short and turned slowly toward her, his mouth agape. "Say what?"

With a sigh, she closed her eyes and nodded. "It sounds like a lunatic raving about crazy impossibilities, right?"

"Not that I'm calling you a lunatic, Raven, but I would love to know which other lunatic put that idea in your head."

She scrunched her face and fixed her gaze on him. "I got a letter from my grandpa."

His eyes widened. "I called Connor Alby a lunatic, didn't I?"

Raven laughed and waved dismissively. "Don't worry. Your secret's safe with me."

An airy chuckle of stunned disbelief issued from the dragon trainer's half-open mouth, and he stared past her at nothing in the woods beyond Moss Ranch. "I appreciate that. What the hell was in that letter?"

"So much I don't understand. Yet." She nodded for them to continue walking, and he fell in beside her on autopilot. "Have you ever heard of a War Mage Athena?"

"Hmm. It's an awesome name but it doesn't ring a bell."

"Yeah, I didn't think so. He said he'd made contact with her and that she was the only person in Havendom who believed him about magic returning. Apparently, she's the one who sent for him before he disappeared from Brighton in the middle of the night."

"Wow."

"I know."

"He really thinks magic's coming back for everyone?"

Raven shrugged. "It's only a hunch. With a trace of proof behind it, I guess."

"That's a smidgeon more than a hunch, Raven."

The young mage turned toward him and pressed her hands together to tip her fingers until they pointed directly at him. "Can you promise to keep my secret?"

William raised his eyebrows and a tiny frown flickered across his eyebrows.

If I didn't know better, I'd say I hurt his feelings with that question.

He studied her intently for a few seconds and fixed her with a steady look. "I hope you know by now that I'd do anything you asked me to."

She smiled and bit her lip. "Well, I'd rather ask than simply assume."

"Okay. I can and do promise to keep your secret." William grinned and the moment of unexpected seriousness passed. "So tell me already. Pretty please with a giant dragon-shaped cherry on top."

Raven barked out a laugh and they continued to walk. "I've seen the proof too—with my own eyes."

"Okay…"

"Oh, fine. Connor Alby has his magic back, okay? He's no longer a spent wizard living out the rest of his days on a goat ranch. He's back in action."

"Ha, ha. Good one."

"Thanks. I'm serious."

He did a double-take and whipped his hat off his head. "Are you kidding me?"

"Nope."

"How did you—" He squinted at the dragon field and released a sigh through loose lips. "Are you sure?"

"All right. I know it's hard to grasp and everyone around here simply accepted my last-minute excuse, which I honestly didn't think would pass as acceptable, but here we are."

William shook his head. "What?"

"Remember that giant hole in my shoulder from that damn elf arrow?"

He snorted. "Oh, boy. Back to when this whole thing started, huh?"

Raven raised an eyebrow and gestured impatiently. "Well it didn't heal itself overnight with a salve, that's for sure."

For a few seconds, the dragon trainer stared at her with his mouth agape, completely motionless. His eye twitched before he shut his mouth with a click and swallowed. "Connor healed that arrow wound...with magic."

"Yeah. It surprised us both, honestly. And you're the only person I've told about this so don't blow it."

William pressed his lips together and tapped them a few times with his fingers.

"Good. I trust you."

"So he had a letter from this War Mage Athena in Havendom because his magic returned."

"Not so much cause and effect, I don't think. Merely creepily perfect timing."

"And he took this long to tell you...why?"

She shrugged. "He said he still had research to do and people to find. I assume because he wants more opinions. But if I were to figuratively read between the lines, I'd say he's putting something of a mage rebellion together. That's because King Vaughn—or his advisors, at least—don't want to accept the possibility of magic for everyone and not only mages."

They stopped when they reached the corner of the fenced-in dragon field. William turned to lean his forearms on the top rung of the fence, and Raven moved beside him to do the same. The two friends were silent as they watched Leander and Zora, who lay side by side a short distance beyond the fence. The dragons only said an occasional word to each other in low voices but mostly, they were content to simply be in each other's presence.

Kind of like this with William right now.

He heaved another heavy sigh and turned to look at her again. "So if he calls you to join him, what are you gonna do?"

"Honestly? I don't think I'll know what to do until the moment actually arrives. Leander and I will decide together and go from there."

William laughed. "With no saddle and no plan. It gives a whole new meaning to 'flying by the seat of your pants,' Raven."

She grinned and looked at Leander. Her massive red dragon familiar raised his head and his glowing yellow eyes settled instantly on hers. He inclined his head in acknowledgment. "So far, I'd say it's working out very well."

The End
(for now)

415

MARTHA CARR & MICHAEL ANDERLE

With her grandfather's discovery fresh in her mind, Raven Alby's responsibilities may have doubled. She's studying to finish her first year of mage school with a dragon, trying to have a personal life while waiting for Connor to send for her, and defending her town from a group of massive beasts wreaking havoc on the kingdom. What she doesn't realize is that it's much easier to fight a brand-new threat than an enemy she thinks she knows. The adventure continues in *WarMage: Undeniable*.

Get sneak peeks, exclusive giveaways, behind the scenes content, and more.
PLUS you'll be notified of special **one day only fan pricing** on new releases.

Sign up today to get free stories.

CLICK HERE

or visit: https://marthacarr.com/read-free-stories/

GOTH DROW

Have you started the Goth Drow series from Martha and Michael? Book one is Once Upon A Midnight Drow and it's available now through Amazon and Kindle Unlimited.

I'm not Goth to hide my Drow heritage, I'm Goth because I'm not a quitter.

My name is Cheyenne Summerlin, remember that name. Somebody should…

The world can't know I'm a Drow halfling. Not yet. I

barely have these powers under my control, but time's up. I'm about to take magic for a test drive. Want to come along?

The black ops government group believe they can run my life... But I have plans of my own.

Watch out magical evil doers – I'm about to crash your party.

But will my training be enough?

Grab your copy today from Amazon or Kindle Unlimited.

AUTHOR NOTES - MARTHA CARR

APRIL 2, 2020

There's something about being pushed to the wall in life that can make us choose to give in and feel resentment, anger and self-pity or... rise up and gain clarity, compassion and new strength. Boy, are we all in one of those times right now.

It's so unique to constantly remember this is a situation that is unique to no one. A shared human experience with no immediate answers that takes a commitment from everyone to make a difference. For some on the frontlines – the medical profession, grocery store clerks, truck drivers, and more – it takes courage and a willingness to literally risk their lives in the service of others.

For others, it's pulling out the old sewing machine and figuring out how to sew a mask or a headband with buttons and give them away. Or play music online every night to sooth a troubled soul and quiet the mind. Or read a story, or host a dance party, or teach yoga, or write an encouraging note in chalk on a sidewalk. The list is becoming endless.

People everywhere are figuring out unique ways to share what they have and reach out across a divide we had to create in order to protect the most vulnerable among us – and yet, we are more connected than ever. It is love personified.

We are all brought into staying in the moment, cherishing what we have, straining to give to others and being gently reminded to take care of ourselves. Qualities we aspire to every day of our lives but never have we ever been forced to do it just to find measures of peace, joy and calm in the middle of a hurricane. But we can do this.

Each day, as I rise I recommit to look for reasons to be grateful – a cool day to walk the dogs, my neighbors' flowers blooming, a good joke from a friend – trust that the universe has my back so I don't have to make things about myself – be willing to be an instrument of peace and not fear – be willing to work with life on life's terms, which right now means taking on the limitations and still look for the blessings within them – help one step beyond what I think I'm capable of – be humble enough to ask for help – and constantly ask of family, friend and stranger alike – How are you doing today? Then let the person answer in as few or as many words as they feel necessary, creating a bond for just a moment.

Someday, this will all pass – it may not be for a while and we may all be very different people when it does. May we come to appreciate each other and ourselves in ever deeper and richer ways. May we value peace and joy and time together over so many other things. May we tend to all those new connections like a vast secret garden and find out we all have green thumbs. May we all look back and see that in the middle of so much loss we all have memories we will cherish forever. And then, may we all get up and go on together, a little kind, gentler and wiser as one, living in harmony the best we can manage – grateful for all of it. More adventures to follow.

AUTHOR NOTES - MICHAEL ANDERLE

APRIL 18. 2020

THANK YOU for reading our story!

We have a few of these planned, but we don't know if we should continue writing and publishing without your input.

Options include leaving a review, reaching out on Facebook to let us know and smoke signals.

Frankly, smoke signals might get misconstrued as low hanging clouds so you might want to nix that idea...

Ok, I want to just be annoyed.

Martha has worked hard to be as calm as she is and it shows. When we speak, she will often discuss how she was when younger and then how she handles things now. Allowing the things she can't change to leave her mind as mist does when the sun comes up.

Normally, my mind doesn't try to worry about stuff except the next item I have on my to-do list or meeting on my calendar. However, there has been a growing frustra-

AUTHOR NOTES - MICHAEL ANDERLE

tion that peaked immediately upon the general 'go stay in your home' directive and now.

I miss being out with people around me.

I'm not very social. What I mean by that is I like to go to restaurants to eat and work, but I'm not there to find new friends or anything. I might get to know the waiters / waitresses or managers because I'm there often (and in Vegas, that is a rarity on the strip.)

So, I am going to take a page out of Martha's book and assume that someday, this will pass and try to remember the blessings that we have as I get out of bed each morning.

Do you maybe want to write?

There are a lot of opportunities in Indie publishing, if you weren't aware. For those who love reading and have ever wanted a chance to see if you can write a book – well now is an excellent time!

There is a LOT of free knowledge on writing and a substantial amount of how to deal with the publishing of your own work all for you to read and learn as you please.

I'll take a moment to plug a group I started – 20Booksto50k® - which is available on Facebook. This free group focuses on the publishing side of the equation to answer questions on the how's and why's and to support those who wish to build a small business publishing stories (your stories or maybe your spouses, siblings, etc.)

I hope you find something you can be grateful for each morning – know that I will be working to do the same!

https://www.facebook.com/groups/20Booksto50k/

I don't dress well.

I used to have long hair when I was in college. It was that 'you aren't in your parents' home, I can have long hair and an earring' time during the 1980's. I shared this rejection of authority by growing my hair long, using hair bands while riding motorcycles.

Yes, I listened to heavy metal and had a Kawasaki EX500... They called it a sport-tourer, I called it fun and thankfully not the death of me.

It was the closest thing to sexy I *ever* had in my notoriously geek life. Except for something recently in the last five years, but that doesn't count.

I'm married. Owning sexy stuff while married takes the sexy out of it. I've lived through the young-family-has-a-van-to-drive days and now I'm in the older-life-kids-out-of-the-house-can-afford-more-expensive-toys days.

Back in the 80's, my hair got long enough that when I rode, I had to use a hair band or rubber band (which HURTS like an SOB trying to get it out of the hair) or spend twenty minutes cussing as I tried to pull a hairbrush through the tangles if I forgot.

I still flinch to this day thinking about pulling the hairbrush through my hair. I am empathetic to any dogs when you have to comb them and they have tangles. I try my best to keep away any pain.

Today I like to wear my hair much shorter because it takes less time to dry.

With the Pandemic, and not haircutting barbershops or anything available, I am trying new ways to style it.

Not very successfully mind you. I'm married, I only have one person to impress and she is usually looking at me strangely. This would be a typical discussion.

Wife: "What is that hairstyle called?"

Me: "Keep it the @#%@# out of my face."

Wife: "… looks nice."

Well, she *SAID* looks nice. Her rolling eyes proclaimed she meant something else.

Mike's Diary: "Sometimes, life just *is*."

So, my company is testing new software to allow us a virtual experience while we work. As of now (4/13/2020), it is performing better than I could have hoped in bringing those who collaborate with LMBPN together, no matter the location or time of day (or night.)

This same software, I hope, will allow us to create virtual meetings with fans, and (I'm trying, but I'm not sure the company behind the software will make it affordable) I want to create a place for fans to get together and create all sorts of fun stuff with LMBPN.

And frankly just have a place to hang a while.

If you would like to know more (and are on Facebook) join us on the Kurtherian Gambit Facebook Group For Fans and Authors

Link: https://www.facebook.com/profile.php?id=127989844503323&ref=br_rs

I hope to have something up to start testing this in the next week or two. We will start with small groups, and possibly move up from there.

Clean is the New Dream

My office isn't messy… exactly. It is lived-in *chic.*

Honestly, a whole *lot* of the lived-in part. (If you add

chic to the end of any descriptor, you immediately sound artsy. No, really, try it.

"That's ugly."

"No, that's ugly-*chic*."

"That man-cave crap has got to go."

"No, that's man-cave *chic*. It stays."

"That's hideous."

"No, that's hideous—"

"If you end that with 'chic,' I will shove my cottony house slippers so far up your ass you will be burping tiny clouds."

"Right. So, what now? I lost my train of thought with that visual."

(You thought 'Hideous *chic*, and that would have worked, #AmIRight?)

I will have to take another set of boxes to the storage room tomorrow after our meetings, and maybe then I'll have a bit of "clean" in my office. Judith cleaned the living room and Kitchen (both places she works from) yesterday, and believe it or not, I am a bit #Jealous of her clean areas.

(Don't worry, I'm having trouble believing it too.)

I'm So Going to Regret This.

So, I have the new 2020 iPad (#SupportApple and #Its-GoodToHaveAppleEmployeesWithDiscountsAsFriends along with #SupportFriendsByBuyingApple), but I don't like using it just as it is.

I want either a Smart Keyboard Folio or the new More Magic Keyboard for the iPad, or maybe something clamshell (but won't that effectively make it a Mac?).

Have I mentioned I'm seriously impatient? I work six often seven days a week (#ThankGodILoveWhatIDo), and when it comes to my technology, I splurge on myself. It's the one thing I can point to my wife and say 'it's a write-off' and 'Don't harsh my (writing) buzz, woman.'

(Actually, only one of those responses works on Judith. #ThankGodAppleDoesn'tRefreshOften and #IReallyDo-Wait2YearsBetweeniPhonesNow.)

I swear Apple better not upgrade their keyboard on the larger MacBooks in 2021, or I might have to try therapy to hold-back on an upgrade (yes, I have the 2021 MacBook 16".) If therapy is more expensive than my purchase, doesn't that make it smarter just to purchase the product?

I think it does.

Are you paying attention, Steve? (#StephenCampbellNeed-saNewMacbook13Pro)

Anyway. My iPad is sitting in its box unopened because I don't have a keyboard for it. I can't get the Magic Keyboard until May at this point, or maybe later. Since I suffer from #ImpatienceIsAThing, I am looking to see if anything cool is out for my iPad that includes a touchpad for mousing around.

You know, if—and this is for the benefit of my fans who might wish to know—I buy a clamshell with touchpad and report that information back here in a future *Author Note*, that's research and something I can write off on taxes, right?

So, I might sacrifice a larger credit card bill on the altar of #DoingItForTheFans.

If you happen to write a review for any of our books, maybe drop a line in the review "I Support Mike and his Magic Keyboard!" (Or, if you hate Apple products, feel free to suggest I buy other technology. Especially really expensive hardware that I can point to and show my wife how frugal' I was with the purchases I have already made or might <snicker> make soon.

Ad Aeternitatem,

Michael Anderle

(P.S. – Apple came out early with the Magic Keyboard... Hehehehe.)

JOIN THE ORICERAN UNIVERSE FAN GROUP ON FACEBOOK!

Made in the USA
Monee, IL
05 June 2020

32488696R00256